Tell me
to stop

The Nanny Chronicles

ELLE M THOMAS

Elle M Thomas

Cover design by The Write Life
Editing by The Write Life
Formatting by V R Formatting

This is an Elle M Thomas mature, contemporary romance. Anyone who has read my work before will know what that means, but if you're new to me then let me explain.
This book includes adult situations including, but not limited to adult characters that swear, a lot. A leading man who talks dirty, really, really dirty. Sex, lots and lots of hot, steamy, sheet gripping and toe-curling sex. Due to the dark and explicit nature of this book, it is recommended for mature audiences only.
If this is not what you want to read about then this might not be the book for you, but if it is then sit back, buckle up and enjoy the ride.

TITLES SO FAR...

Contemporary romance titles by Elle M Thomas:

Disaster-in-Waiting
Revealing His Prize

Carrington Siblings Series (should be read in order)
One Night Or Forever (Mason and Olivia)
Family Affair (Declan and Anita)

Love in Vegas Series (to be read in order)
Lucky Seven (Book 1)
Pushing His Luck (Book 2)
Lucking Out (Book 3)

Love in Vegas Novellas (to be read in timeline order)
Winters Wishes (takes place during Lucking Out)
Valentine's Vows (takes place around three years after Lucking Out)

Falling Series (to be read in order)
New Beginnings (Book 1)

Still Falling (Book 2)

New Beginnings/Falling Series Novellas (to be read in timeline order)
Old Endings (prequel to New Beginnings – Eve's Story)

The Nanny Chronicles (to be read in order)
Single Dad (Gabe and Carrie)
Pinky Promise (Seb and Bea)
Tell Me To Stop (Maurizio and Flora)

Erotic romance titles by Elle M Thomas:

The Revelation Series
Days of Discovery – Kate & Marcus Book 1
Events of Endeavour – Kate & Marcus Book 2

DEDICATION

With thanks to my readers, old and new, whose support means the world to me, and to my newly assembled ARC team. x

Chapter 1

Maurizio

I sat opposite Bea at the kitchen table, both of us going through our own notes about each candidate we'd interviewed that day.

"So, in reverse order . . . third place . . ."

Bea laughed, leaning back in her chair, giving her small baby bump a gentle stroke. She was pretty in a girl next door kind of way with long, dark blonde hair and pale blue eyes. She was funny and an all-round lovely young lady. I was sure I blushed as I recalled the couple of clumsy passes I'd made at her when Sophie first left me. Fortunately, she had not laughed, slapped or prosecuted me, or worse, set her boyfriend on me. She had simply moved on from it and seen them, and me, for what they were, pathetic. I was better than that now and was focused on being a good dad, the one my kids needed and deserved.

"Third for me was the American girl." She scanned her notes. "Nova."

I nodded. "I had her and the Irish lady, Krista, neck and neck."

"And in first place."

when she'd discussed her role, experience, and love of children. What more could I ask for? I blocked out the voice in my head that wanted to remind me of her long golden hair, deep blue eyes, and her curvy, hourglass shape.

The children laughed at something happening on the screen and I laughed too, but my amusement was at myself and the naughty thoughts of the new nanny. Wasn't that normal, though? Single man. Hot nanny. I'm sure women everywhere read that shit in those romance books of theirs.

But this wasn't the same.

She was off limits, and I needed to keep her that way. My thoughts needed to be entirely professional, or my mother would get wind of it, and then she would meddle. Her favourite pastime. She was never happy until I was neck deep in the waters of dating, and this was simply dipping my toes. I wouldn't put it past my mother to push me in the deep end. Head first.

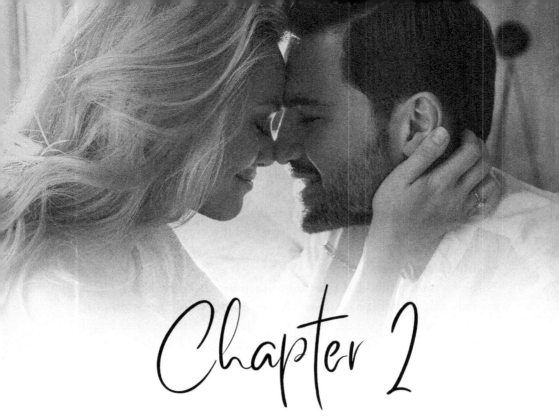

Chapter 2

Flora

"Yes!" I squealed as I hung up the phone. "I only went and got the job!"

My sister, Maddie, rushed to me and hugged me tightly. "I am so bloody proud of you. You are a warrior."

I frowned.

Maddie held my gaze. "You are. You are stronger than you know, smarter than you believe, more beautiful than you see and an all-round badass. You get that from me."

Wasn't that a quote from Winnie the Pooh?

It didn't matter, it was still kind. Sort of.

I laughed. But in all honesty, she was a badass and took no shit from anyone, ever.

Unlike me.

I had never been much of a party animal. She was the original good time girl. During my late teenage years I had overindulged in alcohol but discovered I was a melancholy drunk. Eventually, I showed a little more restraint and whilst I enjoyed a cocktail or a glass of wine, I rarely drank to excess. Maddie was the life and soul of the party sober, but with a few drinks she was off the scale. She was vivacious, loud, confident and would make her own fun wherever she went. I remembered countless occasions when she had ended up as the unofficial entertainment in pubs and clubs; she danced on tables, sang karaoke when it wasn't karaoke night, took part in an open night at a comedy club that we hadn't known was a comedy club. Then there was the time we'd ended up in a back street pole dancing bar and she had left with two hundred pounds more in her purse than when she'd entered, and my personal favourite, the time she'd challenged a huge Hell's Angel to an arm wrestle and won. Yeah, Maddie really was a party animal and an all-round badass.

We were similar, but quite different and it worked. We worked. I loved my big sister and we were close. We were often mistaken for twins, more so when we were younger, but I guess that was understandable as there was less than a year between us.

Maddie had lots of friends, including my own. When the chips were down it was just the two of us, battling for each other. She was my best friend as well as my big sister, had been since our parents died in an accident when I was fifteen. We had moved in with our grandparents and stayed there for a few years before we'd moved out to share a place. I moved into my own place for a time, a couple of years later when Maddie had set up home with her boyfriend who was now her ex. That was something we both had in common, failed relationships.

"Onwards and upwards now. Right, get your tightest jeans, lowest top and highest shoes on because we need to celebrate." Without another word she was heading for the stairs calling for me behind her, "Flora, now!"

It had been a while since I'd shared a big night out with Maddie and as I seemed to have little choice in it, I decided to enjoy it. We started with dinner, at a very fancy restaurant, the tiny portions for the three courses doing nothing to soak up the bottle of wine we'd shared, then we hit a bar for cocktails and then a new club, or at least new to me. Of course my sister was on first name terms with every staff member there.

There was an offer on the spirits which Maddie made full use of. I watched her down yet another double something before heading to the dancefloor, dragging me behind her. I already knew she was going to have the mother of all hangovers come the morning, but for tonight, she was happy and having fun.

We danced for what felt like hours, the music sounding as if someone had put mine and my sister's soundtrack together and were now serenading us with it. I was going to miss Maddie when I took up my new job. She was the one constant in my life and had always been there for me. A frown marred her face as she stopped dancing and looked across at me.

"Come on," she shouted above the music, already taking my hand in hers, leading me to the toilets.

The rather long distance to the bathroom allowed me to fully take in this place; shiny chrome flashed, mirrors reflected lights, it was all accented with soft muted colours giving the place a feeling of luxury and class. The bathrooms were no different. They even had a beauty station with counters to sit at in front of huge mirrors and lighting that made you look like a Kardashian. The toilet doors were a dark grey but adorned with an inspirational quote from influential women. I was distracted as I began reading them, jumping when Maddie pulled me down onto a chaise near the beauty station.

"What's wrong?" she asked with just a hint of a slur.

"Nothing." I was clueless as to what she meant.

"Out there, on the dancefloor, you pulled your sad face."

The penny dropped. "Ah, I was just thinking how weird it will be not to see you every day when I start my new job."

She dropped her head into her hands and rested her elbows on her knees for a few silent seconds before looking back up at me. "You don't have to go—except I think you do—there's nothing here for you. This could be a chance for you to make a good life for yourself. It's a brilliant new start."

I could feel my eyes drying as I stared at her, unsure if she wanted me to go rather than just supporting the move.

"I will miss you like crazy. I can't remember my life without you," she said and sniffed loudly. "But I want you to be happy and fulfilled and I have a gut feeling this is the right move for you."

I nodded, fearful of speaking for a few more seconds. The tightness in my throat and the fire burning there threatened tears. "I think you might be right." I smiled, taking her hand into mine. "But do not ever say there is nothing here for me, our grandparents are here, and you, my big sister."

With a single sob, she pulled me in for a hug, a move I reciprocated and clung to her even when she attempted to release me. I wasn't quite ready to let her go, not yet.

Fortunately, our night had proven pretty tame after our little emotional heart to heart, resulting in a good night out with only a thick head for me the following morning rather than a fully-fledged hangover.

Maddie appeared in the kitchen and looked a little bleary eyed. She headed straight to the cupboard that housed the headache tablets. She'd had more to drink than me the night before. The way she winced at my simple breakfast of fruit and yoghurt confirmed her fragility.

She sat opposite me with a glass of water. "Are you sure you'll be okay living that far away from me?"

I laughed at her concerned expression.

"Two hours in a car and probably less via a direct train."

She still stared.

"If I'm not, I will come straight back and I will call you, often."

She nodded now and offered a small smile. "Promise."

"Scout's honour."

"Neither of us were ever scouts, Flo."

"You're splitting hairs, but I have a good feeling about this, and I haven't had one of those for quite some time. Plus, when I was having a wobble last night, you were the one telling me this was the right thing to do."

"Okay, I was the one saying that, wasn't I . . ." She sighed, sipping her water gingerly. "Go and knock them dead, but always remember I am here for you, forever. We have each other, and even though I'm not there to straighten it, you better make sure that you remember you are a bloody queen, so keep your crown on straight and knock them all out."

I leapt up and circled the table so I could engulf my sister in my arms.

"Thank you, for everything, but I just turned twenty-nine years old and need to get my arse in gear. And if ever my crown needs straightening, I know where to find you."

She sniffed back tears. "Yeah, you and me both, and you can't be twenty-nine because that would make me almost thirty and I refuse to be older than twenty-five."

"Sorry, my mistake." I stuck my tongue in my cheek, trying not to laugh.

"Too right. Now, when do you need to leave?"

"I'm going back at the end of the week, just for the day to sort the final details and then it should be the week after that."

"Well, in that case, we had better make the next couple of weeks count, but not now because I need to go back to bed."

————

I nervously knocked on the front door and waited for a sound or sign of movement. Seconds passed by and as I pulled my phone out to check that I had the right date and time, the door flung open.

Mr Walker, my new boss, greeted me in a casual outfit of tracksuit bottoms and a tight white vest that clung to the obviously hard toned muscles of his chest and abs that were damp with sweat. I was staring and needed to stop. Looking up at his face, he rubbed a towel over his thick, dark head and face. Again, I stared. Dropping my gaze slightly, I took in his biceps that glistened, tracing my glance down his tanned arms, corded with muscles before finishing at his hands that he was drying. With a smile that made his dark eyes twinkle, he extended a hand to welcome me.

"Miss Maynard." He smiled. "Flora?" he queried, as if gaining permission to address me informally.

I smiled back, "Yes, Flora." I wasn't a big fan of formality, especially not if I was going to be living and working in someone's house.

"Time got away from me. Come in, then. Bea has taken the children out for a while. I thought we could chat and finalise details before I unleashed them on you."

I laughed at his way of making them sound like a pack of wild beasts, but at the same time glowing with love and pride for them.

"They're a handful," he added, as if justifying his own words.

"I'm sure they are. I've never known children not to be, in their own way."

He nodded as he stepped back and followed me into the hallway, passing me so he could lead me into the kitchen that was a perfect fusion of modern and traditional, the large number of windows basking the room in light.

With a cup of tea in my hand, I looked around, waiting for Mr Walker to return from his shower. I avoided dwelling on thoughts of him wet and naked and instead wondered how things would work here, with me and the other nanny, Bea. This was her domain and whilst I would be taking over from her, I hoped the handover of the baton would be a smooth one.

"Right, sorry about that, but I'm sure you'd rather speak to me when I'm clean than drenched in sweat and smelling like the children's week old socks." He laughed at his own reference, whereas I sat staring at him, jaw slack as my mind continued to hang onto the image of him in well-fitting jeans that slouched in just the right way and a white t-shirt. Now I couldn't decide whether I would have preferred his earlier sweaty and smelly self or the current one . . . all clean and fresh . . . as delectable as Tom Cruise following the beach scene in *Top Gun* . . . the jury was out because both had their own attractions, much like the man himself.

I reminded myself, not for the first time since my initial interview, he was my boss which meant he was out of bounds for anything more than eye candy, and there was no harm in looking, was there? I could appreciate the menu and not order from it.

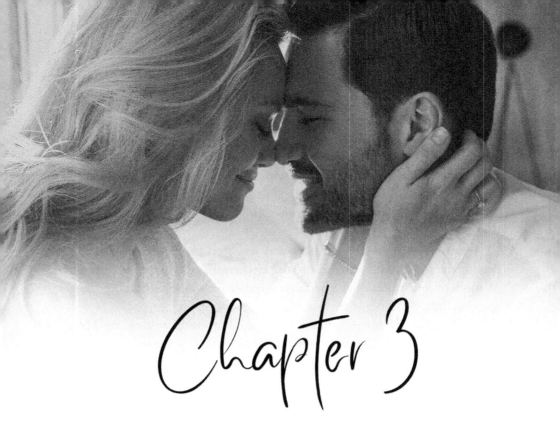

Chapter 3

Maurizio

I sat down opposite Flora and picked up my own cup of tea, focusing on anything that wasn't the way she was looking at me. Whilst not an Adonis by any stretch of the imagination, I knew I was attractive, or at least women often found me to be. I was tall, like my father, but everything else I got from the Italian side of my family, the naturally bronzed skin, dark hair and eyes, and on occasion, the charm. I hadn't intentionally been flirting or aiming to be suggestive when I'd said about being sweaty, but I think it came across that way. I'd noted the way Flora had swallowed, hard, had flushed and taken in my whole appearance before her face, neck and chest took on a slightly deeper shade of pink. She really was very cute.

I smiled, hoping to relax the woman opposite me, but the truth was that my smile had been entirely natural, a sign at my happiness that she found me attractive and was reacting to me. Under other circumstances I might be concerned by that, had she just started working in the firm of barristers I was a partner in. Maybe I should be more concerned as I was not only employing her, but she was also going to be living in my house. However, I admitted, if only to myself, that the attraction was entirely reciprocal and so long as we both knew we weren't crossing those professional lines, and we weren't, where was the harm?

The sound of the children charging through the house interrupted every thought I had. Showtime.

After introducing the children to Flora and explaining again that she would be here with Bea to take care of them and then alone once their current nanny went on maternity leave, I retreated to my office. I didn't want anyone to feel uncomfortable or pressured by my presence, plus, under normal circumstances, I was unlikely to be around when the children were in either nanny's care.

An hour or so had passed when I heard loud laughter that I immediately recognised as Rosie's. I looked out of my office window and watched on as some kind of chasing game took place. Bea seemed to be watching on with Craig who wore a large smile at the scene of his sister lying on the grass giggling as Flora tickled her, having caught her. My son was quieter, more reserved than his sister. Craig loved Bea, but then he couldn't remember a time when she hadn't been there, so I expected it to take a while for him to bond with Flora. I found myself smiling and laughing as I continued to watch the images of my children, happy and carefree, just as they should always be.

This felt right. Flora belonged here with us and any doubts, of which there were just a few, disappeared right then.

With Rosie all giggled out, Flora stood to her full height, straightening from her earlier bent position which had afforded me a glorious view of her round behind. Before my mind could take that thought any further, she turned to face the house, her face still beaming with the biggest of smiles, aglow with genuine pleasure from playing with my daughter. Then, her expression turned a little more serious, almost coy as our eyes met. I was uncertain what to do; run, hide, or with my own expression becoming more intense, I could simply continue to hold her glance until she looked away. I did none of those. I waved at her and smiled. I could have kicked myself for the wave alone until she waved back, a small flush staining her cheeks, but that might have been from the chasing of the children. I turned away and allowed myself a slightly bigger smile. Yes, Flora was exactly the right fit here. For the children, obviously.

I left it another hour before I ventured out to find them. They were all sitting in the conservatory that was situated off the kitchen, the children playing with their toys, while the women chatted and laughed together. I was pleased to find they'd seemingly hit it off.

"Flora." They both jumped at my interruption. "If I could steal you away for a few moments, I'll show you around and finalise the details." I smiled, so as not to scare the woman off at the possibilities of the details. The job was already hers.

"Of course." She got to her feet.

"I'll see you when you get back then," called Bea, the broad smile hinting at her thoughts as I led Flora out.

I gave her the full guided tour of the main house as this would be her place of work and then led her to the accommodation above the garages.

"You can access your home from the side door to the garage," I explained as I led her through the door at the furthest point of the upstairs of the house.

"Okay."

She sounded nervous, awkward even, maybe she felt both and I was unsure why. I came to an abrupt stop so that the poor woman almost collided with my front as I spun to face her.

Her face looked conflicted as she seemed to consider whether to speak or not.

"Flora, what is it?"

She swallowed hard, sucked in a deep breath, and then spoke. "Am I to assume that you'd rather I didn't enter my rooms from the house, Mr Walker?"

Her question left her in one big rush of air.

I laughed and she flushed. Presumably she thought I was laughing at her. I wasn't, only at her misunderstanding and what seemed to be her assumption that I was being a snob, or an arsehole. "Sorry. I wasn't clear. There is no issue with you using the access here as far as I am concerned, but I meant the side entrance was for you, for your privacy, and call me Maurice, please."

"Ah, okay, thanks." She was still a little pink in the cheeks.

"Plus, I don't think you'll want to traipse through the house in the dark after a night out any more than I'll want to find you passed out on the landing."

She looked flustered again.

"And what you do in your own time is your business, Flora, and none of my concern. I wasn't insinuating or suggesting anything."

With a short nod she seemed relaxed once more.

"I'm sure your boyfriend won't want to be dragged through the house when he visits you either." I forced a smile, feeling flustered myself now, wondering why my smile wasn't given more freely when discussing Flora's boyfriend.

Her eyes were wide and slightly startled now. "I, erm, no, I don't, no. I mean to say that I don't have a boyfriend, so no visitors."

I nodded, my smile broadening and feeling entirely natural with that information. "Good. Right. Let's finish the tour and then there are just a couple of housekeeping matters."

Turning back to the door that separated her living quarters from mine, I grinned. Relieved that there was no boyfriend who would be visiting her.

I knew why I felt that way, but it was ridiculous to give the thought any time because there was no way she and I would ever be anything aside from employer and employee.

Chapter 4

Flora

T he feeling of embarrassment was subsiding as a larger dose of idiocy took over. I could have simply said that I didn't have a boyfriend. *I don't have a boyfriend.* Five words were all I needed to utter, but instead I had rambled. If I really thought about it, I was certain that by five words in, I was no closer to addressing my non-existent boyfriend than a stammered *don't*. Mr Walker, Maurice, made me nervous. Nervous like a man never had before, but why? Yes, he was going to be my boss and part of that package made him my landlord too, but still. And okay, I had eyes in my head, he was attractive, very, and I did fancy him in a look don't touch kind of way. The way he'd looked at me a couple of times had made me think it wasn't a one-sided attraction. Did the unknown make me nervous? I wasn't sure what he'd do at any given second, would he act on that look? However, I should try to remain calm around him and not make myself look any more stupid than I already had. I needed to focus on my work, on the children and make this a long and successful career move as well as fulfilling the children's needs.

I followed behind as I was shown around my rooms; an open plan kitchen and lounge with a few doors off the main room that housed the bathroom, cupboards, the boiler and heating controls. Maurice stopped at the final door and flung it open before disappearing through it. I again followed until he turned to face me in. The bedroom. "If there is anything else you need or would like, please say and I will ensure it is here for you."

"Thank you." I offered him a genuinely warm smile. His offer was beyond generous as the accommodation was not only furnished but furnished to a very high standard. "But everything I could possibly want or need is here."

A sudden rise in temperature, or maybe a charge in the air moved through the room. He stepped closer and his gaze dropped to my lips. He licked his own, but his eyes never left mine as he spoke. "I'm pleased. I want you to be happy here."

"I'm sure I will be." I was uncertain of anything at that moment, and that probably included my own name, but what I did know was that I desperately wanted to be happy here.

"Good. That makes me happy too."

"I'm glad you're happy."

He grinned and I vowed to stop speaking. I closed my eyes to gather my thoughts and was startled to find him much closer upon opening my eyes again. Shit! He was going to kiss me and I knew I'd be unable to stop him. I wouldn't want to.

"Let's finalise the last couple of details. In my office." He looked startled, as if he had no recollection of apparently preparing to kiss me.

He turned, and once more, I dutifully followed him all the way back to his office.

Sitting opposite him, I answered all of his questions relating to my bank details, tax information and associated benefits with my role and then he stunned me by explaining that my credit card would be delivered once I started work.

"I don't need a credit card." The words came out with a slight stammer. I had no clue what the hell was going on here. Why was he getting me a credit card and what was I expected to give up in return?

"I beg to differ."

For the first time, I got a glimmer of the barrister he was stern, forthright, and not used to being argued with.

"I don't want your credit card." This time my tone was firmer, and the words were better strung together.

His eyes lifted until they held mine, their journey only halted momentarily to stare at my lips again. "Flora, you need the credit card."

My mouth opened to object once more, but he continued to speak.

"If the children need something or there is an unexpected expense for the house, food even, it makes sense for me to pay direct rather than you paying and me reimbursing."

I nodded. That made perfect sense, plus, I might not have the funds to cover the costs in the first place.

"Also, if you were unable to pay at the time, you would need to contact me and if I am with a client or in court, I may not be available."

"Of course. Thank you." I still wasn't happy about this, but what could I say? I refuse to have your credit card Mr Walker, or maybe I could just stick it in a drawer somewhere. He'd never know, would he? The little voice in my head that asked how I would explain myself in the event that one of the situations he'd described occurred and I had no means of payment, made a fair point. Looked like I was having a credit card.

He smiled and either I was imagining things, or he was watching my lips again. I licked across the dryness of them and watched, slightly amused, when he leapt to his feet and hurried for the door. "Right then, Flora, let's get you back to Bea and the children and then I can drop you back at the station in time for your train."

———

I'd been back home for two days, and I was struggling to talk about anything that didn't involve my new job. Maddie listened to me rave about the kids and Bea, and of course, Maurice.

"So, what's Daddy like?" she asked with a suggestive wiggle of her perfect shaped brows.

I shook my head at her, mainly at her calling my new boss, Daddy. "Never call him that again."

She shrugged and I saw the intention in her blue eyes. Maddie never gave up that easily. Hence her repeated question. "So, what's he like?"

"He's nice. Seems a really good dad and Bea says he is. She gets on with him really well which gives me hope that I will too."

"Hmmm," my sister muttered.

"What's, 'hmmm'?"

"Him and Bea, do you suppose there was more? Maybe that's why he and his wife split..."

I had wondered that when I'd first seen the easy banter between them, but then she'd spoke about her boyfriend, and it was clear she was head over heels for him. "She's got a boyfriend and they seem very happy. They're having a baby, so, I think not."

"He's available then?"

I laughed at Maddie's deadpan expression and air of optimism. "He is off limits."

She shrugged. "He's not my boss, maybe you could introduce us."

My mouth dropped open, horror spreading across my face.

"Oh my God!" Maddie moved closer until she was sat on the edge of the coffee table, putting us eye to eye as I shifted my arse on the sofa. "You like him, like, you know, *like-like* him."

I could feel the heat radiating from my face as I struggled for words, and as much as I wanted to offer my sister a denial of her accusation, I couldn't. Apart from anything else, she would see through me because she could read me like a book. "He is off limits," I repeated. "*Please drop it.*" There was no way I was entertaining the idea of anything actually happening with Maurice, certainly not with Maddie who'd never let this go if I gave her even a whiff of encouragement.

"Flora, I get why you might choose not to pursue things with him, but I am just excited to see you showing an interest . . . it's been too long. So, if you choose to friend-zone him . . ."

I frowned at her choice of words. He wasn't my friend and although he and Bea seemed to have a friendly banter, I didn't really think they were friends either. I didn't believe he was the sort of man to become the cliché of the rich, single dad who ended up shagging the nanny. No. He would keep things professional I was sure.

"Whatever." My sister waved off my unspoken objection. "You've boss-zoned him, better?"

I was beyond relieved when my phone rang giving me the get out I needed.

We'd managed to avoid the 'Maurice' discussion for another week until I was packing up my old and trusty car for the journey to my new home and workplace. My emotions were all over the place as I turned to face Maddie. I was naturally nervous, but there was excitement there too, bubbling in my belly while a knot of sadness sat in my chest at the idea of moving away from my sister.

"Just be careful."

"I will. I'll keep to the speed limit and take it steady," I promised as I found myself pulled in for a hug.

"Good, but that's not what I meant. I was thinking when you get there. With the boss."

I rolled my eyes and shook my head. "I don't need to be careful with the boss because there is not and will never be anything more than employer and employee, regardless of how hot he is."

"Tell me how hot he is again," she demanded with her almost customary wiggle of brows.

I laughed, glad that she wasn't going to make this a big or uncomfortable thing. "Really hot, scorching, but I have to go, so use your imagination and it still might not be hot enough."

"Damn! I need photos, send me *all* the photos."

With a final hug and another giggle, I got into my car and sending a prayer to the heavens that it would make the journey in one piece, I set off for my new job, home and life.

When I finally arrived at my destination, several hours later than planned, I was a little embarrassed. My desire for my car to arrive in one piece hadn't quite panned out. The fact that I was climbing down from the cab of a breakdown truck confirmed that whilst my car was in one piece, it wasn't actually working. With the recovery driver already out and preparing to unload my car, I turned to find the children looking out of the largest window to the front of the house, their faces full of excitement and wonder while their father was striding towards me.

"Flora," he called, a frown creasing his brow.

"Sorry," I began, sensing some kind of annoyance or at least an objection to my heap of a car being deposited on his pristine drive where his own immaculate and perfectly working car sat in front of his beautiful house.

"Are you okay? What happened?" Already walking around my car, he examined it. "Well, it doesn't look like a collision."

"I broke down." I couldn't help but smile back at my boss who seemed genuinely relieved that I was safe, despite the eyesore of a car that was about to take up residence on his driveway. "I'll look into finding a garage as soon as I can—"

The recovery driver cut me off with a chuckle, gaining mine and Maurice's attention. "Sorry, but it might cost more to put right than to replace it."

"Shit!" I muttered, wondering just how long it would take me to be able to get a replacement. "Sorry," I quickly added, thinking cursing and profanity might not be appropriate while my boss was within ear shot, especially as my role was to care for his young children.

He waved off my curse. "I'd be inclined to agree." Taking the keys from the driver, he turned to me. "Leave it with me, Flora. I'll have someone collect it tomorrow unless you know someone yourself?"

I smiled across at him as the recovery driver climbed back into his truck with a wave and a cheerio. "No, I have no clue of anyone locally. Thank you."

He extended his arm with a warm and welcoming smile that seemed to be directing me to head into the house.

"After such an eventful trip down, let's get you a drink." He glanced down at his watch. "Tea maybe, it's a little early for anything stronger."

As much as I could have gone for a glass of wine after my morning, he had a point. "Oh, my luggage," I stammered, heading back towards my car that was packed to the rafters with my belongings.

Maurice shook his head and wore an expression that suggested there was no room for debate. "After tea."

I demonstrated my acquiescence by walking towards the house where the children were still in the window, waving and smiling, their expressions contagious judging by the returning wave and smile I offered them.

Nursing a cup of tea that Maurice had made for me, saw me sitting opposite the children who watch on in horror as I dunked a jammie biscuit into my cup.

"I don't think you should do that," Rosie told me.

Slightly distracted, it took a second to realise she was referring to my biscuit that at that precise second broke, dropping back into the hot liquid, splashing over the side slightly.

Maurice laughed before taking my cup from me and offering me a towel to dry my hand and the damp patch on my top.

Rosie stared at me and if she didn't do a complete role reversal so I felt as though I was the three-year-old.

"What happened to your car, Flora?" Craig hadn't spoken until that point.

"It broke." It was the truth and I didn't think the little boy would want the life history of my knackered car.

"Did you break it, or crash it?" He didn't wait for a response. "Is it because you're a woman driver? Uncle Nico says–"

Maurice cut him off. "I don't know that we need to hear the gospel according to Uncle Nico, but Flora's car broke because it is old and a little bit tired."

"That's what Uncle Nico said about Nonna," Rosie told us, a frown creasing her brow until her father laughed followed by me and Craig.

"Again, I don't think we need my brother's words of wisdom."

Any nerves I'd had dissipated in the moments I had shared with this family I thought I could become very fond of.

Chapter 5

Maurizio

T he first week since Flora's arrival had passed quite smoothly. She was friendly, warm and had a welcome air about her that endeared her to everyone she met. The children were growing accustomed to her presence, and although Craig was less keen on change, Rosie seemed to have taken to Flora almost immediately from the tickling game in the garden. Bea had befriended her and was showing her around the local area and had introduced her to a few people, but for the most part, Flora seemed to keep herself to herself.

Our relationship was developing, and by developing I meant that she didn't seem petrified of me anymore, or perhaps not as much, which was good. I wasn't an ogre. Far from it, and I found I wanted to show her that more than anything. I was pretty easy going and as such tried to be friendly and welcome her into my home.

My attention was gained by the sound of the doorbell ringing followed by the children squealing with excitement. Opening my office door, I went to investigate.

"I miei bellissimi nipoti."

The children were dancing around my mother who regularly spoke to them in Italian and always encouraged them to speak it. I couldn't argue that they were indeed her beautiful grandchildren.

Their voices grew louder and louder with each of them trying to gain her full attention with calls of 'Nonna' echoing around the hall.

Bea stood nearby with Flora, both of them falling under my mother's gaze. "Bea, how are you, and the bambino." She rubbed her hand across Bea's belly.

"I'm very well, thank you, and the baby appears to be very hungry judging by how much I'm eating."

My mother laughed. "A strong and handsome boy then, like his father." She winked, her appreciation for Bea's possessive boyfriend clear.

"He'd like the idea of that." Bea rolled her eyes.

My mother's attention fell to Flora. "I'm Carmella, Flora... fiore, no?"

Poor Flora looked startled.

"Mother," I called, hoping to distract her.

"Ah, Maurizio, mio principe. I didn't know you'd be home." She strode towards me and with a dip from me and a stretch from her, she kissed each of my cheeks.

"I was just about to make tea," Bea said, ushering Flora towards the kitchen.

"Perfect," my mother replied and turned to follow the nannies and the children who could surely sense the possibility of a biscuit or some other treat. My mother quickly turned back to me, a mischievous twinkle in her eyes. "She seems sweet—shy—bellissima."

I rolled my eyes but didn't disagree.

"And beneath that I think you might discover una donna appassionata."

I laughed. Only my mother could go from describing Flora as sweet to passionate in six words. "Come, drink your tea, and no matchmaking."

"Of course," she responded as she sauntered towards the children, calling to them to show her something exciting.

. . .

I looked over the remnants of tea and cake, while the children, having devoured the cake and washed it down with milk, were now drawing and colouring. My mother was her usual charming self, telling Bea and Flora all about her home in Italy and sharing stories from her time spent there.

Several times she involved me in her conversation with the simple prompt of, "Tell them, Maurizio."

Every time she used my full name, Flora looked startled, unlike Bea who knew that it was my actual name. The fourth or fifth time it was used, my mother noticed Flora's reaction.

"It is his name, my dear. His given name, Maurizio." She overemphasised her Italian accent, making me laugh.

"But Maurice is fine, or Mo."

Flora flushed a little while Bea said nothing.

"I like it," Flora seemed to blurt out. "Your name. Maurizio. It suits you."

I smiled across at her and thought I might have flushed myself now.

"You are as wise as you are beautiful," my mother told Flora before turning her attention to me. "See, what did I tell you? Maurice is an ugly old man's name," my mother accused, making the other women and my children laugh. "Maurizio is handsome, strong and sexy, no?"

I was unsure whether she expected an answer, not that I intended to give her one, unlike Flora who opened her mouth so that her 'yes' slipped out just after my mother added one more word of her own, "Virile."

Flora looked like she wanted to crawl up her own arse, and why wouldn't she? I briefly allowed my mind to wander to her arse. Peachy, toned, and begging to be touched. Bea roared with laughter as her phone sounded with a message.

She checked it. "Seb. He's waiting for me. We're going to see Carrie and Gabe tonight."

"Get off then," I told her, not that she needed my permission, it was just past her clocking off time after all.

She got to her feet and with all of her goodbyes said, she left, along with my mother who suddenly seemed in a hurry to leave me alone with the children, *and* Flora.

Flora nervously shifted around me for the first few minutes. She seemed happy and confident when talking to the children, but with me, not so much so. It seemed I still made her nervous. At least she was no longer petrified.

"Oh, I had a call earlier. Your car has been fixed."

"Really?"

I chuckled at her surprise. I had been astounded when the local garage had said they could probably ensure it lived to see another day, although the mechanic had said it might not last months and certainly not years. The car was hanging on by a thread. It was an old Mini that almost dated back to when they were popular the first time around. It was way past its best and quite possibly a death trap between the unreliable engine and flaky red paintwork that held the thing together along with the rust. "Yeah, I was as surprised as you."

"Did they say how much?" Nerves coated her words.

"He owed me a favour." It hadn't been my intention to say that, or to pay for the repairs, she did understand that's what I'd meant, right? I would have happily offered her an advance on her salary to cover the cost of repair. Then I'd heard her concern which suggested she might not have the funds to pay for the work. I had no clue how much the bill was, but that didn't matter as I had committed to paying it.

"Oh, thank you. If you're sure?"

"I am, and you're welcome. I am in court tomorrow but not until lunchtime so once Bea arrives, I can drop you off to collect it."

"Thank you," she repeated.

"No problem."

"I, erm, should be going . . . you'll want to enjoy your evening."

Her cheeks were pink and as I stared at her, considering the option of inviting her to stay and have dinner, her complexion deepened until it was red. I didn't doubt that my evening would have been far more enjoyable if Flora remained.

Her breathing hitched a little and I could now see that her chest and neck were colouring up while she nervously toyed with the ends of her hair that were held in a ponytail.

"Goodnight, Mr Walk—" She stopped dead, remembering that we were on first name terms here. "Mauriz...Maurice."

She virtually ran for the stairs, almost tripping over her own feet as she called to the children that she'd see them in the morning.

She had almost called me Maurizio. I grinned smugly. She really did prefer Maurizio over Maurice. Maybe that would be my sole mission in life, to get her to address me as Maurizio.

"Right then, my little rug rats, let's get you fed, watered and ready for bed.

Chapter 6

Flora

"Buggery bloody bollocks!" I cried as I dropped onto the sofa. After stammering and spluttering at him in the kitchen, nearly calling him Maurizio and then almost falling on my face, I didn't know how the hell I was ever going to talk to him again.

I was not a naturally clumsy or bumbling person, and yet, around Maurice, I was becoming very much that way. Why? I had no clue. I mean, he made me nervous, not in a scared or fearful kind of way. He was a nice man, friendly, funny, and had gone out of his way to make me feel nothing but welcome since I'd arrived.

A nagging voice in my head persistently reminded me that he was gorgeous, his height making me envision all the ways he could lift me. He was a wonderful father, and that was always a turn on when it came to single men. I couldn't even allow myself to think about how he smelled. I wasn't sure I had sufficient adjectives to describe his aroma, even to myself.

"So much for not thinking about his smell." The sound of those words aloud rather than in my head spurred me into action.

What was happening to me? I pushed all thoughts of crushes and attraction from my mind because that would be ridiculous, wouldn't it? I hadn't been a teenage girl for a long time and needed to stop acting like one.

I got to my feet, intent on sorting dinner, having a shower and spending the night in front of the telly. Maybe I'd phone Maddie and catch up. That would take my mind off thoughts of my boss and making myself look a prat.

Or maybe it wouldn't because we all knew what the topic of conversation would be when it came to my sister.

I ate a dinner of spaghetti hoops on toast and before a shower I phoned Maddie. She answered on the first ring.

"Hey there baby sister! How are you? Are you okay?"

I laughed at the panic I detected in her voice believing that I was calling because there was a problem. "I'm fine, I just thought I'd call for a chat."

"Ah." She sounded awkward, as though she wanted to give me the brush off but didn't quite feel entirely able to.

"Are you okay?" I suddenly became concerned that she may be the one with a problem.

"Yeah, yeah. Sorry. Now's not a good time." Her voice turned into a whisper. "I have a date."

I laughed, assuming her date must be there if she was whispering. "And is that your way of him not hearing you telling me that you have a date?"

She laughed herself. "Yes, now bugger off. I'll call you tomorrow night and we can have a proper catch up."

"It's a date. Maybe not as active as tonight's but a date, nevertheless. Have fun and be careful."

"Yes, Grandma," Maddie replied with something between a huff and a laugh.

· · ·

As a gossip with Maddie was postponed, I changed my shower for a bath and a large glass of wine. The water was nice and hot and the bubbles high enough to hit my nose. I cautioned myself with the consuming of the wine, just in case drowning by bubbles was an option. I had lit a couple of candles, savouring the large bath that allowed me to lie at full stretch whilst sipping my wine and listening to an equally well chilled playlist of tunes I'd found listed as *Beach Spa*. It was tranquil, sleep inducing potentially and made me think of far off sunny climes.

Lying submerged in the water wasn't something I did often, but when I did, I enjoyed it. My mind kept returning to Maurizio and my departure from the kitchen earlier. My initial horror had now faded and although I still felt a bit of a knob, I was able to laugh about it. The biggest problem that I faced was this ridiculous crush I had. Even if my attraction to him, my inability to coordinate my limbs and failure to string a sentence together served as some kind of amusement, I wasn't sure how long that would last, so I needed to get over it, and quick. I came up with a quick, get over him, rather than under him, list.

No more thoughts of how handsome he was.

No imagining him naked.

No thinking about how it would feel for him to lift me before pushing my back against a wall and...

Finally, certainly no fantasies of said wall or how his kisses would infuse fires across my lips and body.

I needed to get a grip, grow up and see Mr Walker, Maurice, for what he was. My boss. Only my boss.

Looking down at my hands, I could see they were shrivelled like prunes and with the water beginning to cool, I drained the wine from my glass, got out from the bath and wrapped myself in freshly laundered towels with a renewed determination to make my life here, my work, a real success.

The following morning, I woke early and was already in the family kitchen before anyone else was awake. With my fresh determination from the night before still going strong, I felt good about the day ahead and the days that would follow. I would not be the silly nanny, acting like a schoolgirl with an adolescent crush on my boss, who was somehow incapable of stringing together coherent thoughts or words. I would be professional, an adult. I was almost thirty, not thirteen. I switched on the kettle and got out the breakfast things for the children so that when they arrived with their father, they could pour cereal into their bowls.

Maurice called a cheery good morning, a greeting I returned. I could do this. I could keep this professional and rather than friendzone him I could 'bosszone' him, like Maddie had said when she had figured my attraction to him, well, that's what I told myself and believed it until he brushed past me to make some tea. The feel of his body briefly and accidentally making contact with mine had me doubting whether any zone would be secure enough to contain him. My whole body heated from the outside in, and I was sure my heartrate had increased along with my breathing. I found I was doing something of an internal chant. *Calm down, calm down. Rein it in, rein it in. He's just your boss, he's just your boss.* The strange little mewl that left my partially parted lips suggested my chant was flawed and totally ineffective.

And then there was the divine aroma that was all him. God, he smelled amazing. Good enough to eat.

Shit!

This was going well!

The thought of eating him would ensure that he was naked and aroused, and those thoughts were enough to have me wondering what would happen next. His mouth on mine, working its way down my body, devouring every inch of me until he was lapping at my core. While he may have missed the low mewl I had made at the feel of his body touching mine, albeit briefly, there was no way he couldn't have heard the louder moan I uttered with thoughts of his mouth all over me and the way I would consume him with greed until we both came undone because of each other.

He moved back behind me, pausing to give me a cup of tea. I opened my mouth, preparing to utter the words thank you but no sound beyond a deep moan came out. Amazing. Now, when I needed to put the letters together to make normal words, all I could do was murmur sex noises. Great.

"Morning."

The jolly cry from Bea entering through the back door broke the moment, thank goodness, and allowed me to regain the power of speech and normal breathing. Who knew how quickly that ability would be taken from me again.

Chapter 7

Maurizio

Part of me had cursed the arrival of Bea that morning as she had not only interrupted us, but she'd also shattered the moment we'd been sharing. I guess the moment had been a hell of a lot more than just a moment because if the charge between us had intensified much more and her heavy breathing and moaning had continued, I might have ended up spinning her around, pinning her against the nearest surface, and kissing her breathless. And they were just the first thoughts I had when it came to her. Considering my children were sat at the table, pouring cereal into bowls, it was probably for the best that Bea had arrived at that precise second or Rosie and Craig may have been traumatized forevermore.

After greeting Bea, I made my excuses and with a time agreed to take Flora to collect her car, I headed to my office with a cup of tea in hand.

For an hour or so I busied myself with emails and the final preparations for the case I was due to defend in court starting that afternoon.

Stiff from sitting at the computer, I got up, turned to look out of the window at nothing whilst I stretched. I arched my back slightly until everything began to loosen with a few cracks here and there. I might need to make an appointment with the chiropractor, see if he couldn't get a few decent back cracks out of me. Or maybe I needed a massage . . . I actually meant a sports massage but somehow my thoughts deserted me and returned to Flora and the potential of her hands on me. The image of those oiled hands moving across my skin, the feel of her on me. I needed to lose all thoughts of this nature. Blowing out a breath with a bend of my neck as I moved it from side to side, I turned back to face my office where Flora stood in the open doorway which caused me to jump.

"Sorry. I was going to knock, but the door was open."

I watched the colour stain her cheeks. "That's okay, come in."

She looked awkward, shifting from one foot to the other as if she was considering crossing the threshold but had decided against it. I wanted her to come in and join me. To be confident enough to tell me what was going on in her head. With that intention in my mind, I curled my hand, summoning her in as I retook my seat.

Cautiously putting one foot in front of the other, she entered.

"Close the door."

Three words.

Innocent words that halted her progress as she came to a dead stop that almost saw her trip the distance between her and my desk.

With a hard swallow, she turned and gently clicked the door closed. I didn't doubt she was rethinking closing the distance between us, but all I could do while she had her back to me was to drink in the shape of her peachy arse which was encased in tight fitting stone-washed denim.

She spun suddenly, startling me and causing a blush of my own to creep up my cheeks, sure she knew I'd been ogling her behind.

I gestured to a chair, but with a single shake of her head, she declined, but did at least speak now. "I didn't want to disturb you, but you said you'd be able to take me to collect my car once Bea arrived . . . I mean it's fine if you can't. I can grab an Uber if you give me the address."

"Of course, sorry. I was working and forgot, but we can go now if you're ready?"

She nodded. I leapt to my feet and followed her towards the door where she came to an abrupt standstill and turned so quickly that my front almost collided with hers.

"Oh." She gasped that one word as I stood over her, one of my feet coming to rest between hers, our bodies close enough that I was almost pressed against her chest that I swore was heaving.

We froze in that moment, or was it that time stood still, with me, looking down, gazing into her blue eyes that told me everything I needed to know. This feeling, the pull towards her, might prove to be many things but the one thing it wasn't was one-sided. She felt it too. Was that why they said eyes were the window to a person's soul?

"Flora." I had no idea what that one slightly breathless word was, what I meant to say or convey in my utterance of her name.

She said nothing. She just nodded.

I leaned in, incapable of doing anything else. I wanted the taste of her on my lips and there was nothing that would stop that. "Say my name."

"Maurice."

Her reply was instant and did absolutely nothing but irritate me.

I shook my head and got exactly what I wanted from her.

"Maurizio."

My heart was ready to leap from my chest at the utterance of my name spoken by her for the first time. There was no denying the curl of my lips that continued until I was flashing my teeth at her.

I leaned in closer. She smelled delightful, vanilla, coconut and something else that begged me to devour her where she stood. Devourment would have to wait. My lips edged ever closer and that's when I saw her nervousness and hesitation. I pulled back slightly, what if this wasn't the right time? Although, would there ever be a right time for this? It was crazy. Of that I had no doubt, and yet, I couldn't think of anything I wanted to do more.

"Tell me to stop," I implored her, needing her to be one hundred percent on board with this and to suffer no regrets in its aftermath. For fuck's sake, this needed never to happen regardless of whether she was on board or not!

"Stop," she managed to whisper.

I stepped back and nodded. "Of course. If you'd rather get an Uber, I understand."

"It might be best, for us both, to have some distance."

I felt a strange sense of annoyance at her suggestion but, it was for the best because if we were confined to the small space of a car, then we both knew her whispered stop would be long forgotten.

"Grange Road, that's where the garage is, and they know you're collecting it this morning."

She nodded. "Thank you. Have a good day."

"You, too. I'll see you later."

With a slightly forced smile from us both, I stepped back and allowed her to open the door, leaving me behind with a hammering heart, a raging erection, and head full of conflicting ideas and thoughts.

The journey into work was difficult. Between roadworks, traffic, and some road closures, I was cutting it fine getting in a few minutes before I would need to leave for court. I still felt rather confused after the altercation this morning and wondered how things had got so heated so soon between me and Flora. I wanted her so badly, like I might just fucking die if I never got to kiss her. Yet, with space between us, I could see things more rationally. Things could go horribly wrong, in fact, they were more likely to go wrong than not, and then I'd be without a nanny and that would be grossly unfair on my children. Why the hell was I thinking with my cock? My children deserved better. Flora deserved better. The logical half of my brain was saying to end it before it got started, but the other half was saying to simply do it because this was inevitable so why fight it? I had to keep thinking about the consequences of my actions. That would be the only way to survive this.

The phone on my desk rang and because I was so engrossed in thoughts of Flora, I jumped, startled to realise I was still at work and losing the plot, clearly. I snatched the phone up and after identifying myself, I sat back and listened as I was told that the case I was due to defend that afternoon had been dropped by the CPS. This sometimes happened, but even in this instance it was bloody last minute. With a call to my client made, I realised I would be spending the afternoon in the office which even with my Flora consumed thoughts was a safer place than home.

Lost in work, and actually making a good go at pushing her from my thoughts, my desk phone rang. Upon answering, Flora marched up front and centre again as I spent the next ten minutes or so, making arrangements for a new car to be ordered for her. After she'd arrived on the back of a recovery truck, or at least her car had, I'd decided to add a car to her employee benefits, not that she knew that yet.

With a satisfied smirk, I began to pack away for the day, but those actions were thwarted when there was a knock of the door and the appearance of a junior colleague.

"You okay there, Rai?"

She hesitated in the doorway, a frown plaguing her browline. She entered and closed the door behind her.

"Looks like you'd better take a seat."

Rai explained that she had just taken a call from the representative of a very prominent celebrity who had been arrested and charged with the serious crime of rape. The evidence looked damning. His representative wanted to arrange a meeting that evening to discuss the case and also wanted me to represent him.

I looked at the clock on the wall, it was almost five so if I didn't leave soon, I was going to be late home.

"If I can get the nanny to stay on the clock I can do tonight, otherwise, it will have to be tomorrow."

Rai viewed me with suspicion. Before Sophie and I had split, I wouldn't have hesitated to stay behind. If she'd been lucky, my wife might have gotten a quick text, but now, things were different. *I* was different. The call to Flora was easy and she was more than happy to stay on and take care of the children. I smiled as she assured me she would bath them and put them to bed if I wasn't back, which I was unlikely to be. In the time since Flora had joined us, she had slotted in seamlessly. A lot of the credit for that belonged to Bea who had been amazing in her handover and befriending of Flora. The children had quickly adapted to the changes and were both thriving under the care of both nannies. Although, I had noticed that Bea was already beginning to take more of a back seat in some of the more mundane duties and I imagined this would only increase and move into more and more areas of my children's lives.

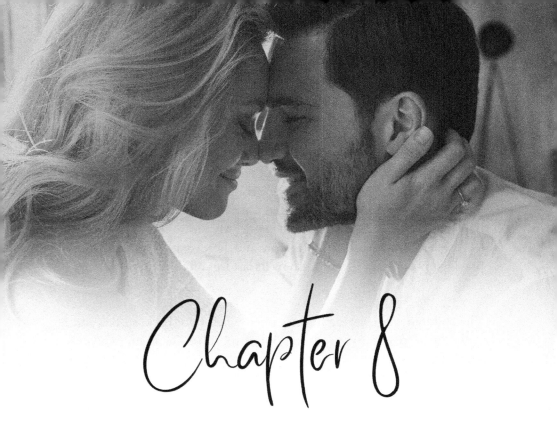

Chapter 8

Flora

So much for putting Mr Walker, Maurice...Maurizio on ice. God, that had sounded good, saying his name like that. It felt like intimacy on the tip of my tongue. But whatever his name, I wasn't doing so well with the bosszone. I still couldn't believe how close we'd come to kissing in his office. I'd nearly ended up with his tongue in my mouth at the very least.

"Bugger," I muttered as I got out of the Uber and made my way into the garage where I was greeted by a friendly man who seemed to know who I was.

He held out my keys and smiled. "Your boss called to say you were on your way. She's all ready for you."

I followed the point of his finger to where my car was parked on the other side of the road.

"I best pay you then."

He frowned. "All done."

I reciprocated his confusion with a frown of my own now.

"Your boss has already settled the bill."

"Oh." I had no other words, well not for the man before me, but my boss, that was a different matter because when I'd previously asked about cost, Maurice had simply said the guy owed him a favour. I had taken that to mean that he was doing a cheap job.

He handed me my keys with the warning words of, "I don't know how long she'll last. She's been well loved." My car was on its last legs.

I offered him a final thank you and headed back to the house, praying my car wasn't going to show its last legs on the ride home.

The children were playing in the garden when I got back, so Bea and I took the opportunity to sit outdoors to supervise them while we chatted.

"How are you finding it? All settled in?"

I stared at her and was unsure how to answer what should have been a simple question. My reaction must have been funny as I watched her laugh at me.

"That good, huh?"

"Sorry, yeah, all good. I love it here and the kids are great, and you and my rooms."

She flicked the dark blonde plait her hair was in and quirked a disbelieving brow at me.

"What?"

"Nothing," she replied, but her nothing was anything but. It spoke a thousand words.

Unsure if I wanted her to shut up and leave things be or if I needed a confidante who I could share my worries and concerns with, I said nothing.

"I don't know what else to say, but if you want to talk, I'm here."

I viewed her with suspicion. I didn't know her, not really, and she could easily throw me under the bus if I shared too much.

"The offer's there. No pressure." She shrugged. "You should meet my friend, Carrie. You'd like her. Everyone does."

I searched her tone, demeanour and expression at those last two words for anything akin to bitchiness, but there was none. Her pale blue eyes smiled as much as her mouth did. She was totally genuine in her belief and sentiment that everyone loved her friend.

"I don't have any friends or know anyone yet, so, that would be nice," I agreed as Rosie came running back to us.

"Craig has just done a wee in the bush down there." The little girl put a hand on her hip, horrified and disgusted at the idea of peeing in the garden.

Bea shook her head and got to her feet, ready to go and deal with Craig and his rogue, outdoor peeing behaviour.

"Let me," I offered. I got on with both of the children, but of the two of them, Craig was still a little resistant to my presence here at what he viewed as Bea's expense.

Rosie stood at my side, ready to escort me. Sensing that she may want her brother's chastisement to be greater than anything I intended to deliver, I told her to stay with Bea to keep her company. When she looked ready to object, I repeated my words but now it was more of a directive than a suggestion which she picked up on.

When I reached Craig, he was sat in the corner of the garden. His legs were pulled up so his face that was covered by his hands rested on his knees.

"Hey." I sat next to him and waited a few seconds. "I heard you got caught short."

He moved his hands and turned his head slightly, until he was looking at me. His very confused expression suggested he was unsure what my words had meant.

"You needed a wee . . . maybe left it a bit late to get inside to go?" I phrased my words as a question, allowing him to simply agree, not needing to make the kid feel scared or ashamed. In the grand scheme of things, a three-year-old little boy weeing in the garden wasn't exactly major in my book.

He nodded and looked as if he might cry.

I shuffled a little closer and draped an arm around his shoulders that I used to pull him in. "It happens to everyone."

He looked up, a small disbelieving frown creasing his brow.

"It does!" I laughed. "I have had to find somewhere quiet and private when there have been no toilets around."

"Really?" The tiniest of smiles tugged at his lips.

"Really. I promise you. I mean it. Everyone has done it at some point in their lives."

"Am I in trouble?" A wobble entered his voice as the possible consequences returned.

A shake of my head was my response. "I don't see why you would be. It's not like you do this all the time and it was an emergency, right?"

"I thought I might wet myself."

The shake of my head was now replaced with a nod. "So, an emergency, but you know, even if you had wet yourself, that would have been okay, you wouldn't have been in trouble for that either . . . accidents happen."

"I love Bea . . ." his voice trailed off. "But I like you. I'm glad you're our nanny too."

The smile cracking my face was my only response along with offering my hand so we might both get to our feet.

Bea had a doctor's appointment so planned on leaving early, but before she did, we managed more chatter while the children, who had exhausted themselves running around, took a short nap.

"You were saying earlier that you were enjoying life here . . ."

I looked across at Bea and laughed at her lack of subtlety.

"Sorry, well, I'm not sorry, but I can't do tactful very well."

I laughed again and she joined in.

"My friend, Carrie, she makes me look like a diplomat."

My laughter turned into a roar that saw me almost choke on my own saliva. "You're really selling her to me, aren't you?"

With a cheeky grin, she shrugged. "So, how are you finding things, really?"

"I wasn't lying to you earlier. I do love it here and talking to you, the kids and my rooms are great."

She nodded. "And Maurice?"

I couldn't tell if she was simply fishing for gossip. The question was undoubtedly loaded, but did she have ulterior motives? Studying her face, I saw nothing but sincere openness and it gave me no cause to question her intentions. She'd gone so far as to invite me to join her friendship group and to the best of my knowledge, Carrie was her only real friend.

"Maurice? Maurizio." I overemphasised his name and we both giggled.

"Yes, Maurizio," she said with a put on thick Italian accent that would have fitted better as a voice over for a pasta sauce advert.

"He's strange."

She arched a brow and her voice bestowed confusion at my choice of the word. "Strange?"

"Maybe not strange." I wasn't sure what to say about him but tried to find the right words again. "He has made me feel very welcome here. He paid for the repair on my car."

Bea looked startled at that. Clearly this wasn't his usual behaviour.

"He never really mentioned it and when I tried to pay, it was all done and dusted."

"I see."

"Do you? I'm not sure I do. Sorry. He is nice, more than nice, and he loves the children and I know he's been through a tough time with his wife and stuff."

Bea nodded. "And there's always the added bonus of him being attractive, he's very easy on the eye for a slightly older man."

I laughed and couldn't deny what she was saying. I wouldn't embarrass myself by attempting to dispute it.

"You've noticed, then?"

"It would be very hard not to, wouldn't it?" I wasn't lying, it would.

"It would. Just be careful. He's still on the rebound and you're new . . ."

Her voice trailed off as my face morphed into a horrified expression at what I perceived she was saying, that he was probably only looking for a convenient bunk up and I was new enough to replace without too much disruption.

Before either of us spoke again, my phone rang, speak of the devil. The boss needed me to stay on the clock until he got home. I had no problem with that and was happy to feed, bathe and put the children to bed if he wasn't back. Aside from that, I was even happier that my conversation with Bea had been cut short and by the time I got off the phone, she'd needed to leave so I didn't have time to think about it beyond that.

Although, I was going to think about it. Why lie to myself?

Chapter 9

Maurizio

Two hours later I was getting my head around the alleged rape my new client had been accused of and charged with. A lot of the evidence seemed circumstantial, but there was probably enough to make a decent case. Add to that my client's reputation as a bad boy, a womaniser, some resurfacing social media posts made during his ill spent youth and a few stupid errors in judgement that he'd made on the night in question, I could see why he'd come to me. Not to be arrogant, but I was good at what I did, the best, and whilst I was expensive, I was worth every penny when a case came to court.

"Right, let's go over it again."

My client, RadMan, otherwise known as Peter Grey, sighed.

I levelled him with a hard expression. "I need to know everything there is to know in order to defend you. When you're under oath and the prosecution make you go over and over your account of events and reveal something I don't know, I may not be able to repair the damage." My tone was firm. He knew I meant business. Now, I like my near perfect success rate, but if we lose your case I will still go home to my house and children." And nanny, I thought. "You, however, will be on your way to prison for a lengthy stay." I let that rest in the air for a second, nudging back in my chair like I had no worries at all. "So, shall we go over it again or shall I go home in time to put my children to bed and you can think about your life choices?"

Rad laughed. "There's a reason you charge so much and have the reputation you do."

I shrugged but continued to stare at the man opposite me.

"Fine! I went out with some friends . . ."

Rai continued to record everything while I listened and fired questions for the next two hours.

By the time I pulled up outside my house, I was exhausted but smiled, happy to be home. The thought of Flora also helped push away some of the fatigue the day had left on me. I took a moment to again consider how well the time she had been with us had gone. How my home was running with effortless ease and the precision of a very expensive clock. I considered the pull I felt to her, the obviously mutual attraction, and wondered just how much of a train wreck acting upon that could turn out to be. I refused to be drawn on that particular question. I'd had enough questions tonight. Instead, I looked at the house. A few lights were on; the upstairs landing, lamplight from the lounge and the kitchen, which was fully illuminated.

I grabbed my things, strolled to the door and unlocked it. I was greeted by the smell of garlic, tomatoes, basil and a variety of other gorgeous aromas that suggested food had been cooked. My stomach grumbled in protest at being deprived of food since a quick sandwich at lunchtime. I dropped my briefcase in the hall next to the table where I placed my keys and wallet before heading to the kitchen where the smells were emanating from, but it wasn't the food that caused me to pull up short, it was Flora.

She stood, barefoot on her tip toes, reaching up, stretching to retrieve a glass from a high shelf and as she did so, I remained frozen on the spot, mesmerised by her. She wore short pyjamas in a soft looking cotton. The top fitted like a cropped t-shirt, while the shorts clung to her peachy arse and as she stretched there was a tantalising amount of cheek protruding from each leg . . . barely a handful and yet that was all I could think of, cupping her behind and allowing my grip to tighten so she could feel my possession but without hurting her.

Briefly, my mind went back to Sophie, my wife, the woman who, months before had left me and the children. When we had first been together and early in our marriage, we had been unable to keep our hands off one another. Had it been Sophie I had walked in on like this I would have marched across the room and had her naked and spread out on the floor or a surface, with me inside her. My hands would have been covering every inch of her body and my mouth claiming hers. When the children had been born, things had changed and then continued to do so until there was very little intimacy between us. I allowed myself an internal chuckle that the reason for that may have had something to do with the fact that she had left me because she had been having an affair with another woman and had recently confirmed that she was a lesbian, not bisexual, but a lesbian, so I guess I was never going to be enough for her.

I avoided wondering why she had married me or had the children. Had she always been gay, or had she not realised until she'd met the right person? Maybe none of it needed labels and it was just a case that she had realised our relationship didn't fulfil her or make her happy, and her current one did, regardless of gender. I had offered the option of being bi so as to give her a way back to me and the children. She'd rejected it. Maybe she was stronger than me and I had simply given her that as an option for us to carry on as we had been and in turn had been hoping to make my own life easier. I needed to stop thinking about this, torturing myself with ifs, buts and maybes. If I was honest, neither of us had been happy for a while, not really. Sophie had moved on, and my attraction to Flora suggested I might be able to do the same. However, I did need to speak to Sophie and discuss next steps for the children and both of us. Perhaps I should seek legal advice, too, in terms of the children and formally starting a divorce.

Returning my attention to Flora, I watched as she stretched further, the muscles in her legs tensing until everything was taut.

"Do you need a hand?" I asked, unsure if I meant with getting a glass or whether I was thinking of her arse in my hands again.

She spun to face me, her body dropping to its natural height as the glass that she'd finally got hold of came flying towards me. I jumped forward, just about catching it before it ended up in a million pieces on the floor.

Her breathing was fast and she clutched her chest which was completely covered and yet, the way the fabric clung to her curves drew my eyes until I was sure I could see her actual breasts rather than just the curve of them, although there was no mistaking the bullets of her nipples that pushed against the fabric of her top.

"Sorry," we both said in unison, me for giving her a fright and her for throwing the glass in my direction.

We stared across at each other and a tension settled between us.

"I was getting a drink of water," she said pointing towards the glass I still held.

I offered it to her. "And I was just coming home."

We both laughed at our pathetic attempts to diffuse the crackle in the air.

"Would you like a drink of water?" she asked and flushed as she heard her own offer of my water from my tap in my kitchen.

"No, thanks, I'm fine, but you go ahead." I didn't want her to feel awkward because as much as this was my home it was her place of work and an extension of her home upstairs. Plus, the only reason she was here now was because she had done me the favour of staying over.

"I should go, home, upstairs, to bed . . . there's some dinner in the fridge . . . pasta with chicken and vegetables . . . I saved you some, but if you don't want it you don't have to . . ." Her rambles trailed off as she allowed an over exaggerated and forced yawn to leave her mouth.

"Okay. Thank you, for tonight, the children, dinner, staying over . . ." Her rambling was clearly contagious.

"I'll be off then." She seemed reluctant to leave and I was enjoying some adult company in the evening, even if it was infantile and a little awkward.

"Okay."

She made to pass by me and I grabbed her wrist, the air threatening to ignite around us as my touch appeared to burn us both, especially judging by how we jumped. This was bad . . . I mean it was good, but like really bad, and if I was a wise man I would let her go and never consider touching her again.

"Or you could stay, and I'll open a bottle of wine . . . we could chat, get to know one another." The wise man had pissed off for the night, and I was clearly a fool.

Chapter 10

Flora

Get to know one another. That's what he'd said and that was my cue to leave, and quickly. Or it should have been.

He looked at me, taking in my silence and waited. Presumably he wanted a clue or indication of whether I wanted him to open the bottle of wine or not.

I did. Absolutely, yet I had no clue if the wine was simply an invitation to enjoy a drink and a chat, or if it was more. Like kissing more. Touching more. Sex more.

He stepped closer. "Flora, wine?"

I was like a rabbit caught in headlights.

With another step towards me, my breathing hitched as I inhaled his scent . . . the aroma of fading aftershave, washing powder and a unique smell that I thought might be all him. I didn't need alcohol. I was already getting drunk.

"Or tea?"

I thought he was as aware of my giddy state as I was.

Tea was safe, wasn't it? Clearly, I thought so. "Yes, tea would be nice."

"Go into the lounge and I'll bring it through."

He smiled at me, seeming genuinely happy that I had agreed to have tea with him.

A few minutes passed before he appeared with two cups, me on the sofa while he took a chair.

"You got your car okay?" He immediately continued. "I saw it outside."

I was immediately irritated by him bringing this up in such a way when he clearly knew that there couldn't have been an issue collecting my car as he had paid for it. "Presumably, you'd have known if I hadn't got it okay, considering you picked up the tab."

He looked confused. "I told you the bill was sorted."

"And I thought the mechanic was doing a cheap deal, not that you were paying regardless."

"Oh. Sorry. I thought, when we discussed it, what I meant was clear and you'd looked concerned at the cost, so I wanted to help."

My annoyance began to lift slightly. "I will pay you back–"

He cut me off. "There's no need."

"There's every need. So, you can either take it directly from my pay or I will arrange to transfer it to you."

I had no clue what the cost would be, so my offer was potentially bold.

"Of course. I can take it from your pay, maybe over a few months?"

I was grateful for the offer. "Thank you."

He offered a single nod of his head and although it was accompanied by a half-smile, he looked irked, but I had no intention of taking money from him that I hadn't earned.

"The children went off to bed okay?" That was a welcome change of topic.

"Yes, no problem. They're incredibly well behaved."

He laughed and the area around his eyes crinkled, but even that was attractive.

I gave myself an internal nudge to focus on the conversation.

"Give it time and I am sure you'll be privy to a meltdown or twenty."

I shrugged. "Perhaps that's part of their charm."

"Perhaps it is. What made you want to work with children?"

I recalled that question being asked in my interview but presumably he wanted the personal answer rather than the standard one. "I didn't know what I wanted to do for a while. I was a little lost I suppose." Why had I said that? It was true but he didn't need to know that. I noticed a quirk of his brows and a tilt of his head but rushed on, brushing over it. "I worked in admin and retail, all sorts and then one day, I was sitting in the park feeling a little disillusioned with life when I got chatting to a little girl who was there with her mum. The mum had a baby in a sling and this little girl was desperate to play and chat. I played and chatted, and for the first time in a long time I felt as if I was contributing something and I was happy. The mum, it turned out was looking for a nanny for when she returned to work and kind of offered me a job. I enrolled in evening school and trained while I worked for the family. I loved it. I don't know that I ever chose being a nanny, it chose me I think."

Looking across at Maurizio, he was beaming as I enthused about my introduction to the world of nannying. "A vocation. Did you stay with them long, the family?"

"About four years. They moved away, although they offered me the chance to join them in America, but I chose to stay at home." Before he probed into the reason for that, I moved on. "I worked for a couple of other families and then went to work in a nursery, which was different, but a good experience."

"You prefer working with families?"

I laughed as I imagined saying no. I was tempted to do just that to see what his reaction would be.

"Absolutely not fishing for compliments here."

I laughed again but answered his question. "I do. It's more personal and I enjoy the familiarity of a family and a home."

"That makes sense, although there must be times where the familial aspect is a double edged sword."

"I suppose it is. My last family went through a separation and eventually a divorce and it was hard to almost be in the middle of it, trying to protect the children." His face dropped and I panicked that I had somehow reminded him of his own children being stuck in the middle of their parents' marital breakdown. Quickly I tried to lighten things again. "However, being in a family allows me to share in the magical moments too, like Craig getting caught short and weeing in the garden to the horror of Rosie."

Maurizio laughed, a genuine booming sound. "When you've gotta go . . ."

"Indeed, but Rosie didn't quite see it that way."

He laughed again. "Yeah, no grey areas, it's black or white for my girl."

"Does she get that from you? You being a barrister, wrong and right, legal or illegal?"

"Trust me, the law is many things, none of them entirely black and white."

"How was your day?" As I asked the question, it occurred to me that I'd never really thought about the details of his job, and we certainly hadn't talked about it.

He crinkled his nose and furrowed his brow a little. "Long. Something, a case, came up late, but it was okay."

"You enjoy your work?" I got the impression he did and his nod confirmed it.

"It wasn't my first choice of career, but I do, and I'm pretty good at what I do."

I was surprised by that. "What was your first choice?"

"Astronaut until I was about seven, then I wanted to be a magician and by the time I was thirteen, professional rugby player seemed like a good choice."

I laughed at the astronaut and magician at least. The thought of Maurizio wearing a tight rugby shirt and those teeny tiny shorts made me feel many things, none of them were amusement. My cheeks heated and when I glanced across at him, I suspected he'd noticed.

"And finally law?"

"Indeed," he replied with a smile. "I've always been pretty decent at debating and offering a persuasive argument, so maybe it was an obvious choice."

"Can I ask something, about your work?" I felt slightly nervous in case my questions and thoughts somehow offended him.

"Of course, I'm happy to answer any questions you have."

"You defend people." I knew he did, both Bea and his mother had mentioned it. "What if someone is guilty and you help them avoid justice, prison, do you feel guilty?"

He sipped his tea and seemed to be studying me before a small smile curled his lips. "That old chestnut." He smiled but explained, "I am lucky that I can choose who I defend and who I don't. If someone is innocent, or I believe them to be, I will defend them to the best of my ability, regardless of the crime. If I believe someone is possibly guilty, I would still defend them. If I knew they were guilty and the crime was one I considered dangerous, I would be disinclined to take them on."

"That must be hard, to know if they're telling the truth."

He shrugged. "Not as hard as you might think. I have dealt with a lot of people and crimes, plus, professionally I can quickly spot a hole in an account of events."

That made sense.

"The case I agreed to take on today is an allegation of rape."

I stared at him, my mouth hanging loose in shock.

"I am satisfied he is innocent of that charge. His actions ultimately left him open to such allegations, but he didn't rape anyone, of that, I am sure."

"What if he did?"

"He didn't," Maurizio told me, his tone sounding slightly antsy.

"But if he did or if it goes to court, will you question the victim?" I could feel my anxiety rising at the thought of a rape victim being cross examined and having to *prove* themselves.

"As she would be the prosecution's star witness, of course, but I should stress, again, she wasn't raped." He looked at me intently and for a few seconds remained silent, as did I, unsure what to say. "It must seem very odd to you, to imagine victims of crimes having their day in court and the defence trying to pick holes in their story and cast doubt on their account of things, but the thing you have to remember is that the onus is on the prosecution to prove guilt, and everyone has the right to be defended."

I nodded and offered him a warm smile. His explanation made sense and reassured me that he really was a nice man and all round decent human being. "Innocent til proven guilty?"

"Exactly, but like I say, I choose who I defend and if someone is guilty or their crimes offend me, I wouldn't defend them."

"Really?" I was unsure if I believed that. Would he really turn down work? Would he be able to?

"Yes, really." His tone was suddenly firmer. "My role isn't as cut and dried as simply proving their innocence. Sometimes, if they are likely to be found guilty it can be more about getting them the best outcome possible. And for the record, I have turned down cases and will again if I felt it were needed. One case involved crimes against children. Even I wasn't convinced of this guy's innocence, and the evidence was pretty damning, so I said no. I have to come home and face my children, Flora, and I wouldn't be able to live with myself if I allowed someone to go out into the world knowing they were capable of causing real harm to others. I also have to face myself in the mirror."

With my empty cup still in my hand, I decided I should go. We'd talked and had tea together, which had been the plan. "I should go."

Already on my feet, I placed my cup on the coffee table and made my way to the door that led into the hall. Maurizio followed me. Turning, I came to a standstill.

"Thank you for the tea, and the chat."

"You're welcome, anytime. I enjoyed it."

My pulse hammered in my neck, my palms sweated as my whole body began to radiate heat. Looking up, I stared into his big, dark eyes that were hypnotising me, drawing me in.

Maurizio's hand raised until he was pushing some loose hair behind my ear and as his touch withdrew, his thumb brushed across my cheek. I leaned into his touch, closing my eyes, savouring and enjoying the contact and sensations it triggered within me.

"Flora," Maurizio called, prompting me to open my eyes to find his face had moved closer to mine.

Oh God, what should I do? I wanted him to kiss me, could think of nothing I wanted more at that second, but knowing I shouldn't want it scared me.

"Tell me to stop," he said.

He knew this was a bad idea, too, and his words confirmed that.

"Tell me," he implored.

So, I did. "Stop."

He nodded but made no move or comment.

"I should go—to bed—my bed—alone—to sleep—goodnight."

All those words had spilled from my mouth with no thought or plan in mind and I didn't doubt that was clear to my boss who I had turned my back on without so much as a look backwards.

By the time I reached my own home, I was beyond red and embarrassed. "You stupid bloody fool!" I hissed to my reflection. "Shit!" How the hell was I going to face him in the morning, or ever again for that matter!

I was supposed to be catching up with Maddie tonight, but I knew she'd smell a rat before hello left my lips, so I text her and said I was going to bed with a headache and would catch up with her soon, which I would, when the moment was right for me. I crawled into bed rather than simply climbing in and with the covers pulled over my head, I hoped and prayed that when I woke up this would turn out to have been a dream . . . well, nightmare, but whichever, so long as it wasn't real.

Morning came all too soon, as did the realisation that last night had really happened. With a groan, I got out of bed, washed and dressed. It wasn't like I could avoid facing my boss as I worked and lived in his home.

I nervously headed into the kitchen where I found Bea and the children. I looked around, catching Bea's attention.

"Looking for something? Someone?" She smirked.

"What? No!" I protested a little too weakly. The last thing I needed was for Bea, or anyone else to get the wrong impression about me and Maurizio, or to spread those impressions off as gossip.

She chuckled. "Okay, whatever you say. Maurice has already left for work by the way. He said he'll be back no later than five."

I nodded, unsure what, if anything I should say.

"What are you up to tonight?" Bea asked.

I shook my head. "Nothing." Well, not unless I somehow ended up in a tryst with our boss. But I kept that thought to myself.

"Then come out with me. Carrie and I are meeting up for dinner. We're both pregnant and off booze but you don't have to be."

I must have looked hesitant.

"Think about it," she added with a warm smile.

Suddenly it occurred to me that my hesitation may have come across as ungrateful. "Sorry, I'd love to. Thank you."

"Great." Bea sounded genuinely excited that I'd agreed to join her and her friend. "I know I've said it before, but you'll love Carrie. She really is great."

The children interrupted us as they argued about what was the best choice for breakfast that morning.

My day had been good. I'd go as far as to say fun. We had just got home from the park and while I told Bea to sit down and catch her breath, I set about getting some snacks sorted for us all.

"Would you like milk, water or juice?"

Rosie answered first. "Milk, please. Did you know that milk helps to make you bones and teeth grow strong. It has a special ingredient . . ." She seemed to think hard. "Daddy called it calc, erm, calm, erm, what is it?" she asked.

"Calcium," I suggested.

"Yes!" she squealed. "My daddy is so clever, Flora. He knows really big words." The pride beaming from her smiling face took my breath away for a second as the adoration she had for him took me back to being a little girl myself.

Emotion stuck in my throat as I replied. "Yes, he is."

"Uncle Nico calls him a smart bum, but uses a bad word," Craig told me.

Rosie and I giggled before Craig continued.

"Ass is the bad word."

I howled while Rosie's faced morphed into complete horror. "Craig!" she cried, a hand on her hip. "We're not supposed to say that even if Uncle Nico does."

Suddenly my mind went to Uncle Nico who seemed something of a rogue. Returning my attention to the children, Craig looked worried. "Maybe don't say that again, okay?"

He nodded and offered me a small smile.

"Would you like milk too?"

"Yes, please. Flora, can we have biscuits too?"

"Of course." I leaned down and ruffled his hair before turning back to Rosie. "Why don't you go and turn the TV on and I'll bring your snacks through."

With the bikes they'd taken to the park already away, and the remnants of our picnic discarded, I took their snacks through and found the children huddled together on the sofa, snoring. Clearly, all the excitement of the day had taken its toll and they were exhausted.

Looking down at them I couldn't get over just how cute they were. I wondered what it was like for them, to have never known an existence without the other. Their other half. From the second they were conceived the other had been there. The first person they'd each seen was the other. My sister and I were close, really close, but the two children cuddling had a closeness that was unimaginable. My next thought related to their mother who I believed had walked out on their father and somehow managed to leave her babies behind, too. I tried not to be judgemental, but I was struggling here. I knew that she was a lawyer like Maurizio and assumed she worked long hours as he did at times, but surely, even if she hadn't been able to take them, you'd want to be in regular contact with them. Perhaps she was and I was unaware of it. There was no reason why I should know the details but in the time I had lived and worked here, the children's mother hadn't visited, not once. I'd seen a picture of her in the children's room and there were a couple of photos dotted around the house of them all when Rosie and Craig were babies.

"They look so angelic when they're sleeping, don't they?"

I jumped at the sound of Maurice's voice. Still clutching my chest from the shock of his appearance, I laughed at his observation. "They're also angelic when awake."

He smiled as he came to stand at my side. "I wonder if you'll still say that in a year's time?"

I turned to look at him in profile and almost wished I hadn't. He really was a very attractive man and in that second I was catapulted back to the previous night. I think we both were if the tension between us was anything to go by. He turned to face me and smiled. God! Not for the first time, I was questioning my decision to tell him to stop the previous night.

"I should take the milk and biscuits back into the kitchen." I was flailing, unsure what to say or do to diffuse the tension and remove myself from being under his scrutiny. "Bea might need some help." Jumping from one random topic to another, confirmed my floundering.

He reached for me and gently gripped my wrist as he said my name, stopping me dead in my tracks. My skin felt as if it had been burnt. The tingle and singe had me gasping, then breathing deeply and noisily as my chest heaved, my pulse quickened, and my palms grew damp . . . and other parts of my anatomy, considerably lower down.

Although I didn't make any attempt to shake free of his hold, I think he thought I was going to. He tightened his grip ever so slightly, never once taking his eyes off me.

"Flora, Bea looked exhausted so has left for the day."

"Oh."

I whispered that one word but had no idea what his words meant. Did he mean that I didn't need to help her as she'd gone, or was it more that he was telling me that my very obvious excuse for leaving was null and void?

"I was going to ask you if you wanted to have dinner, but Bea informs me that you have plans with her and Carrie."

I nodded.

His grip loosened until he was no longer touching me, a move that left my skin cold and bereft of his touch. "I'll take it from here, with the kids. Treat yourself to an early finish and have a lovely night with the girls."

With the glasses of milk and biscuits on the tray I'd carried them in on, I returned them to the kitchen and ran upstairs as fast as my feet could carry me. I really had no idea just how many times I'd be able to resist my boss or continue telling him to stop.

Chapter 11

Maurizio

"Daddy."

I screwed my face up until it was contorted in a combination of disappointment that my daughter was still awake and resignation that I was going to become embroiled in at least two more bedtime stories and possibly a lengthy discussion. "Yes, sweetheart." Turning, I saw Rosie fidgeting until she sat up in bed, looking at me expectantly.

"Can I ask you something?"

Maybe I'd get away with the story telling if she was going straight in with asking questions. "Of course."

My daughter patted the space next to her on the bed and I dutifully took my place there.

"Does Bea have to leave?"

I looked down at her confused little face and wondered what was going on in her head. "Well, you know she is having a baby, so she'll need to take some time off to have the baby and take care of him, or her, won't she?"

Rosie nodded.

"I mean, if she still wants to come and visit, she can. Then when she's had some time with her baby, she can come back and work here, if she wants to." I resisted the temptation to lay the groundwork for the fact that Bea may choose not to return to work. Actually, I very much doubted that her boyfriend would want her to come back, and I thought that once she had her own baby in her arms, she'd be totally on board with that.

My daughter continued to frown, meaning my response was either not the one she wanted or there was something else on her mind. When she started to speak it became clear it was the latter.

"Like Mummy?"

"Mummy?" I sat straighter with a start at the introduction of Sophie, but unclear which part of Bea's maternity leave was like Mummy.

"Well, she left for a little bit and then she came back." Her voice broke. "But then she went again, and she phones us, but she doesn't visit so much."

Fucking hell! Why had I never thought of it that way? My poor baby girl. All this shit had no place in her young and innocent mind. If Sophie appeared right now, I might just fucking throttle her with my bare hands. I didn't want my wife to be unhappy and she clearly had been with me. My ego had taken a bit of a chink in its armour when she'd announced her discontentment, more so when I realised her life with me had been a lie of sorts for some of our time together, if not all of it. She was their mother and I got that she needed time to get her own shit together and to explore her new relationship, but not at our children's expense. The reality had been that 'her return' had been fleeting, no more and that had clearly done Rosie and probably Craig more harm than good, but this had still been her home so even if I'd wanted to at that stage, I couldn't deny her the opportunity to return, could I?

"I could speak to Mummy, see if she is able to visit soon." I had no idea if this was possible from Sophie's end.

Rosie nodded. "Can Mummy come back home, if she wants to?"

What was I supposed to say to that because the real answer to that was no. A big fat fucking no. Not because I held any malice for her but because we were done. Forever. And no matter what she decided, I wouldn't be her fallback guy, no matter how much I loved my kids. I had far too much self-respect for that. Plus, my mother would kick my arse back to Italy a dozen times over if I gave Sophie so much as a sniff of another chance.

"Darling, no." I felt like a complete bastard as fresh, hot tears rolled down my little girl's beautiful face. "Mummy will always be your mummy and Daddy would never keep you from seeing her, you nor Craig, but Mummy and Daddy can't be together anymore. We both love you so much, more than anything or anyone, and that will never change."

She nodded. We'd had this conversation when Sophie first left and a couple of times after, but not for a while and clearly Bea, another constant in their life moving on had prompted these worries.

"I know things might feel a little strange when Bea leaves to have her baby, but that is why Flora is here, too, so we can all get to know each other and become friends."

Rosie nodded again. "We made cakes with Bea today."

I let out a short chuckle at the turn in conversation. "Did you save me one?"

"We saved you two . . ." Her voice trailed off.

"But . . ."

She giggled. "We ate them, me and Craig."

"No!" I cried as quietly as I could so as not to wake my son who let out a little snore.

She giggled again at my horrified expression. "Flora said we can make biscuits tomorrow."

"That sounds nice. Will you save me one of those then?"

"I'll try."

I laughed at her non-committal response.

"Flora let us help her cook pasta last night . . . she put tomatoes and green stuff in it and lots of vegetables, but they were nice." She looked agog at the idea of green stuff, which I assumed were herbs or spinach, being put into her dinner. "We saved you some of that," she added as an afterthought.

"Thank you. I will have that for dinner tonight then. If you're okay and ready to sleep?" I was starving, but if my little girl needed me to stay and hold her hand or anything else, then that is what I would do.

She shook her head as she let out a yawn, confirming that she was ready for sleep.

"Night, my sweet girl." I leaned down and kissed her goodnight. "Do you like Flora?" This wasn't me fishing, this was me making sure that I had made the right choice in employing her as Bea's replacement.

"She's funny and plays with us. Before, Craig did a wee in the garden—"

My laughter cut off my daughter's tale. She didn't need to know I already knew this story so I let her carry on.

"Daddy . . ." She frowned at me disapprovingly. "It's not funny. He didn't need to do that. There are lots of toilets in the house."

She was right, there were.

"Sorry, sweetheart. Maybe I should have a word with Craig tomorrow."

She shook her head. "Flora spoke to him. She sat with him on the grass and chatted." Another frown creased her brow. "I wanted to go with her when she was talking to him, but she wouldn't let me."

I smiled, partly at my daughter's dismay at missing out on front row seats to Flora speaking to Craig, but also at Flora's handling of the situation, in private, discreetly, in a calm and dignified way. Just as it should be.

"And she likes us to help her when she cooks and stuff . . ." Rosie was back on why she liked Flora. "Oh, and she's pretty and smells nice."

I felt the smirk spread across my face. She was pretty. Gorgeous, in fact. And fuck it, she did smell really nice. Nice enough to eat. I couldn't think of her in that way, especially not eating her, specifically not when I was tucking my daughter up for the night. With a final straighten of the bed covers and another kiss, I prepared to leave.

"Night, Daddy."

. . .

As I sat in the kitchen with the pasta from the night before and a beer, I stared down at my phone. With Sophie's number already selected, I braced myself for the call I needed to make, if only to get some idea of when Sophie planned on seeing the children. The first mouthful of pasta in my mouth had me moaning as the flavours burst against my taste buds. This tasted divine and immediately I imagined the taste of the cook herself.

"Fuck," I said with a laugh aimed at my own obsessive weirdo behaviour. I felt my cock stiffen slightly at the thought of Flora's taste on my tongue. I was like an adolescent all over again.

Looking back down at my phone I decided I might need to be a grown-up for a little while. I snatched it up and hit dial and waited for the call to connect.

Chapter 12

Flora

Any nerves I'd had at meeting Bea's friend, Carrie, disappeared within seconds of us all taking our seats at a table in a local bistro. She was funny, warm, friendly, and very chatty. For the first five minutes she spoke about her daughter, Charlotte, and the baby she was carrying and then went on a twenty-minute rant about her husband, Gabe, who, it appeared, was getting increasingly protective of her as her pregnancy progressed. She swore, laughed and threw in the odd hiss as she went over the struggle she'd had to get out without him and then reeled off all of the rules he'd laid down for her.

"He's a bloody nightmare," she finally finished, but then a huge grin spread across her face. "But he's mine and I love him."

Both Bea and I laughed at her admission, not that it was a surprise, not even to me because every time she said his name, spoke about him or revealed another fact, she beamed. She was totally head over heels for her husband.

Once Carrie had finished, Bea launched into her own little rant about Seb. Her rendition of Seb's overprotective routine included him banning her from taking a bath in case the water in the tub somehow drowned the baby, to him becoming a nutrition expert who spent hours in the supermarket checking labels. The one that amused me and Carrie the most was his sudden refusal to have sex because he didn't want to hurt the baby by poking him in the head.

Carrie snorted loudly, while I ended up losing some of the wine I'd taken a good gulp of down my nose.

"This might be absolutely none of my business, but just how hung is he?" I asked and while Bea laughed and gave me a wink, Carrie put her fingers in her ears and began to hum loudly.

"Well, not to do my man a disservice, whilst his concerns for our unborn baby's risk of a serious head injury are ill placed, he is beyond adequate."

"No!" squealed Carrie. "I can't sit opposite him at family functions knowing details."

Bea and I sniggered more than a little immaturely, before Bea waved her friend's concerns away.

Once Carrie had removed her fingers from her ears and was picking up her glass again, Bea squealed three words quickly, "Like a horse."

Tears ran down my face while Bea roared with laughter.

"For fuck's sake! How the hell am I going to face Seb when he sits in my house having his hair, nails and make-up done by my daughter, knowing he's packing?"

Bea shrugged as I continued to cry with barely contained laughter as I drank my wine. "You two would be out of control with alcohol, I am sure."

"Well, once these babies have hatched, we'll show you how hard core we are," Carrie said before turning her attention fully to me. "Now that we have provided amusement via our men, tell us about you. Boyfriend, ex, someone in your sights."

"Ouch!" I cried as I was kicked beneath the table.

"Sorry, was that you? I didn't mean to kick you." Bea looked embarrassed, unlike Carrie who laughed again.

"I think the kick was meant for me."

Carrie rolled her eyes at her friend and it suddenly became clear. Bea had intended to kick her in an attempt to warn her about going down the line of conversation that was my romantic past or present, and presumably, Maurizio, who was now on her conversational radar.

"Sorry," Bea said again, but this time it wasn't for the kick, maybe more for having discussed me and presumably Maurizio.

"No problem. I have no boyfriend, the most horrendous track record, and possibly even worse taste when it comes to the opposite sex."

"Let's drink to the opposite sex," said Bea, raising her alcohol-free cocktail for us to clink.

I laughed with a shake of my head. "Did you not hear that I have really bad taste in the opposite sex?"

"That's because you haven't tried things with the right man," Carrie chipped in.

"Oh God! You two are like a bloody tag team."

They looked at each other then back to me and smirked.

"Well, I'm not looking, so . . ."

"And that is when it happens," Carrie shrilled, as if issuing a warning. "Look at us, neither of us were looking."

"What happened with the Walkers?" I was fishing but I thought it was a reasonable question to ask. She had never visited or had access to the children to the best of my knowledge since my arrival, so, where was she and why was she absent?

"I'm not sure that's really our business," Bea replied and sounded prickly.

Judging by Carrie's expression, I was not the only one taken aback by her response.

"I'm not asking for specific details. I was just curious as to why she didn't see the children and if there was something I should be aware of. I wasn't being nosey or looking for gossip." I'd taken on the same prickly tone. I did admit, internally, that there was more to my quest for knowledge, just a little.

"Of course not," Carrie said now, throwing Bea a sideways glance. "Sophie left, suddenly. Long story short, she had been having an affair with another woman and she left. The children remained with Maurice and had Bea to care for them and that caused the least amount of disruption to their lives. Sophie came back very, very briefly and then went again."

Still, Bea said nothing.

"I don't understand how she could remain away from them. Her relationship with their father is irrelevant in all of this."

"I don't have any answers on that. I don't understand it either." Carrie sounded genuinely perplexed, as I was, but in no way judging Sophie, perhaps, unlike me.

"Maybe none of us need to because it's none of our business."

Carrie and I both spun to face Bea who looked conflicted.

"I'm not being a bitch to you Flora, really I'm not, but I knew Sophie, liked her, and although she wasn't a friend like Carrie and you are, for a while she felt like one, so talking about her makes me feel uncomfortable."

Perhaps I had been naïve to have not thought about Bea's relationship with Sophie, but truly, I hadn't seen that coming. Watching on as Carrie stretched over and patted her hand, maybe she hadn't either.

"I'm going to the toilet," I told them, hoping that my return would allow us to revert back to simpler, easier topics, even if that did mean dealing with their answer for everything attitude.

"And then we'll talk about Maurice when you return," said Bea. Her words earning her a high five from her friend. "Like your doe-eyed expression and the rise in temperature when you're together."

I couldn't help but like them both, I was relieved that my broaching of the subject of Sophie hadn't damaged things in our fledgling relationship, but they were going to be a pain in my arse with their need to fix me up and make me as 'happy' as they were, especially as there was only one man who currently made me 'happy'.

There was another glass of wine waiting for me when I retook my seat.

"So, Maurice," Carrie said with a glance at Bea.

"You could cut the sexual tension with a knife," Bea told her friend while I sat there, unsure what to say, especially as I considered Bea's flat tone.

"Come on, Flora, you can tell us anything. When I first moved here,

I knew nobody and then I met a few nannies, one of whom was Bea. She became my friend and helped me through the minefield of things between me and Gabe."

Bea took things up now. "Same for me. I had a few friends, but nobody especially close until Carrie. She introduced me to Seb and when things got serious, or just tricky, I went to her and if nothing else, she listened to me."

I nodded, understanding what they had, but doubting if I could fit into that friendship with them. Especially as I recalled earlier what had felt like Bea warning me off. Although, it had seemed she was warning me off discussing Sophie rather than fancying the pants off her estranged husband.

"Maurice likes you. Like I say, the sexual tension is unmistakable." Bea looked at me and waited for a response.

"He is very, very handsome, and smells better than anything I have ever known."

"Yay!" Carrie let out a loud cheer. "You are seriously fucked if you are already hooked on his smell."

I laughed, and Bea joined in too.

"Come on, tell us all about how he smells and then we'll move on to his bum . . . I love a nice tight bum . . . and don't ever tell my husband I said this, but old Maurice is packing some seriously biteable booty."

My laughter increased, but she was absolutely right.

Watching their eyes grow wider as they seemed to sense some kind of admission or revelation from me, I knew I needed to play this down because, apart from anything else, there was no me and Maurizio to discuss. Not really. As lovely as these two seemed. and Bea had been nothing but friendly and welcoming, I didn't know them well enough yet to trust them to be confidantes and I didn't want to compromise Bea or our relationship by inadvertently making her uncomfortable about Maurizio or Sophie again.

"But he is my boss, and totally out of bounds."

They exchanged a glance that said they weren't buying it.

"There's no harm in window shopping though, is there?" I asked, raising my glass in salute before clinking it against theirs.

"I won't point out that my husband was also my boss."

With a shake of my head, I laughed. Laughter they both joined in with.

"I thought I recognised the sound of witches around a cauldron."

I snapped my eyes in the direction of the male voice that had interrupted us to find an attractive, younger man, at least younger than me, standing at our table wearing a beaming smile that showed off his dazzling white teeth.

Both Carrie and Bea leapt up and engulfed him in a group hug. "Ash!" they cried in stereo, making all three of them laugh.

Turning to me, Carrie made the introductions, "This is Flora, she is Bea's replacement with the Walkers. Flora, this is Ash, he's a manny for a family at the far end of the village."

"Manny?" I wasn't sure if I'd heard correctly.

"Yes," he confirmed offering me a hand and a smile. "I am a nanny, but as I am a man, these two thought they were so bloody witty by making me a manny! They have watched too many reruns of *Friends*." He rolled his eyes but grinned at the other two women.

"Join us," Bea said. "We are both on the wagon, but Flora isn't so you could keep her company."

"I'd love to." With a wink in my direction, he took the space next to me.

Chapter 13

Maurizio

I was like an anxious father as I paced the room and continued to periodically check through the window to see if Flora had returned home. She hadn't. I'd spoken to Sophie and although she was a bit wishy washy initially, when I explained how concerned Rosie was at the idea of Bea's departure, she agreed that her contact needed to be more frequent and consistent. She'd committed to getting back to me over the next few days with some concrete dates and times to visit and hopefully take the children overnight to reassure them that although their parents were no longer together, they would always have us both and be our priority.

Unsure what else to do, despite the fact that I had work I could be getting on with, I meandered through to the kitchen and put the kettle on, not that I wanted tea or coffee.

It was from my position standing in the window that I saw head-lights coming up the drive. When the car eventually came to a stop, I saw it was a taxi, one Flora was climbing out of, and then I watched as she dipped back in to kiss Bea and Carrie goodnight. I liked them both, although I knew Bea better than her friend. I was transfixed at the sight of Flora in body hugging jeans and a casual sweater as she swayed towards her entrance to the upstairs. She disappeared briefly from sight, and I wondered if she had fallen, but then she reappeared, her hair slightly dishevelled, as she held her keys in the air as if in victory. She'd dropped her keys. I laughed at how happy she was to have successfully bent down to retrieve them.

Should I go out? Say hi, invite her in for the tea I didn't want. She had passed the kitchen now and it was now or never. So, without much in the way of thought, I flung the side door open, almost knocking her over but certainly startling her judging by her jump and shriek.

"Fuck!" she muttered under her breath as one hand went to her chest, as if clutching her hammering heart.

"Sorry. I was just wondering who was creeping around out here." Had I really come up with that lame excuse for appearing at the back door? Checking who was there? Well, who else could it be? Although, my use of the words *creeping around* might have suggested that I was expecting to find an intruder rather than the most beautiful face that looked back at me. Beautiful, ruffled, and rather tipsy.

"Me," she whispered then held her hand in the air as she giggled. "I'm creeping around," she said and blew her wayward hair off her face making it fly up.

I laughed now. She was fucking adorable.

"I have my keys," she told me proudly, her keys held aloft again.

"You do," I agreed.

"I'm going home." She pointed towards her door. "Maurizio." She giggled again as she uttered my name.

It sounded amazing the way she said it, and every time she said it, I liked it a little more.

"Perhaps you'd like to join me for tea first." I'd had no intention of doing that, the tea or the invitation, and I couldn't help thinking it was potentially a bad idea.

"I'd love to."

With a cheesy grin, I turned my back and prepared to lead her in. I spun around quickly to say something, but when I did, she was staring at me. Checking me out. Checking my arse out. Probably due to the alcohol, she didn't try to offer up any excuses, she just gave another giggle and muttered something about Carrie having a point. I had no idea what to make of that other than assuming my arse had been a topic of conversation and although my contact with Carrie Caldwell hadn't been extensive, it appeared that she appreciated my arse, as did Flora, the latter was a fact I appreciated more than the former.

Once she'd shut the kitchen door, I turned to Flora again and put the kettle on. "Sugar?" I felt a sudden determination to remember how she took her drinks.

"Just milk," she replied on another little giggle. Then with a snort added, "I'm sweet enough."

I stared at her, not doubting for a second how sweet she was, my mind awash with immoral thoughts of just how sweet she'd taste on my tongue. The flush that crept up her cheeks suggested that she was either embarrassed by her own words or was aware of the thoughts in my head. I quickly returned to the tea making and grabbed a couple of cups and added teabags.

We sat in the lounge with our tea made and for a couple of moments, silence surrounded us. I wasn't sure that it wouldn't turn awkward as giggly, tipsy Flora disappeared. Suddenly, she was replaced with a quietly confident version of herself who was a sight to behold. Buoyed by alcohol but relaxed enough to chat freely, she led the conversation.

"If you could see one artist, dead or alive, in concert, who would it be?" She leaned forward, waiting for my response.

"The King."

"Michael Jackson?"

I did nothing to hide my horror. "Michael Jackson is not *The King*. Elvis Presley."

"I'm sure Michael Jackson is considered The King of Pop," she replied, total faith in what she was saying.

"Maybe. But I am talking The King of Rock 'n' Roll. What about you?"

"Abba. The greatest pop band in the world. Like did they ever have a bad song?" She didn't come up for breath, answering her own question. "No, they didn't. Banger after banger."

A smile curled my lips at her sheer enthusiasm and confidence of this woman, even if alcohol was still facilitating this. "Favourite film?"

"That's tough one. Depends. Nothing where an animal dies, nor where the girl gets her heart broken and no dead parents." She choked on the last two words. "Why do kids animations always kill the parents?" She sniffed back tears and in the blink of an eye shouted out as if she'd just won a prize. "*Dirty Dancing*. What about you?"

I shrugged. She was right, it was a tough one. "Not *Dirty Dancing*."

She pulled a face and bobbed her tongue out.

I liked sassy Flora. "Maybe *The Godfather*, or *Heat* with De Niro and Pacino.

Flora grinned at me. "Are you really a barrister or are you on the other side of the law? A bad boy?"

The way she almost whispered those two words, her voice turning husky before she licked her lips gave me ideas on just how bad I could be with her.

"Depends. Do you like a bad boy?"

"Depends." She flushed as she repeated my own word. "On the boy."

"Boy or man?"

"Man."

We both jumped when my phone sounded with a message from my brother. A message I had no intention of responding to.

The interruption had been enough to move her away from the path we were previously on. One I imagined being paved with me telling her exactly how bad I could be for the right woman.

"If you could only eat one food for the rest of your life, what would it be?"

Her. That was the initial reply that I contained in my mind. I wondered if she'd remember this tomorrow and if she did, would she regret it. I knew that if she didn't remember it, I would be the one with regrets.

"Come on, one food?" She repeated making me laugh again, something I'd been doing a lot more of since this woman entered my home and my life.

Chapter 14

Flora

We sat on a long, soft, chenille sofa which was easily big enough to accommodate four adults. We'd taken opposite ends of it after discussing films and music, and I think we both realised how late it was and for a few long seconds we each remained silent and stared at one another. The truth was that whilst I knew we had been talking almost non-stop since he'd found me loitering near the back door, the details of what we'd said were a little sketchy. That was almost certainly due to my slightly tipsy state, but I recalled banter and a suggestion of him being a bad boy.

Maurizio directed the conversation to the safer topic of the children. "Rosie and Craig are very fond of you," he said, making me smile.

"I'm very fond of them, too. They really are a credit to you, and their mother." I was clearly intent on discussing the children's mother tonight. He looked quite relaxed at the mention of his ex-wife. Was she his ex-wife or perhaps their divorce wasn't quite finalised as they had split relatively recently.

Where was I going with these thoughts?

I watched him and I could have sworn he blushed at my words of praise for him.

"I don't know that I should take the credit, not really, their mother and Bea, have done most of the raising."

I continued to study his expression and was unsure if he was simply being honest or if it was something else. How did he feel about that fact with hindsight? Did he feel that the raising of the children had been the job of their mother and the nanny who was paid to fulfil that role? Maybe, maybe not. Could it be guilt that I saw on his face, guilt for having not been as involved as he might have been in the children's upbringing? I reasoned to myself that as they were still only three, almost four, most of their upbringing was still to be done.

The silence hung between us. One of us needed to end it.

"Well, you seem very involved and hands on now, and no matter who has helped to raise them, they are lovely."

My kind words caused a smile to light up his face, one I reciprocated as I nervously nursed my empty cup. Maurice looked at it in my hands. "Maybe next time we could do this with wine."

Next time. I had no idea what that meant, *next time.* Did that mean the next time he sobered me up slightly after finding me drunk outside? Or did next time mean that he had enjoyed spending time with me and would like to do it again without me being tipsy beforehand?

"Next time," I said, sounding flustered to my own ears, but quickly changed the topic to wine. "Do you know much about wine?" Without giving him chance to reply, I blustered on. "I know what I like and always tend to order or buy the same brand. That is where my wine knowledge starts and ends."

He laughed. "Mine isn't much better," he admitted, somehow shocking me. "My brother fancies himself as a wine buff, whereas I know which wines I like and kind of understand which of those goes with what and I stick to that formula."

"If it works," I said with a smile. Him discussing his brother somehow pleased me. As if him choosing to share information about his family with me meant something. "I initially imagined you might be an only child with how dedicated your mother is."

He laughed. "That's one word for her, *dedicated*. However, I am not an only child. I have one brother, Nico and a sister. I am the baby of the family though. What about you? You mentioned a sister before . . . just the two of you?"

I nodded as I continued to nurse my cup. "Yes, just me and Maddie. I'm the baby too, by just under a year. We're very close and best friends."

He looked pleased at the knowledge that I had Maddie.

Maurizio was already closing the distance between us to relieve me of my cup. He paused, up on his knees on the cushion directly next to me.

"I, erm . . ." My voice trailed off, clueless in what I should say or do. All I could think of was him closing the distance completely, until our bodies touched. I closed my eyes, unsure if that was an attempt to block out my thoughts of him kissing me, pulling me closer and pressing his body into mine. If I was being completely honest with myself, I would have acknowledged that the real reason for closing my eyes was to better visualise the images of my own fantasy of what might happen next.

After what felt like forever, I opened my eyes and was greeted by the sight of my boss frozen to the spot where I'd last seen him.

"Flora," he whispered.

"Yes." My voice was husky, something I'd never noticed before.

"This is a bad idea."

He wasn't wrong and I refused to deny it. I nodded. His face came closer, so close I could feel his breath caressing my cheek.

"Tell me to stop."

I shook my head.

"Tell. Me. To. Stop."

He repeated his request, plead, whatever it was, but it carried a very different undertone with his punctuation of each word.

Again, I shook my head. "I don't want to."

He nodded. "But you need to. You've had too much to drink . . ." His voice trailed off. He was right. I needed to make these decisions with a sober and focused mind, not a tipsy head and a desperate and needy body.

"I should go," I managed to say, my words stammered, but before I moved, his hand reached up and his fingers stroked across my cheek. "Maurizio." His name left my mouth on a moan as I moved closer.

"You should go."

His fingers stroked lower until his thumb pressed into my lips, forcing them to part.

I landed a single kiss to it, and found myself roughly pulled against him, his hand moving until it fisted in my hair, while the other one held my hip, drawing me closer still, his arousal clear.

"Flora."

I gazed into his eyes, already drunk and now at risk of becoming stoned on the aphrodisiac of him.

"You really should go."

I nodded, and somehow got to my feet. I turned for the door.

"Goodnight, Flora. You really are sweet enough already."

I laughed. I knew what he'd been thinking when I'd said that in the kitchen.

"And you really do have the best bum I have ever seen."

He laughed as I left the room, and I heard him contradict that I hadn't seen it. Yet.

I entered my rooms from the house and whilst more sober than I had been when I first returned, I was still a little merry meaning opening the door was something of a challenge, but a challenge that I overcame.

With the door open, I headed for the bathroom, shedding my clothes across the bedroom area as I went. With my teeth brushed, I climbed into bed expecting to fall asleep quickly. I didn't. Sleep was elusive. I lay on my back, then moved from one side to the other, even resorting to lying on my front for a very short time. All to no avail. I lay there wide awake with thoughts of my boss, his bum and just how sweet he might find me filling my mind. Just the memory of his breath touching my face, the offer of a promise of a kiss ensured my breathing became rather rapid as my heart soared, and my sex became slick with arousal.

"Oh God!" I groaned, desperate for release, for his touch. Why did I drink tonight? If I'd remained sober, I could have made a rational decision. Right now I could be under Maurizio. God! I loved his name. We could be kissing, touching, fucking and coming. I could be coming with him inside me.

These thoughts were not helping my inability to sleep or my rising horniness. The fact that one of my hands was between my thighs and the other was stroking the flesh of my breast confirmed this.

Maybe this is what I needed and as I was flying solo, I could and would do this for myself. With my lower hand teasing me from the outside, tormenting my own body, hinting at what might have happened, I focused on my breast, circular movements decreasing until I reached my nipple that I rolled then squeezed. A low moan escaped me before I turned my attention to my other breast and briefly allowed a finger from my other hand to dip into my wetness that I spread along my length, avoiding my clit, needing to make this last. With my breathing coming fast, my legs spreading farther and farther apart, and my finger sliding inside my body, I wasn't sure how long I'd be capable of making it last.

Chapter 15

Maurizio

Once I had put the cups into the dishwasher, I allowed myself a little chuckle at the fact that Flora had checked out my arse. Not only that, she'd admitted to it, although that had probably been down to the alcohol. I really did like her. She was the sort of girl a man could lose his mind over. Every time we got close to making the attraction more, and by that, I meant taking it further, when I gave her the get out, when I implored her to tell me to stop, she did. Except tonight she had admitted that she didn't want to, but knew it was for the best to stop things before it went too far, and it was the right thing to do. If we had ended up shagging tonight, she could have regretted it in the morning, not because it hadn't been what she'd wanted, but because she hadn't made the decision with a rational and straight head. When it happened, and it would, she was going to be stone cold sober, we both were, and with that realisation, I stopped dead in my tracks. It was going to happen. Maybe not tonight or tomorrow, but it seemed inevitable and when it did, it would be fucking amazing. I needed to stop thinking about this. About her. I needed to go to bed and get some sleep. Well, sleep might have to wait until after a little self-gratification in the shower.

With the house locked and in darkness, I climbed the stairs, stopping briefly to check on the children. They were both fast asleep and safely tucked up in bed. I really was incredibly lucky. I now needed Sophie to step up and start to be their mother. I gave each of them a kiss and left before I woke or disturbed their peaceful slumber.

I turned towards my own room but stopped when I heard a strange sound coming from down the hall. A weird little cry, muffled almost, and I knew exactly where and who it had come from. Flora.

Running on autopilot, I made my way to Flora's door that was open. I prepared to knock but didn't. The cry that was a little louder and slightly more breathless prevented me from doing so. Slowly, I entered and made my way across her living area, not stopping until I reached her bedroom door that was ajar. I took a deep breath, a very deep breath, and moved closer.

Fuck! This was not what I was expecting. Not that I had expected anything. I hadn't put much thought into it when I'd followed the unmistakable sound of pleasure, although, the sound of Flora's pleasure was like music to my bloody ears, like a siren's call, summoning me. I was only sorry that as I stood at her door, like a peeping Tom in the making, that I wasn't the reason for her moans of sexual satisfaction.

I was hard. Rock hard and as much as I wanted to reach down and touch myself, to move into the open doorway and watch her, I wasn't going to. This was wrong and an invasion of a dozen different things, including her privacy. I turned to leave, knowing the fantasy of how this could have turned out was going to provide me with my own porn to get myself off to, and then the world stood still for me. One word left her lips. A single word. A name released on a gasp that said she was coming.

"Maurizio."

If that wasn't an invitation to watch, I didn't know what was.

"Oh God, yes, fuck me, please, Maurizio."

Any self-control I'd had was well and truly gone because I was now standing in the small, open space of the door, watching Flora naked with the covers thrown off, leaving her body fully exposed. She was magnificent and as it was my name she was calling, she was mine, kind of.

"I'm going to come."

I had no clue how to play this. Should I charge in and tell her that she was indeed going to come? For me. That I was going to watch her as she came undone and was going to enjoy every second of it? Or should I remain here? Concealed, unless she looked directly at the opening of the door? If I made my presence clear, would it spook her, embarrass her and make her stop? That was the last thing I wanted, so I chose to remain in my current position.

She had one, maybe two fingers inside her pussy, pumping them in and out, her speed increasing as she got closer to release while her thumb was rubbing her clit. Her other hand was cupping and kneading each breast in turn, squeezing the perfect pink bud of her nipples until she arched off the bed. Fuck, if this wasn't the best seat in the house I didn't know where was. Her legs widened further, and her hips bucked as her pleasure built again, taking her to the point of no return. My own hand had slid under my clothing where I wrapped my fingers tightly around my length I was sliding along. I was going to come before she did if she didn't take the final fall over the edge soon. I felt like a teenage boy watching his first porno and I would look like one too if I ended up covered in my own cum.

"Maurizio."

Her use of my name centred me, although I did have to check that she wasn't staring at me, aware of my presence. She wasn't. She was stoned on her own pleasure and oblivious to anything else right now.

"Yes, yes," she began to chant. "Please, make me come, let me come," she begged.

I made a mental note that when, not if I fucked her, I would insist on her asking for permission before she came.

"Lick me, Maurizio," she cried as her whole body came crashing down. Everything flailed and thrashed as she rode the storm of her orgasm. Her fingers pumped relentlessly before everything became too sensitive and her legs tightly closed.

Fuck! That really was in the top two experiences of my life and the other was the birth of my children. The way she called to me, totally believing I was there and doing that to her was a real aphrodisiac. She had asked me to lick her, meaning she imagined me between her thighs, pleasuring her with my fingers and mouth. Nothing would give me greater pleasure. One day, Flora, one day.

As she calmed a little, I realised that if she looked this way, even briefly, she would see me, so I pulled my hand from around my cock and prepared to leave, knowing exactly what scenario I would be replaying once I got back to my own bedroom and could deal with the agonising ache in my groin.

I took one final look and could have sworn for the tiniest fraction of a second that her eyes passed by the door, lingering a little, but then she closed them.

Chapter 16

Flora

"Good morning," I called merrily as I entered the kitchen. It was early, so early that Bea hadn't yet arrived and the children were still sleeping meaning it was me and Maurice.

He looked a little awkward and flustered. "Morning."

I reached for the kettle and made tea for us both. "Thank you, for last night."

He looked beyond awkward now. "Last night?" he almost stammered with a slightly awkward expression crossing his face.

"I may have been a little tipsy." I laughed. Surely if either of us was going to find this morning difficult, it should have been me, not him. Unless it was because we had shared another weird, almost kiss moment where he had yet again told me to tell him to stop. I wasn't sure I had last night though.

"Ah." The penny dropped. "No problem. Any time. Did you sleep well?" The uneasiness had returned with his last question.

A yawn and a stretch seemed to come out of nowhere, startling us both. "I did, thank you." I could feel the magnitude of my grin as I recalled lying in bed before sleep. "You?" I asked, wondering if either of us was going to raise the topic of our obvious attraction and strange interactions.

"Eventually," he replied with a far-off smile that prompted a big, bright, cocky smile from me too, and in that second he seemed to regain his equilibrium. "I enjoyed last night."

I was thrown slightly, unsure what to say in response. "You did?"

"I did." He was up on his feet and standing behind me, close enough that his front almost covered my back.

I could smell him and as usual his scent assaulted my senses. In that second I wanted him. My body wanted him, and he knew it.

"We should do it again."

"Again?"

"Hmmm, all of it."

"All of it?" I needed to find my confident self again, the one with the upper hand or there was a good chance I'd need to change my knickers before the children woke. Everything was pulsating and preparing for pleasure.

"Every second. We could even make it last a little longer, together."

Fuck. He knew. "It?" My confidence had clearly gone into hiding or hibernation, not that the latter was likely as it was anything but cold around here.

"It." He emphasised each sound in the word and if even that wasn't sexy as fuck.

"It."

"It."

I wondered if this conversation was ever going to move forward from us each repeating the word *it*.

"With a nice bottle of wine and more conversation and everything else from last night."

Any remaining doubts I might have had about his knowledge of last night disappeared at that very second. He knew. That is why he was a little shaken this morning. He was embarrassed or uncomfortable, but now, he was enjoying this cat and mouse game with me.

"Daddy!" Rosie's squeal broke the moment and the atmosphere, and not a second too soon for me.

"Until *it*," he whispered, so close to my ear that the skin there and all along my neck came up in goosebumps. His hand rested on my hip and as his fingers gently squeezed, I let out a tiny gasp while my body softened and moistened further. Yes, new underwear before breakfast was needed.

"How's my beautiful girl this morning?" he said and for a second, I wondered if he meant me, but turning, I watched him scoop his daughter up into his arms and not that I thought it was possible, he became even more attractive which was the last thing my imagination, libido, addled mind, or increasingly damp underwear needed.

Bea and I had met up with Carrie for lunch in the park and my mind was anywhere but with them. I gazed into the distance and watched the children playing with bats and balls. Not one of them had an accurate aim with the ball or a decent return with the bat, but as they laughed together, none of that mattered. They were happy and having fun.

"Boo!"

"Jeez!" I shrieked, jumping from my seat at the picnic bench in response to Carrie's immature act.

"Sorry. I didn't mean to scare you half to death, you just looked deep in thought."

"Are you okay?" Bea asked, sitting next to me so I was flanked by her and Carrie.

"I'm fine."

"You're quiet," Carrie said.

"She has been all day," Bea added.

"Bloody hell, the tag team are back." I laughed, which seemed more like a huff at this moment in time.

"Are you hanging?" Carrie suddenly asked.

"She didn't look to be when I arrived this morning, her and Maurice were . . . shit! Is it you and Maurice?"

Bea had arrived at the split second he had picked Rosie up meaning she had walked into an atmosphere that was probably thick with sexual tension.

"Did something happen between you two?" Carrie asked, taking what appeared to be her turn to speak.

"We're all friends here. You can trust us," Bea said with a sincerity I totally believed. She had been nothing but nice to me since I'd arrived. "I know you're probably unsure about that, especially after my offhand response when you asked about Sophie, but you really can trust us."

"Seriously, Flora, it can be lonely if you bottle things up when you're new to town with no family around you. We are here for you if you want us to be." Carrie rubbed a hand over mine.

I felt guilty at holding out on them and while I didn't want to divulge all of the details of what had happened, I did want to share something, if only to try and order things in my head.

"We almost kissed."

"O-k-ay," drawled Carrie.

"Like a friendly kiss?" Bea asked.

Her question, while aimed at me was responded to by Carrie with a loud guffaw.

We both turned to look at her. She looked completely unapologetic. "If it was a friendly kiss, we would not be having this conversation." She turned to me. "Tell us what happened."

I explained what had happened when I'd returned home. Everything until I went to bed.

"What holds you back?" Carrie asked while Bea said nothing.

"Everything. He scares me and it would be wholly inappropriate. He's my boss."

Bea still said nothing, unlike Carrie, "I can relate to that, all of it. I was in exactly the same position with Gabe and look how that turned out." She grinned and rubbed a hand across her bump.

Bea did speak now. "Carrie, with all due respect, you and Gabe are not the norm. Far from it. I reckon there are hundreds, even thousands of nannies who have fancied their boss, shagged him and then ended up on the wrong side of the fallout."

I nodded. I agreed with what Bea was saying and although reluctant to, Carrie did too. She didn't need to say as much, her face said it all.

"So, what's the advice, ladies?"

"Talk to him and see if there's a way forward."

I smiled at Carrie's optimism.

"I'm going to sound like a bitch now, but what I am about to say is for you, for your wellbeing, professionally and personally. Do not talk to him in any way that isn't professional. Move on. Find a boyfriend or a hobby or anything that doesn't involve Maurice. He is a lovely man and a wonderful father, but those children do not deserve to be stuck in the middle of any of this and that is without considering Sophie."

"Sophie?" I had no idea why she would impact on anything moving forward as she and Maurice were separated and she had already move on.

"Yes, Sophie. Despite how things are now, she is still their mother and she loves them."

I was beginning to regret sharing any of this with them. Was I really being given wise words of advice or being warned off Sophie's man? "She might still be their mum, but what I find strange is the lack of an appearance since I've been here." Unsure where my words or the accusatory tone that carried them had come from, I immediately felt awkward.

Carrie nodded while Bea shook her head. "It's hard for her."

I frowned and realised that perhaps Bea and Sophie's closeness wasn't in the past and I now suspected that she may be in contact with her. Despite her claims that I could trust her, could I?

Carrie was clearly on the same page as me. "You need to be very careful, Bea, or you may well find yourself on the wrong side of this. You cannot play both sides and come out unscathed."

Bea considered her, and suddenly this felt different, as though it was nothing to do with me anymore.

"Oh," Carrie said now as if fully realising that Bea had indeed been playing both sides. "Whilst I can't say that I know how it feels for Sophie, or how hard it is, I know it's considerably harder for the kids, so she needs to get her head out of her arse and step up before it's too late."

I liked Carrie. I mean, I liked Bea, but I liked that Carrie looked at this from the point of view of the kids who were the truly innocent ones in this.

Bea looked back to me and continued. "I'm just saying, it's not been very long since the split and it must be hard for him, knowing that she left for another woman. Maybe he sees you as a conquest, an ego boost."

"Ignore her," Carrie said with a scowl aimed at Bea. "Her hormones have hardened her to romance and love."

"And hormones have made you even soppier than before." Bea looked back at me again. "Only you can decide what you do but be careful with Maurice. He's lonely . . ." Her voice trailed off and I observed a glance being exchanged between the other two.

"What? If I am missing something here, please enlighten me."

Carrie looked across at Bea, almost in deference.

"Shit! It seems like a long time ago and it wasn't anything, not really. A mistake, misunderstanding, call it what you will."

"Go on." My guts churned and my head began to pound as I felt nervousness rise.

"When Sophie first left, Maurice struggled. Kind of carried on as normal and some of the responsibility for the children fell to me. More than it should have. Carrie warned me that the lines could blur for him, that he could replace Sophie with me."

"Right . . ." I felt sick, suspecting what was coming. Had he done the same with Bea as he was doing with me? Saying all the right things and I was falling for it, hook, line and sinker, unlike Bea it seemed. How stupid was I to think he might have liked me as I liked him? That this was in anyway real.

"He, erm, made a couple of passes at me. Clumsy, drunken passes that he apologised for and they were no more than that."

I nodded, although, I was fighting the urge to cry.

"Are we going home to make biscuits?" asked Rosie as she appeared at my side.

"Yes, we are, so let's make a move." Already on my feet, I called Craig over, happy to be leaving this conversation and regretting ever being drawn into it. how was I ever going to make sense of everything now?

Chapter 17

Maurizio

I was meeting with a client who had a pending trial that I couldn't lose. I didn't take loss very well, not even if the odds were stacked against me, but with this one, I would be a laughingstock because nobody should have been able to lose it. It was full of flaws and loopholes, and I was amazed that the prosecution were still pushing forward with it, but then my client was rich, influential, and I suspected that they wanted to be seen to be serving justice. To make an example of him in a high-profile way. The man was an arsehole of the highest order, and I could see the attraction of hanging him out to dry, however, the ones who would come out of this tarnished would be them, not him.

The idiot was now rambling about suing and taking the Crown Prosecution Service to the cleaners. I let him get it off his chest with the occasional nod, but my mind was elsewhere. My mind was at home with Flora.

There was something off with her. Since that night, several weeks before when I had watched her pleasure herself, she had been distant, almost angry in a way. We spoke still, but it was short, curt, and always related to her work and the children. She was pissed off with me, of that I was sure, but had no clue why that might be. Maybe she was home sick or something. I knew for a fact that she was going home at the weekend to see her sister because it was her birthday. I needed to speak to her and see if there was anything I could do to resolve that because she was amazing with Rosie and Craig and really was the ideal replacement for Bea.

With Flora away and the children having a weekend at the coast with my mother, I was going to be at something of a loss. Pushing those thoughts from my mind, I focused on Sophie. We had spoken a few times about her taking Rosie and Craig for an overnight stay. I had even suggested this weekend and had gone so far as to invite her to stay in my home, her former home, in order to make it easier for them. She'd declined, although she had seen them a couple of weeks before, one Saturday afternoon we'd met at an adventure playground and called them with a little more regularity. I didn't get how she could do this, but then, I didn't need to. My job was to be a good father and to give our children stability, a permanent home, continuity of care and most of all, unconditional love. The last one was the easiest and most natural thing ever.

Returning my attention to my client, I put all thoughts of occupying my weekend, my family and Flora from my mind and focused on work, but decided I was going to cut the day short and spend a little time playing with my children and maybe I'd even get the chance to speak to Flora.

My earlier plan had worked out in part. I had got home and taken the kids to the park and for a long walk through the woods where there were puddles and mud aplenty so lots of jumping around in wellies. Bea had now dropped a couple of afternoons, so it was only Flora working and I had invited her to join us or to take an early finish. She took the latter and not only was I fuming and disappointed, but gutted. She cited the unexpected opportunity to meet up earlier than planned with a nanny friend, not Bea nor Carrie but someone new, Ash, whoever she was. I had no objection to that, and no right to any either and the thought of her making new friends, her own friends, pleased me because if she was feeling home sick, this might just ease it.

Now, it was late, well, half past nine, and with the children sleeping soundly, I poured a scotch, added some ice and flicked around the TV channels, pausing occasionally on anything that wasn't reality TV or a soap. I thought I heard footsteps on the stairs so getting to my feet, I hit mute on the remote control. Nothing. I was imagining things. Then, I had the sensation that I was being watched. Turning, I found Flora standing in the doorway wearing a pair of short pyjamas covered in *Sylvester and Tweety Pie* cartoon characters. I was more of a *Daffy Duck* kind of guy, but that cat and bird were growing on me.

Our eyes locked and the sizzle in the air was back. The attraction and promise of something amazing hung between us.

"Sorry," she said looking sad.

"For what?" I wasn't aware I was owed an apology.

"For taking the early finish."

I waved her apology away. As pissed off as I'd been earlier, she had every right to have made the choice she had. "Would you like a drink?" What the fuck was I doing here? This was going to be another *tell me to stop* moment and she would, and I would end up confused and in agony from blue balls that I'd end up taking care of myself.

She sauntered into the room and took the glass from my hand before taking a slug of the amber liquid. I might just add nights out to her contract because every time she'd been out or more specifically, had a drink, she became confident and unafraid to take what she wanted, whereas when she was stone cold sober, she was nervous and less inclined to speak up.

I watched as she swallowed the liquid. The way her throat moved was seriously fucking sexy and I needed not to think of what I would rather she was swallowing right now. The moment was broken when she began to choke, coughing and spluttering. With a short laugh, I leapt to my feet and patted her back, removing the glass from her hand.

Flushed, she pulled a distasteful expression. "It's whiskey."

I nodded and fought a grin.

"I don't like whiskey . . . it burns."

She threw in a little cough while I laughed out loud.

"Why did you drink it then?"

"Not a clue," she replied, making me laugh again, and then I stopped.

We were almost toe to toe, she was staring up at me while I gazed down. I found myself becoming lost, drowning in her eyes, and praying that one day I might get the chance to be lost at sea in all of her.

Neither of us spoke, and yet there was noise everywhere, deafening. I swear I could hear our hearts beating out of our chests and our breathing filled the room. Reaching down with no thought, I stroked a thumb over her cheek, then lower, down her face and neck until I reached her pulse. Fuck, it was hammering away, maybe even more rapidly than my own. I slowly tracked my way back up until my thumb came to rest on her full bottom lip that I traced. Her eyes filled with something now, a little fear, nerves, but most of all desire. There was no mistaking that.

She allowed her lips to part a little and she breathed out a single word, "Maurizio."

Fuck! My cock that had been ramrod hard, stiffened further and just her utterance of my name had me all but ready to come right there. I pressed my thumb gently past her lips and found her wet tongue waiting for me.

Chapter 18

Flora

What the fuck had I been thinking when I came down here? Clearly, thought and common sense had no part in the situation I now found myself in. I had come back from drinks and dinner, and had gone straight to my own rooms. After last time I was not risking another almost moment with Maurizio, especially now, knowing that hitting on his nannies was common for him. I liked him, a lot, but if he thought my salary each month included me, all of me, the intimate parts of me, he was wrong. I refused to be a notch on his bedpost and more than that, I would not prostitute myself into an entirely compromised position with my boss.

I'd talked it through that evening with Ash. We'd met fairly regularly since we'd been introduced, with and without the children we cared for and although it had only been a few weeks, we'd become close and our friendship had grown. Tonight we'd agreed that I deserved better. Me and Maurizio, together, had mistake written all over it. In fairness to

Ash, he hadn't done much talking but had done plenty of listening and that was perhaps what I'd needed, a sounding board to confirm all of the things I knew.

Yet, here I was, having decided that going to bed alone, touching myself whilst thinking of him was a bad idea, I was standing in front of him having choked on the hideous tasting whiskey he'd been nursing. His thumb had skimmed from my cheek to my neck and now it was pressing against my lips.

God! He was gorgeous and did things to me nobody else ever had. My body reacted to him, to his mere presence on the most basic level. Just being in his company saw my pulse racing, my skin flushing, my breath hitching and between my nipples pebbling and my nether regions softening and moistening, there was no doubting how desirable I found him or how turned on he made me. He was as near to perfect as could ever exist.

Gazing up as his thumb pressed against my mouth, all thoughts of my conversation with Ash had disappeared from my mind. I couldn't deny how much I wanted him. How much my body needed him. I knew I should stop this because there were only so many of these encounters we could share before I was going to find myself fucked senseless by him. Although, I was currently unfucked senseless, so maybe the alternative was better . . .

"Maurizio." What was the matter with me? Of all the things to say to stop this, a single utterance of his name was not conducive to that.

His eyes flickered then darkened with his name leaving my lips and then with no effort on his part, I granted him access to my mouth, my tongue eagerly greeting his thumb. I drew him into the damp heat of my mouth and set about showing him what he was missing. I sucked, licked, lapped, and circled his digit as if it was the hard length of his erection that was clearly visible through his trousers.

I heard a loud groan and as much as I was enjoying myself, it wasn't mine . . . it was his. He knew this was what I'd do to his dick given the chance and he could feel my mouth along his length already. A hand slid into my hair and pulled my head further down onto his thumb and another low rumble of a moan escaped his lips.

"Fuck!" he hissed, and I swear had it really been his length in my mouth, I would have been sure he was about to come.

Suddenly, he pulled his hand away and stared down at me.

"You are going to need to tell me to stop in the next twenty seconds or I am going to tear your clothes off and fuck you so hard the neighbours will need a cigarette afterwards."

I released a single laugh, but said nothing, although, in my head I was screaming the word stop.

"Flora," he whispered as a tortured expression spread across his gorgeous face. "Tell me to stop." He stepped closer and placed his hands on my hips, as if preparing to lift me.

"I saw you."

He frowned.

"You watched me."

I was being inarticulate and his confusion was growing.

"Before. In bed. My bed. You stood in the doorway and watched me."

He looked seriously uncomfortable and I was unsure if he was regretting that night or maybe regretted not knowing I'd seen him. I wondered what would have happened had I called to him. I knew exactly what would have happened.

"I touched myself." I offered him a tiny smile, not wanting him to retreat or regret that night.

"You did. I heard you moaning and followed the sounds. You said my name."

I felt the heat of my flush as I nodded.

"I had no idea you were aware of my presence . . . although I could have sworn you looked my way."

I nodded again.

"You looked phenomenal."

I flushed further but had no idea what to say.

"When you came. I've never seen anyone look more beautiful."

"Thank you." Not my finest moment in terms of a retort, but it was all I had.

He smiled, a half, lazy little smile that made him even sexier than before. "Do you want me to tell you what I did when I left you?"

I shook my head and for a second, he looked lost and entirely perplexed. Did he think I didn't want to know? That I hadn't wondered what he had done? If he had touched himself? How had he touched himself? Nothing could be further than the truth, I really did want to know exactly what he'd done, all of it, and as I sensed him preparing to withdraw, I spoke. "Let me see what you did."

Chapter 19

Maurizio

L *et me see*. Three words, and everything changed in that second.
I had no clue what had made her come down here tonight and
I didn't care. I was just glad she had. Even with her sassy and
confident routine that didn't come entirely naturally to her, I couldn't
have dreamed how this evening would develop. The truth was that
currently, I had no idea how it was going to end.

I reached for her hand and almost dragged her from the room. With
zero reluctance, she followed, almost running to keep up.

We climbed the stairs and entered my bedroom where I released her
hand and headed for my bathroom, shedding my clothes as I went.

She followed me and stood in the doorway as I turned on the
shower and stepped into the cubicle.

I stood beneath the hot water and closed my eyes. Immediately I was
back to that night where I'd watched her pleasure herself. I rolled my
neck and shoulders, loosening myself up, then with my eyes open, I
reached for the shower gel. I washed my chest, arms and neck before

sliding my hand lower until it reached my erection that was throbbing with anticipation. With a firm grip I took a hold of it at the base, my whole hand closing around it and then, slowly, slid along the length of it.

Looking across to where Flora stood, I fixed her with a stare. Her eyes dropped to where my hand continued to move along my shaft. She licked her lips, but I was unsure if that was because of nervousness or arousal . . . maybe a combination of both.

I relaxed against the tiled wall, fighting the urge to flinch at the coldness against my skin, but my eyes remained on her.

"Yeah," I moaned as I skimmed the crown of my erection with my thumb.

My balls were beginning to tighten, and I knew this wouldn't take long. It didn't take long last time, but my stamina tonight was that of an adolescent virgin.

"Flora, fuck!" I groaned, allowing my other hand to drop down and cup my balls that were ready to explode.

"Maurizio."

Flora calling my name was the final nudge I needed. My eyes, still locked on hers watched her expression of wanton desire as I came, streams of white covering my hand and belly made my release even sweeter.

She smiled at me, her eyes on mine, and fuck me if that didn't make me begin to stiffen again. She had enjoyed her little power trip, knowing she had done this to me, metaphorically brought me to my knees simply by being under her gaze.

Her eyes dropped back down to where the water was washing all evidence of my release away. I summoned her to me with the curl of my hand. She stepped closer, slowly, but there was no hesitation in her movement. When she came to a stop at the shower cubicle, I opened the door and reached out for her. With my hand laced through her hair, I pulled her head to me, preparing to kiss her.

She grinned. "Isn't this where you tell me to tell you to stop."

I arched a brow. She was assured, bold and a little cheeky. I liked her attitude, a lot.

"Have you been drinking?" I needed her not to be drunk, not that I thought she was.

"One glass of wine . . . a large glass, but just the one . . . Dutch courage maybe, but not drunk."

"What did you need courage for? For coming downstairs?"

She shrugged, as if considering her own reason for the drink. "For needing to ask you something?"

I stood still and stared at her. "Ask me anything you want?" I was clueless as to what she might ask, but I had nothing to hide.

"Bea . . ."

She looked ready to flounder, but maybe that's why she'd gone with Dutch courage because she pushed forward.

"You and Bea. Was there something between you two, something like this?" She flicked her finger between us.

I wasn't exactly thrilled to think Bea had possibly warned her off me because of a couple of stupid, drunken passes I'd made, not that I was proud of myself for them either, but she'd asked a fair question and I needed to reply. The last thing I wanted was for her to think that I saw anyone who worked for me as some kind of employee with benefits. That was not my style. Ever. And as for her asking if there was something like this, like me and her with Bea or anyone else, that pissed me off a bit, but only because the thing between us was like nothing I'd ever known.

"I made a pass at her, possibly two . . . I was drunk, my head was all over the place when Sophie first left. I'm neither proud nor making excuses for it, but it happened, she rebuked me, I woke up with a hangover, and apologised with a heavy dose of embarrassment. But there was never anything between us and there has never been anything like this." I flicked my finger between us, copying her earlier movement.

"Good," she said and looked very pleased with that information, her grin spreading across her face and lighting it up until I could have sworn that the light alone was illuminating the room.

I grinned down at her, wondering how the hell I wasn't ripping her clothes off and devouring her.

"Any more questions?"

"Nope."

With my lips lowering towards hers, barely stopping myself from consuming her there and then, I managed to speak. "Tell. Me. To. Stop."

She grinned, her top teeth grazing her lower lip, making her appear every inch the seductress, but the hitch in her breathing and the pulse in her neck hammering away revealed a little of her nervousness.

"No," she replied, and I swear her lips puckered, preparing for my kiss, not that I was entirely sure anything could or would prepare either of us for it.

Her hand stretched up and with her fingers teasing their way through my hair, I prepared to close the final distance that remained between us.

The sound of crying stopped us both dead in our tracks. We both pulled back and looked towards the door, my bedroom, and the rest of the house beyond it.

"Craig," I said, recognising my son's cry.

I grabbed a towel and wrapped it around my waist and headed past Flora to seek out my son.

"Sorry." I was sorry for what could have been being so abruptly brought to an end.

"Me too. Go."

I offered a final smile, for her compassion, lack of annoyance and genuine desire for me to go to my child.

Chapter 20

Flora

After my night in Maurizio's bathroom, when Craig had woken from a bad dream, we hadn't really spoken about what could have been. The idea of the children being away all weekend had made me seriously consider cancelling my visit to see Maddie, but when I called her with an excuse all lined up, she sounded so excited that I backed down and finalised my plans with her. I was going to wait until Maurizio returned from work on Friday night and then I was going to drive home and stay until Sunday morning.

My car was all packed up and ready to go when Maurizio returned home at the same time as his mother.

"Flora," she called to me before being ambushed by her grandchildren who were excitedly chattering about the fun they were all going to have.

"Hi, Carmella," I said with a smile.

"I'll leave you all to get sorted then." With a quick hug for the children and a wave for Carmella, I headed back into the house to grab my phone and keys before heading off, but not before exchanging a strange smile and knowing glance with Maurizio.

My car seemed to be struggling more than usual by the time I parked it outside Maddie's house. I was barely outside when my sister was running barefoot down the path to greet me. I found myself engulfed in her arms and was disappearing beneath her kisses.

"Look at you! You look fabulous," she gushed before lunging back in for another hug.

"Anyone would think you'd missed me," I teased.

"Maybe, just a little bit," she replied, already pulling me in to be hugged again before grabbing my bags from the boot and taking them into the house.

"So, the arsehole was married all along?" I stared, agog at my sister's revelation about her last boyfriend.

"Yup! When the wife came into the restaurant and started shouting the odds and throwing names around, I could have died."

I felt my sister's mortification at being outed as the other woman in a crowded restaurant when she had no clue her date had a wife. The thought of her having to sit there and be humiliated in that way made me sad, but more than that, angry.

"And has the dickhead been in touch since?"

She looked at me and dropped her gaze.

"Really? And you gave him the time of day? Why?"

"I like him," my sister replied, leaving me unsure what to say.

"You like him . . . and his wife, presumably he likes her?" I shook my head, fuming at him and Maddie.

Her mouth opened several times, but no words came out.

"Ah. Is this where you tell me that his wife doesn't understand him?"

She shrugged and suddenly looked ashamed, something I didn't want her to feel.

"Please, be careful. He's a douche and is going to hurt you one way or another, and if he doesn't, his wife might."

In spite of the situation, we both laughed.

"So, enough of my disaster zone love life, tell me about yours."

I blew out a breath that ended up coming out something like a blown raspberry.

"That good, eh?" Maddie moved closer and patted my knee. "We're a bit shit at men, aren't we?"

"I dunno if we're shit, but we were spoilt with role models." We exchanged a sad smile as we each thought of our parents and the love they shared, the sort of love you only usually find in swoon worthy romance books and films. Our grandparents still shared the type of love most of us only ever dare dream of. "We do like to complicate things, don't we?"

She raised a questioning eyebrow and like that the floodgates opened until I had given her a blow-by-blow account of my time with Maurizio.

We both sat in silence and then, she spoke. "He is seriously fucking hot then?"

I laughed loudly. "Yes, yes he is."

"And he watched you touching yourself?"

"Yes."

"And then you watched him?"

"Yes," I repeated again.

"But we're still waiting for the main act?"

My laugh became more of a cackle now, but I did nod.

"And his kids are away this weekend with his mother?"

"Yes."

She rolled her eyes then shook her head. "What the bloody hell are you doing here then? Shouldn't you be back there with Maurizio?" She overemphasised his name making me wonder if she would ever be able to say it without sounding as though she was advertising a pasta sauce, very badly.

I shrugged at her.

"Not that I'm not pleased to see you."

"Good. Plus, Maurizio will still be there when I get back, and it's your thirtieth tomorrow."

"What's the real story with him and his wife and how are things going with Bea?"

I knew she meant between me and Bea rather than Maurizio and Bea, but with the words out, I figured I might as well tell her exactly what I knew, but the truth was I still knew very little about him and Sophie.

Chapter 21

Maurizio

Friday night came and went, as did Saturday morning and afternoon. I was bored. I'd spoken to the children who were having a wonderful time with my mother, but I hadn't heard from Flora and that pissed me off. We hadn't agreed to keep in touch, however, I was irked by the lack of communication. The voice in my head pointed out that I could have as easily contacted her, but I ignored it.

I needed to get out.

I arrived at the bar where I'd agreed to meet, Nico. We didn't meet up as often as we used to, outside of family gatherings, but we were only ever at the end of the phone and always up for a meet up and tonight I needed it.

Nico was already there when I arrived. I spotted him at a high table surrounded by four stools.

"Here he is." Nico leapt to his feet and thrust a glass of scotch in my hand before we took seats opposite each other. "Not that I'm not thrilled for the opportunity to catch up, but what's her name?"

I laughed at his very accurate summing up of my reason for making contact, yet still attempted to deny it. "We're not all hopeless cases like you, you know."

He laughed, unbothered by my accusation. "And yet, you called me."

"Kiss my arse, Nico."

"Wouldn't be the first time," Nico threw back, the banter already flowing back and forth.

"You said we'd keep those times between ourselves." I laughed with him and then shocked him and me. "Flora. Her name is Flora."

"Shit! Hold that thought. We need more drinks."

He was already on his feet and heading for the bar and as I watched the barman filling our order, I laughed again as I saw four glasses having very generous measures of scotch added to them.

Nico watched me down another scotch. I'd lost count of how many had gone before this one and as I swallowed it, the burn it caused made me think of Flora and her attempt at drinking my whiskey, only to cough and splutter her amazement that it was whiskey. Whiskey she didn't like that burned.

"So, Flora is the nanny. You like her, she likes you, and there is no way back for you and Sophie?"

I nodded.

"The nanny that Mama says is beautiful and such a sweet girl?" He laughed and arched a brow at our mother's meddling where her boys' love lives were concerned.

"Mama is right, but I need her not to know about this."

Nico laughed. "Maurizio, you are an open book where women are concerned and Mama is like a blood hound with a big juicy bone with us and women."

I rubbed my hands over my face hoping that when I revealed it again, my thoughts and mind would be clearer. They weren't.

Nico wasn't done clarifying the situation. "She, Flora, is hot as fuck and seriously into you, as you are her and although you've never really got it together, you want to. You both want to?"

"Yes."

"You are both single and consenting adults, so what's the problem?"

It sounded so simple when he put it like that, but it really wasn't, far from it. "She's my children's nanny."

"I know, you said."

"If we get together and it goes to shit, the kids lose their nanny." I thought that was more than adequate as far as explanations went.

"You could get a new nanny." Nico was staring across at me, a deep frown creasing his brow.

I shook my head at his lack of understanding my point.

"But the children like this nanny."

"Oh right. But they liked the old nanny, right, Bea?"

"Ye-es." My drawled out reply confirmed I was beginning to see the point he was trying to make.

"So, if you fuck it up between you, and she no longer wants to be your children's nanny, you could get a new one. To replace her for Rosie and Craig, not to try again with another." He sniggered, unlike me, not that I couldn't see where he was coming from. "Also, by the time she has realised you're more trouble than you're worth, Bea could be back."

Before I had a chance to really consider any of those scenarios, he continued.

"Maurizio, I am calling bullshit here. I accept that her being the nanny kind of complicates things if it all turns to shit and as the nanny, you can't fuck her and move on."

I saw red and immediately got to my feet, stepping closer to my brother, ready to punch him if he continued in this way. "Do not speak about her that way. Flora is a wonderful woman. She's sweet and kind, and does not deserve to be spoken about so disrespectfully."

The temptation to take a swing at my brother was strong whether he said anymore or not. Perhaps that was what I needed, to fight. What I actually needed was Flora, naked and writhing as I drew every last ounce of pleasure form her and forced her beautiful features to contort in pleasure with me insider her, but as I wouldn't be doing the latter, the former might be the only way to work off this tension and frustration.

The sound of my brother's laughter interrupted all thoughts, whether they be of pleasure or violence. As I stared at him, he paused, possibly sensing my violent thoughts. "Baby brother, you have it real bad if my use of the word fuck has you so wound up and getting all chivalrous. What I meant was that her role in your home and with Craig and Rosie means you can't simply act on your desire and attraction and move on like you could if you picked someone up in a bar or a club. I really didn't mean to disrespect the lovely Flora or antagonise you."

I wasn't sure about the latter, but I believed he wouldn't deliberately show such disrespect towards Flora so I retook my seat. Nico had, however, made several good points about the ease with which I could move on from a night with someone I casually picked up rather than pursuing things with Flora. Unfortunately, I didn't want to pick someone up, I wanted Flora. I didn't have time to think how that might look or what I should do next when I saw a couple of men draw alongside our table and for the first time, I noticed just how busy the bar had become.

"Maurice," one man said, Gabriel Caldwell, Carrie's husband.

"Gabriel."

I offered him an outstretched hand and was in no way surprised to see that the other man with him was Bea's boyfriend, Seb. Seb and I didn't not get on, but we didn't get on either. He knew that I'd made a couple of clumsy passes at his girlfriend, the same passes Flora asked me about in my bathroom. As a consequence, Seb had marked my card and held a certain amount of distrust towards me. I didn't blame him for that, but he had no need to be suspicious of me because there was only one nanny I was interested in, and it wasn't his.

Nico was already shuffling around the table so that he was sitting next to me. "If you guys want seats, we have a couple free."

Gabriel didn't hesitate in taking a seat, while Seb, a little more reluctantly, followed his friend's lead.

I introduced Gabe to Nico first, just by his name and then moved onto Seb and foolishly added the information of him being Bea's boyfriend.

"Do you have a nanny, too?" Nico asked Gabe with a laugh that confirmed he thought he was being humorous.

"Not anymore," Gabe replied and then continued. "I married her so now I have a wife."

"Shit!" Nico laughed, believing what Gabe was saying, but genuinely amused. "Is it something they put in the water around here? You have a nanny, now a wife." He pointed at Gabe. "And your girl-friend is his nanny, one of them . . . the pregnant one." He wagged his finger in the direction of Seb then finally turned to me. "And you have another nanny, one you're totally bewitched by and for some reason I can't figure out, she seems rather taken with you too, but you're too much of a pussy to do anything about it."

"You're a fucking arsehole," I told my brother, but couldn't deny his summing up or his insult, even if I hadn't wanted that knowledge to be shared with either of the other men present.

Seb looked stunned, but quite happy to discover I had a new nanny in my sights, not that Bea was ever truly in them.

Gabe on the other hand, laughed as he picked his glass up. "You, mate, are fucked," he told me. Then raising his glass as if in a toast said, "To nannies, each and every crazy, fucked up in the head, and down-right delightful one of them. And to those of us who are doomed to love them."

"To nannies," added Seb as we all clinked glasses and I sent a silent prayer that I might be fortunate enough to be one of those Gabriel Caldwell described as being doomed. I wanted to be doomed to love them. To love Flora.

Chapter 22

Flora

M addie looked rough, courtesy of the vodka, wine and
cocktails last night. Friday night we had a glass of wine each
and then stuck to tea. Yesterday was Maddie's birthday and
we had partied until the early hours. I was slightly more sensible than
my sister and had moved onto water as I knew if I ended up hungover,
I'd be in no fit state to leave the bathroom never mind drive home later.

"It was a good night though?"

Maddie dropped her head to the table but did throw a hand with a
thumb up into the air, making me chuckle.

It had been a brilliant night; food, dancing, drinking, and lots of
laughter. The sound of my phone alerting me to a text saw Maddie raise
her head slightly.

"My friend, Ash."

Her nod was soon replaced with a frown. "Ash as in Alison or Ash as
in Ashley or Ashton?"

"I dunno." I had no clue what Ash's full name was.

"Ooh," Maddie sat upright quickly and apparently regretted it judging by how she held her head now. "Shit!" She winced but now had the bit between her teeth. "But Ash is a boy?"

I shook my head at her mischievous expression. "Yes, he is, but he is just a friend, a nanny friend."

"Hmmm. A friend? A nanny friend you said."

Laughing, I answered. "He is. Bea and Carrie introduced us . . . they introduced him as a manny, male nanny."

"*Friends.*"

"Apparently so."

"Gay?"

"Maddie!" I shrieked. Why did everyone assume that? That any man working with young children must be gay. Although there were others who assumed far worse. "He is many things but none of them are gay."

"Ooh—"

I cut her off, wanting to shut this down right now before she decided that there might be something between me and Ash. "Just a friend. He is seeing someone." I had no clue if he was, in fact, as far as I knew, he wasn't, but she didn't need to know that. "Now, shift your arse, we need to meet Grandma and Grandad in an hour."

We went to a local pub for lunch where we met our grandparents. They were quite possibly the nicest people in the world, although, of course, I was biased. They had raised us and neither Maddie nor I had ever wanted for anything. I felt sure they hadn't given a second thought in taking us in, despite the fact that they were at a point in their life where they had gained some financial security and in turn freedom and an opportunity to enjoy their lives independently, and then we had been orphaned. Sitting with them, eating lunch, chatting and laughing, I realised just how lucky we were to have them, and to have the bond we did and always would have. Earlier, for much of the weekend, I'd felt some regrets about not staying at home with Maurizio while the children were away, but now, more than anything, I was glad and felt blessed to have spent the weekend with my family. Maddie was always good fun and time with her was my only real constant in life and I loved my grandparents, so it had been good to see them. They asked about my new job and home. I'd told them, and about the children, Bea and Carrie, but kept details about my boss to the bare minimum beyond the fact that he was my boss and a barrister, that he was kind and had made me feel very welcome.

With my car repacked and my sister still nursing the remnants of her hangover, I kissed her goodbye and began the journey home with a promise to arrange for her to visit me soon.

It was probably only a couple of hours drive back to Maurizio's house, but in my car, it was closer to three, maybe three and a half with a couple of stops along the way.

I was drinking a cup of coffee from a machine at my last planned stop of the journey and checked my phone. Should I have made contact with Maurizio while I'd been away? There was no real need to as we weren't generally inclined to casually text throughout the day. Our contact via calls or text was restricted to changes to our day, my working day, or in relation to the children and none of those things had been present that weekend. I reasoned that no, I had no need to have made contact. A small sigh escaped my lips when I realised how disappointed I was that the need to contact him or to be contacted by him wasn't there.

I'd been back on the road for another half an hour or so when my car began to make a strange noise. The engine laboured, threatening to stall, and then with a loud bang and steam coming from beneath the bonnet, it stopped.

"Shit!" I cursed, already relieved that I was on a relatively quiet road with a parking cut out.

I managed to get it parked safely then walked around the car, unsure what I was looking for or what to do. I'd cancelled my breakdown cover when money was tight, just after I'd moved. With hindsight, landing at my new home and job on the back of a breakdown truck might have been an indication that the time wasn't right to cancel my cover.

Reaching back into the car, I grabbed my phone and dialled the breakdown service who it seemed wanted a ridiculous amount of cash to rescue me. They did give me the number of a local garage. It seemed it was a one man and a one truck operation, and he was already rescuing someone.

I began to pace and then wondered if I would be better calling the garage who had most recently repaired my vehicle, but I didn't have the number or the name and as it was, I had very little signal for internet access. Maybe if I walked down the road, towards a village, I might have more luck.

About half an hour later, I found myself entering a coffee shop with free internet access. I searched for the garage as I sipped a cup of tea and ate a chocolate muffin. The mechanic who had repaired my car answered but told me it would be a couple of hours before he could get to me. In the grand scheme of things that was a win, so I agreed to wait for him. I'd drink my tea, finish my cake, use their bathroom facilities and then take a slow stroll back to my car.

It was another hour before I left the coffee shop and felt a chill in the air that was followed by the first drops of rain. Looked like I was going to be cold and wet by the time I got back to my car, but at least I'd be on my way home soon enough.

The decision not to wear a coat was a bad one when I found myself less than halfway back to my car and absolutely drenched courtesy of the rain that had turned into a torrential downpour that showed no signs of abating, neither did the cold wind that was freezing me until I was unable to stop shivering. I didn't think I had ever been so wet before. I made a very bad attempt at running back to the car, but I was many things and none of them a runner.

Just when I thought things couldn't get any worse, a speeding van went through a huge puddle at the very second I stepped alongside it. My earlier belief that I hadn't been so wet before was now surpassed by this moment and that is when a bright flash of lightning lit the sky above me, followed shortly afterwards by a loud rumble of thunder rolling overhead, and that is when I began to cry.

Chapter 23

Maurizio

After a very heavy and even later night, most of Sunday morning was spent in bed fending off the hangover from hell. I didn't drink to excess often, but once Nico is added to the equation, it's a foregone conclusion that a hangover will be had. That was further compounded by the addition of Gabe and Seb who both knew how to put it away. I recalled that by the end of the evening we were like old friends, so much so that they were calling me Mo, something only those closest to me did.

By lunchtime, or at least two in the afternoon, I had managed to drag my arse out of bed, shower, drink some juice and eat some toast. As I re-entered my bedroom to dress, the stench of stale alcohol hit me, so I threw on some track bottoms and a t-shirt before opening a window then put clean bed linen on.

I wasn't exactly house proud or house-husband material, but I was pretty domesticated and knew how to operate household appliances. In all honesty, that had been put to the test since Sophie left. With the washing machine on, I thought my afternoon plan might be as simple as a cup of tea and a boxset on the TV while waiting for the children to return that evening. The children and Flora.

I had genuinely missed Flora being around, maybe too much. Whilst I had missed the children being there, it had been nice to only have to think of myself for a couple of days. It hit me in that moment how long I had done precisely that for. After Sophie and I married we continued to make our own plans but to fit in with the other, however, once the children were born, that had changed, for Sophie at least, whereas I had simply continued as before. I was beginning to see how difficult that had been for Sophie and that even with Bea working for us, it had still been her role to juggle multiple plates and make sure none were dropped. The truth was that as time had gone on, our marriage and relationship had suffered as we each began to make our own plans with no regard for the other unless it involved the whole family.

Since Sophie had left, I had questioned how much I had driven her to leave, and I wasn't stupid enough to believe that I had played no part in it. My mother had cast Sophie entirely as the villain in this particular piece, but I knew that wasn't entirely accurate because I could have been a better husband. However, that was the past and I just needed to support Sophie to be the mother our children needed and deserved. Thinking back to the night before, I briefly recalled a conversation with Nico, Gabe and Seb about exes and children, not that Nico really understood the intricacies of that, but the other men seemed to, not that I fully knew their stories. However, they made sense when they spoke about needing to facilitate the relationship with the absent parent, leaving the channels of communication open and not making threats or ultimatums, but also knowing the importance of consistency of presence over everything else. I'd give Sophie a while longer and I had to give credit for the more frequent contact of late, but the children deserved to know where they stood and if they were seeing her every day or on holidays and high days, or most likely, something in between.

With a cup of tea in one hand and the TV remote control in the other, I pushed thoughts of the past and my children's possible futures aside, and settled on the sofa and prepared to chill when my phone rang.

By the time I disconnected the call, I knew I would not be chilling. I was going to find Flora, who was stuck at the roadside in the middle of nowhere. I grabbed my keys and headed for the door.

I'd been driving for about an hour when it started to rain. At least Flora would be able to sit in her car and stay dry. The rain was relentless and even with my windscreen wipers on their fastest speed, visibility was poor. When the mechanic called, he explained that Flora's car had finally given up the ghost. That wasn't a problem. I'd bought her a new car a few weeks before and it would be available this week. The problem, however, was that she was in the middle of nowhere and with the addition of horrific weather, she could be vulnerable.

"For fuck's sake!" The flash of lightning followed by a loud crack of thunder that I swore shook my car, made me jump. "Amazing." Because obviously this is what was missing from Flora being stuck at the roadside.

The temptation was to put my foot down, but that would be reckless and while Flora brought out an element of that in me, I wasn't recklessly dangerous. I was sensible, usually. Safe. I reminded myself that I was a father and my children did not need to be semi-orphaned by me speeding in this weather. Briefly, I wondered if Sophie would step up if I wasn't there. A few months ago, there would have been zero doubts in my mind, but now? Well, I wasn't so sure. I needed to speak to someone, a solicitor, a family specialist maybe, and find out what my rights and options were for securing a future for my children. Then, I needed to speak to Sophie and discuss the children and our divorce and then I needed to update my will. With the seriousness of reality kicking in, I eased off the accelerator and opted for a slower, but safer arrival.

My Satnav directed me to a village. It seemed to be a single street with shops and houses on both sides, small and quaint, but well-appointed with good facilities. I drove past a school, a pub, a shop, a playing field, tennis club, then a youth club. I was impressed. It was a nice location and if I was looking for somewhere farther away from the rat race, this place would be a serious option, not that where I currently lived could be described as inner city. As I imagined I'd be heading out of the village, I found more shops along a heavily flooded part of the road; a boutique, a hair and beauty salon, an off licence, a butchers, a bakers . . . I laughed. I was only missing the candlestick maker. There seemed to be a card and gift shop combined with a haberdashery and then a coffee shop opposite a closed garage.

"Your destination is on the right."

I stared at the garage and pulled over. This was not my destination. Couldn't be. When Flora called the garage near home, she'd given him a location on a B road. She hadn't mentioned a garage or a coffee shop, and she would have done. I opened the map on my phone and zeroed in on my current location, then using the directions and location information the mechanic had given me, I found her most likely position. I took another look around, just in case she was hidden nearby, but knew she wasn't. All I could presume was that due to the rural location, there were limited postcodes around here.

"Right." I sighed. "Flora, I am coming to find you." I put the car back in gear and with the storm seeming to be getting worse, I set about finding her.

Chapter 24

Flora

The closer I got to my car, the worse the storm got. The rain continued to lash down and with every crack of thunder and flash of lightning, I cried a little more until I could barely see beyond the end of my nose between the thrashing rain and my own tears. I gave up trying to see and dropped my head, watching my pumps getting wetter and wetter. I really should have worn a coat and possibly boots, although I wasn't convinced that any coat or boots I had packed in my car would have been any match for this horrendous storm. The loudest clap of thunder I had ever heard boomed causing a loud sob to escape from me as fresh tears of fear, trauma, and my past ran down my face and mingled with the rain there.

Eventually, I was almost back at my car, I risked a glance up and could see it still parked where I had left it. Unfortunately, there was no sign of the pick-up truck, but at least I could get in from the storm and change into some dry clothes.

I fished my keys out of my pocket, but with my hands dripping, I dropped them into a large puddle just a few feet from my car. Bending, I reached to pick them up when I heard an engine getting closer, the flash of lights suggested the other vehicle was pulling in behind mine. I straightened, just as another bout of thunder and lightning roared around me, this time even louder, and I could have sworn a bolt of lightning struck mere inches from me, taunting me. I literally leapt in the air and ran for my car, all thoughts of the other vehicle forgotten, but with shaking hands, I struggled to open the door.

A loud, almost blood curdling scream left my mouth when a hand appeared over mine, steadying my grip on the keys.

"Hey, ssh," were the words I heard, and even with only one word and a sound spoken, I recognised the voice.

Spinning to face him, the floodgates of my emotions erupted. I cried. Immediately he tugged me to him, comforting me and although the storm continued around us, I suddenly felt a little safer.

Pulling back, I looked up at him. His eyes were fixed on mine and with no words exchanged, he leaned in and kissed me. The second our mouths met, I was lost to anything that wasn't him. My lips softened and parted, inviting him in. His tongue licked across my lower lip and then he accepted my invitation. Our tongues duelled and yet rather than do battle, they seemed to meld together, working as one. His arms were wrapped around me and somehow, I entangled myself in and around him. My arms were around his neck, holding him tight and close while my legs were wrapped around his hips.

The sound of a loud claxon blaring brought things to an abrupt end. We both laughed as the passing lorry seemed to applaud the show we had been putting on.

"Come on, let's get you dry." Maurizio took my keys and after shutting me in his car, ran back to mine to retrieve my overnight bag.

When he joined me back in his car, he offered me my bag.

"Thank you. How did you know where I was?" Panicking that he might think I was being short with him or incredibly conceited to think he had come to my rescue, I continued. "I mean, I assume you weren't just passing and saw my knackered car." I avoided the thought of what he had witnessed in terms of my own, sad, dishevelled and rather hysterical performance.

"The garage called to let me know you had broken down and that it might be a while before they could get to you."

"Ah." I was unsure why the mechanic had felt it necessary to call my boss, but I was glad he had, even if the reason was probably because Maurizio had ensured his last bill for repairing my car had been settled.

"And I was looking for you, not the car. Couldn't give a shit about the car."

The air was crackling again and the atmosphere was as thick as it had ever been. I found myself turning in my seat and realised Maurizio's movement had mirrored my own. We were staring at each other again, our bodies taut liked coiled springs or wild cats, circling each other, waiting for the optimum moment to pounce. The question was, who was going to pounce first?

The first move was made by Maurizio and whilst that wasn't a shock, the sensation of his hand gently cupping my chin and his fingers stroking across my damp and tearstained cheek was.

"Flora."

No more words followed for long seconds as the previously sexually charged moment became equally as emotional. His eyes bored through me, as if he could see me, all of me for the first time. I felt bare and exposed and it should have made me feel uncomfortable or ready to shut down, but it didn't, quite the opposite happened. If anyone was going to see me laid bare and completely vulnerable, there was nobody else I could think of that I'd want that to be.

"You looked sad."

It wasn't a question, not even a statement really, more of a musing he was mulling over.

I didn't want this discussion. Not now, maybe never.

"Maurizio." I stopped because I had no clue what else to say at this moment.

He continued to allow his fingers to travel back and forth across my face for a few more seconds and then he pulled my face closer, as if preparing to kiss me again.

"Tell me to stop."

And there it was. The point where he handed things over to me. We had been here so many times before and I was past the point of putting this off. It seemed inevitable that the attraction between us would be acted upon. I ignored the voice in my head telling me that if it went wrong it would leave behind a very awkward situation that could ultimately cost me my job and my home. This was meant to be and whatever followed, well, we'd deal with it one way or another.

"No."

He cocked an eyebrow at my determined reply, and in return I cocked mine back at him, almost daring him to stop.

He leaned in closer until his lips almost touched mine. "Tell."

The sensation of his breath on my face made me swallow hard.

"Me."

He rested his lips against mine and I allowed them to part once more.

"To."

The hand that had been on my face had slid into my hair so he was now cradling my head while his lips pressed more firmly against mine.

"Stop."

We were frozen in our position and possibly time as this moment seemed to pause, waiting for someone to move it forward or end it.

"Never again."

Chapter 25

Maurizio

Never again. That's what she'd said and it was all the confirmation I needed. This was potentially a bad idea, the worst, and yet there was nothing I wanted more. Nothing more than Flora.

The storm continued around us but somehow cocooned us, giving a sense of safety to be in my car. Flora was calmer, less fearful, almost oblivious to the thunder, lightning, lashing rain and howling wind that continued to battle all around us.

In the blink of an eye, my lips captured hers, our kiss turning passionate as soon as my tongue met hers. I was unsure what my arms were doing but before I knew it, they were all over her, wrapped around her, pulling her closer until she was virtually in my lap. That is when I realised she was still sodden from being caught in the storm.

"You're wet," I told her, breaking our kiss and pulling back.

With a slight flush covering her neck, chest and cheeks and a strange glimmer in her eyes, I laughed, realising what her reaction to my words was.

"Your clothes, from the rain."

"Ah." She flushed a deeper shade of red at her own misunderstanding and my grasp of things.

She pulled back and snatched her bag open to retrieve some dry clothes and a towel that she threw into my lap. With her wet jacket tossed in the footwell on top of her shoes, she roughly dried her hair on the towel, leaving it beautifully dishevelled in what looked like natural waves. I was transfixed by her as she discreetly began to remove her clothes. She lifted her hips enough to slide her open jeans down her thighs and then she pushed the towel beneath her so that when she lowered her hips, she was sitting on it. Her t-shirt sat low enough that she revealed nothing beyond the length of her pale legs. Suddenly, she reached back into the bag and pulled out something small, white and lacy—knickers.

Fuck me, she was about to put on dry knickers which meant she was going to remove the wet ones she was wearing. I needed to look away or I'd be removing everything else for her and devouring her right here in my car parked in a layby. I prepared to look away, out of my window, but as she rubbed the overflowing towel over her legs and then as her hips rose once more, I was mesmerised. I quickly snapped my gaze away. I gave her enough time to change her underwear, and then I looked back, but fuck me, if I hadn't mistimed it. She was just pulling her top over her head, revealing her upper body. Fortunately, she had put trousers on over her dry knickers. But there she sat in her bra, a lacy number in a pink colour and I couldn't take my eyes off her. Her chest was heaving as she watched me watching her and along with goose pimples across her chest, I could see her nipples beading through the lace of her bra, those tightly pulled buds a slightly darker shade of pink than the bra.

My mouth dried and my cock stiffened a little more. I needed Flora like I needed my next breath. I didn't doubt that I was going to be balls deep in her within the next five minutes if she didn't stop watching me watching her nakedness or at least cover herself up. I could think of nothing better than being buried inside her, but not here. When I finally got my hands on her it was going to be somewhere I could take my sweet time and savour every second of her.

Or maybe not because she chose that very second to reach behind her back to unfasten her bra. If I saw her tits, all bets were off. I knew it and apparently, she did too.

"Maurizio," she murmured as she prepared to lower the straps down her arms.

"Flora." I reached across and slipped a finger beneath one strap and prepared to help her.

We both leapt apart as the sound of a pick-up truck sounding its horn screamed around us.

"Fuck!" I hissed, both disappointed and relieved to have been interrupted. "The garage . . . get dressed." I could have kicked myself at the sharpness that had entered my voice when I saw her embarrassed flush and clouds of shame flickering in her eyes. I paused and leaned in. "Now isn't the time or place . . . but when we get home . . ." My voice trailed off as she smiled and pulled her dry top over her head.

By the time Flora's car was loaded onto the back of the breakdown truck with a destination of a scrapyard near home, and its contents were loaded into mine, it was getting dark.

Our earlier close encounter had calmed somewhat, but I think we both knew that it wouldn't take much to reignite the heat and fireworks, but that really would be better in the privacy of home.

We chatted a little, about Flora's weekend with her sister and mine with Nico. She laughed at my description of my hangover and the sound warmed me. She in return suggested that her sister and I needed to think of the consequences to our actions and went on to expand on her sister's delicate state that morning. She said very little about her car, almost resigned to its fate, although I sensed she was worried about replacing it. Part of me was tempted to blurt out that her new car would be arriving that week, but a bigger part of me resisted, unsure how she might respond to that.

When I pulled up in front of the house and with the engine turned off, we both sat in silence, staring through the windscreen. Unsure if I should say or do something, I waited, hoping Flora might give me an indication of where her mind was at and what she wanted.

"We should go in." Her words came out as a statement for the most part, although I was sure I detected some uncertainty in them.

"Yes . . . unless you don't want to." We both knew I wasn't referring to her not wanting to go indoors.

"I want to."

I turned to look at her now and found her gaze falling upon me.

"If you still do . . . I want to."

I felt a broad grin split my face before I laughed. "This is like being a teenager and knowing there's an empty house behind that closed door."

She smiled at me as a flush crept across her cheeks. "I guess the only difference is that we both know what could happen once that door closes behind us."

She was right. "Could?" I suddenly queried, wondering if she was having second thoughts about this despite her earlier claim to the contrary.

"What *will* happen," she corrected as her pink cheeks reddened.

I got out of the car and went round to the passenger door, opening it to offer Flora an outstretched hand. She took it and together we walked hand in hand to the front door, both of us knowing what awaited us inside.

Chapter 26

Flora

This was happening. We were really doing this. I was nervous, but there was more to it than that. I was excited. I knew if this was a flop then it would complicate things, but I couldn't help but feel that it wouldn't be. I felt like this was going to be a defining moment in my life and hopefully for the right reasons.

The feel of my hand wrapped in Maurizio's felt right. I hoped my palm wasn't clammy with nerves because this might have been more animalistic than romantic, I didn't want it to become awkward, although I was struggling to speak. Maybe speech was unnecessary.

Walking to the front door seemed to take forever but once it opened, everything picked up speed. I quickly found myself pressed against the back of the door while Maurizio studied me briefly before lowering his mouth to mine, pausing as his lips were about to land against my own.

"I don't know what this will mean . . . for us." Maurizio's expression was suddenly serious.

I refused to let the weight of his stir make me question the repercussions of this. "Nor do I." The truth was that I was blocking out the reality of what it might mean for us afterwards.

"It could be bad. Really bad. Disastrous."

"It could." I had at least rediscovered my voice, even if my words were essentially a repetition of his.

"Last chance. Tell me to stop and I will, and we need never speak of it again."

I smiled up at him, loving his integrity in wanting me to stop this and whatever the consequences to it might be. "I don't want you to stop. I don't know what this is, the attraction, but I want to find out. Don't stop."

That was it. His lips continued their journey until they clashed with mine, and I had never been so glad to have defied his demand to stop this than I had ever been about anything else before.

He parted my lips with ease and as his tongue found mine, we embarked on a battle of sorts until everything I was softened and succumbed to his body that crushed mine.

We kissed, although that seemed a totally inadequate description of what we were doing and how it felt. This was like no kiss I had ever known before and I feared it may ruin any other kiss I might ever experience, or at least ruin any other person that might ever kiss me. Why was I thinking about other kisses when all I wanted were Maurizio's? Was I already preparing myself for the end? Like this definitely couldn't last and my gut knew it?

No.

I wasn't going down that road.

I tuned back into his kiss, the way his lips created fires that would continue to burn for a long time.

I had no idea how long we had been in this position, our lips, tongues and arms somehow entwined, but time no longer seemed to matter or make sense. Somehow one of my legs had snaked around his hip, allowing him to get even closer, his body pressed into mine.

"Maurizio," I quietly moaned when our kiss broke, albeit briefly.

My use of his name seemed to act as encouragement for him to return his lips to mine. Suddenly there was a strange sensation against my thigh, right up high, almost against my most intimate folds that were already softening and moistening from his kiss alone.

"Maurizio, what's that? I can feel something."

I felt his laughter vibrate against my neck that his mouth was now teasing. He had clearly misunderstood the meaning of my words.

"I should hope you can feel something, I'd be very disappointed and a little insulted if you couldn't."

He laughed again. This time I laughed too just as the sensation I felt earlier struck once more.

"Maurizio," I called, a little more insistently now. "Can't you feel it?"

A confused expression spread across his face as realisation dawned. The vibrating had stopped and almost immediately began again.

"My phone." Maurizio reached into his pocket and retrieved his phone. "My mother," he told me, holding the display towards me.

I nodded, unsure if he was somehow asking permission to take the call, but as far as I was concerned that was unnecessary, even if yet another of our moments was being broken; she was his mother and she was currently caring for his children. He dipped in and delivered a single kiss to my cheek before connecting his call, whilst still standing with my leg around his hip.

"Mama . . . no, of course." He laughed. "I bet they are, but only if you're sure. No, that's fine . . . hey, you two . . ."

He continued to chatter, quite obviously to the children, and then he hung up, returning his phone to his pocket and his full attention to me.

"My mother and the children have had such an amazing weekend and with the weather forecast promising sun and warm temperatures, they'd like to stay another night."

"I see." I honestly wasn't sure that I saw anything.

"Meaning . . ." Maurizio leaned in closer, as if preparing to resume his kissing of me.

"Meaning?" I asked a little breathlessly and rather optimistically.

"We have the whole night with no interruptions."

I fought the grin that was desperate to break out. "Do you suppose she'll ring back?"

Maurizio looked confused. "You want my mother to ring back?"

I shrugged. "Not necessarily your mother but the vibrate mode on your phone was rather pleasurable."

"You're." He rested his forehead against mine. "Going." His hand slipped around my neck until he gripped the back of it. "To." He pulled me closer. "Get." His breath danced across my lips. "More." He smirked. "Pleasure." My breath hitched. "Than." His eyes bored into mine. "You've." I could feel myself flushing as my temperature rose. "Ever." A moan sounded around us as his lips gently touched mine. "Known."

Before I could respond in any way, I was being lifted until I was hanging over Maurizio's shoulder and he was climbing the stairs. He paused at the top and looked between his room and the landing that led to mine.

"Your place or mine?" I asked, still hanging over his shoulder, unsure why he seemed to be deliberating this as much as he was.

"Yours."

I felt a little insulted by his reluctance to take me to his bed. A hand rubbed across my ass cheeks, and he spoke again.

"Yours for starters, I have plans, and then we go to my bed."

Chapter 27

Maurizio

This day was just getting better and better and might be the only cure for a hangover I would ever rely on. I allowed myself a small, satisfied smile at Flora's bristling at my suggestion for taking this to her room, I assumed her irritation was because she had taken my words to mean that she wasn't welcome in my bed. Nothing could be further from the truth, and she would be in no doubt about that by the time morning came.

I couldn't believe my luck, to have her here, literally in my arms, well, thrown over my shoulder, but clearly the stars were aligning for me with my mother's plans for an extended stay away with the children, meaning that tonight it was just me and Flora. All night and I was going to make it count.

My hand was still caressing her behind as I made my way to her rooms. The door was unlocked so I headed straight in and didn't stop until I was depositing her in the middle of her bed. She looked up at me and fuck me if she didn't look beautiful in her aroused and dishevelled state.

"I want you naked and I want a do over."

She lay perfectly still, gazing up at me, her face a picture of confusion.

I retreated until I stood in the doorway then repeated, "I want you naked and I want a do over, but this time I am watching everything and you're going to know I'm here."

"You mean—"

I nodded. We both knew what I meant.

A flush crept up her cheeks but in spite of it, she sat up and began to remove her clothes. Her top came first and then she shed everything else until she was down to her underwear.

I drank her in, every inch of her luscious skin that had the slight glow of a fading tan. Immediately, I imagined her soaking up the sun in a bikini, the two of us lying together enjoying the heat on our skin, the slightly salty taste of her skin combined with the sea. Fuck! What I wouldn't give to be on a deserted beach with her, just the two of us, but that would have to wait because right now, here was perfect. Wherever we were, she was perfect.

Slowly, almost shyly, she reached behind her and undid her bra. With her arms folded across her front, she drew the straps down her arms until she was casting the lacy fabric aside, revealing her perfect breasts to me. Large, but not too large. They would overfill my hands slightly and her luscious pink nipples that were hard and beaded, begged to be drawn into the wet heat of my mouth where I would suck on them, graze them with my teeth before biting into them, gently at first and then more firmly. My own erotic thoughts almost made me miss Flora sliding her knickers down her legs before tossing them in the direction of her bra.

She lay back against her pillows and briefly closed her eyes as her hands began to skim across her own flesh; her neck, chest and then she cupped her breasts. I prepared to demand her eyes stay open and on me, but as she closed in on her nipples, the deep blue pools of her eyes were mine. All mine.

Holding her gaze, I was determined not to miss a second of this and the way she fixed me with her stare, I knew she didn't want me to. I was in awe of her confidence as she continued to explore her own body. Her back arched slightly as she pinched her nipples before skimming further down her body until one hand made its way between her thighs that were splayed, offering me an unobscured view of her body opening up.

"Fuck!" I all but growled as I licked my lips, desperate to taste her.

She gave me a tiny shake of her head as her fingers began to delve lower, stroking along her own length, avoiding her clit, simply dancing around it.

Her mouth formed an 'O' as she released a tiny moan of my name. I had the willpower of a thousand men because somehow I held back despite how close I was to coming there and then.

I thought back to shy, less assured Flora, and then reminded myself of her confidence on the occasions where she had been buoyed by alcohol, but she paled when compared to this woman before me. She was a fucking goddess and whether she realised it or not, she was mine.

"Maurizio."

My moaned name left her lips for the second time, the bottom lip that she bit down into once more while I continued to watch her; her chest rose and fell rapidly, her fingers danced through her own wetness before finally circling her clit. A loud groan sounded around us as her hips bucked at the sensation.

"Show me, tesoro mio. Show me what you want."

Her movements paused briefly as she fixed me with a stare, her eyes glittering with lust and desire and then with one hand still teasing each of her breasts in turn, she allowed her fingers to slide inside her, fucking herself for both of our pleasures.

"Oh God, yes, fuck me, please, Maurizio."

"With fucking pleasure." My clothes were already falling to the floor and I was stalking towards her. As hot as it was to watch her pleasure herself, my control was spent, and I needed to be the one touching her and making her moan rather than simply the thought of me.

In what felt like a split second, I blanketed her body. Nothing had ever felt so right as our naked flesh pressed together. My lips immediately found hers, open and inviting, and I was suddenly a man on a mission to kiss every inch of her body.

"Oh God, yes, fuck me, please, Maurizio." Her repeated words were filled with desperation and pleading for me to give her what she needed.

The same words uttered as that night when I'd found her touching herself, but unlike that night, I was going nowhere and I fully intended to fulfil her needs. Every last one of them.

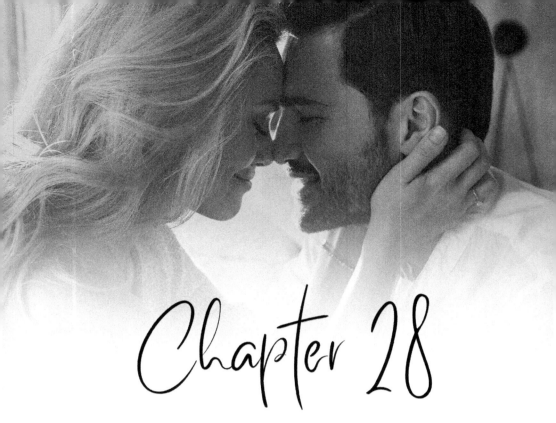

Chapter 28

Flora

The sensation of his body touching mine felt better than I ever dared imagine it might and as I gazed down and saw the top of his head between my legs, I had a feeling things were about to get even better.

"Fuck!" I cried as my fingers tightened in his hair. His breath warmed then chilled against my intimate flesh a split second before his tongue ran along my length.

The feel of his mouth on me there was beyond anything I had ever known and while I was basking in it, it also felt too much. I attempted to pull away or push him away, but apparently he wasn't on board with that.

"Not a fucking chance, tesoro mio," he rasped his second utterance of the Italian word I didn't know against my flesh as he gripped my hips more firmly and pulled me back against his mouth.

He hadn't shaved that day and the slight scruff he was sporting on his face abraded my inner thighs as he set about devouring me, and I liked the contrast of his soft tongue and rough stubble.

"Maurizio," I moaned as his tongue began to lap against and around my clit while a finger slid inside me.

My muscles tightened, clenching and holding his finger tightly, as an ache in my belly and pelvis began to build.

The calling of his name seemed to be taken as encouragement judging by the sensation overload he unleashed on my body. With my muscles relaxing a little, a second digit was added to the first and they pumped in and out in perfect rhythm with his tongue that was worshipping my clit.

"I can't stop," I muttered, warning him of my imminent release.

He paused, very briefly. "Good."

One word and then he returned his attention to me and my pleasure.

A garbled scream with the utterance of his name merged to leave my mouth as a cry of pleasure and passion. My body convulsed with the intensity of my orgasm and instead of easing up or releasing his grip on me, Maurizio continued to pleasure me, wringing every last ounce of my delirious release from me until I felt boneless and exhausted, yet craving more of this man.

He crawled back up my body, "Dolcezza."

Yet more Italian but before I could ask about it, we were kissing again, the taste of my pleasure passing from his lips to mine and if that wasn't an aphrodisiac, I didn't know what was. I could feel the length of him, hard and in need, pressing against me and I wanted nothing more than to feel him inside me. My arms were already around his back, holding him tightly and pulling him closer and my legs were now joining the party as my ankles crossed on his behind.

"Do you have any idea how beautiful you are when you come?"

I had no idea if his question was rhetorical.

"You are, like should be illegal to be that beautiful."

I laughed at what I perceived to be his flattery. His expression intensified and his eyes turned darker.

"I wasn't laughing, and I wasn't fucking joking."

I felt strangely chastened so tried to look away.

"No!" His tone was commanding and dominant. "Look at me."

I immediately complied.

"You are a beautiful, but when you come, the sight of you, the knowledge that I am the one giving you pleasure, well, that is indescribable, my lady."

His words couldn't be described as romantic, I was sure, and yet they tugged at my heartstrings, the sincerity of them as well as his desire for me.

"Maurizio." That was all I had in response. I reached for his face, stroking his bristly cheek and chin, then smiled up at him, a smile he returned.

"That is never going to get tired, my name on your kiss swollen lips. Do you want me as much as I want you?"

He slid the hard length of his desire back and forth along me, then stopped.

"Yes, more than anything."

In that moment, his hands were everywhere, holding me, touching me, pulling me closer.

"Where do you keep condoms?" He pulled back, kneeling between my open thighs where I was on display for him once more.

My eyes dropped from his face, down his body that glistened with sweat before I reached his erection that already glistened with pre-cum. I licked my lips and wondered how he would taste.

"Condoms?" he repeated, regaining my attention.

His gaze flitted between my lips, my exposed intimate folds and the bedside table where I assumed he expected me to keep condoms.

"I don't have any."

He stared and said nothing. Maybe he needed me to expand.

"No need . . ."

He silently stared.

"I don't have sex . . ."

Silence dragged on.

"Not for a while . . . I wouldn't do that . . . fuck . . . not here . . . not without you."

He leapt from the bed as if he had been burned. Panic rose as I wondered if I had said something wrong. Had I come on too strong and frightened him off?

"Yeah, well, you better remember that, but now, there is a need and you will be having sex, a lot because I intend to fuck you every way I can think of and then I am going to think of some new ways."

He turned to leave.

"Stay exactly where you are while I get condoms."

I watched his back and sexy arse leave my bedroom and could barely believe what was going to happen. What had already happened.

Lying, spread out, waiting for Maurizio seemed to last a lifetime. I assumed when he said he was going for condoms, he was going to his room to get them, but as I wondered just how long he had been gone, I questioned if he had gone to buy some.

Tired of waiting, I got up and went in pursuit of him and I didn't have to go far before I found him, halfway between his room and mine.

"I thought I told you to stay where you were."

"You did, but you were gone too long."

He quirked a brow as he held up a box of condoms.

"How many of those do you need?"

"All of them." His answer, just like his naked stance, was cocky and self-assured. "Now, tell me, where would you like to be fucked first, your bed, mine, or right here on the landing?"

Chapter 29

Maurizio

She looked slightly startled by my question, but only for a split second and then a broad grin spread across her face.

"I'm tempted to say right here on the landing," she admitted, and somehow it wasn't entirely a surprise.

Reaching for her, I pulled her close enough to kiss. "Your choice if you want to risk the friction of the carpet on your arse, back, knees, but know, I will fuck you anywhere and everywhere."

She laughed and stretched up to land a delicate kiss to my lips. "Then take me to your bed."

I had no idea how long it took us to get as far as my bed because we seemed incapable of not kissing and touching with every step. The journey wasn't as straight forward as it might have been. By the time we fell onto the bed I was working my way down her body again and had one of her nipples in my mouth while the other was making do with my fingers teasing and squeezing it.

"Maurizio," she called, her hands in my hair, tugging the ends gently.

I kissed my way back up her body until my lips rested against hers and our eyes were fixed on each other.

"Tell me you want me." I needed her to have no doubts about this.

"I want you, all of you, right now."

"Then you are going to get exactly that."

The temptation to slide inside her was strong, but not without a condom, so, with a brief retreat to sheath myself, I returned to her and positioned myself at her opening. I kissed her, gently at first, but soon enough, passion and need were running this show, our kisses were intensifying until our desire was ready to ignite.

Slowly, I edged closer, the very tip of me finding her heat. I wanted to savour the moment when I first entered her, stretching her, feeling her clenching around me.

"Baby," she groaned, her legs wrapping around me and her ankles crossing on my behind, encouraging me in.

"Greedy," I teased, although I was using every ounce of my self-control not to drive inside her in a single thrust and claim her as mine right there and then.

"More," she moaned, her hips tilting in an attempt to draw me in.

"More," I repeated, sliding inside her a little more.

"Hmm," she muttered, but her face suggested she may have gotten a little more than she'd anticipated.

"You okay?"

"Yeah, just give me a second."

"Whatever you need."

She smiled up at me.

"What?"

She giggled. "This is where I boost your ego and tell you that you're a lot to take and I'm out of practice."

Fuck, if I didn't want her even more, not because she was boosting my ego and complimenting my manhood, but I loved the idea of her being out of practice.

"I am trying really hard to take this slowly with you, but you're not making it easy."

"More. I want more."

I slid back slightly and then drove forward giving her a little more than before.

"Yes. Shit, that feels good."

Her head dropped back, exposing her neck to me and I wasn't about to turn down that invitation. My mouth dropped to her neck and as I kissed and caressed the soft flesh there, finding the spots that made her moan and her body soften further, I continued in my mission to fully occupy her until I was buried as deep inside her as I could be.

"And now, this is where it's going to feel even better." I was unsure if I was warning her or myself, but as I began to drive back and forth, I was seeing stars.

I'd had sex before, a lot, and had always enjoyed it, but this was something else. The physical feelings and reactions were second to none but when I looked into her eyes as I drove deep inside her and our bodies reacted to each other and the stimulation, well, that was like nothing I had ever known.

The feeling of her body squeezing me, driving me ever closer to my release meant this wasn't going to last as long as I had hoped, but the way she was moving in perfect time with me and the succession of pants she was releasing, interspersed with nibbles to her lip and an almost tortured expression crossing her face, the concoction was going to see me coming undone in a split second.

"I need to touch myself," she seemed to announce and I took that to mean that she was close to coming but needed a little more stimulation.

"Fuck!" I groaned, the memory of her touching herself almost being the catalyst to me embarrassing myself and coming before her.

Quickly, I adjusted my position so that I was kneeling between her thighs, giving her access to her clit while I continued to fuck her.

I paused, staring down at the sight of her before me, naked, my cock buried inside her while her fingers reached down to find her clit.

"Spread your legs," I demanded, unsure if I was going to shoot my load if she did as I told her. "Show yourself to me."

She obliged immediately and the sight of her wet and glistening with my cock driving in and out of her was my very own pornographic image.

"You need to come."

She nodded, possibly thinking I needed her to come, which I did, but what I had actually meant was that if she didn't come soon, I was going to get there before her.

"Maurizio," she called, her eyes fixed on mine as her fingers circled her clit for the first time.

"That's it, show me how I make you feel."

"I'm going to come. Fuck me hard . . . make me come. . ."

Her voice trailed off into a series of moans and cries as her whole body convulsed while I fucked her hard, possibly harder than she'd expected and then everything went black as I exploded inside her, one hand in her hair, pulling the golden strands firmly while the other one gripped her arse and pulled her closer to me, my fingers digging into the soft flesh there, most likely leaving my mark. I hoped leaving my mark.

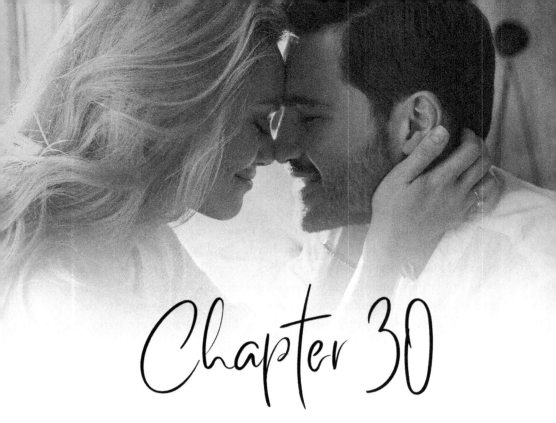

Chapter 30

Flora

Waking I noticed that the space next to me in Maurizio's bed was empty and only the tiniest amount of warmth resonated meaning he hadn't been there for a while. I checked the time and saw it was a little after seven. Not late, but still something of a lie in for me on a weekday.

Looking around, I wondered what I should do. Was this going to be awkward? It hadn't been last night, but that was then . . . and this is now. There was a severe lack of my clothing in this room, however, there was a t-shirt of Maurizio's, but could that be the catalyst for awkwardness to descend, me strolling into the kitchen wearing his t-shirt, reminding us both that last night had really happened. Moreover, would it force our hands in addressing what happened in the cold light of day and whether either of us regretted it?

As I considered all of these questions and possible answers, I realised that no matter how amazing the sex between us had been, and it had been absolutely phenomenal, it could be our undoing once reality struck. What had I been thinking when I had all but begged Maurizio to fuck me? I hadn't been thinking, not with my mind anyway.

I needed the bathroom and then I should get dressed, fully. Leaping from the bed, I made the short dash to Maurizio's bathroom where I was startled to find my face reflected back in the mirror. My hair was all over the place, my eyes looked wide and sparkly . . . jeez, I looked stoned, not that I had a point of reference for that, and my lips looked a deeper shade of pink and swollen. I'd never really thought lips could become kiss swollen but they really were. Sitting down on the toilet, I let out a cry as my inner thighs tightened and throbbed.

"Shit! He's broken me." I laughed at myself thinking that if I had to be broken, there was no better way for it to happen.

Coming face to face with my reflection once more, as I washed and dried my hands, I looked at my naked body that carried some finger marks where Maurizio had gripped and held me. I needed to get dressed and stop reliving the feel of his touch and kiss.

Re-entering the bedroom, the doubts and possible fall out of sleeping with my boss began to infiltrate my mind again. There was no reason why I couldn't go back to my own bedroom where all of my clothes were and then I'd go downstairs like I did every other morning, but in the meantime, I needed not to be caught wandering around the house naked. Grabbing Maurizio's t-shirt, I threw it on from my position now sat on the edge of the bed.

I prepared for the walk of shame, albeit from one end of the house to the other when I almost leapt from the bed at the site of Maurizio opening the door, looking like he should be on the cover of a magazine wearing just a pair of grey joggers and carrying two cups of something steaming.

"Oh, you're up." He sounded disappointed.

"I was going to get dressed." I heard the nervousness in my voice.

"I thought we could spend a little time together . . . I made tea."

He offered me a cup before rounding the bed and climbing in.

Following his lead, I moved until I was sitting up in bed next to him. I sipped my tea and felt stifled by the awkwardness I'd feared might descend.

"I called Bea and gave her the day off."

"Oh." I hadn't considered Bea arriving for work, not even when I thought about going downstairs in Maurizio's t-shirt. This really had the potential to implode. Bea may not be here today, but when I did see her, how the hell was I going to face her? No, that wasn't it. it was more that I feared she'd take one look at me and know that I'd slept with our boss.

"Well, the children won't be back until this evening so there seems no point in her being here, plus, as I said, I was hoping we could spend some time together."

I turned to face him, wanting to give him a get out from this . . . whatever this was, but when I saw his handsome features, I wanted to simply lean in and kiss him, pull him to me, feel his skin against mine before getting lost in his touch.

"Flora." My name was a gentle whisper on his lips. "Are you okay? About last night . . . do you regret it? Want to forget it, or at least pretend it didn't happen?"

I opened my mouth, desperate to assure him that I had no regrets, but before the first word left my mouth, he spoke again.

"I don't. I certainly could never forget it. I don't know that I can pretend it didn't happen either . . ." His voice trailed off.

Placing my cup down, and turning so we were looking at each other, eye to eye, I considered my words. "I don't want to forget it. It was more than I imagined it might be, but I don't want it to be awkward, for either of us, nor the children and Bea."

He nodded. "Neither do I, but I don't want it to stop."

I stared at his expression, wondering what he meant by *it*.

"No! I don't mean sex! I mean I do, but not just sex. I'd like us to get to know each other better, but the children need consistency. Sorry—"

I cut him off. "I know, and they have to come first. Can we agree to be discreet then? I have no desire to be seen as someone on the make or to become the stereotype of 'the nanny who falls for the handsome single dad'."

His grin was unmissable. "As you're the nanny, that would make me the handsome single dad."

I laughed. "I suppose it would."

"And you're the beautiful nanny, not just the nanny. So, we're going to do this, us?"

I nodded.

"With discretion, on both our parts?"

I nodded again.

"Then let's seal the deal . . ." Maurizio leaned in, one hand cupping my chin, drawing me closer until our lips met, ". . . with a kiss."

From that kiss to seal the deal, we had ended up making love before showering and dressing and now we were driving in Maurizio's car, heading into town.

"Don't you have work?"

He frowned. "A little, but there was something I needed to do first."

"With me?"

His responding nod caused me to flush as I wondered if him *doing* me was in fact the thing he'd needed to do.

A short laugh followed. "Flora, I needed my fill of you this morning, I can't deny that, and seeing my finger marks on your skin, only made me want you more, as did your begging to be filled by me, but that wasn't the actual thing I was referring to."

"Oh. Well, that's not at all awkward, is it?"

He smiled across at me and reached over to give my knee a gentle squeeze. "Let's grab some food and then I'll tell you why we're out and about this morning."

Chapter 31

Maurizio

F lora spied a little café in town. "The cakes here are to die for,"
she told me, already preparing to cross the road.

"I'm going to need more than cake to sustain me." That was
true, but the café she had indicated was somewhere I was reluctant to
enter with her. It was a popular pitstop in the village, especially with
local nannies and parents, mainly mums with their children, and I knew
our plan for discretion would be blown if we were seen there sharing
lunch.

She turned, a sultry expression spreading across her face. "And I
really think you're going to need some sustenance." Her tongue darted
out and licked across her full bottom lip.

"You are such a temptation." Leaning forward, I pushed some stray
hair behind her ear. I needed not to get distracted by her, especially not
here, in public with the possibility of an unwanted audience. "But
food."

"They do a decent all day breakfast too." She was already heading across the road, leaving me to follow in her steps.

The bell on the door announced our arrival which I realised was the point of it, but this also resulted in several sets of eyes landing on us, a few I recognised, accompanied by smiles. I didn't dwell on whether the smiles were welcoming or judgemental. Quickly, everyone seemed to return to their own lives leaving me and Flora to find a table. I spied one in a corner towards the back, and although I didn't want to flaunt the fact we were here together, I didn't want to appear as though I was ashamed of that. The only other table was in the window. This was the sublime to the ridiculous. Flora stood next to me, waiting for an indication of where we were going to sit.

Determined not to make her feel inadequate or like a dirty little secret, I gestured to the window. While she sat, I headed to the counter and ordered for us. There was one person in front of me, so not exactly a queue but it gave me the opportunity to watch Flora, study her. She gazed out of the window and then reached into her bag, pulling her phone out. She looked down at the screen and grinned. A sharp stab to my chest caught me off guard, especially when I realised it was due to not knowing who was making her smile that way. Specifically it was the fact that it wasn't me. I'd never been a particularly jealous person. I was possessive over anyone who was mine, but not jealous.

With our order in, I made the short distance to where she sat, aware of eyes on me again, unfortunately not Flora's. Taking the seat opposite her, she looked up and smiled, still typing.

"Sorry, two seconds, my sister is in full flow."

Relief washed over me and the heaviness lying across my chest like a lead weight lifted. Her sister. I could live with that.

"Is she okay?"

Flora threw her phone back into her bag. "Yeah, she's fine. What cake did I get?"

I laughed at the eager expression spreading across her face and the glint of excitement in her eyes at the prospect of cake. "I considered getting you real food, but I wasn't willing to run the risk of denying you cake."

"Very wise." Her squeal of delight signalled the arrival of our food and as I looked to the server, I realised there were still several sets of eyes trained on us, and despite my earlier reservations, I didn't give a shit.

We were back in the car, driving further away from home, but not by much, and Flora was still enthusing about her cake. When I first pulled into the car park, she looked concerned.

"Is there something wrong with your car?"

I got out and quickly, making my way to my door. I stretched out my hand, she accepted it and dutifully allowed herself to be led indoors.

We were greeted as soon as we entered. "Mr Walker," the salesman called.

I smiled at him and then turned to Flora. "I hope you like it."

The salesman immediately latched onto that. "You are going to love it. Her. She's a beauty and I can see the two of you being very happy together."

Flora looked between us and seeing her annoyed face, my nerves kicked in.

"This way," the salesman called, already striding across the shiny garage showroom floor.

"Maurizio." That was all she said. No other words, but my name was enough for me to offer her an explanation.

"You need a new car." I attempted to walk away.

"I didn't need you to get me one," she hissed, anger really kicking in.

"Flora, please—"

She cut me off and turned to face me, pulled her hand free of mine "No! Why would you do this? Is this my reward for not telling you to stop? Last night had nothing to do with any kind of gain as far as I was concerned, certainly not a pay off."

Her burgeoning annoyance paled next to mine and seeing her flinch, I assumed my expression conveyed my absolute fury. "Is that what you think?" I whispered the words, refusing to become a sideshow here, but they were as much as a shouted chastisement than if I'd raised the roof off this place. "I considered it some time ago, around the same time your car first appeared on my drive on the back of a breakdown truck, so last night has nothing to do with this. I thought it could be added to your employee benefits . . . you can transport the children when you need to, safely, and also have the convenience of a reliable vehicle."

"Oh."

I shook my head. Her 'oh' was insufficient.

"After you paid the repair bill on my car without telling me . . ."

A cold stare was my initial response. "The bill I thought I had told you about and when it became apparent you were unhappy with that, I agreed to deduct it from your wages, that bill?"

She apparently had nothing else to offer me.

"And to be entirely transparent in this, I haven't bought you a car, I have leased it so you'll only need to add petrol and I'm sure my accountant can make it tax deductible."

She reached for my arm, her mouth opening, possibly preparing her apology when the salesman called to us again. I strode towards the other man, leaving Flora to follow me.

I was unsure how Flora was likely to react to the news of her new car, but I hadn't expected her to suggest the car was essentially payment for having sex with me. That was still bothering me when she parked it next to mine on the drive.

Flora had attempted a couple of apologies, but I hadn't been in the mood to accept them and if I had, I certainly wasn't prepared to do it in front of the salesman. Maybe now though.

"Sorry," she called behind me as I made my way to the front door.

I stopped immediately and spun to face her. "Yeah, me too. Maybe I should have told you about it rather than springing it on you, but I thought I was doing a nice thing."

"It is a nice thing—"

"So nice that you assumed it was payment in kind for last night?" I could feel my anger rising again.

"Sorry," she repeated, and as I looked across at her, nervously toying with the car key, I could see and feel the sincerity of her apology.

With a deep, calming breath, I stopped, allowing her to catch up with me. Taking her hand, I looked down at her. "I can see why you might have thought this was a reward of some kind, but I don't operate that way, and I really did arrange this some time ago. It just took a little longer than I had originally anticipated, so even if last night hadn't happened, I would have still given you the car."

"Thank you." She allowed a small smile to curl her lips. "It's very generous of you and I love it."

"Then there's no more to say." With her hand still safely tucked in mine, I led her towards the house. "I have some work to do, but as the children aren't here, take the rest of the day off and relax."

As much as I would have liked to have spent the day with Flora, in or out of bed, I couldn't, I really did have work to do. Once I settled into work mode, I became fully immersed in it and as such kept Flora off my mind. That was something that was an advantage and a disadvantage of the particular personality trait I had of being quite focused and single minded. The pro: I was professional and never left loose ends. The con: other things ceased to exist in that moment. As a consequence those other things sometimes got bored of waiting for my attention. Those things were people. People like Sophie, although there had been more than my neglect of her involved in the breakdown of our marriage, but the other people, my children were totally innocent. I had been doing better at being present and drawing a line under work and focusing solely on them. They were my priority, always had been, but I needed to show them that. Then there was Flora, the greatest distraction and temptation that had ever walked the earth.

With the work done, I went in search of Flora. I had given her the day off, so she might not even be at home. I went into the kitchen, and from there I could see her car still parked next to mine. Presumably, she hadn't gone out. With downstairs showing no sign of her, I moved upstairs where the door was slightly open and I could hear her chatting. With no response from anyone else, I assumed she was on the phone.

"You do not need to know that. Ever." She giggled and the sound of it made me smile. "Maddie!" she shrieked.

Her sister.

"I am not telling you that!"

She sounded horrified but also amused and then I realised what was the subject of this conversation, or should that be who?

"I wish I had never told you how scorchingly hot Maurizio was."

My ego was seriously swelling to know that not only did she consider me scorchingly hot, but she had discussed me with her sister.

A loud squeal made me jump before she began to sing some nameless tune as if drowning her sister out.

"What did I tell you?" she asked, laughing again. "Never, ever call him Daddy."

I laughed myself, but loved the playful banter she shared with her sister. When we'd spoken about interests and family previously, she had mentioned her parents, her grandparents and her sister, but that had been it. Maybe that was it in terms of family and as for friends, she hadn't mentioned anyone besides Bea, Carrie and another nanny, Ash, so maybe she didn't have old friends. Suddenly, I thought back to rescuing her in the storm and how upset she'd been, almost too upset for just getting stuck in a storm with a broken down car.

My thoughts were interrupted by Flora calling her sister's name. "Maddie, look just to shut you up, and without details, it was the best sex of my life. Toe curling, sheet gripping, calling to God, amazing sex, happy now?"

Yeah, my ego was beyond pleased that I'd come in search of Flora. The truth was that last night had been everything she'd said, but as far as I was concerned that was the start, not the peak, so she'd better prepare for more toe curling, sheet gripping, calling to God, amazing sex. In fact, that might be my plan for the next couple of hours before the children returned.

The remainder of the afternoon was spent in front of the TV watching one of my all-time favourite films, *The Shawshank Redemption*. I had given Flora first choice on what we watched, but she'd told me to choose, so I had. I wasn't entirely sure it was her type of thing, but she'd watched it.

"What time is your mum due back?" She was already sitting up, stretching and then facing me.

She was beautiful with her face free of make-up, her hair piled high on her head and dressed in track bottoms and a simple t-shirt. I could already feel the blood in my body rushing to my cock.

"Maurizio." Her call of my name was a reminder that she had spoken to me, asked a question.

"Sorry."

She smiled, knowing exactly what I was thinking about, or at least what I was thinking about doing.

I checked my watch. "About an hour."

"Shame. I was considering a little siesta."

I looked back at my watch as if checking again would give us more time and as I returned my gaze to Flora, she was moving to straddle my lap.

"What about your siesta?"

"An hour wouldn't be long enough." She grinned and if it didn't cause a chain reaction of my own megawatt smile.

"Did you have something else in mind?"

"I did." She offered no further explanation but did lower her lips to mine where we began what was becoming almost a ritual of our tongues duelling before mine overpowered hers as my hands grazed over her body, pulling her head closer, moving to stroke her face before travelling lower, cupping her breasts, squeezing and rolling her nipples until she became breathless and her hips began to thrust against my rock hard arousal that I thought might never get enough of her. "Maurizio."

And there it was, the mere utterance of my name that in such a short time had become a plea, confirmation, and so much more.

"I want to taste you," she told me as my hands came to rest on her hips, pausing her sliding across my length that was telling me to throw her down and fuck her right here, even if there was a chance my mother might interrupt things.

"Taste me?"

Her reply came in the form of her sliding to her knees in the space between my slightly splayed legs. Looking up from beneath her partially lowered and heavy looking lids, she looked like sin personified. Her hands reached up for the waistband of the track bottoms I wore, minus underwear, and my erection sprang free. Watching her eyes widen and the slow lick of her tongue across her lips caused my cock to lurch as I imagined just how it would feel to be inside her mouth, the sensations that the heat of her mouth and tongue pleasuring me would bring. She continued to look between my face and my erection for a few seconds longer which is when I reached down and held myself, still for a split second before I began to move my hand along my length, the first pearl of pre-cum appearing immediately.

No words were uttered by either of us, although a slightly strangled hiss that was mine sounded around us before her hand covered mine for a couple of strokes and then her mouth covered the very tip. Slowly, she sucked, licked and caressed me until she had lowered herself over me a little at a time and then she began to move, still slowly as she built her rhythm and then her pace increased while she cupped and stroked my balls that were heavy and aching already.

The sight of her golden waves spread out in my lap as my pleasure built and threatened to literally explode was both heaven and hell. Reaching down, I gathered her hair and held it in one hand like a pony-tail so I might have a view of her beautiful face and the erotic image of my cock being covered and revealed by her mouth. The visual along with the physical sensation was reducing the time this was likely to last, but in this moment I wasn't sure I cared. I was drunk and stoned on her, this lady who was everything. Tesoro mio. That two-word thought coincided with her pulling back and almost releasing me but only enough so that she could circle my crown with her tongue. This show was just getting better with every second, every second that pushed me closer to release and I knew it was going to be like nothing I had ever experienced and whilst pleasurable it was going to be tinged with glorious pain.

"Flora." The use of her name was accompanied by me inadvertently tugging on her hair that remained in my hand.

A low hiss and aroused groan was her only response, causing me to tug her hair again and if her hiss and groan weren't a little louder. She liked that. She found that little area with her tongue that had me growling and ready to come and with a small, cocky smile she returned to moving along my length, driving me to the point of no return.

"Flora," I warned, "I'm going to come."

Her efforts increased as did her caressing of my balls and then the world stopped spinning as I came, the first spurt arriving with a roar while the subsequent ones saw me thrusting up to meet her mouth in a sea of cries, moans, groans, expletives, and a sheen of sweat.

When the earth returned to spinning, my breathing was still erratic, and Flora remained on the floor between my legs wearing a small, almost shy smile that seemed to hide what had just happened. Her hair was no longer in my hand but I swear a few strands remained wrapped around my fingers.

I gazed down and prepared to speak but had no clue what to say when I realised her eyes were fixed on my cock that was hard again, assuming it had ever returned to anything else.

"Oh, yeah, I need to be inside of you, and I definitely need to make you come."

"I could get on board with that." Her teasing smirk was accompanied by a twinkle in her eye.

"Could you get on board with me having you on all fours, fucking you hard while I pull on your hair, forcing you to look at me as I drive into you, both of us knowing how wet and desperate your pussy is as it squeezes me, begging for more until you come all over my cock as you call my name?" I wasn't sure I had intended to give so much detail to her, but watching the earlier glint in her eye light up with nothing but desire confirmed she was totally on board now.

"How long do we have?"

That question reminded me of the imminent return of my mother and children. A quick look at my watch confirmed we were running out of time for all I'd like. "Thirty minutes." I was considering all I could do in thirty minutes when the sound of tyres on the gravel drive alerted us both to my mother's arrival with the children, a little earlier than planned. "Shit!" I'd been grateful for the extra night but a little longer would have been even better. Quickly redressing, I prepared to make an offer of later or something similar when Flora spoke.

"Thank you," she said, already leaning in to land a single kiss to my lips. "For rescuing me, for last night, this morning, for the car, just thank you."

Already on her feet, she was exiting the room when the children's squeals and the thudding of feet signalled their approach.

"Hey, you two," I heard her say before the children appeared, rushing in for hugs and kisses.

"I missed you," I told them, hugging them more tightly, and I meant it, I had, but had they been another half an hour, I wouldn't have been disappointed. Could my life get any better? At that second, I didn't think so.

Once the children were in bed and the remaining work I needed to do was done, I allowed myself to think about the events of the weekend. I didn't even try to fight the broad grin splitting my face as I recounted each and every second of the last couple of days, especially not the time I'd spent with Flora. Gabe and Seb had been right, I was fucked where she was concerned, just as they had been with their own nannies. Just the thought of Flora made everything somehow better. It was inevitable that my thoughts would go back to that afternoon when she had given me the best blow job of my life.

After checking on my children who were both sleeping soundly, I made my way to Flora's door and knocked gently. Just a few seconds later, she opened the door and didn't look entirely surprised to find me there, although, who else would be knocking on this door aside from me.

"Good evening, Mr Walker."

Was she teasing me?

"Really, Mr Walker?"

She shrugged and offered me a lopsided smirk. "I am practising my discretion."

"And you think Mr Walker will come across as discreet when I favour the informality of Maurice?"

"Perhaps, but honestly, there is no way I can be trusted to call you Maurice because it will come out as Maurizio and then—"

Her words were stemmed as I rushed her, somehow pulling her against me and lifting her at the same time, my lips covering hers and her back being pressed against the wall.

"Maurizio." Her breathy gasp of my name against my lips that were retreating only served to arouse me further and remind me of how many times she'd said it over the last couple of days and how much I'd liked it. The truth was that every time she said it, lust and desire kicked in and went straight to my groin. Perhaps some formality might be for the best, although the way she said Mr Walker made me as horny as her Maurizio did, or was it simply the fact that she was speaking to me that made me horny?

"I'm sorry that the children's return interrupted us before I could give you your release."

"It's okay."

"It's not, so let me make it up to you."

"Now?"

"Now."

"Here?"

"Here," I confirmed, and immediately wrapped her legs around my hips which is when I noticed that her hair was damp and piled on her head and the only thing she wore was conveniently a long t-shirt that barely covered her arse. As things stood, it wasn't covering her arse or anything else in her current elevated position and I now knew she was minus underwear. "Hold on." She followed my instruction and wrapped her arms around my neck allowing me to drop one hand between us while the other skimmed across her taut nipple. The hand between us quickly discovered the damp heat of her arousal, pleasing me to know she was as pleased to see me as my erection was confirming I was to see her.

With ease, I slipped a finger inside her, teasing and stretching her slightly before moving to circle her clit. Her legs immediately tightened while her fingers and nails began to flex and dig into my neck and shoulders. I alternated between sliding a finger inside her, then two and moving to circle her clit with her own arousal, each movement eliciting louder moans and harder scratches to my shoulders.

"Come on, let me see you fall apart for me." My words saw her face contort further in pleasure.

"Maurizio," she cried as she moved ever closer to the release that would not abate from this point.

I resisted the temptation to point out that her discretional Mr Walker was long forgotten.

"Please, Maurizio, fuck me."

I wanted nothing more, but this was not about me, and the truth was that I had no condom within easy reach and there was no way I was going to stop her from embracing the pleasure of her glorious release.

"Next time, but this is for you, tesoro mio, just you." And with a final thrust of my fingers and my thumb pressing down into the soft flesh around her clit, she did indeed fall apart, and I had never seen anything or anyone more exquisitely stunning in my entire life.

Several days passed and any opportunities for alone time with Flora were non-existent beyond stolen kisses before the children came down to breakfast. She had been busy all day with the children and in turn, I had been busy with work, even having a couple of late nights where my mother had stepped in to care for Craig and Rosie. It wasn't that Flora wouldn't have stayed on the clock for a few extra hours, she would have, and had done in the past. No, it had been my decision to ask my mother because, well, I wasn't entirely sure. I thought it may have been some subconscious desire for Flora's role in my life to be clear. Yes, she was employed as my children's nanny, but outside of that, she was so much more, and I never ever wanted her to feel as though her job and the salary she received for that had any bearing or influence on her role in my life outside of that. It didn't entirely make sense to me, not even in my own head, but that is how I rationalised it. Flora herself had spent time with her friends too, meaning we seemed to have constantly missed one another.

Chapter 32

Flora

My overthinking was at risk of overwhelming me. Every thought I had came back to Maurizio and the things we'd done together just a week before. There was no part of my life that wasn't wrapped up in and around him. I lived in his house where every surface, corner and item screamed his name. I cared for his children who carried physical resemblances as well as character traits, not to mention their constant chatter of him. My encounters with Carmella and her use of single Italian words and endearments set my mind to Maurizio and the times he'd said things in Italian to me. I wondered what those words meant. Even if I could say them, who would I ask, Carmella? I laughed, thinking they may not be suitable for her as Maurizio's mother. The car I drove had been chosen by him with me in mind. Even going to bed at night conjured thoughts of him, the scent of the man, his taste and the feel of his skin against mine as he drew pleasure and sensation from me in a way I never knew was possible. Even entering or leaving my home into the main house screamed

Maurizio's name much as I had that night when he had come to me and made me come whilst pressed against the wall!

"Penny for them."

I shrieked, startled by Bea's voice.

She laughed. "Oh dear."

"What? 'Oh dear', what?"

"How about we take the kids to the park and then we can drink some half decent coffee and indulge in a very acceptable slice of cake. Then while they play you can tell me why you have that look on your face."

"What look?"

She shook her head at me, a little disbelievingly. "The one I saw Carrie wearing before she got things straightened out with her and Gabe. The same one I saw looking back at me in the mirror when things between me and Seb were up in the air."

"Ah."

"Yeah, ah."

We were, as Bea had suggested, drinking coffee and eating cake together when Carrie and Ash appeared before us. I scowled at my colleague, suspecting some kind of intervention.

She shook her head. "Coincidence."

Ash took a seat next to me and explained his presence. "My lot are off to look at new houses, meaning they are picking the kids up from school and eating out, so I am off the clock."

Carrie came in for hugs from us each in turn and explained that she and her daughter, Charlotte, had been to the dentist meaning the little girl had finished school early, hence them being in the park at the same time as us. I still wasn't convinced until she began drinking her cappuccino through a straw.

"Bloody anaesthetic for a filling."

It was then that I noticed her slightly slurred speech. Okay, maybe this wasn't an intervention, which was good. I neither wanted nor needed one.

Barely two minutes passed before I seemed to blurt out, "Apparently

I have a look that you two had before finding your happily ever after."
Perhaps I did want an intervention after all.

Carrie stared at me as a frown creased her brow and her lips pursed,
well, as much as they could purse with her partial, temporary paralysis.

"What?" What had I said?

"I don't do happily ever afters, nor Prince Charming if that's your
next stereotype for me finding happiness with a partner and making a
family."

Seemed I had hit something of a raw nerve.

"Sorry." I was ready to make my own apology when Carrie interrupted me with hers.

"I have issues, but continue telling me about your look." She sucked
up some stray saliva before resting a hand on her growing belly. "Tell me
how you come to be wearing your finding happiness face?"

A few seconds passed before I committed to speaking, wary of
breaking the discretion Maurizio and I had agreed to. "How did you
know, both of you, that you'd met the right man?" I was changing tack
and turning this on them.

They exchanged a glance while Ash gave me a playful elbow dig.
"What about me? Perhaps I have my own Miss Right stashed away!"

We all turned to look at him, knowing full well that he didn't. I
especially knew this because Ash and I had discussed the topic of love
lives several times.

Bea and Carrie guffawed their response about Ash's Miss Right and
began to answer me.

Bea stepped up first.

"I'm not sure there was a specific moment for me. Seb was funny,
sexy, charming, and really goofy. He made me laugh, a lot, and he was
safe."

"Safe?" I wasn't sure I understood.

"He didn't want a girlfriend, a wife, a family, the happy ever after."

I definitely didn't understand now. He pretty much had all that she
was saying he didn't want.

"He didn't want those things and neither did I."

Carrie huffed her disbelief.

"Okay, we thought we didn't, but that made him safe. I wasn't risking my heart because he was all about a good time and never about feelings and emotions . . ." She paused. "Until he was, until we both were, and by then it was too late. I loved him, he loved me, although neither of us was ready for that bombshell nor an unplanned baby."

I'd only seen Seb a couple of times and he was besotted with Bea and their unborn baby. I looked across at Ash and saw his disbelief as clear as mine.

"I know, I know, he's super daddy in waiting now." Bea laughed. "But he was scared . . ." Her voice trailed off again, but this time she looked sad as her gaze moved as far as Carrie who took over.

"Long story short, Seb was hurt in the past and his funny, manwhore Uncle Seb routine was a front."

"Mummy!"

We all turned to see Charlotte with her hands on her hips, her face stern as she approached us, but Carrie was her only target.

"What has Daddy said about saying bad words?"

"Sorry," replied Carrie contritely, the roles of the two seemingly reversed.

Turning to me, Charlotte smiled. "Mummy sometimes says bad words, and Daddy, but Daddy doesn't like it. My Grandma says really bad words."

Carrie and Bea laughed, laughter the little girl joined in with.

"But Daddy says she has a broken brain sometimes so she can't help it." Quick as a flash she changed topic to Seb. "Uncle Seb is so lovely. He loves me lots and lots and he loves me even more than lots and more than anyone in the whole wide world."

I felt strangely emotional at the obvious love and adoration radiating from this little girl towards her uncle.

She gave Bea a sideways glance that was slightly frostier. "Uncle Seb is funny and kind, and oh so handsome—"

"And that is a direct Seb quote," Bea interjected to the little girl's clear irritation.

"And do you know what else, Flora?" Charlotte's focus was all mine again.

A shake of my head was my reply.

"Sometimes my Uncle Seb even likes Bea." And as quickly as she'd entered the conversation, she was gone, calling to Craig and Rosie who were in a nearby sandpit.

My mouth hung open, while Ash struggled to stifle laughter, Carrie shook her head and Bea looked rocked.

"She adores Uncle Seb and they've had this true love thing going on a while, and it's always been a little exclusive so she's getting used to him having another woman in his life." Carrie reached over and gave Bea's shoulder a pat.

"I thought she was warming to the idea." Bea looked a little upset.

"She is," Carrie assured her. "But you were kind of suggesting that he wasn't funny, kind and oh so handsome."

Bea nodded, although she clearly agreed with Seb's own quote that Charlotte had recycled for us.

Ash deflected attention by explaining that his sister had hated him so much as a baby that she'd put him outside in his pram and locked the door. This was the same sister who was as good as a second mother to him now. "Kids just need time to adapt to change, and you know this, we all do, we know kids, it's our job."

Carrie turned her undivided attention to me. "I fancied Gabe from the get go, even if he was a bit scary. He was my boss and like you, I lived with him so was scared for my home and job if we acted on the attraction, but from the second I met him there was a tension between us, and when I moved in with my clothes spread across the landing and he handed me my tiny scrap of underwear, I think I knew."

"The underwear he nicked and kept," Bea said, possibly oversharing. Ash and I were rapt.

"Yeah, well, as serial killer as that sounds, it worked out. We were meant to be together, and I can't ever imagine a life without him and my children."

The sound of fake vomiting from Ash made us all laugh as the children appeared talking about ice-creams.

"I might go and mend a few fences with Charlotte," Bea said and Ash got to his feet too.

"I'll get another round in," he said, indicating the empty cups surrounding us. "Let's get ice-cream!" he squealed, encouraging the children to join in and follow him and Bea into the café.

"So, what's your story, yours and Mo's."

I frowned at her use of Mo.

"He got drunk with Gabe and Seb when you were visiting your sister, him and his brother, and they all bonded and he is now referred to as Mo in our house."

I laughed. "He told me he ended up hung over, but not about the bonding."

"Boys will be boys. But you're deflecting, tell me about you and him."

"I think I might have messed it up."

"How?"

I told her that we'd had sex and that he seemed to be retreating, even using his mother as his primary childcare provider out of hours.

"I'll come back to the retreating, but how hot was the sex?"

I laughed. "Like nothing I have ever known. Nothing else has ever come close."

"You're fucked!" Carrie laughed at her double entendre because I was on both counts. "Maybe he's trying to draw a line between Flora the nanny and Flora the, what did you say he called you?"

"Tesoro mio or something like that."

She grabbed her phone from the table and repeated it.

"My treasure." The computer voice said.

"Wow! So maybe he's separating the two sides of you, but you'd need to speak to him to know that. But he didn't blow cold as soon as you and he'd had sex?"

"No," I heard the hesitation in my own voice.

"What?"

"I hope I can trust you."

She nodded.

With a deep breath, I spoke again, unsure why I felt safe speaking with Carrie in a way I didn't with Bea. "It's been going on for a while. Not the sex but the attraction and pull, which you probably already knew. We kept ending up in clinches and compromising positions, sometimes minus clothes, but he's never withdrawn like this before. After our almost moments there would be a little tension I suppose but it was quickly replaced again with the attraction and usually another almost moment."

When Carrie nodded, she actually looked as though she knew what I meant.

"The day I arrived at Gabe's house, my clothes ended up strewn across the landing, much to his disgust, and he picked up my tiniest, laciest item of underwear and dangled it from his finger to return it."

I giggled.

"That is the item he ended up keeping and doing unthinkable things with."

My eyes were out on stalks at the possibility of those unthinkable things but also found it kind of hot.

"I did walk into his bathroom one time before we were together properly and found him," she looked around before whispering the last two words, "touching himself. I then offered to help him 'finish'."

"Same," I said and then expanded. "He saw me." I was crimson and burning hot. "I didn't know he was watching me that time, I mean we did it again, together, and he showed me what he did." I wasn't anywhere near as articulate as Carrie but I think I got the gist of things across.

"Yeah, you're fucked and he might just need some time to catch up, especially with the kids, and let's not forget, you're his treasure."

Carrie grinned while I rolled my eyes, but inside the butterflies were throwing a party.

"I know that for Gabe, the one thing that made him hold back was Charlotte and not confusing her."

"Makes sense."

"But talk to Mo. However, never forget your own worth."

I took that to mean if I discovered that Maurizio had doubts or regrets. "You sound like my sister."

"She sounds really smart."

We both laughed as Ash and Bea returned while the children set about getting the huge ice-creams into their mouths rather than all over their faces.

"Should we even ask what you two have been talking about?" Ash asked.

"You can, but we won't tell you." Carrie laughed but continued. "We've just been chatting and discovered that we have a lot more in common than we first thought. A lot more."

I hoped I wasn't blushing or pulling an expression that suggested what we had in common related to masturbation, sex and hot single dads. I was relieved when my phone sprang into life, startling us all. Maurizio. I quickly read his text, letting me know that he was working late. Again. And that his mother had agreed to take care of the children once I clocked off. Again. Well, it worked well in pissing me off and making me certain he was avoiding me.

Ash looked over at the phone in my hand. "You want to get together? Go out?"

I shook my head. "Not out, but you could come to mine and we can have take-out and wine." I looked across at the other two women. "You're welcome to join us, minus the wine."

They both shook their heads. "Gabe and Seb are comparing car seats tonight, so we'll need to give it a miss," Carrie said.

I was unsure what to say.

"Not even joking. They check reviews and even draw up a list of pros and cons before scoring. They have already done pushchairs and cribs," Bea explained, making me and Ash laugh before agreeing a time for him to come over.

Chapter 33

Maurizio

F ive o'clock had come and gone and it felt as though I might be making some headway on the work that I needed to do in preparation for a court hearing the following week. In my head, I reckoned I could be done here by seven, half past seven at the latest. I had asked my mum to watch the kids for a couple of hours and if my timings were accurate, by the time I got home, Rosie and Craig would be ready for bed. I could do story time and kiss them good night, and then seek out Flora. Perhaps if she hadn't eaten we could have dinner, a glass of wine, and enjoy each other's company and not sex, well, I wasn't ruling that out but I actually wanted to spend some real time with her, chatting, getting to know each other, and then the sex.

That was when Raj appeared in the doorway. "Don't shoot the messenger."

"What?" I might not know the details but I sure as hell knew the words she was about to speak were going to ruin my plans.

"Leigh has had to leave, so she won't be coming to help out tonight."

"Shit! Where the hell is she and why are you telling me and not her?" I was angrier than Raj expected judging by her expression as she came closer.

"Mo, her dad has been taken to hospital with a suspected heart attack, she left in a bit of a hurry."

"Oh." I felt guilty, of course she needed to go and telling me personally wouldn't and shouldn't have been high on her list of priorities. "Just the two of us then?"

Raj looked a little awkward.

"Don't tell me you're bailing as well?"

"No, of course not, well, not entirely, but I only have a sitter until nine."

"We'll aim for a nine o'clock finish then, and if we're not done, I can finish up."

She nodded and offered me a smile. "We don't all have a Flora on speed dial."

Her comment was accompanied by another smile, but somehow it didn't sit right with me, not because she was wrong, she wasn't, but I didn't have her on speed dial like I wanted to. I shook thoughts of Flora from my mind and literally focused on the papers in front of me. "Let's do this."

Climbing into my car at ten o'clock brought a sense of relief. I would definitely have missed bath time and kissing my children goodnight, but there was time for me to catch up with Flora, wasn't there? Maybe. It would be half ten at the earliest before I arrived home, and it might take another half an hour to see my mother out, unless she stayed, which she was welcome to do, but that would definitely put an end to any Flora shaped plans I might have.

I hit a little traffic as I was leaving the town centre due to Friday night revellers—how old was I? *Friday night revellers.* Regardless of that, it added another ten minutes to my journey meaning by the time I parked my car next to Flora's it was almost a quarter to eleven. Rather than entering the house immediately, I took a slight detour to Flora's side of the house and could see lights still on, presumably meaning she was still awake.

Ducking back round to the front of the house, I found my mother in the hallway preparing to greet me. She fussed and offered to make me something to eat, I declined her offer. I wasn't hungry. Not for food anyway.

"If you're sure?" My mother's frown confirmed that she was less than thrilled that I'd missed a meal.

"I am, Mama, but thank you." Leaning down I landed a kiss to her cheek. "You are welcome to stay, it's late and I don't like to think of you driving home alone."

A loud pfft sound left her lips as she waved my concerns away.

"I am a grown woman and have managed to get myself home safely my entire adult life. Now, as you won't eat supper, please promise me you'll eat a hearty breakfast."

"I promise." I was hoping by breakfast time I was going to have worked up an appetite like never before, however, my mother did not need to know that.

With another kiss and a warm hug, I walked her to her car that was parked at the side of the house, affording me another opportunity to check if Flora's rooms were still illuminated. They were. Quickly returning my gaze to my mother, I blanched as I realised she had seen exactly where my attention had been. However, surprisingly, she chose not to pursue me and Flora, she simply gave me a wink before getting into her car and disappearing down the drive.

Leaning back against the stone wall of my house, I wondered if I should call Flora, go up to her rooms or invite her down to join me. As much as I wanted to simply turn up unannounced and devour her, as I had done before. Too long before, I didn't want her to think she was a booty call, no more and no less. She wasn't. My thoughts we shattered by the intoxicating sound of Flora's laughter followed by her muttering something I didn't hear, meaning she had been with a friend this evening, perhaps Bea or Carrie as they were the only friends I knew her to have. There was her sister of course, so maybe she was on the phone as I hadn't yet heard another voice, and then I did. A man's voice.

Moving into the shadows, I watched as she stood on her doorstep, the man leaning forward to kiss her, and fuck me if she didn't allow him to. My blood was boiling in an instant and not due to arousal as it usually did where Flora was concerned. I tried to reason that it wasn't a passionate kiss and there was no holding or touching to accompany it, but still, it was a kiss from someone who wasn't me.

I took a step towards them and then retreated. No. I would not do this, not now, not ever. Whilst I thought we had an understanding that what we were doing together was exclusive, I'd obviously been very wrong if she was kissing another man. I acknowledged that things had been difficult, busy for me, and I hadn't been able to speak to Flora nor spend time with her, but I deserved better than this, didn't I? If she had come to me and said she needed more, or less as it seemed, I would have respected it, but this?

"Fuck!" I hissed at myself and as I heard the man's voice shout something about the banging of her headboard, I had heard enough, and the only plan I now had was a glass of something strong and going to bed alone.

I had no clue what I was going to do about Flora because I wasn't sure I could be trusted not to lose my shit, sack her, and then end up on trial for killing that fucker, whoever he was who had come into my home and literally stolen her from under my nose.

An hour or so later, with a couple of glasses of whiskey downed, I decided to call it a night. I didn't need to metaphorically cry into my glass, and if I continued drinking it might not be metaphorical, plus my children did not need to have a hungover father come Saturday morning.

Placing my glass into the sink, a note on the fridge door caught my eye – *Bea's Baby Shower – Saturday – 2pm. Don't be late! Bea & Seb x*

Shit! I had no clue how I was going to face Flora so soon, and God forbid she tried to act as if she hadn't been cheating on me. Was it me? First Sophie and now Flora. I pushed that thought away and reread the note. Of course I would go, for Bea, and the children would have fun playing with their friends who would be there.

Maybe I did need to speak to Flora, but not tonight.

Heading to bed, I checked on the children before moving towards my own room where I paused at the door and then I heard her voice again, just one word. My name.

"Maurizio."

And if my treacherous cock didn't turn hard as steel in that second. Seemed I was going to be speaking to her tonight. She had taken that decision out of my hands and if that didn't piss me off more.

Turning, my resolve to remain mad at her began to dissolve as I drank her in wearing her short and vest pyjama things that clung to her curvy, hourglass figure, teasing and tempting me, while her long golden hair cascaded down, framing her beautiful face, her deep blue eyes, warm and twinkling with warmth and desire seemed to bore into me. On some level I acknowledged and felt reassured that she hadn't been wearing so little when she had been kissing her boyfriend, fuck buddy, whatever he was.

"Are you okay?"

No. No I wasn't. Far from it.

My cold laugh startled her enough that she appeared to take a step back.

"Why?" That's all I could muster, and she looked confused by my question, genuinely confused. Had I misread what I had seen? I didn't think so. "I saw both of you outside."

A look of recognition and understanding filled her face and then it was gone, replaced with anger, no, cold, hard fury.

"And what precisely do you think you saw?"

Her eyes were aflame with rage, and although I probably shouldn't, I found her as attractive as I ever had.

"I saw you with whoever the fuck it was with his lips on you and fuck knows what else." I was seething now, just saying the words aloud infuriated me. "And I hope the banging of the headboard was worth it."

"You are an idiot," she spat. "A total fucking idiot. Not that I owe you any explanation when you don't trust me enough not to hide in the shadows to spy on me." She didn't pause long enough to let me dispute her allegation and with barely a pause, she continued. "However, for your information, you sanctimonious arsehole, *whoever the fuck it was,*

was Ash, my friend. So, unless you're suffering from illusions or delusions, what you actually saw was nothing more than two friends who had shared a takeaway and a bottle of wine saying goodnight."

Now she did pause. Staring at me, she appeared to wait for me to say something, and I had nothing except complete belief in what she'd told me.

She let out a single laugh. "Do you know something, Mr Walker?"

Fuck! There was no warmth in it. There was certainly no arousal from it on my part. I had ballsed this up badly. I had seen something innocent and had overreacted. I should have spoken her, maybe even made my presence known outside and given her an opportunity to introduce me to Ash, the nanny who I had assumed was a girl not a boy. Seems I had got that horribly wrong, too. Briefly, I remembered that she hadn't told me that, but quickly reprimand myself because she didn't need to tell me Ash was not one of the girls. I had assumed he was. That was on me.

"Sophie lied to me, cheated, sorry, I just saw you say goodbye and got it wrong. I shouldn't have assumed and got angry."

She shook her head. "No, you shouldn't, and yet you did. Maybe it's my fault for letting my guard down. I can't say you didn't warn me, you did, every time you told me to tell you to stop, but I ignored your warnings and enough red flags to cover the house in bunting—"

"No." I interrupted her, knowing where this was going, where she was taking it and now, in this moment, I knew for certain that the only thing I wanted was to make this right and for her to forgive me.

"Yes. It was a mistake. We were a mistake. I don't do mistrust and jealousy, it's destructive and damaging, and I won't do that to myself. I know my worth, so, let's forget what happened between us."

Opening my mouth to object, she didn't give me the chance. With an expression of dogged determination, she continued, my heart sinking with every word she said. I had fucked up in spectacular style and she was taking no prisoners in handing me my arse. I needed to stop her before she said anything else, anything that would end this.

"Flora." The desperate whisper of her name as I stepped closer seemed to register briefly, but before I could consider taking a second step, she waved her hand, dismissing me.

"No, this is me telling you to stop, Mr Walker. I should go to bed, and I will see you on Monday. Have a good weekend."

She turned, leaving me speechless, regretting ever telling her to tell me to stop because now she was using it against me.

Unsure of what to do, I stood, impotent, and did precisely nothing.

With a sudden and sharp turn, she startled me, causing me to all but flinch.

"Oh, and one last thing, do not awaken feelings in the next woman who comes along and takes your fancy if you're not man enough to deal with them, and her like an actual adult. No, this is actually the one last thing, the banging headboard you clearly heard about was yours. I was feeling a bit jittery since we, you know, fucked."

The venom in her delivery of the word *fucked*, cut me deep. It was so much more than that, but I had made her doubt that, like she was nothing more than a convenience, a port in a storm, her earlier reference to knowing her worth confirmed that. She was anything but.

"I know you've been busy with work, but I felt like you were avoiding me, especially by asking Carmella to help out with the children rather than me, so, I got jittery. Ash told me that rather than bottling things up, I should put my big girl pants on and make the first move, not stopping until your headboard was banging against the wall like a barn door in a storm. Me coming down here was me doing precisely that."

With a final turn away, I watched as she walked from me, sadness washing over me as I acknowledged that I really had messed up. Badly. I hadn't trusted her and that had hurt her and now I feared she might never forgive me.

I had no idea how long I lay in the dark, desperately wishing sleep would come and take me away from my own miserable thoughts that became stronger each time I replayed the night's events with Flora. Rolling over again before punching my pillow, I grabbed my phone from the bedside table and sighed that it was two in the morning. I needed to sleep because my children would be up in around five hours and then we needed to attend Bea's baby shower. Shit! That was going to be awkward with the tension between me and Flora, something Bea would pick up on, not that anyone could miss it if tonight was anything to go by.

Even with my eyes closed, I could have sworn there was a flash of light. I was delirious clearly because when I opened my eyes, there was nothing. The sound of something akin to an explosion caused me to shudder and leap up in bed. Thunder. Maybe not delirious then, just a storm. Shit! A storm. The sound of a petrified cry saw me up on my feet with only one destination in mind. Flora.

Chapter 34

Flora

"He's a wanker!" I was fuming. How dare Maurizio even imply that what he saw on my doorstep was anything other than a friendly goodnight kiss. "I hate him."

My reflection in the bathroom mirror that clearly showed my eyes preparing to overflow with tears disputed that second statement. I didn't hate him. I liked him, a lot. I had thought he liked me too. I still did, kind of, but he didn't trust me. I understood he'd been hurt, felt betrayed by Sophie, but I wasn't her and I refused to be punished for her mistakes. When I'd told him that mistrust and jealousy were destructive and damaging, I'd meant it, and had been hurt by both things in the past. I refused to put myself through it again.

I just needed to get through the weekend and on Monday, go back to being the nanny. Maybe I could look at getting a flat of my own or something. I briefly recalled Bea talking about the available flat she'd had. I hadn't really had enough time to build up savings, but I'd manage. I'd have to.

With my teeth brushed, my face washed, and a touch of moisturiser added, I climbed into bed and begged sleep to summon me, determined to move on from how awful today had proven. It wasn't like things could get worse, was it?

A couple of hours later, I was woken from my surprisingly sound slumber by the horrific sound of a storm outside. The sound of rain bouncing off the ground and the windows was interspersed with loud cracks of thunder, while my curtains did nothing to mask the forks of lightening illuminating the sky.

It seemed things could get worse judging by the fact that I was now sat up in bed, my knees tucked into my chest with my hands clamped over my ears while my eyes remained screwed tightly closed hoping to block out the murderous sounds that taunted me from outside and my own thoughts that were intent on slowly breaking me from the inside.

I had no clue how long the storm had been going when I found myself curled in a ball behind my front door with a blanket over me. It hadn't been my plan to end up there. I didn't know that I'd had a plan, not really, but I had found it impossible to escape the sounds, sights and smell of the storm in my bed, so had gotten up, hoping to find somewhere in my home where I might feel safe. There was nowhere. Opening my door, I had been uncertain where I was planning to go, or had I? There was only one place I wanted to be. In the safety of Maurizio's arms. The last time I had felt safe in a storm had been the day my car had broken down and Maurizio had rescued me. That thought alone saw tears coming faster and harder. He had felt like my safe place, and now without him, I didn't have one.

There was a loud, deafening crack of thunder that I swore was directly above me, coming for me, taunting me, planning to claim me, having missed the chance previously and that was when the small amount of self-control I had was lost. My tears and crying paused briefly as a loud and traumatic cry tore from me.

The world around me was shaking, or that might have just been me as I seemed incapable of remaining still. My breathing was erratic and I was unsure if I could hear or feel it, maybe both. Nausea washed over me and suddenly I felt out of control, like an inflatable dinghy lost at sea in choppy waters. The erratic breathing I'd previously noted had changed until I was fighting for my next gasp of air. Shit! I was falling headlong into a full-blown panic attack and I was unsure if I could fend it off. I couldn't even begin to muster the self-calming strategies I'd previously been taught, but then why would I? It had probably been five years since I'd had one. Everything was beginning to blur and as much as passing out would give me some relief from the overwhelming fear and horror I currently felt, it would also see me alone, more alone than I currently was with my thoughts of sadness, loss and grief that were momentarily keeping me company. The pounding of my heart began to increase until I thought it might literally burst from my chest, and then, it slowed, calming as warmth enveloped me. A sense of safety wrapped around me as the internal weight I had previously felt was replaced with the weight of arms encasing me while soft words of comfort and security washed over me. The noise of the storm still played in the background but somehow it was being drowned out by the words I couldn't quite make out. Feeling limp and lax, I realised where I was, in Maurizio's arms.

It felt as though there was a breeze blowing across my face and I was weightless. A constant and comforting ssh sound vibrated against my head before something soft dipped beneath me a split second before the warmth and safety of Maurizio's arms left me. A small moan of objection sounded from my throat before he was back again, holding me, comforting me.

"It's okay. I've got you. I'm not going anywhere."

At some point I realised that I was on a bed, lying down with Maurizio as the storm continued somewhere in the distance but it couldn't touch me, not here, not with him. Then, silence and darkness, nothing. Sleep had claimed me and once more the arms I trusted held me and kept me safe.

Wearily, I prised my eyes open as I felt something stifling me while light seemed to tempt my eyes to open. My vision blurred slightly as I recognised my surroundings, Maurizio's bedroom. The events of the night before began to unfold in my memory and the unmistakable crying induced swelling of my eyes made sense. The window nearest to me had sunlight peeking through along with the break of day and if that didn't feel like mother nature having another little dig because of course after the hellish storm of the night before, what I really needed was a glorious sunny day to wake up to.

"Hey, how you feeling?" Maurizio's arm that I'd only just realised was thrown over me tightened its grip around me, pulling me back so I was tightly held against his chest. He was the thing that had been stifling me in my sleep.

"Fine, yeah, good . . ." I was rambling and if I wasn't careful I'd be well and truly lost in a sea of positive adjectives.

The bed dipped beneath me signalling him moving behind me. Before I knew it he was over me, his eyes firmly fixed on mine. "That was not a trick question and it's okay not to be okay, last night—"

As if I wasn't embarrassed enough by the whole debacle of the previous night, I did not need to face the most handsome of faces and perform a postmortem on the disaster it had become.

"It's fine. I'm fine. Sorry, I should go . . . to my room and leave you to your weekend." Any attempt to move from my prone position was futile as Maurizio moved again so that he straddled me, caging me in for all intents and purposes.

"The only way you are leaving here is with me. If you want to go back to yours, we can. If you want to go downstairs, we can, but the key to this is *we*. The storm last night, how distressed you were, goes beyond being a little jumpy. I saw that the day your car broke down, but last night was off the scale."

"That's none of your business. I am none of your business. I ceased to be the second you accused me of being a liar and a cheat." Rationally, I knew we'd moved on from that, kind of. The fact that he had come to my rescue and comforted me again suggested to me that he realised he had been the idiot I had accused him of being the night before, not that we didn't need to have a conversation regarding accusations and mistrust, particularly if we wanted to move forward in any way that wasn't purely employer and employee. Did I want to move forward and continue whatever it was we had started? *Stupid question, Flora.*

"Flora, it's early, let's talk before the children wake up, please." There was a hint of pleading in his voice, but it was unnecessary because despite my own protestations, I wanted to talk to him.

Once we arrived downstairs, Maurizio sat me in the lounge while he made tea for us both, and I was still nursing the remnants of my first cup when he broached the subject of his misunderstanding of me and Ash.

"I can't apologise enough for what I accused you of. I saw you with Ash and not knowing who he was, I made terrible assumptions and on the back of them, I said some terrible things to you. I am sorry, sorrier than you might believe. If I could turn the clock back I would, but I can't."

"No, you can't and that means it can't happen again. We all make mistakes. Mistakes we need to learn from rather than repeat them."

He nodded. "I should, perhaps, have put my brain into gear, much as I would at work. God! What an idiot I am. I work in facts and proof that support actual evidence every day in my professional life, and yet, last night, seeing you. . ."

I watched as he swallowed hard after his voice had dropped off.

"I suppose, but then I don't want to be part of your working day and I don't want to spend time with your professional persona. I want you, the man behind that who reacts on an emotional and personal level."

He frowned his confusion that on one hand I had criticised him for reacting in a way that was emotional and not well thought out, and yet here I was rejecting the offer of an analytic reaction. His frown only served to make me smile in that instant.

"If you see me, as you did last night, I don't mind you asking me questions, maybe even feeling a little jealous, just a little, but you don't get to accuse me and throw unpleasant allegations around. It might be a cliché, but if we don't have trust, we don't have anything."

"I just need to know that I haven't fucked this up completely. Us."

"No, but I'm still not sure what we're doing Maurizio."

His smile at my use of his name was contagious, especially judging by my own spreading across my face. "What do you want us to be doing?"

I laughed at how suggestive his question was and that laughter was soon replaced by horrification as his expression morphed into one that confirmed that he had not been thinking of sex! Neither had I and yet in that second, with eight apparently innocent words uttered, I had gone straight there.

"What I mean is, what do you want from this, from us?"

I shrugged, unsure what to say and what not to say. I wasn't expecting promises and pledges, nor declarations of undying love, but I wanted to be more than a means to scratch an itch.

"Flora, we agreed to be discreet, and I think that remains a wise option, but tell me what you see this as. I am not looking for specific labels here, just an inkling of where you're at with it."

"I like you. I wouldn't sleep with you if I didn't. I trust you and feel safe with you, and that is a little scary considering this, is so recent, and you're my boss."

"Good, you should trust me and feel safe with me, and I like the fact that you wouldn't sleep with me if you didn't like me." He grinned, a confident and cocky aura surrounding him.

"I can live without labels, certainly for now, but I don't want to feel like I really am some sort of cliché; the nanny sleeping with her boss, and if I am simply a notch on your bedpost, then please, tell me now so at least I know where I stand."

"I would also appreciate not being the cliché of a boss who sleeps with his staff. Despite what Bea may have suggested, intimated, whatever, I have never approached a staff member to pursue anything that wasn't professional before." He seemed to reconsider his words and the meaning behind them. "Bea, we, there was never anything between us. I was in a bad place after Sophie left and she helped a lot more with the children. I leaned on her more than I should have and because my mother had never been Sophie's biggest fan, I wanted to keep her at arm's length as much as possible, if only to keep her dislike of my children's mother to a fairly silent contempt. Anyway, without making excuses for my actions, I overstepped the mark and misjudged things, perhaps because Bea was taking on some of Sophie's role, I don't know, and as I said, I am not making excuses, but there was nothing between me and Bea . . . obviously she was already with Seb, but there was no real interest from me, not really. Sorry if I sound like a dickhead."

He had hit the nail on the head. *He did sound like a dickhead.* That wasn't entirely fair because there were some extenuating circumstances involved and he and Bea were still on good terms. It wasn't exactly music to my ears, knowing those lines had blurred or whatever thought process had been behind his clumsy passes at Bea. I watched him closely and considered how I felt. Confused. I replayed his words, his account of events, and compared them to Bea's version before considering my next words.

Chapter 35

Maurizio

And then I waited. Seconds passed, several, and then she offered me a simple nod. What did it mean though? Did she accept my explanation and wanted to build something with me? Or was it an acceptance of me being a dickhead?

"I understand, and Bea said very similar."

The frown that creased my brow had nothing to do with Flora, nor Bea really, but was more to do with my discomfort and dislike at being discussed as I clearly had been. I prided myself on being a good person who was not the subject of gossip. I liked to keep my private business just that, *private,* and through my own stupid actions, it wasn't. I ignored the voice in my head pointing out that the relationship I had now embarked on with my children's nanny was likely to make gossip about me more likely than ever.

"However . . ."

Cocking my head slightly, I braced myself for impact.

". . . regardless of what you were going through, it was inappropriate, and Bea should have been safe from your clumsy, drunken passes, but I accept you made a mistake and regret it."

Flora was right and I had nothing more to add in terms of a defence. Flora suddenly began to fidget in her seat, her glance flitting between the clock on the wall and everywhere other than me, suggesting she was avoiding the next conversation, the one we originally came down here to have.

"Flora, I'm not going to force you to give me a blow by blow account of what happened to make you so fearful last night. Last night and that day when your car broke down, but I'd really like to know something of what made you so frightened."

Her eyes fixed firmly on my face and with a hard swallow, she began to speak. "My parents died in a car crash during a storm."

She looked startled by the bluntness of her own words, not as startled as me but definitely taken aback.

"I'm so sorry." It sounded wholly inadequate to offer sympathy wrapped up in two short words when Flora had lost both of her parents in such a tragedy, one that she had been clearly traumatised by. I couldn't imagine how it might have felt for her to have lost both of them together and as glad as I'd been that she and her sister were close before, I was beyond grateful for it now. As I tried to order my thoughts and consider what else to say, she continued and my mind was blown completely.

"It was my fault."

The urge to dispute what she was saying was strong and yet I couldn't. One because I didn't know the details of the horror that had befallen her family but also because I wasn't sure that's what she wanted from me. Although I was certain that it wasn't her fault, how could it be?

"Maddie and I were supposed to go to a camp with school. I only wanted to go because of Maddie. She had lots of friends, still does, whereas I had a very small circle and my sister was the main member of it. The day before we were due to go, I found out that Maddie's boyfriend was going too. He was her first boyfriend and when they were together, nobody else existed."

Flora laughed, startling me until she explained.

"I wasn't all that interested in boys and found them to be either irritating or intimidating. There was a boy I had a crush on but he shut me down when my friend did that whole, *my friend really likes you, do you like her?* As such, I didn't fully understand how Maddie and Harry were so oblivious to anything that wasn't the two of them." She giggled. "I get it now though."

I wasn't so foolish as to belief that she had only begun to understand the obsession of her sister's teenage romance since we'd become involved, however her slightly lowered eyes, the flush across her cheeks and the coy smile she was wearing suggested she might have rediscovered it of late.

"What happened?" As much as I was enjoying the image of adolescent Flora that was being painted, I didn't see what this had to do with her parents dying and her part in it.

"When I found out Harry was going to camp, I tried to back out, but I couldn't, so the night before, I pretended to be sick so my parents wouldn't send me, and it worked. With Maddie away, my parents who had planned a date night for just the two of them at some fancy restaurant, ended up changing their reservation to a more family friendly place with me as the third wheel. We had dinner and as much as I hadn't wanted to go to camp, I was a bit moody and missed Maddie. I complained about the food and was generally sulky. As we left the restaurant, it started to rain, something else I complained about. When we all went out together, my dad drove and my mum rode up front with him, as much as anything to stop me and Maddie arguing about who was sitting next to him. However, that night with it just being the three of us, I called shotgun and got away with it. The rain got worse and visibility deteriorated as the storm began to increase. There was rain, thunder, lightning, wind, even hale descended at one point. It really was a storm of biblical proportions."

Where this was going was clear to me, but I still didn't get where Flora's guilt came from beside her being the reason for her parents' change of restaurant.

"The route back home was one my father knew well but some of the roads were narrow and had no lighting aside from the headlights of the car. A song came on the radio as we approached a particularly precarious road that had a hill one side of it and an inadequate fence that over-looked a sheer drop into rocks and a valley below."

Potentially the reality of this was far worse than I might have imagined. Staring across at Flora, she looked blank. It was as though she was reciting a script rather than reliving the most horrific of memories. Her voice sounded as indifferent as her face remained expressionless. I would have expected tears or a few broken sobs, at the very least the stammering of words that were heavy with emotion, but there were none. She continued to speak, and I refocused on her words rather than worrying about the conflict between her emotional state and that of her apparent calmness.

"I had turned the radio up and was singing along, but as we began driving on that road, my dad turned it down. I turned it back up and he shouted as he turned it back down. I shouted back at him and said I wished I'd gone with Maddie. My mum was trying to calm everything down but between mine and my dad's raised voices and the deafening storm she was barely a whisper. My dad told me he'd wished I'd gone with Maddie too, and that is when the brightest flash of lightning I had ever seen, well, until last night, lit up the sky and that coincided with the sound of thunder shaking the car."

Relief washed over me as I observed Flora's emotions kick in, the wall of her feelings coming down a little. She swallowed hard before dropping her head until it rested in her hands, albeit briefly. Raising her head, she looked back at me and the first tear rolled down her cheek.

"It all happened so quickly. A tree was hit by the lightning causing it to fall and it would have hit the car had my dad not swerved. I just remember the light and noise of the storm along with my own screams as I willed it to stop and for everything to be okay, but as he swerved more lightning struck above us. It was truly blinding, so much so that the next thing I knew, we had crashed through the fence and we were hurtling towards the trees and the valley below. I don't know how long it took for us to come to a standstill . . . it had felt like a lifetime."

I don't know that I planned on interrupting her but the next thing I knew, two more words left my lips, possibly more inadequate and impotent than my earlier, *I'm sorry*. "Oh, Flora."

Tears were accompanied by a few breathy sobs as she waved away my words and my attempt to move to her, to comfort her.

"I remember hearing my mum crying and calling out to me while the car was falling but by the time we landed she was silent. When I turned to see why she was quiet, there was blood everywhere and she was already dead. Her window had been smashed and a piece of glass had hit her neck, puncturing the carotid artery. I don't know that I knew she was gone, but the blood scared me as did her silence. My dad was still alive at that point and trapped behind the wheel. The driver's side of the car had taken the brunt of the impact. He talked to Mum and when she didn't answer he began to cry . . . I think he knew. He was in a bad way himself and needed help, but he was more worried about me than himself. He kept telling me to get out of the car in case it fell any further or maybe he was worried it might explode. I didn't want to leave them. I pleaded with him to be okay, to get out of the car with me, but he couldn't. I don't know how long we were there or the time that passed before I got out of the car to find help. He told me how much he loved me, me and Maddie, how much him and Mum loved us and how happy and proud we made them. I kept apologising for being such a pain that night and for not going with Maddie. I even confessed that I hadn't really been sick so could have gone to camp, but of course my parents already knew that. I kissed him, one final time and with a promise of finding help, he told me he loved me and that he would be there when I got back, that he'd hang on and then I left them."

Somewhere between her waving away my attempt to move to her and her finishing that sentence that sounded like an admission of guilt *and then I left them*, I had gotten up, pulled her to me, held her and now we were huddled together, her in my lap while I had everything I could wrapped around her. With the volume of her cries increasing, I held her tighter. Instinctively, I rocked her, gently at first and then with slightly more force as if that would give greater comfort, although I wasn't sure who I was hoping to comfort most, me or her. I had no words to offer her, not a single one, not least because I had no understanding or comprehension of what she had gone through, well, nothing beyond the facts she had shared.

A heavy silence sat around us after a length of time I had no way of measuring.

"It was dark and I was scared. I tried to find my way to a road or where someone who could help might be. The storm continued for hours and I lost my way so many times or I hid, desperate for shelter and protection from the elements that had already hurt me so much that night. By the time I found someone, although, they actually found me, the sun had started to rise and it was too late. A rescue team went to the scene to recover the car and the bodies. My dad, he was dead too. I took too long, Maurizio, he hung on like he'd said until he couldn't wait any longer."

She was hysterical now, tears running down her face faster than she could wipe them away. I felt like the world's biggest shit for having forced this revelation, and yet I was glad to know about her fear of storms. I also knew that from this day going forward she would never face another one alone.

Chapter 36

Flora

Having never told anyone in such detail the events of that night that haunted me in my waking hours as well as my sleeping ones, not even Maddie, I felt both unburdened and troubled; having shared the events of my parents death with Maurizio and him showing no negative response to my confessions had made me feel lighter, but the heaviness of reliving that night weighed down on my shoulders as I got ready for Bea's baby shower.

After my meltdown that morning, I had lost an amount of time. I was unsure if I had fallen asleep or just blocked out the time that was missing from my memory. One minute I was being held by Maurizio and the next thing I knew, I was waking up on my bed with a note at my side telling me that he would see me later, that he needed to get the children's breakfast and that he was honoured for me to have shared something so personal.

This afternoon was a happy occasion. Bea and Seb were revealing the gender of their baby. Celebrating their move into parenthood in a matter of a couple of months and they were allowing me to share that with them so I would focus on the good in my life, the present and the future, whatever that held rather than the pain of my past.

Casually dressed in a summer, floral tea dress and wedged sandals, I skipped down to my car, leaving the house via the separate entrance my home benefited from. I allowed myself a small smirk at the familiar sight of mine and Maurizio's cars parked side by side. Was it because of our recent closeness, and I didn't mean sex, that gave me an intensified rush at the image of anything that linked us as if we were an actual couple. My head told me that this thing between us, whilst intense and special to each of us, it was earlier than early days and it could fizzle out as easy as it had fizzled in. My heart on the other hand was heading for a place with picket fences and happily ever afters.

The sound of a car unlocking startled me, especially as my keys were still in my handbag.

"Flora!" Rosie's cry coincided with the appearance of Craig running towards me.

"We're going to have cake and play with Charlotte and meet Bea's baby," Craig told me excitedly as I became aware of Maurizio's approach.

"We won't be meeting the baby just yet, sweetheart, but we will have cake and Charlotte will be there to play with."

"The baby isn't cooked yet, is it?" Rosie took my hand in hers and gave it a squeeze as she looked up at me, her big brown eyes smiling as much as her mouth.

"Cooked?" Maurizio looked between us.

"That's what Flora said about Bea's baby, and Carrie's, they're not cooked."

Maurizio's smile and quirk of his eyebrow warmed me far more than I was sure it should have.

"Ah, cooked, I see." Dropping to his haunches until he was eye to eye with Craig, Maurizio explained to him, "What Rosie and Flora mean is that the baby isn't ready to born yet. He, or she, needs to stay in Bea's tummy for a while longer and then when they've got bigger and stronger, you can meet them."

Craig nodded while Rosie watched on with a warm and loving smile for her brother and her father, but why wouldn't she? Her brother was literally her other half and her father, well, could this man be any more perfect in his little girl's eyes? Or attractive, I added for myself? I didn't think so, but then every time I pondered that question, he disproved that he couldn't be.

"Let's get you two strapped in and then we'll be on our way."

The children climbed into the car while Maurizio held the door open for them.

"I'll be off too," I told them all, a small wave confirming my intention to get into my own car.

"You're coming to Bea's party too? You can sit next to Daddy," Rosie told me rather than asking.

"I am, but I'm going in my car."

"Why?" Craig asked. "There's lots of room for you, isn't there, Daddy?"

"It does seem foolish to take two cars rather than one."

"I don't want people to get the wrong idea."

Maurizio, having strapped the children in and closed the door, turned to face me. "What would that be then, the wrong idea?"

What did he want me to say to that? I wasn't even sure what the right idea was never mind the wrong one. Was he playing with me, teasing me or provoking a reaction from his question? His next words suggested my face showed the confusion I felt.

"Sorry. I'm not being an arsehole, but us arriving separately when we're travelling from the same starting point and heading for the same destination might be more likely to trigger the wrong idea, or more likely the right idea."

He made perfect sense as did the three-year-olds who were staring at me until I followed their father to the passenger door where he paused before opening the door for me.

"Are you okay? Shit...no...that was a stupid question . . . I meant after this morning rather than what happened with your parents—"

I cut him off. He was usually so confident and articulate but my revelations from that morning had rendered him a babbling mess. Trying not to overthink the impact of him knowing about my parents, I replied. "I know what you mean, and I am, thank you."

"Good, and if I didn't say this earlier, whether you believe it or not, it wasn't your fault. Now, we need to go or we'll be so late the baby might just be cooked!"

Bea's baby shower was intimate and when we arrived there were a few people already there; Carrie, Gabe, Gabe's parents, some of the other nannies we knew including Ash and several other people I didn't recognise. Gabe and Carrie, perhaps Carrie more than Gabe were leading the celebrations so that at one point Maurizio and I ended up manning the barbecue which was fun. Okay, fun might not be the first adjective you might think of when barbecuing but it was, although that might have had more to do with the fact that it allowed us to spend time together, talking and laughing. Our plan for discretion might have been hampered slightly if the knowing glances exchanged between Bea and Carrie were noticed by anyone other than us, whereas Ash made very immature gestures to me when nobody was looking. It was after one such incident that I decided to introduce them.

"Ash, this is my boss, Maurizio . . ." I stammered slightly at my use of his first name rather than using a more formal term or at least the name most others used, Maurice. The flush spread across my face from my neck and despite the sunny day, the warmth I felt radiating from me was nothing to do with the heat of the weather and everything to do with the fact that I may have intentionally made a faux pas with my indiscretion.

"Ash." Maurizio extended a hand, ignoring my use of his name and my awkwardness.

Ash gave me a sideways smirk while the two men still shook hands. "Maurizio."

"Ash is a manny," I announced, causing both men to face me as Bea and Carrie came to stop alongside us accompanied by Seb and Gabe. I continued, "Because he is a man and a nanny, a manny."

Ash shook his head, but had released Maurizio's hand, Maurizio who was looking at me with genuine amusement and something that looked similar to endearment.

"A manny?" Maurizio asked.

Ash replied. "Yeah, don't judge her too harshly because these two . . ." he pointed between Carrie and Bea, ". . . they think they're funnier than they are and it's rubbing off on your gir—" he cut himself off while I stared in disbelief that he had slipped up in that way.

I could have sworn that my other friends choked while Seb openly sniggered and Gabe muttered something about, *I told you, Mo, fucked.*

"Nanny, your nanny!" Ash shouted, drawing more attention from the people around us, including the children who were playing nearby.

"Ash, Flora is our nanny, not Daddy's," Rosie told him.

"Daddy is a grown up so he doesn't have a nanny," Craig added.

"Yeah, you'd think so," chipped in Seb with a single laugh that was cut off by Bea smacking his arm while Gabe chuckled, possibly more at his friend's chastisement than the comment itself.

If I had thought Carrie and Bea were a tag team, they had nothing on their men who were like a comedy double act. Charlotte moved closer and as she spoke I thought that the children might be more of a tag team than any adults I'd previously labelled that way.

"Sometimes daddies do have a nanny because that's what my daddy used to say about Mummy before she was my mummy, he called her *my nanny.*" She giggled while her father stared wildly and Carrie blushed. Seb laughed, earning himself another smack from Bea. "And Uncle Seb called her nanny too, he still does sometimes and Daddy says bad words when he does but Uncle Seb laughs."

Uncle Seb was still laughing and as it became clear that he was about to get another smack, from Bea, Charlotte intervened.

"Bea, we don't hit people, it's not nice, is it, Mummy?"

Carrie looked conflicted. She had clearly told the little girl that hitting people was wrong but knew that Bea wasn't really hitting Seb. "No, we don't, or we shouldn't hit people, but Bea was—"

This kid was ballsy beyond belief and had a confidence most grown women would be in awe of. I certainly was and whilst I loved that about her, I was glad I didn't have to deal with it on a daily basis.

Having cut her mother off, she turned to her beloved Uncle Seb. "Are you okay, Uncle Seb?"

Maurizio wore a huge grin as he watched the little girl stretch up and rub her uncle's arm.

"Do you want to play with me and Rosie and Craig, we have kind hands, don't we?"

Both Rosie and Craig nodded, the latter offering Seb a hand, an offer he accepted and was dutifully led away by Craig and Charlotte leaving Rosie to disapprovingly shake her head at Bea whilst standing with one hand on her hip.

"Bea, you can't hurt people. Kind hands," she said, repeating Charlotte's earlier words and then with a final shake of her head, she followed the other children.

Bea looked shell shocked and as she rubbed a hand across her swollen belly, I thought she might cry.

"Sorry," began Gabe. "You know how she is with Seb."

"She hates me, and I swear she is bringing in reinforcements with Rosie and Craig."

"I'm sure she doesn't hate you," I offered, hoping to reassure her but she looked doubtful.

"She doesn't," Carrie said with certainty. "But she loves Uncle Seb beyond words and although you were giving him a dig for being a smart arse, she doesn't understand that."

Bea nodded.

"So, you'll need to find alternative ways to punish him if you can't use kind hands," Ash said, making the rest of us laugh at his impersonation of the children with the last two words.

Maurizio spoke in what felt like forever, addressing the whirlwind nature of Charlotte, directing his words to Gabe. "I like your kid, I mean she's scary but likeable, but honestly, I'm kind of glad that if she chooses to go into law that I'll be retired before there's a possibility of being pitted against her in a courtroom."

Gabe's mum suddenly appeared and linked her arm through Bea's. "Right then, Mummy, are you ready to tell the world if we are backing team blue or team pink?"

With a smile splitting her face, Bea happily allowed Christine to lead her away.

Chapter 37

Maurizio

We had barely gotten two minutes away from the baby shower when the sound of the children's snoring sounded around us.

"I'm sorry," Flora blurted out, reaching across the space between us to rest a hand on my knee before quickly retreating and folding her arms across her chest.

I didn't know what she was apologising for, although, I could hazard a guess.

"Our plan for discretion. I think I may have blown that with my fumbling attempt to introduce you and Ash."

I shook my head. She wasn't wrong, her introduction would have told anyone with eyes, ears or an ounce of common sense that we were more than employee and employer. However, Ash wasn't surprised to see us together. "Flora, I think *us* was many things to Ash, none of them a surprise, after all he was the one who suggested making my headboard bang like a barn door in a storm."

Gazing across at her, I allowed myself a half smirk at the small flush of colour across her cheeks along with a coy smile. "Exactly. Nothing to apologise for."

"Do you suppose anyone suspected anything about us? You and me being, well, whatever?"

Suddenly all warmth and lightness left me with her inarticulate phrasing of the word whatever. "We need a conversation about us and the discretion."

Before I could say any more, I heard her breathing change and as she responded her voice carried a nervous and sad lilt. "Of course."

"Flora, you misunderstand," I told her as we turned off the road and headed towards the house. Other than the gentle snores of my children, the space around us was filled with silence until my car came to a stop next to hers, and then, with my seatbelt undone, I turned to face her. "I don't want you to think that we are a dirty secret or a temporary stopgap for me. It, we, you are neither. I like you, a lot. I was nervous about us, you know that. I wanted it but wasn't sure it was wise and as such, I didn't want it to happen . . . I obviously wanted you, but the complication of a relationship, especially one with my children's nanny is what I didn't want to happen because it had the potential to be messy. It still does and for the children, it would be disastrous for them to lose you, but from the second you didn't tell me to stop, there was no going back. Discretion was a pipe dream."

"What are you saying?"

Fuck me! I was a barrister, paid handsomely to be articulate and she sounded and looked as if I made no sense at all.

"Today, we had a nice time, didn't we?"

She nodded and a smile lit up her face.

Reaching across the space between us, I took her hand and pulled it to me, kissing her knuckles before lowering my own hand that still held hers into my lap. "Even when I thought there was a good chance that Charlotte was going to take Bea down, I had fun."

She laughed and I was certain I could feel the vibration of it rattling in my chest, my heart. I was well and truly fucked with thoughts like that. When did I get flowery and all romantic? Yup, fucked, just like Seb and Gabe had told me weeks, months ago.

"I want to have more fun, with you, tesoro mio ."

"Fun?"

Shit! Did she think I meant sexy fun because I didn't. Obviously, I did want more sexy fun with her but that's not what I meant right now.

She giggled and I realised she knew I hadn't meant that.

"You naughty minx."

"Naughty? Do I need to be punished?"

My mouth went dry and the world stood still. Did she want to be punished, and what was she thinking might be a suitable punishment? She was fucking with my head and in the fifteen minutes since we had left the baby shower, I had worked through the whole spectrum of feelings and right now horny was in pole position.

"Sorry—"

I cut her off because apart from anything else, I didn't want her to be sorry, not for speaking her mind and sharing her thoughts, even if she hadn't meant it and was playing with me. "Something else not to be sorry for and with no pressure whatsoever, we can talk about that later, but for now, let's focus on the other fun. The being together, enjoying spending time together and getting to know each other kind of fun."

"Me too."

Raising her knuckles back to my mouth, I kissed them again. "Then let's do that."

"And discretion?" With her eyes lowered she looked awkward but was that because she did or didn't want to be discreet, or perhaps she was still unsure whether she could truly believe what I was saying.

"Look at me." My tone was sharper than I had intended but it served the purpose of focusing her gaze on me once more. "We can be as discreet as you want or don't want, however, we are in a relationship, a non-professional one and whilst I don't think the children need front row seats to that right now, in time, I'd like them to know about us."

She looked stunned, but why wouldn't she be, I was and the words I'd uttered had been in my brain at some point before I spoke them.

"We don't need labels, at least not now, unless you do, but it's just us and whether other people know it or not, *we* know it . . ." I reached across and undid her seat belt, trying and failing not to watch as it recoiled, moving slowly across her body, tantalisingly so as it passed through the valley between her breasts, her magnificent breasts that just the thought of had my cock stiffening further and twitching. "And feel it . . ." My hand moved to her face, pushing a stray lock of her golden curls behind her ear, then stroking along her jaw until my thumb rubbed across her lips that parted a little, inviting me in. "And believe it, right?" Before she answered my hand had moved to cup her head, my fingers flexing between the strands of her hair and then I was pulling her to me, determined not to stop until my lips and hers were one.

"What does it mean, tesoro mio?"

I had wondered how long it was going to take for her to finally ask this. Her pronunciation wasn't too shabby either. "My treasure, and you are."

She grinned. "You said something else when you, you know."

I laughed at her flustered face and language as she recalled me being between her thighs, my mouth bringing her pleasure. "Dolcezza means sweetness, which you are, in every way, especially on my tongue."

The taste of her was an aphrodisiac and might just be my undoing, but right now, I needed the taste of her lips so closed the remaining distance between us. We fitted together perfectly, our lips blended as one and our tongues worked in perfect harmony. I was drunk on her, unaware of anything that wasn't her. Right up to the point where the sound of a car moving through the gravel of the drive got louder.

Breaking our kiss, I felt as flustered as Flora looked and in the split second it took me to turn and see the driver and the car coming to a stop next to mine, I came down to earth with an almighty bump. "Sophie." The irony of my car being sandwiched between those of my wife, my soon-to-be ex-wife and the car I had handpicked for Flora, the woman I had just committed myself to.

I was unsure how much Sophie may have seen until I saw the smirk spreading across her face. She knew that Flora and I were together even if she hadn't seen us kissing. So much for not giving my children a front row seat. Had they woken, that is exactly what they would have had.

Rediscovering the power of speech and movement, I briefly looked at Flora. "Sorry." It was my turn to be apologetic now, even if I didn't know what for, except I did. Sophie and I were dead and buried but her reappearance was going to be a mindfuck for Flora, and I suspected for me, too.

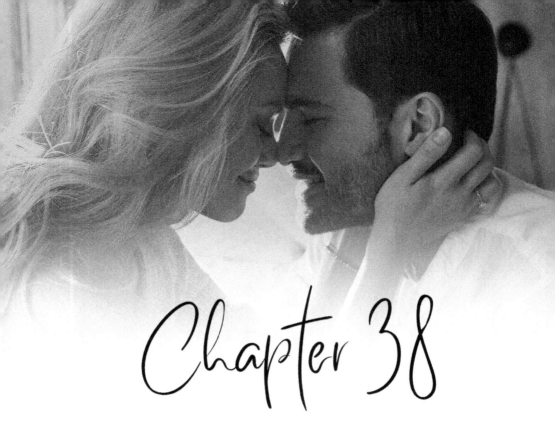

Chapter 38

Flora

O ne word, or at least a name, Sophie. That was all it had taken for Maurizio's words and sentiments to come crashing down. Watching him leave the car, leaving me behind him and approaching her had been hard. Even harder had been watching them hug, seeing the couple they had once been, although their contact and affection was platonic rather than romantic, of that I was sure. However, nothing could have prepared me for the children waking up a few seconds later to see their parents together and their excited cries of Mummy and Daddy were like daggers to my heart.

I couldn't wait to be away from them. All of them. My hasty exit involved a stumble from the car, the rubbing of my nerve induced sweaty palms down my thighs and an introduction to Sophie. I don't know how I might have expected Maurizio to introduce me, but *this is Flora, the children's nanny* was not it. I pushed down the voice in my head pointing out that those words were factual, accurate, no more, no less. Instead, I told myself that the children's nanny was *all* I was. Maurizio's kisses, words, and everything else we'd shared were long forgotten in that moment, perhaps forever. I had never met this woman before. Her contact with the children had been non-existent, then infrequent and over the last few weeks, or even a couple of months, it had become a little more regular, but of course all arrangements were between Maurizio and her. There was no need for me to know or be involved in any of that because it really was nothing to do with me, and yet, in this exact second, even that felt like the sudden unveiling of a red flag before my eyes, taunting me.

The children had run around their parents as if they were some kind of attraction or national treasure, which I suppose they were in their eyes. That is when I noticed that at Sophie's feet was a bag. A suitcase. She had come home but where did that leave me, me and Maurizio? That really was my cue to leave and with words I couldn't remember, I began my departure, not stopping until I was running for the back door to my home, not the front door I imagined entering the house by just a matter of minutes before everything changed.

I had barely made it through the door when the first of my tears began to fall. My phone was already in my hand and I was hitting my sister's name on the screen. Straight to voicemail. I didn't want to startle her with a sobbing, messy message, so simply hung up and followed up with a quick text to the effect of 'nothing important, catch you later'.

With Maddie out of the equation, I considered my friends, Bea and Carrie would be otherwise occupied after the baby shower and as if my hands had already got that memo, I found Ash's name on the screen but before I could hit call, there was a knock on my door, the one from the house.

I reasoned it would only be one person until I prepared to open it and then panicked in case it was Sophie, but what would she want with me? Would she want to introduce herself? Talk? Warn me off? With a deep breath and nausea washing over me, I pulled the door back, revealing Maurizio. He stood, gorgeous as ever even with the expression of concern he currently wore.

"Hey." He was already stepping forward, preparing to enter. "Are you okay?"

It was obvious that I wasn't, and I assumed my face was a little tearstained.

"You've been crying."

"What do you want?" The authenticity of the impatience in my voice surprised me but the truth was that if he was coming to dump me or at least cool things between us, I needed to remain composed, and this was how I stood the greatest chance of achieving that.

"Hey," he repeated, reaching for me. "This changes nothing between us regardless of what you're thinking."

"How? How can it not? Your wife has come home."

"Ex-wife." He corrected, as if that was the issue here.

"You're divorced?" Okay so maybe that was an issue if I was hung up on that technicality too.

"Not yet—"

An exasperated growl leaving my mouth was my interruption not that Maurizio saw it as such.

"I have filed for divorce and Sophie has engaged her own solicitor to represent her. So, we are divorcing, we will be divorced, and it shouldn't take long because we are both in agreement with it."

"Why is she here?" At any other time, listening to him speak about his marriage being over and legal steps being taken to officially end it would have been music to my ears. What did that say about me? I answered my own question and hoped I'd done so in my head and not aloud. *Because you love him.* I sure as hell wasn't going there or sharing that particular nugget of information with him. Hell, I was brushing it under a carpet in my mind and had no plans to ever uncover it.

"For the children. She has been a mess. She knows that's no excuse for isolating herself from them and she has been doing better with contact of late."

I stared, astounded that he thought that was any kind of adequate explanation. "Why is she here, with a suitcase?"

"Ah . . ."

And there it was.

"She's going to stay for a while, to reconnect properly with the children, and we need to go through some things regarding the divorce and the division of assets and the children."

"And she can't do that from whatever rock she's crawled out from under?" I sounded a bitch and I didn't care.

"You have nothing to be jealous of, Flora, this changes nothing between us."

There was no prepared reply to that in my head and even as I opened my mouth, I was unsure what I was going to say, but then no words were spoken, not by me anyway.

"I have to go, the children are waiting, but once they are in bed, I can come up and we can chat."

"The children and Sophie." I stopped short of uttering the words *your wife* although they were on the tip of my tongue.

"The children," he replied and reiterated with a much firmer tone.

A nod was my only reply.

"I'll come back, okay?"

Another nod, and then he turned and left, leaving me alone with an entire catalogue of conflicting thoughts and feelings as well as more tears.

The seconds dragged into long minutes and they in turn stretched before me into hours filled with overthinking and an overwhelming sense of nervousness.

Should I call Maddie and talk it through? She'd probably come down here and kick Maurizio hard in very delicate places for getting me in this state, although it was my own spiralling thoughts of scenarios that weren't real and the imaginary fallout from them that currently had me crying and panicking.

What the hell was I going to do? There were only two real outcomes from this. One where I got Maurizio, and one where I didn't. I suppose they were the two outcomes from any new relationship, but the difference here was that if I lost him, then I needed it not to be because Sophie got him. The reality of working here with the children following a break-up now that I'd crossed the line with Maurizio would be bad enough, possibly impossible, but I would not be able to stay here and watch on as he rekindled his marital relationship before my eyes on a daily basis. Surely, if they reconciled, I would be the last person Sophie would want to be here, in her home, with her children.

My head was spinning while my heart was hammering away in my chest so fast and hard that I swore I could feel it pumping in my veins. I had no clue how long I was going to have to wait for Maurizio to return, but I needed to calm down, even just a little.

We will be divorced and it shouldn't take long because we are both in agreement with it. That's what he'd told me, and I was desperate to believe that, but what if they weren't in agreement? What if Sophie wanted to remain married and to live in the same house as her children on a permanent basis? That was perfectly reasonable, at least the bit about the children anyway. Or what if she wanted to give the impression of one big happy family. I had no idea why anyone would want to do that, but my mind continued to create a whole new scenario to freak me out. So, assuming she pitched the fake, happy marriage situation successfully, would she suggest that Maurizio and I could continue to see one another, perhaps on the understanding that we kept it locked down and behind closed doors? Would she really expect me to stay on as the nanny by day and be no more than Daddy's dirty little secret?

"What the hell is the matter with you?" My reflection in the bathroom mirror offered no reply as I washed my hands. "That is not real. That is not happening."

Pacing back to the kitchen, I grabbed a half open bottle of wine and a glass and poured a drink. A large one that I settled on the sofa with and called Ash rather than Maddie. While both of them would listen, Ash was more likely to offer rational advice rather than threatening to cut Maurizio's balls off. I retold him the events of the day from arriving back at the house, not that I was sure I made sense, but when I finally came up for breath, his long, loud sigh suggested that he'd gotten the gist of what had happened.

"What does she want? Why is she back here? Have you spoken to Bea in case she has the inside track of this? Sorry, I'm rambling, but this is a real mind fuck!"

I chuckled, not that there was an ounce of amusement in this whole situation beyond the fact that Ash had asked the same questions I had asked myself. "I have no clue. Hopefully, he will answer some of those questions when I see him later, oh, and I haven't spoken to Bea, and if you do, don't say anything, please."

"Of course not . . . His pause was barely that as he launched into another question. "What about Maddie, have you spoken to her?"

I explained my earlier call and subsequent message as I refilled my wine glass and checked the clock. Half past nine, surely Maurizio would be here soon. If he wasn't there was a good chance that I'd be drunk. The children would have normally been in bed by half seven so what was taking so long. Presumably the children were taking longer than normal to settle due to the excitement of Mummy being home. Just the thought of Sophie's name and the word home in the same sentence made my head spin.

"Maybe we can meet up in the week, with the girls, and I might know more about this disastrous turn of events."

"Yeah, keep me posted and I will round the gang up."

The rap of a knock on the door startled me, but at least Maurizio had arrived.

"Sorry. I have to go, Maurizio's here."

For the second time that night, I opened the door and found the most attractive man I had ever seen standing before me; a smile, warm eyes and dark wavy hair damp from the shower. He wore grey trackpants with a simple white t-shirt and bare feet that somehow Maurizio managed to make effortlessly glamorous, classy even.

Chapter 39

Maurizio

The sight that greeted me when the door had been opened was nothing short of perfection. Flora was dressed in a pair of black leggings and a plain black t-shirt, but she looked as good as if she had been wrapped in a designer gown and dripping in jewels, not that the latter did it for me, unlike Flora who very much did do it for me.

Today had all in all been a shit show to end all shit shows. We'd shared a genuinely nice time at Bea's baby shower, then returned to the cluster bomb of Sophie's return. What was the main problem was her turning up here, unannounced with her suitcase and a plan to move back in. We had already agreed that I would buy her out of her half of the house in the divorce and divide all assets equally so never in my wildest dreams had I ever seen her back here, staying, living in the house, even on a temporary basis, and one way or another, this would be temporary, it had to be.

Flora moved away from the open doorway and as I watched her

back getting farther away, I followed. She moved into the kitchen and picked up a clean glass and an almost half empty bottle of wine, filled the glass then returned to me, offering me the glass before sitting on the sofa having picked up her own half-filled glass from the table.

We sat in silence at opposite ends of the sofa, both of us staring at one another, perhaps waiting for the other to speak. She looked beautiful, as she always did, but her eyes were red, a few dark circles beneath them, clearly the result of crying. Crying because of me, us, Sophie, assuming they weren't one and the same. I needed to reassure her that Sophie's reappearance wouldn't change things between us, although that wasn't strictly true because a lot of things were going to change, that was inevitable, but Sophie really was no threat. I'd already spoken to her about things, although I had done most of the listening to be fair, however, right now, I needed to be exactly what my children needed but also what Flora needed too. I was confident I could deliver on that, not that it wouldn't be problematic at times. However, the biggest problem in delivering the reassurance I knew Flora needed and I wanted to give would be with information missing. She would want to know why Sophie was here and for how long and I couldn't answer those questions, not with complete honesty.

"Maurizio," Flora's voice burst the bubble of internal dialogue I was lost in, and the plea in her tone pulled me up short.

"No, it's okay." It wasn't, but I wanted to make it okay and I was scared that if I let her continue she would call time on us and I wasn't ready to let her go, not yet. Not ever, so I needed to stop her from continuing.

"Do you want to end this?"

The break in her voice was like a dagger to my heart. She was hurting. I was hurting her.

"I'm scared, Maurizio, scared of being hurt by this and losing you. I don't know if I can pretend. That's a lie, I can't, and I can't forget, but most of all I can't watch you with someone else—"

My wine glass was quickly placed on the table and hers joined it soon after so that from my new position next to her, facing her, I could reach for her face, gently cupping it and pulling her face to mine as the first tear escaped her glistening eyes.

"You won't, not ever." My lips covered hers and although I didn't fully know what I was promising with my words, I hoped my lips would. That they would tell her that I felt the same way as her, that nothing and no one could ever make me forget or pretend that *we* hadn't happened. The idea of having to watch her with another man made my blood boil and freeze at the same time. I recalled that night I had overheard her conversation with Ash, overheard and completely misunderstood, and that was bad enough, but now, I wasn't going to let her go, she was mine. The feel of her moving closer, softening against me while I deepened our kiss, taking possession of her mouth and tongue, her breathy gasps and her fingers lacing through my hair, holding me closer as we ended up in a semi-reclined position, me over and against her until her phone rang.

Pulling back, she looked gloriously flustered before pushing her hair back and snatching up her phone. "Maddie," she told me before answering. "Hi, Mads, no, sorry, it was nothing . . . I was hoping to chat and catch up but it's fine, all good."

Her voice was something of a shrill and if I couldn't already guess what she had been hoping to chat with her sister about I did now. Me. Us and how hurt and scared she was. Scared of losing me. She risked a glance in my direction, aware that I now knew she had called her sister who she was attempting to reassure and brush off before revealing any more details to me. In that second it became clear to me that she would never lose me. I was all in, mind, body, soul, heart. Fuck! She had my heart as much as I had hers, meaning this attraction between us, the laughter, happiness, the inexplicable and indescribable sense of weightlessness and zen was down to her and my feelings for her. Even without factoring in the totally amazing sex and shocks of electricity that shot through me every time we touched, she made my heart happy and completed me.

I loved Flora.

With a few final words between her and her sister, she hung up and returned her attention to me. "Are you okay? You look pale."

I was in a state of shock at my own discovery so it was no wonder that I was pale, but I was okay. Stunned, taken aback, but okay, really okay. A smile was my immediate response. "I should be asking you that if you needed to call Maddie. I'm surprised you haven't got Carrie, Bea and Ash here to lynch me or repack Sophie's case."

I'd intended for my words to be amusing and light-hearted but the mention of my ex's name had put paid to that judging by the frown marring Flora's brow.

"Maurizio, what are we doing? I'm scared and you can tell me that it will be okay but how can it be if you and Sophie . . ."

The temptation to pull her close and offer her repeated words of reassurance was strong but that's not what she needed from me. "There is no me and Sophie, not like you mean. She is moving back in, temporarily," I added hastily, although I had no idea how temporary it would be. "She wants to spend time with the children and has reduced her workload to facilitate that."

Flora opened her mouth and closed it again but presumably wondered where that left her professionally.

"Your role here is safe." That sounded fucked up when heard aloud, so much so that I attempted to clarify. "Your job. Being a nanny. You might be able to get some more free time if Sophie wants to spends time with the children, but your salary won't be affected." This was getting worse. "Sorry, I'm trying to tell you, reassure you, but without it sounding like the us side of things is a part of your job because they are very different."

She nodded and offered me a reassuring smile.

"You wouldn't believe based on this level of inarticulation that people pay handsomely for me to talk on their behalf and make an undeniable, compelling defence for them, would you?"

Her laughter confirmed that she understood what I was attempting to say, and it warmed me to hear it.

"You might be overcharging."

"I'm worth every penny, I'll have you know." I was at risk of whiplash with the speed and frequency with which the mood and atmosphere was changing. This time to one that was charged with anticipation and desire as she moved closer until she was straddling me.

Her hands came to rest on my chest while mine settled on her hips, our eyes holding the other's gaze.

"Why is Sophie really here?"

"I've told you. No more than that. I swear on my children's lives that there is nothing between me and her beyond us both wanting what is best for the children."

"Please don't hurt me, Maurizio."

"Tesoro mio, never."

"Do not lie to me or make me look stupid for believing you."

"I promise."

A single nod was her acceptance and then, once more we kissed, our lips joining us as one which felt exactly as it should be as arms and legs moved together until we were making our way to her bedroom.

Chapter 40

Flora

My early worries and insecurities had passed and now, naked and lying beneath Maurizio, I felt reassured that there was no need for me to worry about Sophie. Had she maintained contact from the start, she would have been someone I crossed paths with regularly, but for whatever reason she hadn't, so this, her being involved was new, or at least that's what I told myself, not that I didn't think being in the same house as her, working with her children and sleeping with her husband wasn't a weird combination.

"Flora," Maurizio groaned my name as he moved lower, capturing a nipple between his lips before drawing it into the wet heat of his mouth where his tongue lapped against the sensitive, bullet like nub.

My groans were the ones I heard now as he sucked harder before allowing his teeth to graze over the tip.

"Maurizio, please," I begged, needing more. More of his touch and attention, everywhere. The moisture between my thighs was increasing and as I attempted to close my thighs, to tighten them and squeeze them together, to gain some relief, his hand set about pinching and rolling the other nipple whilst never taking his eyes off my face. The obstacle of his body lain between my spread legs was counterproductive to relief.

"Not yet, but soon. I'm going to make this last because once I make you call my name and come apart for me, I am going to need to be buried inside you, fucking you, until you've screamed yourself hoarse, and then I will be powerless to do anything beyond filling you with my cum."

The things this man did to me with his words alone should be illegal. I stifled an internal giggle to think that even if they were illegal I would still do them and as he was such a great barrister, he could get me off. The sensation of Maurizio's fingers moving slowly through my arousal made me realise that I wasn't far from getting off instantly.

"Like that, yes," he encouraged, his fingers beginning to make their way into my molten centre while his thumb focused on my clit.

"Maurizio!" I cried, my volume increasing with every touch that drove me ever closer to release.

"Come, for me, show me how I make you feel!" His words were spoken with dominance and authority and that along with my own body's reaction to them were my undoing. "You are fucking beautiful," he told me as he crawled back up my body until our noses touched. "I want you so much."

"You have me." A broad grin cracked his face.

"I do, don't I?"

I could feel the tip of his erection nudging my entrance and then he was gone, kneeling up on my bed while I lay before him, spread out like a meal. That wasn't the worst idea I had ever had. His laugh caused me to look up at him questioningly but clearly my thoughts had been written across my face.

"My tongue is going to savour every inch of you later, but for now . . ." He pulled me into a sitting position. "Turn over, on your hands and knees."

I dutifully obliged and almost immediately heard the sound of foil being torn. Until that second I hadn't even considered if there were condoms in my room. The sensation of a hand coming to rest on my hip triggered a low moan of anticipation.

"You keep making those noises and I am going to embarrass myself before I've even entered you."

"And then we'd have to do it again, slower."

"Good point, so make all the noises you want because they, like you, are as sexy as fuck."

I deliberately repeated my earlier moan and was rewarded with a low chuckle and a single smack to my behind and then the sensation of being stretched and filled.

"This hadn't been my intention when I came back up here. I wanted to talk, just talk."

If the depth of sincerity hadn't been present in Maurizio's voice, I might have thought he was backtracking and was about to tell me that the kissing and the sex had been a mistake, but it was there.

"Are you regretting it?" I asked with a smile and a giggle as I rolled onto my front and looked at him propped up on the pillows of my bed where we remained.

"What do you think?" He pushed the hair back off my face. "In fact, I think you said we should do it again."

"That was if you embarrassed yourself and it was over all too soon, and you didn't."

A smug and cocky smirk curled his lips. "Is that a complaint?"

"No, but I have just done myself out of seconds, haven't I?"

He threw his head back and laughed and the tiny fragments of doubt and concern over this whole thing dissolved. "Maybe not." He paused. "You're okay though, about us and Sophie being here for however long she's here?"

The last bit threw me a little. I had no idea how long she planned to stay, but neither did he. I was missing something here. "It will be weird and perhaps a little awkward, but I guess it'll be okay for a few days." He looked horrified. "A few weeks." I was fishing and his face said it might be longer than that. "Maurizio, please."

He interrupted. "Flora! I don't know how long she needs to stay here."

"But—"

He cut me off completely now. "I have said I do not know and there is nothing more I can add. Sophie has her reasons and they're not mine to share."

Okay, so there was something I didn't know about and he wasn't going to tell me. It was frustrating and yet reassuring at the same time that he would keep her confidence and whether it was wise to do so, I decided to take a slightly different route.

"What happened with you and your wife?"

"Can you not call her that, please? It's like you're accusing me of doing something I shouldn't be, and I'm not." Maybe this was a bad idea, but I had committed to it now.

"She is your wife." I was poking the bear because although she was technically his wife, he had given no indication in the time I had known him that he viewed her in that way.

"Flora!" He snapped and ran a hand through his hair whilst giving me a warning stare.

"Sorry. What would you like me to call her?"

"Sophie will suffice."

"What happened with her, between the two of you?" I sounded nervous rather than angsty now and judging by the butterflies fluttering in my stomach, I felt as I sounded. She hadn't been a threat to whatever was happening between Maurizio and me until earlier that day.

"Happened? When? When we met, the end, the in-between?" His voice was flat, any feelings he might have on the subject of Sophie, indecipherable now.

Fighting the urge to say all of the above, I settled with the truth. "I'm not really sure."

"Sophie was no longer happy or fulfilled by our marriage is the crux of it, but it was more than that."

I nodded, knowing that based on things I'd heard from Maurizio, Bea, Carrie and even Carmella, his summing up seemed accurate.

"I guess we had a fairly typical history. We met, fell in love, and I think we believed we wanted the same things."

Obviously they had been in love, but hearing him say it hurt me, there was no denying it but I attempted to mask it so he would continue. "You believed?"

He nodded and looked a little sad. "We didn't. I wanted a home and a family . . ." A loud sigh sounded around us. "The children weren't planned and although we both wanted them, Sophie struggled with the loss of control. She was ambitious and knew her career would be compromised by being a parent.

My frown caused Maurizio to laugh. Loudly.

"That is not me being chauvinistic, I swear, but Sophie would need to take some time out to give birth at the very least and no matter how brief a time, she knew it would impact her career. The compromise to that was a nanny. Bea. Twins was something of a surprise and the effect physically was significant for Sophie. Even so, she returned to work when the children were three months old."

"Wow." I had nothing else to say. I couldn't imagine having that professional determination or wanting, or perhaps for Sophie, needing to return to work, missing out on those early weeks of her babies' lives that passed by so quickly.

"It was a lot for us both, but Sophie found it hardest; to be who she needed to be in her career that in a matter of a few months had moved on so much without her, and to fit that in with being a good mum, and she was. Don't let what has happened since our marriage failed to distort how good a mother she was. Our separation was hard on us both, but I think especially on Sophie."

I inadvertently rolled my eyes, irritating Maurizio in that second.

"Flora, you're really not in a position to judge Sophie. You weren't here and you do not know her."

His sharp tone stung. He was pissed off and now I was confused. Was he defending her and chastising me because he still had feelings for her or maybe with her back in the house he was remembering happier times and considering putting his family back together? Perhaps now wasn't the right time for this conversation assuming any time ever would be if it was encouraging my insecurities to resurface so soon.

"I wasn't judging." My protest sounded weak, but why? Had I been judging her? Although I wasn't a parent, I couldn't imagine ever leaving children behind by choice, and in the event that I had to . . . I couldn't think of a situation that would make that a reality . . . but if I did, I'd maintain contact and co-parent, so, I didn't understand her motives and as such, yes, I was judging her.

My thoughts and judgement were also partly due to trying to work out where Maurizio and I realistically fitted into the new picture of a present Sophie because we had never discussed this scenario. I hadn't even considered it.

"You were." His tone was softer again and as I watched him rock his head from side to side and flex his jaw a couple of times, his hair mussed by his hand running through it as he briefly closed his eyes and looked down at me. "I get why because I judged her, rather harshly, but now, she is trying under difficult circumstances. For that, for my children, I am grateful because they deserve to have two parents and Sophie deserves to be their mother and to have her career."

He pulled me close and held me tightly, almost like he was rocking me. He kissed me on the top of my head and I was unsure which of us needed this the most.

Chapter 41

Maurizio

A couple of days had passed since Sophie's arrival and Flora had managed to avoid her beyond a couple of awkward exchanges in the kitchen at breakfast. Bea was taking some leave days so hadn't returned to work since the baby shower. As far as I knew she was oblivious to Sophie's return which had surprised me since she and Sophie had been close previously and I had recently discovered had remained in contact. That didn't bother me . . . okay, that wasn't entirely true. I wasn't bothered by them being friends or whatever they were, but it being kept from me was irksome. In the months where Sophie hadn't seen the children, was she getting updates from Bea? Had Bea told her about me and Flora, and is that what had prompted her return? I knew the reason for her return, and it wasn't me, so the no to the second question was answered with conviction.

"Penny for your thoughts?" asked Sophie as we sat together in my office discussing our divorce settlement and of all things, wills.

"Nothing important," I told her with a slightly forced smile.

She laughed. "If you say so, but I know that face too well to buy that. Is it Flora?"

I wasn't going to be able to hold this smile in place if she kept pushing and assumed any less than happy feelings related to Flora. Along with my children, she was the person guaranteed to force genuine smiles and happiness from me.

"No."

"Maurice, Mo," she offered my shortened name she had used occasionally in softer moments, especially in the early days. "I am trying to be friendly and to reassure her about us."

"I know, but it's weird for her because unlike Bea, she has never worked or lived in the house at the same time as you."

"She's used to having you to yourself."

I supposed she was, but I wasn't going to get into a discussion about me and Flora. It was private and if I was going to discuss it, it wouldn't be with Sophie. "Shall we get on?" Pointing down at the pile of papers on the desk between us I wondered how long it would take for Flora to acclimatise to Sophie being here and just how long I could keep the real reason for her presence from anyone else.

An hour, or maybe two, passed with us shut away in my office. I was getting a headache looking at all of the things that needed to be sorted and agreed by us both when the sound of voices and something of a commotion interrupted.

The knock on the door and subsequent opening revealed Flora looking awkward and she paused on the threshold.

"Sorry, erm, Carmella's here."

The sound of the children giggling and their feet hammering on the floor in the hallway usually brought a big smile to my face, but when it was followed by my mother's voice, I felt a sense of dread. Her speaking gentle and kind words to my children was going to be short lived once she saw Sophie. Was she aware of her presence in the house? Perhaps the children had already told her about Mummy being here as they had with everyone they had encountered recently.

Flora physically shrunk when my mother stood alongside her and managed to fill the doorway despite her tiny frame and stature.

"Maurizio," she addressed me before turning to Sophie, her face blank, suggesting she was not surprised to see her former daughter-in-law here but was masking her true feelings.

"Nonna, look, told you, Mummy is home!"

Rosie's words along with Craig entering the office and climbing on his mum's lap saw my mother's face contort slightly before her fixed expression returned. However, it was the physical recoil of Flora as I moved until I was stood next to the chair Sophie still sat in where I scooped my daughter into my arms that cut me the deepest. Shit! We must have looked like something off the front of a politician's posed family Christmas card. I needed to stop showing Flora the family we once were, the couple she feared we may be again.

"Maurizio!" My mother snapped my name and although I towered over her, she painted an imposing figure. "How could you? After all she has done?" It was as though she suddenly realised the children were present because in the blink of an eye, a warm and loving smile returned to her face and she visibly softened as she gazed down at them. "Daddy, has been silly," she told them and even managed to laugh, a light and gentle giggle almost. "But Nonna is going to help him sort things out now that she knows."

Great, my soon-to-be ex-wife had landed unannounced, my kids were thrilled but I was scared for them, not least because I knew this was not the happy ending they hoped for, my girlfriend . . . shit! I had a girlfriend, and she didn't even know it, but then how would she since I had only just realised it, and now, my mother was speaking about me as if I were a child and was ready to launch into a tirade of abuse and chastisement. At least she wasn't angry enough to rip me a new one in Italian.

"Sciocco," she muttered with a roll of her eyes.

"Children, let's go and get some cookies." Flora's voice was cheery in the extreme, unlike her eyes that looked a little dimmer than usual, but at least her words were enough to summon the children from whatever my mother had in store for me.

"Perhaps I should go with them." Sophie was up on her feet and already moving towards the doorway.

"If you would just *go* that would be the perfect solution for everyone."

"Mama." I got that she was upset and only felt that way because she loved me and wanted to protect me from any more hurt at Sophie's hands, but she needed to stop because Sophie was going nowhere at the moment and no matter what else changed, she would always be my children's mother. "Enough."

Sophie was already closing the door behind her, and I didn't doubt running for the safety of the kitchen or wherever else the children and Flora were. I couldn't allow myself to consider how awkward that encounter might be because I needed to focus on speaking to my mother and getting her to accept that Sophie was back, for the children.

"Mama, this is not what you think it is."

She rolled her eyes so hard I wasn't sure she hadn't been possessed by some evil force. "So, she is not back living in the house and playing happy families? Because all evidence would suggest that is untrue."

"Not like you mean—"

She'd heard enough and her shaking head and flailing arms confirmed that. I wasn't sure that I wasn't going to get hit as she stepped closer.

"That puttana! She is using you, and when she has no further use for you, she will leave again and hurt you and break the hearts of those beautiful babies a little more than last time. And Flora, what about her heart in all of this?"

I was stunned at the introduction of Flora's name. My mother had no clue about us being together. I had deliberately kept it from her, so how did she know? I briefly wondered if perhaps Nico had said something to her, but we both knew exactly how my mother was with the mere sniff of romance in the air, so I quickly dismissed him as the cause of her knowledge.

She laughed as she took the seat Sophie had vacated and gestured to my own. Sitting down, I waited for her to speak because I had no clue where to start but was relieved that she was calmer, her face had softened a little.

"You thought I didn't know. That I hadn't noticed the way you look at her, the way you look at each other? Maurizio, you are my baby, and I can read you like an open book where matters of the heart are concerned. Flora wears her heart on her sleeve so it would be hard not to know. I know you think I interfere." She paused for thought for a second. "I do a little, but that's because I love you."

I couldn't fight the smirk that she claimed to only interfere a little.

"But there is a reason you and Sophie didn't work, many reasons, but you and Flora could. I know you loved Sophie, and that the children need and miss her, but do not make the same mistake a second time because it will only get harder to stand firm in what you won't accept and the hurt for the children will be so much greater."

She was right, and had I been considering a reconciliation with Sophie, this conversation would give me food for thought and possibly prompt me to reconsider, but she didn't understand what was happening here, and again, like Flora, I wasn't sure how much I could or should tell her.

"I love Flora." Those words blurted out loud rocked me more than my mother who offered me a nod and an accompanying smile.

"Then what is happening here, Maurizio? Make me understand why Sophie is living here and Flora looks sad despite you loving her?"

Chapter 42

Flora

Heading back to the kitchen with the children, my overriding emotion was relief. Relief to have left the drama of Maurizio, Sophie and Carmella behind. That feeling was short lived when I heard footsteps behind me a few minutes later and I knew it was Sophie. Facing her, she smiled at me and I returned it, at least I hoped I had as I turned away again. This was probably the first time I had been in the company of the other woman without Maurizio being there. I didn't even have Bea to act as a kind of bolster since she was taking a couple of days off. The previous day, Sophie had been out when I woke up and I had finished for the day before she returned. Maurizio had been to see me last night and we'd chatted, but he had work to do so it had been brief. This morning both he and Sophie had been at breakfast along with the children which was weird more than anything and then they had disappeared to his office. And now, well, now I was in the kitchen with her again while the children sat at the table, colouring and chatting to one another about the trip to the park I had offered them for a picnic lunch with Carrie, Bea and Ash. I briefly wondered if Bea knew that Sophie was back as they had remained in touch. I hoped she didn't or else that might indicate that she was more Sophie's friend than mine.

"Sorry." Sophie broke the silence, causing me to spin and face her with a startled expression that matched how I felt.

"For what?" My tone was sharper than I had intended as I spun to face the other woman, but my system was high on anxiety and confusion, with a heavy side order of jealousy based on the happy family sights and sounds I was currently being subjected to.

She laughed and if that didn't rile me up a little more. "Sorry," she repeated. "For the laughter this time, but my original sorry was for that, back there in Maurice's office. Carmella is protective and although I may not have been her first choice of daughter-in-law, we did get along until I left. I knew she would be hostile, however, it was still a surprise to see her."

I nodded. She wasn't saying anything I didn't believe. Suddenly, I wondered if she was blaming me for allowing Carmella to interrupt and unleash her obvious anger and disapproval. Well, if she was expecting an apology, she'd be waiting a long time for one from me. "I work here. This is not my house and as such, when a family member arrives, I have no right or compulsion to control their movements."

She looked stunned and then with a slight smirk, a raised eyebrow, and a cock of the head she nodded. "I wasn't accusing you of anything. I was apologising for putting you in that position."

"Oh." I wasn't sure what else to say if she was genuine, which she seemed.

"Flora. Mo and I are old news and I am no threat to you."

She sounded nothing but reasonable and her use of *Mo* pissed me off a little. I refused to acknowledge that I called him Maurizio so why wouldn't she use his shortened name that was favoured by his friends.

"He is a good man and deserves to be happy, and although we were happy for a time, we were both unhappy, too. I love Mo as my children's father and the good, kind man that he is, someone I would like to be able to call a friend in the future, but no more. Aside from the fact that sexually . . ." She whispered the last word, presumably to protect the children's ears ". . . I am not attracted to him, we don't want to be married, well, not to each other, but right now, I need him, his friendship, and my children." Emotion seemed to choke her as she uttered that word whilst casting a glance in Rosie and Craig's direction. "I need my children."

Seeing her crestfallen expression and total conviction with which she'd spoken of her need, I believed every word she said.

"I want to believe you."

"You should, and more than anything, I want you to make Maurice happy, he cares, really cares for you, as do the children."

Her eyes filled with tears, causing even more confusion to swim around my mind as I wondered why the idea of Maurizio and the children caring for me made her sad. Briefly I replayed her words, *he cares, really cares for you*. What did that mean? Could she be suggesting care as in love, like I loved him. No. I refused to be drawn into that particular minefield whilst standing in the middle of the current one of my boyf–lover, boss, whatever he was, his allegedly soon-to-be ex-wife and his angry mother. That was all kinds of messed up.

"Sophie, I don't know that this conversation is appropriate." That was the best I could come up with.

"Okay, if that's how you feel, but I needed you to know that I am not a threat to your happiness with him."

"Thanks." Again, that seemed a little lame, but I was becoming uncomfortable and wishing lunch was minus the children and with alcohol. Perhaps I could arrange a night with friends, wine and talk, minus little ears.

Sophie laughed. "I am sorry for earlier and for turning up here and disrupting things . . . it won't be forever, I promise."

As I debated asking how long *won't be forever* was, the sound of Carmella interrupted. "Where are my beautiful babies?"

The children giggled as their grandmother moved closer to them, offering Sophie a curt nod and a very brief, tight smile, but at least there were no raised voices and as she came to rest between Craig and Rosie who were chattering about their picnic lunch, she spoke in English. I busied myself by packing lunch into a bag. Maurizio moved alongside me and covered my hand that held a tub of strawberries and grapes with his larger hand.

"Okay?" He sounded nervous.

"Of course." I forced the words out in a voice that carried a tremble of nervousness and confusion before pulling my hand free and addressing the children. "I just need to freshen up if that's okay, and then we can go," I said louder than was necessary and without waiting for a response, I was heading out of the room, rushing for the stairs that would carry me to the safety of my rooms.

I successfully avoided any kind of conversation or actual interaction with any other adult before leaving the house with the children and as we arrived at the park, I was relieved to see Ash, and the children he cared for, as well as Carrie, Charlotte, and Bea waiting for me, but then I noticed someone else standing with them, Maddie. It couldn't be and yet it was. The next few seconds were a blur and I wasn't sure where the children or the picnic were as I flew across the space that separated me and my sister. Throwing myself at her, hugging her, holding her to me, then pulling back to look at her face so I was sure it was really her, I realised just how much I had missed her.

"Flora, are you sad?" Craig's startled voice drew my attention to him and away from my sister.

"No, sweetheart, I'm happy." Crouching down, I looked between him and his sister as I wiped away a couple of tears. "These are happy tears. This is Maddie, my sister."

Maddie dropped down, held out a hand to the children and smiled. "Hi."

"I'm Rosie," Rosie was already stepping closer before introducing her brother.

"I've heard all about you both," Maddie told the children, her gaze moving between them both, then seeing their expressions questioning who she had heard about them from, she laughed. "Flo, Flora talks about you both and how great you are, and clever, and how much fun you all have together."

"And Daddy? Does Flora talk about Daddy because Daddy is great too and clever, isn't he Flora?"

I didn't even get a chance to respond to Craig's question before Rosie threw in her own little cluster bomb of a question. "And Flora has so much fun with Daddy, don't you?"

No amount of overenthusiastic laughter and bustling detracted from the sound of my friends and sister giggling rather immaturely. One of them, possibly Carrie, added a muttered *I bet she does.*

"Picnic," I shrilled, looking around for the picnic bag that Ash held in one hand, a hand I pulled it free from and with the children following me, I hoped, I headed for our preferred picnic area.

The children were happy to run off and play together, leaving the adults alone and that is when they all launched into questions about what was going on in my life with me and Maurizio.

It seemed ridiculous to keep up any pretence regarding our relationship, so I didn't. Instead, I told them that we had fought the attraction and desire for weeks that turned into months until we couldn't fight it anymore. When I told them that he had rescued me from the storm, only Maddie understood the significance of that. Carrie and Bea made comments about our feelings being obvious to everyone at the baby shower, and Ash nodded his agreement while Maddie watched on.

They were almost up to date with developments when I added the most recent event of significance. "Sophie is back."

Aside from Ash who already knew, the faces looking back at me wore expressions of total shock.

"What do you mean, *back*?" Carrie asked, shuffling closer to me. "If he has led you to believe there was something between you and then cast you aside in favour of the runaway wife, I will–"

"Cut his bollocks off, slowly and one at a time," Maddie interrupted but sounded scarily serious.

We all laughed as we watched Ash wince and cross his legs.

"Not a joke because if he had no true intentions towards you then he shouldn't have encouraged you and made you feel things for him," my sister added, while my friends all nodded their heads.

"Sophie is back?" Bea finally spoke and looked and sounded more shocked than anyone at that fact.

"She is. We went home after the baby shower and hadn't even gotten out of the car when she turned up unannounced and totally unexpectedly with a suitcase."

"But she never even mentioned that she was considering coming home." Bea sounded hurt and a little angry to be hearing about this turn of events second hand when she and Sophie had maintained contact.

"I told you that this was a risky game you were playing, Bea. Clearly you value your friendship more than she does." Carrie sounded cross on Bea's behalf whereas I was unsure how I should feel.

"If we can bring this back around to Flo."

Ash sniggered at my sister's short and to the point comment.

Bea mouthed a simple sorry that I waved off.

"So, what's the current state of play?" Maddie was on a mission.

"She's not back for Maurizio. She wants to spend time with the children, and they are finalising the divorce details."

Maddie and Ash wore identical, dubious expressions while Bea frowned as Carrie smiled. She really was a romantic despite her protestations to the contrary.

"Says who?" Ash reached across and took my hand.

"Both of them. Sophie went to great lengths to reassure me that her return is nothing to do with any romantic feelings for Maurizio."

"She could be lying," Bea suggested with a nod of agreement from my sister who I was still unsure why or how she'd gotten here.

"She's not!" I protested. "She's told me that herself and Maurizio and I are still seeing one another."

"Seeing one another?" Carrie asked. "As in, well, you know."

I nodded. "Yeah."

"Hang on, let me get this straight; he is shagging you while his wife is living back in the house with him and their children?"

"Maddie, it's not like that." I mean, it was exactly as she described, but not in the inferred context. "I don't know exactly what's going on because he hasn't told me and neither has Sophie, but I believe her and him. I love him." Admitting that to other people opened the floodgates of my emotions. "I love him," I repeated between sobs and tears.

Around me I heard muttering, curses, Maddie making more threats against Maurizio, and Carrie telling me that she and I had more in common than we thought and that it was okay because it was meant to be. I wished I shared her conviction in that, but really hoped she was right.

Chapter 43

Maurizio

After Flora and the children had left for their picnic, my mother spent a few minutes with Sophie and then she left, but not before telling me to be careful and to do what was right for me as well as everyone else. Sophie was making calls, so I returned to my office and wondered what the hell I was going to do. I wasn't sure how any of this was going to pan out but what I did know was that however this went, the things I truly wanted was to be the best father I could be to my children and for my relationship with Flora to continue, to work out and to be permanent and out in the open. The difficulty was that I had no clue how I might secure that. How long could I continue to live in the same house as Sophie whilst keeping things from Flora, but perhaps the bigger question was how long would Flora allow me to do those things?

My mother was on board more than she had been when she had turned up here, and although I hadn't told her everything, I'd told her something of the situation, enough to stop her blowing this whole thing out of the water. The sound of familiar voices pulled my focus from my mother and the potential minefield I found myself standing in the middle of. The voices got louder, closer. Sophie, and Nico. Clearly my mother had sent in reinforcements that would either get more information than she currently held or someone who would stop me from falling for Sophie all over again which I knew was my mother's greatest fear. An unwarranted fear, but a fear nevertheless.

Moving into the hallway, I found my brother striding towards me and calling back a refusal of coffee from Sophie. He looked at me, shook his head, and pushed me back into my office before closing the door.

"What the fuck is going on here? Mama is losing her mind and has no idea how the hell this is going to end well for you or the children."

"Well, that answers my question of what brings you here."

"Cut the crap and spill because last thing I knew, you were hot for the nanny and you and Sophie were very old news, so what has changed?"

Pacing to the console table that sat near the window, I grabbed a bottle of scotch and two glasses that I half-filled and took my seat, sliding one glass to my brother.

"That bad?" His question coincided with him eyeing three fingers of whiskey on a Monday lunchtime.

"Worse if you really want to know."

"I want to know everything."

"You could live to regret that," I told him, but was relieved to be able to unload everything to the one person I knew I could truly trust with every fucked up detail of what was currently my life.

"So what are you going to do?" Nico asked almost an hour later.

"For starters, I am going to stop drinking this." I pushed my empty tumbler away and scowled in the direction of the half empty whiskey bottle. "And make some coffee." I was up on my feet and already heading for the kitchen, followed by my brother.

Sophie appeared before us in the hallway. "I'm heading to the shop, do you need anything?"

I shook my head.

"I thought I might cook something for dinner . . . for the children . . . and you . . . you'd be welcome to stay, Nico, oh and maybe Flora would like to join us."

Sophie's offer sounded sincere and her words were kind and genuine, but I could think of nothing worse than Flora being subjected to what would undoubtedly appear to be a family dinner, I mean it would be because as soon as the children were factored in, we were a family, weren't we, as their parents? This situation was already turning messy and was beginning to fuck with my life, the new life I was forging before Sophie returned.

"Dinner?" Sophie asked, attempting to prompt some kind of response from me.

"Erm, no, thanks. I have work to do, and it might be a bit soon for Flora, but you should eat with the children and spend some time with them. I am sure after a picnic with the other children and their nannies they'll have plenty to say."

With a nod and an expression I didn't recognise, Sophie turned to Nico again. "I am guessing dinner with chatty three-year-olds and your brother's ex isn't on your bingo card for tonight."

Nico chucked but shook his head. "Not really, but thanks for the offer."

A shrug was her only response before she turned on her heels and headed for the front door leaving me and my brother to travel the short distance to the kettle and coffee that was more necessary than I'd thought it was if the hammering of my head was anything to go by.

Sitting in the kitchen a few minutes later with a cup of black coffee in my hand, Nico asked the question I had no answer for. "What are you going to do?"

A very loud sigh was my initial response. "I don't know. I need to make the children the priority and then Flora, but then Sophie is going to impact on all of it."

"You should tell Flora everything."

"I can't, I promised Sophie."

Nico shook his head. "Then you are running the risk of a pissed off Flora, misunderstandings, and her believing that Sophie means more to you than she does."

"You think I don't know that? This has the potential to blow up in my face and for me to betray somebody whichever way I turn."

The sound of a car door closing drew both mine and Nico's attention to the front of the house. I stood, my attention rapt at the sight of Flora getting out of her car, laughing and carefree apparently, and then my children appeared, happy and innocent. The smile spreading across my face was inevitable, as it always was at the sight and sound of any of them, but together, it was on a whole new level.

I wasn't even aware of my brother joining me in the window until he spoke. "Who the fuck is that and can I get one of those under the Christmas tree because I have been a really good boy!"

Spinning to face him with a glare, I moved closer until we were toe to toe. "Never, ever speak about Flora that way! Show some respect."

He looked confused. "What the fuck is the matter with you? I assume Flora is the one who was driving the nice new car you bought for her and is being flanked by the children. I meant the other hot blonde, not yours."

Looking back at the people on the drive, I realised for the first time that Flora and the
children weren't alone. I didn't know who the other woman was initially and then I recognised her, having seen images of her in Flora's home. That was Maddie, Flora's sister. I could see a resemblance between the sisters and as such got where my brother was coming from, although, I clearly only had eyes for Flora. I hadn't even noticed the other woman until Nico pointed her out.

"Come on, come to Daddy," my brother said beside me and as I glanced across at him, he appeared to be pretending to reel her in with an invisible fishing rod.

I couldn't help but laugh. "You need to never ever refer to yourself as daddy whilst in my company, and I am pretty sure that she is Flora's sister, so please, a little respect."

"I think I preferred you before the coffee kicked in."

We both laughed and prepared for the women and children to enter the house.

Chapter 44

Flora

Nerves were swirling low down in my tummy as we got closer to the house. Somehow, I hadn't considered Maddie's presence with my friends beyond being pleased to see her and realising how much I missed her. Ash had explained that he had contacted her through social media to ask if she had heard from me since the night of the baby shower when I had spoken to him. They had shared their concerns for me and the journey here was sealed. Once the pleasure at seeing her and filling all of my friends in on the current state of my life had been dealt with, I had truly thought about my sister being away from home. It wasn't that far, a couple of hours, but it quickly transpired that she had planned on staying for a while. Staying with me. That fact along with uncertainty as to who would be waiting in the house, and by who, I meant Sophie, who was the cause of those pesky nerves. Should I have asked Maurizio's permission to have a guest. Casting my mind back, I remembered when I had moved here and he had passed a comment about having my own entrance to my part of the house and boyfriends coming by, so, presumably that meant that house guests were acceptable, not of the boyfriend variety, but still.

As the children let go of my hands and ran towards the house, I noticed that alongside my car was Maurizio's and one I didn't recognise, but Sophie's had gone. Initially, that filled me with relief that there wouldn't be an awkward interaction waiting for me when I got indoors, but that was short lived as I seriously overthought the possible reasons for her absence.

Ahead of me the front door opened, revealing Maurizio and another man, presumably the owner of the unknown car. He was tall like Maurizio and of a similar build with the same dark hair and eyes, perhaps a little older, but not much. As they moved closer, the resemblance was unmistakable. The children squealed and were now barrelling in the men's direction.

"Daddy, Uncle Nico," they both called in unison.

Well, that answered the question of this man's identity. Maurizio's brother. I became aware of Maddie's voice and a tug on my arm.

"Which one is Daddy and is the other one up for grabs?"

I burst out laughing, not only at her use of Daddy, which was bloody weird, but her immediate bounce back of checking the status of the other one. Maurizio was smiling at me while Nico had scooped the children up so that one sat on each of his hips.

"Hey," Maurizio said as we stopped before them. "This is my brother, Nico." He looked at Maddie and offered an outstretched hand. "Maddie?"

My sister scowled.

"I recognise you from Flora's photos."

"Ah, then you must be Da–"

I cut her off. The last thing I needed was for her to call him Daddy to his face. My cutting off wasn't quite quick enough though judging by the matching smirks each of the men wore.

"Maddie, this is Maurizio, my, erm, Maurizio." Why wouldn't the earth just open up and swallow me and put me out of my misery?

"Pleasure to meet you," Maurizio said, politeness personified.

"Hmm, jury's still out for me." There was no mistaking her warning tone or the undercurrent of the inference that he needed to prove himself to her.

Nico had put the children down and was extending his own hand, to me first. "Flora, so pleased to meet you at last. Between Mama and Maurizio, I feel I already know you." He raised my hand and lowered his lips to it and landed a kiss to the back of it, startling me.

"Will you knock it off!" Maurizio said, more of a threatening statement than question as he hit his brother's shoulder.

Nico laughed but did release my hand and quickly turned to Maddie, taking hers now. "Absolutely thrilled to make your acquaintance, Maddie."

My sister giggled and as Nico's lips gently kissed her knuckles I swore I heard her draw in a breath before saying, "Not as thrilled as me."

Maurizio looked as though he had been hit over the head with his wide eyes and stunned expression before muttering something involving *unbelievable* and *of course he did*.

"Shall we go in?" I asked the children, already ushering them through the door.

Nico and Maddie were chatting with the children at the table as Maurizio and I moved around the kitchen making drinks, my focus on the children and trying to think of the best way to broach the subject of my sister staying with me for however long that might be, although I reasoned we were talking a few days, no more.

"This is a surprise, Maddie."

At least I didn't have to worry about raising the subject of my house guest. "For me too. Ash contacted her."

"I see, or at least I think I do. Me, because of me, you and Sophie?"

I nodded. "The girls didn't know about Sophie until I told them. Bea seems hurt by hearing it from me."

"I bet, but Maddie . . . she doesn't like me, does she?"

I laughed, relieved that his concern was not about my sister being here just about her possible dislike of him. "She told you, jury's out. I've invited her to stay, with me."

"That will be nice for you." He sounded entirely genuine.

Nico's laughter sounded behind us and turning we both saw him and my sister getting along famously. "Not as nice as for Nico." Our laughter stopped theirs but at least Maddie was being made to feel welcome.

"Mummy's home," cried Sophie, stemming all the laughter.

"What the fuck! I don't even know where to start, Flo! Daddy is hot, but his brother . . ." Maddie released a long, low exhale. "Marks out of two, I'd give him one!" She cackled at her own quip I hadn't heard for a while as she followed me through my front door. "This is nice and your video calls didn't do it justice. But back to this fucked up situation. Daddy – gorgeous."

I rolled my eyes. "Are you going to persist with the *daddy* thing? Of course you are," I responded for myself.

"So, Daddy, dreamy, but could be a twat. Then we have the wife! Friendly, attractive, kids love her, but her and daddy, no chemistry. Kids are a bloody delight but the real jewel in the crown is big brother, Nico, he is seriously hot to trot!"

"Maddie!"

"What? I don't know that you can judge me when you and Maurizio have been getting down and dirty." She paused as she went to sit down on the sofa. "Is this spot safe?"

"You are bloody disgusting." My laughter sounded around us as I joined her on the sofa. "I am really glad you're here, Mads. I've missed you."

"Me too," she told me as she pulled me into a hug and kissed the top of my head. "Now tell me everything you know about Naughty Nico."

The next couple of days were strange; not awkward strange, but just a little odd. Maurizio and I hadn't seen much of each other. Maddie was staying with me so late night rendezvous weren't possible, and I hadn't been to his bed or in the main house outside of working hours since Sophie had returned. That sudden realisation bothered me now, even with my sister's observation of there being no chemistry between Maurizio and her. However, I now felt like the side chick, the one the wife knew about but turned a blind eye to for the sake of respectability and the family unit.

This whole situation was messing with my head and the banging down of cups and bowls on the breakfast table confirmed it.

"I don't know what the cereal has done to you but I think it's learned its lesson now." Maurizio laughed as I eyed the cereal that had escaped the confines of the box as I had thumped it on the table.

Turning, it had been my intention to snap or to point out that the cereal was the least of my problems, but seeing a freshly showered Maurizio smiling at me with nothing but consideration and care, and perhaps a little desire too, I did no more than smile and more gently add the cutlery to the table.

"That's better. I like to see you smile."

"This is hard, us."

Pulling me around to face him, he nodded. "And for me, too. I miss you."

What did any of that even mean?

With his fingers settling beneath my chin, he tilted my face to look up at his where his eyes filled with sincerity and warmth. "It's true. How long does Maddie intend to stay with you?"

For a few seconds, maybe longer, I was speechless. While I was talking about spending time with him, feeling relatively free to act and interact naturally with him, to spend brief moments together when the children were not around, like now, setting up for breakfast or stolen kisses while they napped or hidden in quiet corners or under the cover of night, but what he heard and what he missed was the sex. The sex that had only occurred in my bed since Sophie had returned. Was that a red flag?

Staring up at him, he seemed to realise what he had said, the meaning of it or at least what he could now see I had heard. "No, not what I meant. I miss you, not sex." He hesitated. "That's a lie, I do miss sex." Again, he hesitated, his look of horror intensifying. "With you, I miss sex with you, but I miss being with you, spending time together, but it's awkward right now with us both having house guests."

Is that really what Sophie was, a house guest? I really hoped so.

"How long is it going to be like this, Maurizio? I know we were trying to be discreet, and particularly with the children I think it would still be wise, but everyone we know already knows about us. I am tired of sneaking around and to the outside world you and your wife are together, in this house with your children."

"Other people don't matter and you know that we are not together."

"Other people do matter. They matter to me and I will not become the village scandal or subject of gossip because I am seen to be shagging my boss behind his wife's back."

"What do you want me to say? I have told you that Sophie and I have things to sort out and that she needs my support with the children." He sounded terse, that made two of us.

"You have told me that, more than once, and guess what? I am no further forward in knowing what that means today than I was the very first time you said it. What is the great mystery here? Why has Sophie returned and precisely what is it that you need to sort out and why does that need to be done with her living here?"

"You have no need to be jealous."

My jaw dropped and my eyes widened until they dried. Was he for real? *I had no need to be jealous.* Is that what he thought my confusion, concern and unhappiness about this situation came down to, jealousy? I mean, I was jealous and that was mainly due to Sophie's presence, but even with my sister's words about there being no chemistry between the man before me and his wife, it was more. I felt uneasy and nervous, as though I was going to end up being on the receiving end of the fallout from this.

"Apparently not if you're to be believed in your account of what is going on here."

"If I am to be believed?" He sounded furious that I might be suggesting that he was being dishonest in what he told me.

"Yes, and at this precise moment, I'm not convinced."

"Morning!"

We both spun to see Sophie enter the room and then under the weight of our stares, she stopped dead. "Sorry, I'm interrupting, I, erm,

I'll go and wake the children." She all but ran to escape the two of us and the atmosphere we'd created.

"This conversation is not over," Maurizio told me, slamming a cup down on the kitchen counter beside me.

"Fine!" I snapped back. "And perhaps the next time we have it, you might have some actual answers."

Chapter 45

Maurizio

The last few days had passed by in something of a blur. I'd been relieved to get back to the office and lose myself in work, not least because it gave me a break from being so close to Flora at home but unable to spend time with her alone. Between supporting Sophie in her attempts to gain some semblance of order in her life, spending time with the children, and the presence of Maddie, there was very little opportunity for me and Flora to be alone beyond the odd fleeting seconds in the kitchen each morning before the children got up or as had happened that morning, Sophie disturbing us. Although, her appearance had been perfectly timed in many ways because after the conversation between us had turned frosty and then accusatory, I could only see it going one way and that was badly. There was a potential of mean words and allegations that couldn't be taken back and of which there would be no coming back from, so for once, I had been grateful of an interruption.

Fortunately, my mother's contact had been brief and my brother had only called me once since leaving shortly after Flora and Maddie had arrived together a few afternoons ago. That last fact was a surprise considering Nico had gone on a full charm offensive with Maddie, but nevertheless, the fewest number of people being around gave less scope for revelations and further muddying of the waters of my relationship with Flora.

I was due in court after lunch and assuming everything went according to plan, I should be home no later than half five, perhaps six, so, with my phone already in my hand, I fired off a quick message to Flora inviting her to dinner, just the two of us, and although I was asking her, there was no real option for a rebuttal. I hoped not anyway. We needed some time together away from the house and the people around us.

Rushing into the house at five-thirty, I found the children eating dinner with Sophie.

"Hey, you two." I leaned in and with a ruffle of the children's hair, I landed a kiss to their cheeks. "You okay?" I asked, turning to Sophie.

"Yeah. I know it's short notice but I have an appointment tomorrow, the call only came through this afternoon. Would you be able to come with me?"

"That should be fine. I am in the office doing some court preparation, so let me know the details."

She nodded but looked worried.

"It will be fine. Everything will work out." I wasn't entirely convinced by my own reassurance but reasoned that was what she needed to hear in that moment.

She nodded again. "How's Flora?" She rose to her feet and moved away from the children slightly. "I'm sorry for all of this, Mo. My presence has disrupted things and although I didn't really catch what was said this morning between you, it was clear you were arguing and that I was a factor in that."

I wasn't discussing this with her, not now, not ever. "She was upset, angry. I get why and things got heated, but it's okay, it will be okay. Flora feels shut out and in the dark."

"Until we have facts and figures, please don't tell her."

My sigh coincided with the sound of cutlery hitting a plate. "You are putting me in a terrible position, you know. Rock and hard place springs to mind." I was heading back to the children.

"She agreed to dinner though?" Sophie asked, following me.

"She did."

"She has barely acknowledged me today."

"Perhaps she doesn't feel the need to acknowledge you under the circumstances." Looking at Sophie's face I wondered if I was about to, in the space of eleven hours, piss off yet another woman in the kitchen.

"Which circumstances would they be?"

I shrugged, suddenly tired of all the angst and aggravation. "You're a stranger to her. One who has come along and disrupted everything in her life."

"I am the mother of the children she is paid to take care of. The same mother whose house she lives in."

Well, fuck me this was going from bad to worse, but I wouldn't have Sophie reinvent who and what she was in this situation or to Flora. "You're staying here Sophie, and this was our house, but since we agreed the financial terms of our divorce, it's my house she's lives in and I am the one who pays her to take care of the children."

"That's me put in my place then!" I was unsure if Sophie was angry or hurt.

"Sorry." I really wanted to not be stuck in the middle of the two women but who knew if that was even possible at this stage.

"I'm a fly in her ointment."

I laughed. "Not quite the phrase I would have used, but you're not the fly I don't think, but maybe your presence in the house and the unexpectedness of it."

"What's oinkment?" Craig asked, breaking the tension and replacing it with warm laughter.

Lacing up my shoes as I sat on the edge of my bed, I glanced down at the illuminated screen of my phone and see a message from Flora asking where we should meet. Clearly she didn't want to come down into the house. I quickly replied telling her I would pick her up. With my shoes on and my feet hanging off the bed, I lay back and reached for the spare pillow. Inhaling it, the faint aroma of Flora remained and filled my nostrils with her scent. I really did miss her and as much as Sophie needed support, I regretted her coming back when she had. The fading smell of Flora saddened me because it meant it had been too long since she had been here, in my bed, my arms.

Before leaving, I went to kiss my children who were already snoring in a sound and peaceful slumber and then as I headed for the front door, Sophie appeared. "Where's Flora?"

"I'm going to collect her."

"Ah, nice, romantic."

"I dunno about that but hopefully we can have an actual date."

"Have fun."

"Thanks." If this wasn't awkward I didn't know what was. "I have to go, and I'll see you in the morning."

Hopefully my date with Flora would be a little less fraught and uncomfortable.

By the time I reached Flora's door, I felt more relaxed and optimistic. When the door opened and a stoney faced Maddie stood before me, those feelings disappeared.

"Maurizio." Her tone was curt and the wave of her arm, inviting me in felt sarcastic as did her use of my name.

"Maddie." I entered and looked around for her sister.

"Just in the bathroom, putting the finishing touches to her make-up."

"She doesn't need make-up, she's beautiful without."

Maddie rolled her eyes.

"Have I offended you in some way because you are rather hostile if you don't mind me saying." I didn't care if she did mind me saying as she was being openly antagonistic.

"It doesn't matter if you've offended me, what matters is how you make my sister feel. She is the sweetest girl in the world and she has had a rough time of things . . . she likes you, but that won't be enough to prevent me cutting your balls off if you continue to treat her like your side chick."

"What?" I was horrified at her words.

"You heard, and don't even try to deny it. When you first got together, you both agreed to be discreet, but there's a difference between discretion and hidden. She thought you had turned a corner and then your wife returned, and for the record, I am not buying this bullshit, *she needs help and support and wants to make things up to the children* or whatever bollocks you and her have come up with. There is something not adding up in this whole situation and you don't need to tell me, potentially you don't need to tell Flora, but do not take her for a fool or I will take you down."

"You're scary." Why they were my only words in response, I had no clue, but she was.

"Not even bringing my A-game but I will be if you hurt her any more than you already have with this ridiculous situation."

"I love her." Maddie looked as though she was going to fly at me, possibly with a weapon of some sort, perhaps one that would support her plan to cut my balls off. What was her problem? She wanted me to treat Flora appropriately, to not take advantage or let her down and when I admitted my feelings . . . Shit! She had got the wrong end of the stick completely. "Flora, I love Flora."

"You love me?"

Chapter 46

Flora

Had I heard him correctly? I had changed my outfit at the last minute, changed from a taupe dress and nude lipstick to a black, lace covered dress so had gone from nude to red lips, otherwise I would have been the one to have greeted Maurizio at the door rather than Maddie. My sister had assured me that she would be nice, but I knew she had reservations about what was going on with Sophie, so her idea of being nice might be different to my own. Now I was on the threshold to the room and he had said 'I love Flora'.

They both turned and I was unsure who looked most shocked by the revelation.

"You love me?" I asked, needing some kind of confirmation that I hadn't imagined his three words, although I knew I hadn't.

"Not how I was planning on telling you." He frowned. "I had no plan, but you shouldn't have overheard it that way."

"You love me?" I repeated, apparently unable to get past this point.

"I do." He moved towards me and taking my hands in his, he leaned down as if preparing to kiss me, but simply held my gaze. "I love you."

My grin spread as his lips edged ever closer. "I love you, too." My eyelids fluttered, preparing to close as my lips parted, awaiting his kiss and then the sound of Maddie, Maddie who I had forgotten was there, interrupted.

"No! Not only do I not need to see this, but she is wearing red lipstick and kissing is guaranteed to smudge, so either go on your date and save it for later or I'll go on a date and you two can continue without me."

With a slight flush and a pant of breathlessness, I looked at Maurizio, deferring to him and for a second he looked conflicted, but it was brief. "We're going to dinner, so thanks for the offer, Maddie, I think, but we'll leave you to your evening."

She nodded and smiled across at me as Maurizio took my hand and led me to the door to take us outdoors.

"Oh, and Maddie, it seems to be a good thing you didn't cut my balls off."

They both laughed and I gained an insight into their conversation that I had missed.

"Just remember that offer has no expiry date."

"Noted," replied Maurizio before adding, "Don't wait up, I'm keeping her for the whole night."

"Then I'll make my own entertainment."

We drove in relative silence, but it was comfortable, our earlier declarations of love out in the open with no uneasiness about them. Briefly, I wondered what that would mean for our relationship and the children, the children and Sophie, but for now, I settled on enjoying this time, his love and the contentment I felt.

My phone buzzed and continued to vibrate in my hand multiple times before I was able to see the screen. It appeared that I was in a group chat with my sister, Ash, Carrie and Bea and the group was named Flora and Maurizio sitting in a tree. I laughed loudly before reading any of the messages and then my screen was filled with references to our love, our almost kiss and oblivion to my sister's presence. Judging by the sheer number of messages I hadn't been alerted to and the recent update that I had been added to the group by Maddie, my friends had been brought up to speed by my sister and were now sending GIFs, memes, comments and rude emojis.

"Is tesoro mio okay?" Maurizio asked, reaching across and squeezing my knee.

"Very okay, thank you, but Maddie has been speaking to the girls and Ash about us, about tonight." I was nervous that he might be angry about this turn of events and us, him becoming the subject of gossip.

"I can only imagine the height of the lascivious nature of the messages."

"Sorry, I didn't know she would do this."

Another squeeze of my knee was the first response. "I can't say I am surprised and so long as they don't add the local school governors, parish council or WI, it's all good."

We both laughed and then Maurizio turned serious again.

"Or my mother, she has absolutely no place in a group chat . . ." he peeped at my screen, "titled Flora and Maurizio sitting in a tree." He laughed, rich, deep, and throaty. "How old are they all? Although I believe the next line of that particular ditty involves k-i-s-s-i-n-g."

"Apparently not with red lipstick."

We were pulling into a curb side parking space and I was certain the temperature had gone up because I was beginning to overheat as Maurizio undid both of our seatbelts and moved in, so close that I could smell him, almost taste him. God, how I wanted to taste him.

"Your mouth, my cock and that red lipstick will be intimately acquainted before tonight is over."

I swallowed hard and if I was hot before, I was sweltering now. His hand inched up from my knee and a quirk of his brows confirmed he had found the tops of my rarely worn stockings. He said nothing as his fingers continued to travel until they paused at the barrier of my lace underwear that was already damp. Pushing the fabric aside, he allowed a finger to trace a path along my length.

A deep hiss left my clenched lips while a broad smile spread across Maurizio's face as his finger moved back and forth a couple of times before he paused at my core. His eyes fixed on mine that were probably wide and expectant, and then he slid inside me, my muscles clenching and holding his finger.

"Maurizio, shit, please."

"My dolcezza is an exhibitionist, uh?"

In that second, I couldn't have cared less if anyone was watching us. His dirty words and touch, together with his heated gaze, were all I was aware of. In that moment I would have happily spread myself bare for him right there in the car.

The circling of his finger saw me sliding my hands through his hair, attempting to pull him close enough to kiss.

"No kissing," he told me. "Your lipstick."

"I don't care."

He laughed, possibly at my desperation rather than the words themselves. "No kissing until later, but I'll happily make you come, on one condition."

"Anything."

He laughed again but this was quickly followed by his finger beginning to move. "Call my name as you come."

That was an easy ask, especially as he studied my face.

His thumb moved as far as my clit that he circled while his finger continued to thrust. Clutching his shoulders, I knew this was going to be quick and intense. Another stroke of my clit and a thrust of his finger followed and then another and then with his nose touching mine, I came. My fingers flexed and clawed his shoulders I was gripping as a pool of moisture left my body and coated his hand that remained in my underwear as he stroked and coaxed every last ounce of pleasure from me, all while I called his name over and over until it was more of a chant.

"You are fucking beautiful," he said, withdrawing his hand and moving back into his seat. "Never seen anything more beautiful." He seemed to muse as he raised his hand and proceeded to suck my arousal from his digits.

I said nothing but stared, my jaw slack, my eyes focused on the movement of his mouth.

"The food here is supposed to be out of this world, but it is going to pale when compared to the taste of you, Flora."

I flushed. How ridiculous that it should be those words that caused me to blush rather than what had just happened.

"Let's eat, and then, when we get home, let's eat." With a grin and a wink, Maurizio was out of the car and circling the vehicle until my door opened with the offer of a hand.

Dinner was difficult, not because of the food, that was great, possibly the most delicious food I had ever tasted. Nor the company, Maurizio was always good company and tonight was no exception, we'd laughed and shared stories from our childhoods, our likes and dislikes in movies and music. Somehow we'd ended up disagreeing on a couple of things that had been thrown up, resulting in me agreeing to watch *Top Gun* and him agreeing to a screening of *Love Actually*. Musically we had now agreed to attending concerts by Pink and The Rolling Stones. No, the difficulty of dinner was my discomfort, and by discomfort, I meant just how turned on I was, so much that I spent most of the evening fidgeting and possibly squirming. Every movement resulted in a knowing smirk and slightly wicked glint in his eye.

By the time dessert arrived, I considered using the spoon to slide the whole thing from the plate and into my mouth in one quick movement. I resisted, just.

"I was going to book us a hotel room tonight, for privacy."

He might as well have thrown a bucket of icy water over me. I was no longer hot and bothered, instead I was irritated by his suggestion and the inference of his words. A hotel room meaning not his bedroom and privacy meaning out of sight and sound of Sophie, or at least that's what I took it to mean. Before I could speak or get up and leave or indeed throw something at or over him, he continued.

"However, I changed my mind because although I wanted privacy and some time alone for us, I didn't want you to feel as though I was hiding you away or even wonder if I was abusing the technical position I hold as your employer."

"I see." I felt foolish for jumping to conclusions.

"Because neither of those would be true. I love you."

My face splitting grin could not be mistaken at the reminder of his feelings for me. "And I love you."

"Yes, you do, which means when we get home tonight, I fully intend to fuck you until you scream my name. I would say until you wake the neighbours, but the house is detached and it's chilly out so the windows are likely to be closed."

In reality, him speaking about fucking me until I screamed meant it wouldn't be quite so chilly after all, if the heat rushing through my body was anything to go by.

"I am deadly serious and by the time I am finished with you, mine might be the only name you're sure of."

Shit! I swallowed hard and the fluttering in my tummy, my disordered swirling thoughts and the ache between my legs that showed no sign of abating no matter how tightly I squeezed them together suggested that my own name would be a very dim and distant memory come morning.

"Should I get the bill?"

"Yes. *Now.*"

The summoning of the waiter coincided with his chuckle.

Chapter 47

Maurizio

The temptation to put my foot down hard was near overpowering because I knew once we got home, Flora was all mine and that regardless of her lipstick, I was going to kiss her, long, hard, and for the whole damn night.

I risked a glance across at her and she looked amazing. The lacy black dress she wore finished between her thighs and knees. Taking in her smokey legs, I remembered the stockings she was wearing and suddenly the idea of removing those stockings and using them to tie her spread eagled to my bed sprang to mind. My mind wasn't the only thing springing, my cock was lurching against the zip of my trousers like it had a life of its own. The memory of discovering those stockings reminded me of the feel of the damp heat of her and then there was the way I'd made her come, the way she'd begged for it, neither of us caring about the public location parked at the roadside near the restaurant. Fuck, that had been hot. Risky but hot.

With my eyes back on the road, I concentrated on getting us home safely and tried to push the ideas of what we'd do once there from my mind.

Pulling up in front of the house, I moved to help Flora from the car, only to find she was already out and waiting for me. She was keen, and that was in no way a criticism. With her hand in mine, we headed into the house and upstairs, pausing at my bedroom door.

"I need to check on the children."

"Of course." She offered me a smile and leaned against the frame of the door that separated me from the children.

It had been my plan to do the quickest check and kiss to the head known to man, but when I entered the room both of my children had kicked off their covers. I set about covering them up, tucking them in and kissing their heads starting with Rosie. As I rose to my feet and turned to repeat the action with Craig, I noticed Flora still leaning against the door frame and watching me intently and despite the semi-darkness she was in, I could have sworn there was heat in her eyes, heat and desire, but different to what had been there earlier, this time it was somehow softer, but equally as intense. With my son tucked in, I moved towards her.

"You're a wonderful father."

"Thank you, but that may not have always been the case, and they make it easy."

Closing the door behind me, I pushed a stray piece of hair off her face and tucked it behind her ear.

"Just the two of us." I could have kicked myself when I heard those words out loud and hoped to any and all heavenly beings that Flora wouldn't be reminded of the fact that Sophie was in a spare room at the other end of the landing to where we stood. I hadn't meant anything by my comment beyond the fact that I had tucked the children in and we could resume our earlier plan.

"Then what are we waiting for?" She reached for my hand and actually led me through the door she was opening.

Once in the darkness of the bedroom, I pulled Flora to me and prepared to devour her in the most delightful of ways, starting with holding her in my arms, pressing her against the wall with my body firmly leaning against hers. I wanted her legs and arms wrapped around me as I owned her mouth and pressed my arousal against her sensitive folds, leaving her in no doubt about how much I wanted her.

None of that happened. She had found her confident self and as such had other ideas and that started with her evading my grasp, and instead pushing me back so that it was me who ended up pressed against the wall with her before me. Her blonde locks hanging in loose waves, framing her face, while she worried her lip, taunting me with the fact that I wasn't yet kissing her. Reaching for her again, my hands got as far as her hips, my fingers fully appreciating the gentle curves of her body before she covered my hands with hers and shook her head.

In a movement I didn't see coming, demurely and with grace, she dropped to her knees and gazed up at me. Her eyes never breaking contact with mine, she reached into her bag, pulled something from it and cast the bag aside. I watched on in awe as she revealed the item in her hand, her red lipstick that she was applying another coat of.

By the time she had replaced the lid and cast the lipstick aside, I was harder than I could ever remember being, which was becoming common place with the woman on her knees before me, the contradictory image of submission and power in one image and if that didn't turn me on a little more. I almost came on the spot when she spoke.

"I think it's time my mouth, your cock, and this red lipstick became intimately acquainted, don't you?"

Her use of my own words that had been used to tease and torment her earlier were torturing me, but fortunately, she was not cruel and didn't make me wait for her to follow through on her words.

Reaching forward, she found my belt and the fastening of my trousers. Slowly, she lowered the zipper before tugging down my clothing, exposing my erection that she gently took hold of. Two or three strokes along its length and I was concerned this would be over before it began. Her eyes were still fixed on mine and then if she didn't offer me a coy smile that really did contradict everything else.

"Maurizio," she whispered as her thumb circled the head of my cock that was already leaking.

She moved closer and the sight of her pink, wet tongue appearing between her lips saw me jerk in her hand. Her smile broadened with empowerment, knowing that I was putty in her hands, metaphorically speaking. Using her thumb and forefinger to make a ring around the base of my cock, and slowly, tantalisingly slowly, she leaned in as she licked along the underside of my length, circling the head.

My hands shot into her hair, pulling against the honey coloured lengths as I cursed between gritted teeth, "Fuck, Flora."

Her mouth covered my crown and she giggled, the vibrations of it going straight to my balls, and then she moved down my length, then back up. Over and over again with her hand varying the tightness and pressure around my base while her other hand began to cup and caress my balls that tightened with every move and passing second. I know I had been the one to make this suggestion, but I had expected to be the one torturing her with pleasure, sensation and anticipation, that's not the way it was going down. I offered myself an internal and rather juvenile smirk at my choice of words in that thought, *going down*. I needed to think of something that wasn't about sex or I would be coming in the next five seconds. Rugby, work, interest rates, they all acted as brief distractions, but as Flora picked up pace and her eyes found mine that were drinking in the reality of my own erotic dream, I was fucked.

"Flora, shit!"

She took my words as encouragement rather than a warning. The cupping of my balls becoming firmer and the suction of her mouth that continued to slide along my length while her tongue lapped the most sensitive parts of me meant I needed to be clearer in my warning.

"I'm going to come."

And if she didn't bring her hand to the party at that second meaning the combination of the caressing of my balls and her tightening grip working in tandem with the movements of her glorious mouth saw me lost in a sea of sensation until I was coming in her mouth whilst pulling her hair until, breathless and spent, I thought I might pass out.

The pop sound as she released me brought me back into the moment and looking down, I followed Flora's gaze to my still hard cock that had a perfect red circle from her lipstick around the base of it.

I was good to go again and fully intended to turn the tables, never more so than when I looked back at Flora, offered her a hand to stand and that is when I fully saw that her lipstick was smeared around her mouth. No wonder Maddie warned me off kissing her, but now, well, the damage had been done and it had been far too long since my lips had tasted hers.

"And now I believe you need to scream my name."

Chapter 48

Flora

"Well, who do we have here? Little Miss I Got Some Last Night and have had to do the walk of shame!"

I laughed as Maddie offered me the cup of tea she had made for herself before making another one.

"Good night?" She immediately waved her hand at me, dismissing her own question. "Your grin and glow suggest it was, as does your freshly showered state. Is that one of Maurizio's T-shirts?" She shook her head.

"Better than good."

"How much better?"

"Like a million times, I am struggling to walk better."

"Fuck!" My sister's eyes were wide as she pulled me to sit next to her on the stools at my small breakfast bar. "Tell me everything."

"Eww! No, you do not want to know."

"I do."

I cackled as I reached for the toast she had already made and had only taken one bite from. "I am not giving you a blow by blow account."

"I'd tell you."

I laughed, more at her accompanying pout. "But I wouldn't want to know." She looked genuinely disappointed. "Okay, but not too many details."

With a grin and a clap, she leaned back into her seat as if this was story time.

Maddie had been near silent as I had told her what Maurizio had said to me about my lipstick and his cock. I also mentioned him saying I'd be screaming his name. I held her rapt attention as I told her that I had taken charge initially and delivered what I had believed to be a mind blowing blow job, followed by Maurizio turning feral.

I hadn't given the details of him undressing me, using my stocking to tie my legs to his bed before settling between my spread thighs and setting about driving me to the edge of orgasm over and over and over again. I had indeed screamed his name, begging him to make me come, but he resisted my calls and continued to edge me closer before withdrawing. I swear that by the time he retreated for the last time, a light breeze, the tiniest of movements from my legs or internal muscles or a simple look from him would have had me coming without further stimulation. He'd stood at the end of the bed between my feet and had studied me, surveyed me almost, and then he had shocked me.

"The next time I tie you up, I am going to have your nipples adorned with clamps."

I had no objection to that. My nipples were and had always been sensitive and I had bought some clamps to try alone, but never quite managed to get the hang of them as I always seemed to be a hand or two short. The shock was more that I had never imagined the man who had interviewed me all those months ago turning out to be such a dirty talking, dominant kind of lover.

"We need to go shopping, tesoro mio, because I also intend to watch you come spread out before me with a vibrator in your pussy and a butt plug or beads in your ass."

I had no idea where all of this was coming from, but I had zero complaints if he planned on following through with these threats.

"I want to know I can make you come for me whenever I choose."

I was at risk of coming right there if he didn't stop speaking.

"But for now . . ."

He dropped to his knees and with no further words began to feast on me. His tongue flicked my clit, circled it over and over before moving until he was dipping into my core, drinking my arousal that was coating the whole of my sex and inner thighs. Then he returned his tongue and mouth to my clit while a finger easily slid inside me all too briefly. The finger was replaced with something bigger, thicker, his thumb and that is when the finger began to stroke and ease into my behind. I had never had any interest in anal play, but the sensations these gentle touches triggered, suggested I needed to broaden my horizons.

"Maurizio," I called over and over as his finger worked its way inside me while his thumb moved faster, in and out, stroking me closer to release. His tongue continued to lave my clit, bathing it in the moisture of his mouth as well as my own arousal, and then with it engorged and swollen, he closed his teeth around it and I fell apart like never before.

The screams of his name sounded pained and desperate, much like me.

"Oh my God! What the fuck did he do to you because whatever it is, I am jealous. You're all red and breathless just thinking about it!"

Initially, I had been embarrassed that the memory of that experience had seen me zone out, reliving it, oblivious to what it was doing to my body while my sister watched on, but now, with my sister's good humour, I felt none of those things, I simply felt happy.

Finishing the last slice of toast, I got to my feet. "I need to throw some clothes on and go down, but if you fancy lunch or something, we can get together."

"Are you going to tell me exactly how he fucked you a dozen different ways and why you're suddenly a sexy dominant?"

I roared as I headed out of the room, knowing that as much as I had taken some control, I was many things, but none of them dominant and that suited me just fine.

. . .

When I arrived downstairs in the kitchen, Maurizio sat alone at the table with a cup in front of him.

"Good morning."

He looked up from his phone and smiled. "Yes it is."

As I moved past him, he reached for my arm and pulled me into his lap and kissed me, gently at first but quickly the exchange became heated until I pulled back, aware of our surroundings that I took in, hoping not to find Sophie or the children in them.

"They're all still in bed. Sophie came down for a drink earlier and explained that the children had watched a movie with her last night and hadn't gone to bed until nine so you might have an easy morning of it. Bea starting her maternity leave has also removed one further interruption."

I laughed, thinking of how many times Bea had walked in on us, not that we were ever doing anything beyond fighting our attraction to one another.

Relaxing into his lap again, I felt the unmistakable bulge in his trousers beneath me. "Missed me?" I wriggled against him, smiling when I felt him stiffen and lurch.

His hand slid into my hair, allowing him to manoeuvre me slightly so that his eyes bored into mine. "Enough that if you tease me any more I am going to bend you over the nearest hard surface and fuck you while I finger your ass."

Immediately, I was catapulted back to the previous night when that is exactly what had happened. Once I had recovered and been untied, Maurizio had crawled over me, kissed me and caressed me until I'd been a ball of frenzied arousal again and that was when he had said those words as he'd gotten off the bed and pulled me to my feet. *I am going to bend you over and fuck you while I finger your ass.* The feel of the chest of the marble sink in his bathroom, whilst cold had warmed me, not as much as the realisation that I'd been in front of a mirror that gave me a ringside view to the glory of this naked man and my own flushed complexion as I'd waited for his next move. I hadn't waited long before he'd positioned me, folded over, arse in the air and legs spread. The feel of him moving closer so his arousal had been clear to me, skimming a touch against me had caused a shudder. His hand had settled between my thighs and he'd explored me until he'd been sure I was ready and then his hand had disappeared and he'd entered me. Slowly, torturously, inch by inch until he'd been fully inside me. Then he'd moved, my moans and gasps had been immediate in response. But they were nothing compared to the sounds that escaped my lips when his hand that had been resting on my lips had made its way to my behind, spreading my cheeks to enable a finger to be inserted there, as he'd done earlier. This time, as he'd pounded me from behind, his finger had matched the rhythm perfectly, stride for stride until I couldn't decipher where the pleasure building within had been coming from. This was possibly the most erotic moment of my life, and then he'd took the eroticism off the scale by holding my hair in the nape of my neck with his free hand, fisting it like a ponytail and then he'd gently raised my head so I saw the moment unfold in the mirror. The reflection of us both passing the point of no return with each other, because of each other.

Maurizio's deep chuckle brought me back to the kitchen where I still sat on his lap. "Good to know last night was memorable."

I flushed and attempted to get up, feeling awkward to have been caught reliving the moments from the night before.

"Hey," he said, pulling me tighter against him. "Last night was phenomenal." A gentle kiss landed on my temple before I froze to the spot when I saw Sophie in the doorway looking as though she was about to retreat had she not been seen.

"Sorry." The other woman looked as awkward as I felt. "I might need to start walking heavier or have a bell attached to me, like a cat." She seemed to be rambling as I wondered if adding the option of moving out would be well received. "At least it was me and not the children," she added, and I regretted having not offered her the alternative option to avoid finding us in the kitchen again.

"Indeed," Maurizio said, then with a smile at me, addressed that issue. "I think we should tell the children that Flora and I are dating . . . obviously not in those terms, but that we are friends."

"Friends that kiss?" I wanted the floor to open and swallow me up but Maurizio simply laughed and nodded. "Mo, can we meet at one o'clock today?"

Why were they meeting? All intentions of getting some actual answers about Sophie's presence in the house had been lost the night before. Lost in lust, orgasms, and declarations of love.

"Of course. Text me the location," Maurizio said, getting to his feet and placing me on mine. "I have to go," he told me as he landed another kiss to the top of my head.

I was dreading being alone with Sophie and was beyond relieved to hear the sounds of the children's chatter as their feet could be heard padding down the stairs.

Sophie made herself scarce for most of the morning and by noon she had left the house looking emotional and fearful. I didn't have time to dwell on either of those things as Maddie appeared as I prepared lunch. The children were playing nearby and turning to see Maddie they smiled and waved.

"Hey, you two, how's it going in the world of twins?"

I laughed as Rosie's face morphed into a disapproving scowl to match my own.

"Daddy says we're twins by birth, not personality."

Maddie turned to me and mouthed *what the fuck*, making me laugh louder.

"That means we are twins but we should be treated differently," Craig clarified, assuming Maddie hadn't understood what his sister had said.

"We always wanted to be twins," Maddie told the children, joining them on the floor where they were surrounded by construction pieces and small world toys.

"Really?" Rosie asked, her interest summoning me to join them.

"We did," I confirmed. "Maddie is my big sister, but only by a little bit."

"A very, very little bit," Maddie told them, holding her thumb and finger apart by the tiniest of fractions.

"But lots of people thought we were twins, especially as we look a little bit alike."

"And you're both girls," Craig said while Rosie nodded.

"Lots of people don't think we're twins because I am a girl and Craig is a boy."

"Hmm, well Flora and I were really close and such good friends, like you two, so we decided we wanted to be twins but we couldn't be, even if we were double trouble."

"We get called double trouble too!" Craig laughed and Rosie joined in.

"You have to be in your mummy's tummy together to be a twin." Rosie was intent on clearing up any confusion on our sibling status.

"And we weren't," I confirmed for them.

"Do you have a mummy?" Craig looked confused. "I haven't ever seen your mummy. Daddy has a mummy, Nonna, and Mummy has a mummy, but she lives a long way away with Grandpa so we only see them sometimes."

"Daddy says we don't need another Grandma as we have Nonna and she makes up way more than one Grandma."

Maddie and I both laughed at Rosie's repeated words of her father but came to a stop when a voice interrupted.

"Ain't that the truth."

"Uncle Nico!" The children called, making a beeline for their uncle leaving me and Maddie to get to our feet.

Chapter 49

Maurizio

The morning had started well, reliving the previous night with Flora, although Sophie's interruption and comments about the children had broken the moment. Last night had been everything I could have dreamt of, and more. Perhaps acknowledging our feelings had somehow brought a few more bricks down in the wall between us. The wall was mainly Sophie shaped. There were still concerns around her living in the house. I acknowledged to myself that we still had work to do in setting out our stall in terms of next steps and moving forward, but I didn't want to push Flora too far, too soon. I loved knowing she lived in my house and I would be happy to share my bed with her every night of the week, but I suspected that she wouldn't be ready for that yet. Suddenly, I realised that although I knew about her family, Maddie and her grandparents and of course the loss of her parents, we had never discussed her romantic history. She hadn't been a virgin when we met, nor did I expect her to be, but I also didn't believe

she was likely to have had multiple casual partners so there must have
been boyfriends, at least one.

The alarm I had set on my phone startled me. I needed to go and
meet Sophie. Perhaps I needed to focus on this afternoon with Sophie
more than Flora's romantic past because one was safely behind us and
the other was potentially going to implode on all of our lives, not least
my children's.

Arriving with a few minutes to spare, I spotted Sophie immediately,
she was hard to miss what with her nervously pacing.

"Hi," I said, wrapping an arm around her shoulders. "How you
doing?"

"I'm scared, Mo," she replied, the first tear escaping and running
down her cheek.

Pulling her close, I enveloped her in my arms and rocked her gently,
desperate to offer reassurance. "It's going to be okay . . ." I couldn't
guarantee that and before I continued or backtracked, her name was
called. Taking her hand in mine, I led her towards the nurse who smiled
and guided us past the reception desk and waiting area into a consulta-
tion room where two doctors sat waiting for us.

The following moments went in slow motion and time ceased to
mean anything. Words, lots of words, came our way and while we both
remained calm, inside I was freaking out so I could only imagine how
Sophie felt. She appeared stoic and emotionless through it all, meaning
she was reeling, and why wouldn't she be, she had just been told she had
cervical cancer. I needed to step up and be the rational one, so, pushing
all thoughts of my children and their mother from my mind, I put my
brain into professional mode and asked the questions she would need
answers to, facts and time frames.

"Is this treatable?"

Sophie squeezed my hand tighter.

"Yes," the doctor replied.

"Curable?" That was the million dollar question.

"Potentially." Not as positive as it could be, but not a no. "But you
should have come back sooner."

I was confused. This was her first appointment, wasn't it? She
looked between us and then facing me, explained.

"I missed some appointments."

"What? Why?"

"I was scared, Mo, and for a little while I buried my head in the sand. When I became ill, I put it down to our separation, the upheaval of everything messing with my body and my cycle. I was in the dentist and read an article about a young woman with similar symptoms and so I acted quickly and made an appointment with my doctor. She sent me for bloods and then a scan. The doctors here contacted me quickly but I couldn't do it, I didn't want to hear them confirm what I already knew, so I avoided. I came home and saw the children and decided that they deserved better than watching me become ill."

"Sophie, better they watch you become ill and recover than die!" I snapped the last part and was furious with her.

"I didn't say it was logical, and I don't want to die and leave my babies." Any semblance of control was lost at that point.

Pulling her in closer, I held her, rocked her, and asked the doctors to go through everything from the beginning and then to talk us through some kind of treatment plan.

I felt like I had been punched by the time I had wrapped my head around the events. Sophie had developed abdominal pain and irregular bleeding and after seeking medical advice had been sent for bloods, a scan and investigation. She had then returned home, changed her number, and managed to ignore all follow-ups from the hospital as she had ignored her cancer diagnosis. She had told me that she had cancer and was awaiting further tests. I had believed her. There was no reason for me not to, was there? She had also asked for me to keep it to myself until she knew the exact details and with the exception of my mother who knew Sophie was ill, if only to keep her meddling at bay, and Nico also knew, because, well, it was Nico. I had kept Sophie's secret. Perhaps, now, with the details known, she would allow me to share her illness with Flora so she might better understand Sophie's reappearance.

My hammering heart thudded in my ears as I tried to take all of this in and order my thoughts and more questions for the doctors.

"You said this is treatable and could be curable?"

"I did. First thing we need to do is repeat the tests and scans to ensure that the cancer hasn't spread. If it hasn't then we will look at getting you scheduled for surgery and possibly some chemotherapy."

"And if it's spread?"

The doctor shook his head. "I'm not able to answer that question until we know what we're dealing with."

"When can you do the tests?" I probably sounded like a dick with my firm tone, but I needed information and a plan, and so did Sophie who was pale as a sheet and clearly struggling to hold things together. I still couldn't think about my poor children in the possible scenarios of how this might play out. They'd found it hard enough when Sophie had left and they knew where she lived. The burn in my jaw and the sting in my eyes caught me off guard. I loved Sophie, I wasn't in love with her, but her health and happiness were important to me. I was happy for us to be divorced which we would be in a matter of weeks, however, I hadn't expected her to die.

"The blood tests we can arrange today. I will take a look at scheduling the scan and we can take it from there."

"Thank you."

"I know this is a shock, for you both, but many patients live long lives after surviving cancer. The nurse here, Becky, will sit with you for a while and I am sure she will be able to answer any questions you may have."

We remained at the hospital for the next couple of hours. The bloods were taken and the doctor had even managed to get the scan arranged within the same day. Sophie had to wait until after the weekend to see the doctors and discuss treatment. If we'd needed it, we could have arranged private doctors and consultations, but the NHS team she had were doing a sterling job and really weren't wasting any time. On reflection, I was unsure if that should frighten me more than reassure me if speed was of the essence.

Sitting in the coffee shop around the corner from the hospital, we allowed the silence to wash over us. I wasn't sure what to say. When she had first returned and told me about her cancer, we had talked at length, but at that point I believed she was on top of appointments and that because there seemed no urgency in treatment, that it was in the early stages, non-aggressive and curable. After today I had a feeling that all bets were off.

"I'm sorry."

Looking up, I found Sophie's eyes on mine, tears threatening to spill. Reaching across the small metal table, I took her hand in mine and gave it a squeeze. "Nothing to be sorry for." Now wasn't the time to point out the error of her ways over the last weeks, possibly months.

"I will never forgive myself if I have inadvertently committed our children to being motherless by playing ignorant."

I couldn't tell her that wasn't the case, but I also wouldn't kick her while she was down. "Sophie, I am sure that whatever happens, these weeks you waited will be irrelevant."

Her brow furrowed.

"Don't get me wrong, if you do that again and play Russian roulette with your health, I will set Mama on you and then you'll wish you were dead."

I hadn't thought out those last words, but they actually diffused all of the tension, making us both laugh. Edging my seat closer, I held her against me, hoping to offer reassurance and comfort.

"Whatever happens, I'm here for you."

"Thank you, but Flora–"

I cut her off. "Flora will want to support you, too. She is an amazing woman and once she knows the details." I sensed an objection. "I won't continue to keep this from her, Sophie. I have fobbed her off at every turn in order to keep your confidence but she deserves to know and to not second guess your reason for being in the house, and even if your treatment is straightforward and smooth sailing we will need Flora in our corner, me and the children."

"Okay, just not tonight. Tonight, I need to be Mummy and to spend an evening with the children, and you, if you want to join us for popcorn and a movie and then tomorrow, I'll pull my head fully from out of my arse."

"Deal, but tomorrow morning, I'm telling her."

"You love her, don't you?"

"I do, and she loves me."

"I'm pleased you've found her."

"Me too. I now need not to bugger it up."

"You won't. Now come on, I want to go home and see our children."

Chapter 50

Flora

Uncle Nico had been with the children for about an hour and had exhausted them to the extent that they were passed out at opposite ends of the sofa while I returned to the kitchen to tidy up. That is where I found Nico and Maddie chatting and giggling like old friends.

"Not interrupting am I? I need to tidy up."

Maddie rolled her eyes while Nico laughed, sounding like his brother.

"Let me tidy up for you," Nico offered and turned to Maddie. "You go talk with your sister."

It seemed I had been interrupting something. What was it that my sister needed to talk to me about and why was Nico in the know? More to the point, why were the two of them so cosy, they'd only met once before, hadn't they?

Maddie shot a scowl Nico's way as he began to load the lunchtime dishes into the dishwasher. "Let's go back to our fellow double troublers then."

Sitting opposite my sister as she nervously twirled the strands of her hair, she looked at me and smiled. "I have to go home, tonight."

"Tonight? Why? What's the rush?"

"I need you to stay calm."

"I can't stay calm when you sound worried and you're telling me to stay calm. What is going on?"

"Tell her." Nico appeared and sat between the children.

Glaring at him, I felt he was overstepping and there was clearly something going on here. "What the bloody hell does this have to do with you?"

"Florence!" Maddie chastened with her use of my full name while Nico laughed, a proper belly laugh.

"She's not wrong, is she?"

Maddie returned her attention to me. "I'm pregnant."

My mouth hung open. "Pregnant?" I managed to say many seconds later.

She nodded.

Turning, I fixed Nico with my hard stare. "Is this you? Have you done this?"

He looked horrified at my accusation while my sister screeched my name again.

"No, this is not me, and I have not done this! I met your sister a week ago, is it?"

"But you knew?"

He nodded. "Maddie and I have been talking, messaging, you know."

Frankly, no, I didn't know, but that wasn't the pressing issue right now. "Maddie, who is the fath–" I didn't need to finish that question. "Him, the married one?"

She nodded. "He doesn't know. I need to go home and tell him and see where he stands."

"Next to his wife is where he stands, I imagine." I sounded judgemental and harsh. "Sorry. Will you keep the baby?"

She nodded. "I should tell him and give him the chance to be involved, but I agree that he is likely to want nothing to do with either of us, but this is my baby, Flo. I know I am Maddie the good time girl, but I have only ever wanted to settle down and have a family. I mean when I was younger, I wanted to live my best life and not risk the hurt of loving, but underneath I wanted it."

I was already crouching down in front of her and pulling her in tight. "You're having a baby!" I squealed, "I'm going to be an auntie."

"Congratulations," Nico said, but I was unsure who he was addressing.

Withdrawing from Maddie slightly, I turned my attention back to Nico. "We need a lengthy conversation about you two and the talking and the messaging."

We both giggled, but I meant every word. I needed to know what was going on between the two of them.

"I wish you didn't have to go so soon."

"I already packed and there's a train in a couple of hours."

"I can drive you."

"No, you can't drive me home and come back here tonight, you'll be tired, plus, the tickets are paid for and non-refundable."

"At least let me take you to the station then."

"Okay. I'd like that."

Maurizio and Sophie returned together just as the children woke up. There was a strange atmosphere and whilst it didn't feel like they had argued, it was strained. I was glad to get out of the house and return to my own space with Maddie. Nico had remained behind and from what I could gather, he was staying for dinner.

Maddie and I were at my car, arguing over who was going to lift her case, an argument I was winning as she had got into the car until Maurizio appeared and took the bag from me with ease.

"I can manage," I protested.

"Of course you can, but I want to help you. If I can't help tesoro mio, who can?" He gently ran a thumb over my cheek and leaned in to kiss me. "You're sad?"

I was going to lose the battle with my tears if he kept looking at me with love and adoration while his touch remained gentle and his tone sympathetic.

"Yes. I wish she would stay."

"She can come back whenever she wants. My home is your home, your people are my people now."

"Thank you." I really needed him to stop being nice and saying such sweet things if I had any hope of keeping these tears at bay until after I had waved Maddie off.

"Let me know when you're back, so I know you're safe. Would you like to have breakfast together in the morning, just the two of us. I'll even cook and we can talk."

"Talk?" My overthinking mind was coming up with a dozen different meanings of *talk*.

"I can explain about Sophie."

He looked sad, scared, upset. "Are you okay?"

Before he could answer, we were interrupted by Sophie calling from the front door. "Maurice, where are you? Come on, we're waiting for you. Popcorn is ready, Rosie has got the sweeties out for us and Craig is choosing the movie for us to watch like old times."

My heart was sliced in two in that moment and the laughter emanating from me was hard and lacked any warmth or amusement.

"Just like old times, Maurice."

"Flora." The use of my name in isolation was a plea but before he could add anything to it, the sound of Sophie and the children calling to him, chanting his name deafened me.

"Daddy, Daddy, Daddy."

He looked torn. "Now is not the time. We both need to go."

"We do."

"Breakfast?"

"I'd like that."

"Good. I love you." I thought he was going to kiss me, but he didn't. He'd said about telling the children that we were friends, but as he hadn't done that yet, a kiss might have been a bad idea, for them anyway.

"Daddy!" A final call saw him retreating and I climbed into my car.

. . .

With Maddie all boarded on her train and a promise for her to let me know she'd got home safe, I drove home. I chatted with Ash on the way and explained everything that had happened with Maddie and Maurizio since we'd last spoken. He seemed less shocked about Maddie that I had been so perhaps I was the last to find out about my niece or nephew. I couldn't disguise the grin at the idea of a baby in the family. Somehow I had always imagined being the one to have a baby first, but apparently not. When Maddie had admitted always wanting her happy ever after with a baby, I hadn't been surprised, not really. She tried being party animal, wild child Maddie, and had done it well for a number of years, usually on the back of another disappointing relationship, but underneath it all she wanted no more than to be loved, valued and to be part of a family again. Wasn't that what we all wanted? It was what I wanted and something Maddie and I, in our own ways, were desperate to recreate. I worried that Maddie would be left alone, literally holding the baby, as the father was married. I really wanted to believe that I could have my happy ever after and family with Maurizio and hoped after he explained about Sophie's presence, I didn't end up on the losing side of a relationship with a married man.

Parking my car between Maurizio's and Sophie's made me shudder as if it was representative of something more, something deeper. I looked across at the lights illuminating the house and noticed Nico's care was still here. Again I wondered about him and my sister, but also if he was enjoying a movie and popcorn as part of the family. I chuckled at what that scene might look like, the three of them on the sofa with the children, most likely watching something animated. I didn't doubt that Nico and Maurizio would most likely be the biggest children there.

Climbing the stairs and entering my home, I felt sad. Although Maddie had only been here with me for a short time, the place felt empty without her in a way it hadn't before she arrived. I sent a quick message to let Maurizio know I was home and he replied immediately with a kissing emoji with the words, *can't wait to claim that kiss.*

I took a shower, redressed in loose fitting pyjamas, put the TV on and flicked aimlessly around the channels, not finding anything to watch. Hitting the off button, I reached for the book I had been reading for the last six months but had got no further than chapter four. As much as I could blame the book, I didn't. My inability to concentrate in recent months was nothing to do with the story, it was all me. Me and the tall, dark and handsome man who was only a flight of stairs away.

Debating how desperate and needy I might come across if I messaged him or wandered downstairs, I decided against it. Curling up on the sofa, I pulled a blanket over myself and began to scroll through social media before quickly becoming bored. Maddie's name lit up the screen with a message to let me know she had arrived home and was heading straight to bed. Sadness washed over me again, imagining her in the home we once shared.. I was genuinely lonely. Desperate and needy were distant memories as I made my way to the door that separated me from the rest of the house. With the door barely open a crack, I heard the sound of Sophie putting the children to bed.

"Daddy will be up in a while and kiss you once you're asleep," she told them.

"Will you read us a story, Mummy?" Rosie asked.

"Of course. I missed our stories at bedtime when Mummy had to go away."

Standing out of sight behind my door, I continued to listen, wondering why Sophie sounded as though she was about to have a breakdown. I reasoned that she was potentially realising all she had missed in the time she had been away.

"What story shall we have tonight?" she asked, clearly trying too hard to be perky and bright.

"*Guess How Much I Love You.*"

The sound of the children's excited cries was drowned out by the sound of a single sob, masked with a high-pitched cry of, "My favourite."

I opened the door fully, preparing to check on Sophie who was clearly upset but before I could speak or gain her attention, the children's door was shut.

Maybe my chat with Maurizio where he explained what was happening with Sophie couldn't wait until breakfast.

Gently padding down the stairs, I heard voices, Maurizio's and Nico's. Following them, I found myself coming to a stop at Maurizio's office door.

"Cheers." Nico's word preceded the sound of glasses clinking together.

Maybe I should leave things for tonight. The two men had moved themselves into the confines of the office and were drinking, and judging by the slight slur of Nico's cheers, they may have been at it for a while. Yes, I should go back upstairs and wait for the morning. Walking back the way I came, I prepared to climb the stairs and had yet another change of heart. Even if we couldn't have the conversation tonight. I could say hi, goodnight, and let him claim the kiss I'd sent him earlier.

Striding back towards the office once more, I immediately regretted my decision when I heard the conversation taking place.

"I love Sophie, always have, and now more than ever I want to make things right and live a long and happy life with her. She and the children are my family and my future and Flora was no more than a dream that could never be."

The words I heard Maurizio speak with my own ears were daggers that sliced through my heart. He loved me. That's what he'd told me, and now, with Nico, he was admitting what he really wanted and that wasn't me. *A dream.* This was more of a nightmare from my perspective.

Fight, flight or freeze were my options now. Well, there seemed little point in fighting if I was the only one who wanted this. Freeze meant staying here and listening to more words that would break what was left of my heart, so, that only left flight, and assuming my legs that felt they might buckle allowed me to, that is what I was going for.

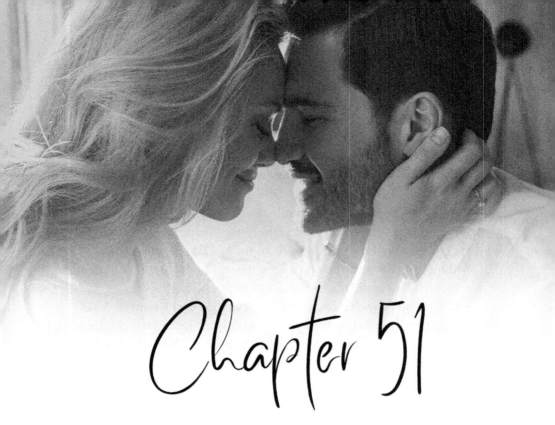

Chapter 51

Maurizio

"I love Sophie, always have and now more than ever I want to make things right and live a long and happy life with her. She and the children are my family and my future and Flora was no more than a dream that could never be." My brother had been goading me all night. We had eaten dinner, the five of us and then watched a movie, but I was wound up. I tried to hide my fear of Sophie's diagnosis and the impact on my children whichever way it worked out.

Nico stared but said nothing, even his silence was him poking the bear.

"Is that what you want me to say? What you think I should say because the mother of my children has cancer?"

"I don't want or expect you to say anything, brother, nothing that isn't true."

"Nico, I am scared, for the children, Sophie, and for myself, but there's so much more than that. I do love Sophie, but not like I love

Flora, however, I need to be there for Sophie and to support her through this."

"That's understandable and the decent thing to do, so, what's the problem?"

"What if Flora finds this too much, or she won't wait?"

"What precisely is it she is waiting for?"

"For me to be free and able to make her mine."

Nico frowned. "You're making a lot of assumptions here. What if she will wait or maybe she won't need to wait because you're already free and she is already yours from where I am sitting."

"I don't want to mess this up because she's the one. Sophie and I were good together, or so I thought, but then I met Flora and she made me see that there was always something missing. She is everything." I carefully considered my next words, remembering what I had falsely said about Sophie when getting riled by my brother who I perceived to be suggesting my future might be with my ex-wife. Although, I did know that he was simply playing devil's advocate. "I love Flora, I think I always have and now more than ever I want to make things right and live a long and happy life with her. She and the children are my family and my future."

He offered a slight cock of his head. "Then you make sure she knows that because apart from anything else, she has one hell of a scary sister."

We both laughed as Nico half-filled our near empty glasses.

The following morning, I woke to the sound of my brother's whistling and my children's laughter. I had clearly passed out judging by my appearance, on the sofa, and I was still fully dressed. My mouth was dry and resembled the bottom of a bird cage, while my head thudded and my stomach lurched.

A cup filled with coffee wafted beneath my nose and if that wasn't almost enough to see me lose the contents of my stomach. Nico laughed.

"How are you not hung over?" I asked as I pulled myself into a semi-sitting position. Seeing me conscious, the children made a beeline to join me and then when they caught a whiff of my hungover aroma, they shuffled away.

"Because, little brother, I can handle my drink far better than you."

I flipped him the bird once I knew the children weren't watching.

He laughed again. I swear he never used to be so jolly. Something about him had changed but I couldn't dwell on that when I needed to keep my stomach from churning, take something for my head and shower, before calling Flora.

"Flora!" I shouted, already up on my feet and immediately regretting moving with such speed. My brain was rattling against my skull for sure.

"Flora isn't here today, Daddy, it's the weekend." Rosie gave me a confused stare.

Grabbing my phone, I sent a quick message to Flora to explain that we would need to move breakfast to lunch.

"I know that, baby, but I was going to see Flora today and make her breakfast." The attention of my children and brother were rapt.

"Why?" Craig asked.

This was not how I had intended on conducting this conversation.

"Because we're friends."

"I thought she was our friend and our nanny," Rosie replied as if correcting me.

"She is."

"Flora is everyone's friend." Craig threw in for good measure while my brother looked on with an amused smirk and a slight grimace, too.

"She is," Nico agreed. "She is my friend, and Maddie, but sometimes we have extra special friends we like to cook breakfast for."

"Bea said Seb cooks her breakfast," my son said innocently.

"And Seb and Bea are friends." Despite my hangover, I felt rather pleased with myself for that response right up to the point where my daughter threw in her contribution.

"Seb and Bea are special friends, though." She giggled. "They're boyfriend and girlfriend and they kiss." She full on belly laughed now and I couldn't help but join in with her.

"Daddy kissed Flora in the car and then Mummy came home," said Craig.

The room fell silent until Sophie's laughter sounded around us.

"Yes, Daddy did kiss Flora, didn't he, and I did come home. But that must mean that Daddy wants Flora to be his girlfriend."

I didn't know what to say or do but as I watched my children return their attention to the TV and my brother beginning to gather his belongings, I realised I didn't have to do or say anything.

"You might want to throw yourself in the shower before you consider breakfast or kissing." Sophie seemed in good spirits considering the last few months but especially the last twenty-four hours.

Last night she had been incredibly upset during the movie and it was fortunate that Nico had been there to stay with the children so I could take Sophie away for a while and allow her to cry which as distressing as it had been, was possibly more appropriate than her earlier indifferent persona.

Sophie was right though, if I was going to cook lunch for Flora, my girlfriend . . . how weird did that sound? But if I was, then I needed to get showered and dressed and make myself presentable before laying all of my cards on the table including making me and my tesoro mio official.

Half an hour later I was washed, shaved and dressed and ready to knock on Flora's door. I checked my phone and saw that my message had gone unanswered, read, but unanswered. I knocked on the door, unsure what reception was waiting for me if she'd read my message and made no reply.

No answer. I knocked again, and again, and again, but still nothing. What the hell was going on. Reaching for the door handle, I hesitated .. . but I needed to know what was going on. Opening the door I was greeted with, well, nothing. Silence. No sign of Flora's presence. Moving through the flat I noticed things looked strange, tidy, not that the place was ever untidy, but it looked bare somehow.

"Shit!" I rushed through the place, the bathroom, the bedroom, everything was gone. She'd left, but why? We'd been on good terms last night. She had encouraged me to spend the evening with Sophie and the children. She'd message to let me know she was home after dropping Maddie off at the station. Is that what this was about, that she missed

Maddie? That made the most sense. She had gone home to her sister. That stung to imagine her thinking of anywhere other than here, with me being home.

I needed to go after her and talk to her, make her see that this is where she belonged, here, with me. If she needed to be closer to Maddie, she could move in too for all I cared. As I passed the kitchen again, something caught my eye, a note resting against a cup, a note with my name on it and her keys. A shudder chilled me as I picked it up, but that was nothing compared to the ice that replaced the blood in my veins as I read the contents of it.

Maurizio,

I love you, but I love myself too much to be an option rather than a choice.

Good luck with your future, one with your family.

You'll never know how sorry I am to have been a dream that could never be.

Flora x

"Fuck!" She'd left me.

Rereading the note, I recognised her words. She must have come downstairs and overheard me speaking to Nico. Overheard and completely misunderstood. I needed to find her and explain what she'd heard, or should that be not heard, and that she was never an option but always a choice. My only choice.

Running back through the house, I found Sophie and told her that Flora had misunderstood something and had left, and that I was going to bring her home.

Chapter 52

Flora

After packing up my belongings, I quickly wrote a note, a very brief note that would get the message across. I didn't need to write chapter and verse containing insults, vitriol or declarations of hurt and pain. No, short and to the point with a reference to his own words would do just fine.

I folded the piece of paper in half, added Maurizio's name and propped it against a cup. Placing my keys next to it, I took a last look around the place that had been my home these last few months and left with my belongings packed in a suitcase and a backpack.

Daylight peeked through the crack in the curtains. God, my head hurt and my eyes were so sore they barely opened.

"Good morning, sunshine." Ash pulled the curtains back and turned to me. "Fuck, you look like shit."

"I feel worse than I look," I replied, my voice breaking, moving to a sitting position in the bed."

"You haven't seen yourself."

"No, but I know how much hurt I feel." I sobbed, acknowledging the pain slicing through me.

"Oh, darling." He joined me on the bed and pulled me in for a tight hug. "Sweetheart, perhaps you should talk to him."

"No! I heard enough of what he had to say. I just need a few days to get my shit together and to stop crying and then I'll go home . . . to Maddie."

"Okay, if that's what you want." Ash pulled me closer. "Maybe you should give Maddie a call and let her know."

I laughed, a single, cold laugh. "I can't speak to her, she'll know something's wrong and then she will be on the next train down here to cut Maurizio's balls off."

"If what you think he said is true, perhaps he needs his balls cutting off." Ash sniggered. I didn't.

"I don't *think* I heard anything. I did hear. Every word he said with my own ears. There was no misunderstanding; he loves Sophie and sees his future with her and the children." The devastation of that reality, the pain I'd felt when I first heard those words only intensified now. Curling up tight with my legs in my chest while my arms wrapped around them, I pulled them close enough so that I could drop my head to my knees, burying my face.

Ash still held me, rocking me, but nothing soothed this pain, and I feared it never would.

"Why does it hurt so much?" I asked between gasps and cries, unsure if I wanted or needed a response but I got one.

"Because you loved so much."

Time passed by and every time I thought my tears had passed, more followed until I didn't think I could cry anymore. My bones ached and my insides throbbed in real physical pain, and my heart was being torn in two. The last time I had felt pain like this had been after my parents had died, the physical pain of grief and loss, and while Maurizio hadn't died, a part of me and the future I thought we might have had did.

Like a child, I cried myself to sleep and when I woke alone I risked looking in the mirror. I looked as though I had been in a fight or mugged, and still I felt worse than I looked. I considered climbing back into bed, curling into the foetal position and crying until there really were no more tears to cry, or perhaps until the pain subsided or at least until I became numb.

That's what I needed, to feel nothing, and maybe to forget for a little while and I knew just how to achieve that.

Ash had been dubious about my plan, but being the good friend he was, or at least the concerned friend, he went along with it.

We had mixed our own cocktails using whatever Ash had available and while they weren't cocktail bar worthy, they were strong and were beginning to kick in, giving me a buzz. It wasn't the usual drunk, happy buzz, but a hazy indifferent buzz, and in that moment, that was a win.

I found a couple of bottles of sour shot stuff and some Tequila in the cupboard and in the absence of shot glasses, I lined up some egg cups and ramakin dishes that I filled. Grabbing the salt and a lime that had seen better days, I added the finishing touches. Ash and I had downed them all, ten, maybe twelve shots and that is when my feeling of indifference shifted to angry. Unsure exactly what I was saying, I ranted, swore, and made awful threats against anyone and everyone who had ever hurt me which led me to talk about my parents. I knew I was at risk of becoming out of control and needed a distraction.

With my phone synched to Ash's smart speaker, I set about devising a playlist. "Music!" I squealed as the first bars of Shania Twain's *Man! I Feel Like A Woman!* rang out. "I am a strong independent woman and I don't need a man."

"Preach it, sister!" Ash called as he pulled me up to dance as I sang loudly.

My independent woman soundtrack only lasted for Kelly Clarkson, Pink! Chaka Khan and the classic break-up song of *I Will Survive* by Gloria Gaynor. Then with Ash looking down at the phone in my hand, I paused at Adele's *Water Under the Bridge*, he delivered a single, "No, no Adele, and no Lewis Capaldi, both musical geniuses who tear your heartstrings out, so no, not tonight!"

"It had to have meant something, right? I had to have meant something to him, didn't I? But how could he have really loved me only to do this, to love and want Sophie?" The tears were back, as were Ash's arms around me, unlike the feeling of indifference and numbness I was hoping for.

The glass in my hand that was still half full suddenly disappeared. "No more alcohol, let me make coffee or something, but yes, you had to have meant something to him."

Huddled in the armchair nearest the speaker, I continued to play my sad songs and cry. Even when Ash returned with coffee, the songs kept coming; *Unbreak My Heart* by Toni Braxton, *I Will Always Love You* by Whitney Houston, *Chasing Cars* by Snow Patrol, until I came full circle to defiance and outrage as the effects of the drink wore off ever so slightly to the sound of *Flowers* by Miley Cyrus pointing out all the things I could do for myself, but the truth was, I didn't want to.

In an attempt to stem the tears threatening to overflow, I continued on my one-woman concert as I moved from angry to regretful, me and Celine Dion warning Maurizio to think twice before committing to the words he'd said and then back to sad I went with Abba of all people. How could they, the kings and queens of the pop anthem and sure fire dancefloor fillers since 1974 be the ones to make me sob? Lyrics I'd sung as a little girl as my mum had been something of a fan and now, although the words hadn't changed, my emotions and interpretation of them had. Barely able to see the space in front of me I now sat in silence as words of a lonely bed, wishing to be somewhere else, of being lonely and waiting for a call. It was me. I was the one of us they sang of, and if I didn't wish I had never left, but I'd had to, he hadn't left any choice, had he?

It was now that I noticed Ash had disappeared and in that moment, I needed him to be my wing man, so I went to find him, and yet again, not twenty-four hours since I'd last been betrayed, I heard him talking on the phone, about me. He was explaining that I was broken hearted and very drunk, that he didn't know what to do or how best to comfort me, and that although I hadn't planned on returning home until I was able to speak without crying, Ash was worried about me so had turned to the only person he knew that might be able to help, Maddie.

I was seething. He had suggested calling Carrie and Bea when I'd first arrived and again this morning, but as much as they were my friends, Bea had a conflict of interest and I knew Carrie would be supportive but possibly insist on thrashing this out with Maurizio, citing the similarities in her relationship with Gabe to ours and holding them up as a shiny beacon of hope. I couldn't do that. I couldn't see his handsome face, or hear his voice, inhale his glorious aroma. That would break me in two, to know that he and all of the things I loved about him belonged to someone else, always had. Plus, my friends were both heavily pregnant and didn't need the added stress of me. Also, I hadn't wanted any drama, and now, the one thing guaranteed to be brought to the party with Maddie on the war path which she would be was drama. Shit!

My anger was being redirected from Ash for telling my sister to Maurizio, Sophie, but most of all, to myself. I decided that before Maddie arrived, and she would be arriving, I was going to deal with The Walkers myself and not allow Maddie to fight my battles. All thoughts of being broken at the sight and sound of Maurizio were gone and I was retreating from my eavesdropping position, heading for the backdoor and leaving to the sounds of Lewis Capaldi's *Forget Me* behind. I was heading back to the house I had ran from the night before, but why, perhaps Lewis was right? I was still holding on.

Chapter 53

Maurizio

The drive to find Flora felt longer than it was and when I eventually pulled up outside the house, I felt sick. What if she wouldn't listen to me? Believe me? See me? I was going to have to get past Maddie first and she had already threatened me and my balls and I didn't doubt her threat was anything but empty.

With a deep breath, I walked down the path and knocked of the door. The sound of voices from the other side were muffled but there were at least two voices making me optimistic that Flora was here still.

I had imagined a dozen or more scenarios of knocking on this door on the drive up here, but not one of them had involved the door opening to reveal my brother filling the space.

"Nico." That is all I had.

My brother looked less surprised at my presence than I was at his.

Neither of us was prepared for Maddie's reaction to me. She was like a blur as she hurled down the hallway at me. "You bastard. You fucking bastard. She loves you and you told her you loved her so what the fuck have you done to hurt her?"

Although I didn't understand why my brother was here, I was glad he was when he scooped Maddie up and prevented her from kicking, punching, or possibly cutting my balls off because her rage suggested her being armed wasn't necessarily an impossibility.

"Put me the fuck down!" She screamed at Nico now.

He did, but quickly turned so that he blocked her path to me and gently rested his hands on her shoulders. "Calm down, yeah. I get that you're pissed, but you have no clue what has happened, oh, and all this rage and anger is no good for you or the baby."

"What the fuck? Have you knocked her up?"

My brother released Maddie but as he spun to face me, I was more concerned about his wrath than hers.

"No, but you speak that way about her pregnancy again and I will be knocking you out, little brother."

"Okay, okay. Maddie, sorry, and er, congratulations."

She sneered in response.

"Why are you here?" I asked my brother.

"Is that really what you want to ask right now?" Maddie asked, coming to stand next to my brother.

I took a moment to see how cosy and right they looked together.

"No, sorry. I need to speak to Flora."

She laughed and shook her head.

"She misunderstood and I need to make her see that, that I love her more than anything."

Again Maddie shook her head.

"Flora!" I shouted from the doorstep, over and over again. "I need to speak to you, explain, I love you, tesoro mio."

Maddie rolled her eyes and briefly moved back into the house, returning with her bag and coat before looking at Nico. "Tell him she's not here."

"She really isn't here. We're going to her now."

"What do you mean?"

"Look, before anyone tells you anything about my sister, how about you tell me what happened."

My head was spinning. I had no clue where Flora was or if she was safe and for all I knew I might have missed my opportunity to explain everything if she hadn't returned here. Part of me wanted to tell Maddie that she had no right to bark orders at me and make demands, but as far as she was concerned, I was the arsehole who had hurt her sister, so for now, I would play by her rules.

"She overheard me talking to Nico. She misunderstood when I said I loved Sophie and saw my future with her." I should have prefaced that statement in some way because she only flew at me again and this time hit me around the head with her handbag. "What the fuck do you keep in there?" I rubbed my head that I had to check wasn't bleeding.

"That is nothing compared to what I will do." She came back for a second attack but again, Nico intercepted.

"Maurizio, are you saying when you said about loving Sophie and all that shit, that she thought you meant it?"

"Seems so."

I fished her note from my pocket and offered it to Nico.

"Shit, she didn't wait to hear you add the context of suggesting that is what I wanted to hear and that nothing was further from the truth because she was everything?"

"Again, seems so."

"Fuck!"

"Quite."

"Right, you need to explain to her and make her see sense. She's devastated, and very drunk it seems."

"Nico!" Maddie screeched. "Don't tell him!"

"Maddie, I will explain on the way, but we need to go to her."

I expected Nico to be attacked, but no, stubborn and bolshy, and apparently pregnant Maddie was a little tamer with my brother. Who knew? Clearly not me!

"Maurizio, she's at Ash's place–"

Maddie's phone interrupted and as she answered it, it became clear that something was wrong. "Bollocks! Where has she gone? I am going to kill her when I get my hands on her, the stupid cow. Okay, we're on the way."

Maddie turned to us and looked worried.

"While Ash was on the phone, Flora has done a runner. She didn't tell him she was leaving so he has no clue where she is, oh, and she hasn't taken anything with her, no purse, phone or even a coat, and to top it all, she was drunk."

"She and I will be having words," I muttered, more to myself than anyone else.

"You'll need to get behind me in that queue," Maddie said, but at least I wasn't the only recipient of her anger. "Ash's is the best starting point I guess."

"Agreed."

"Maddie will come with me, and we'll see you there," Nico said, already leading Maddie down the path.

The journey back was quicker in terms of speed but the knots in my stomach made it even more uncomfortable than the journey to Maddie's. At least I was almost there, about half an hour, and that is when the rain started coming down.

"Fuck!" I needed to find her. "Call Nico," I told my phone. "Any news from Ash?"

Maddie answered, "Nothing new. She's still AWOL."

"I'm going to look for her."

Silence.

"Maddie, it's raining and looking at the clouds, this could be a storm rolling in. She can't be out there alone."

I'd never told anyone about the things Flora had shared with me about her parent's death and her fear of storms, but assumed Maddie would know.

"Maybe getting wet will teach her to go out without her phone, or money or her coat," Nico said.

Maddie and I responded immediately, and in sync. "Shut up, Nico."

"Okay. Nico explained what Flora heard and what she didn't. You go and find her and we'll go to Ash's, but let me know if you find her."

"I will, and if she returns . . ."

"Of course."

Not for the first time, in what was developing into a horrendous storm, I was driving aimlessly looking for Flora, to rescue her and take her home. This time I wouldn't be letting her go, ever.

Chapter 54

Flora

Once the cool air hit me, I realised how drunk I was so had taken the decision not to storm round to casa Walker slurring and making a spectacle of myself and God forbid, scaring the children. Instead, I walked to the park with the intention of grabbing a coffee, but I hadn't got any means of payment with me.

"Bollocks," I hissed as I got to the café.

"Don't think they're on the menu."

I turned to find Gabe, with Charlotte, who eyed me suspiciously.

"I'd ask if you're okay, but you're clearly not, Flora. I am not my wife so have no desire to fix other people's problems in any way that isn't professional, but you seem to have been partying hard this afternoon and you're without cash, so let me buy you a coffee."

I prepared to protest but he continued.

"My wife will have plenty to say if she discovers I didn't help you, so, please, take a seat and let me get coffee. Charlotte, come with Daddy and see if they have the brownies Mummy doesn't let us have before dinner."

The little girl giggled and dutifully followed her father who apparently didn't trust me to be alone with his daughter. Preparing to be offended, I looked into the café and caught sight of myself in the window.

"Shit! No wonder he's taken the kid with him." I looked awful, almost like the victim of an accident with my still red, blotchy and swollen face, but worse than that was the clearly drunk, glazed eyes. I looked like I should live on a park bench or under a bridge. I smiled sadly for a second as I thought of the troll that lived under the bridge in The Three Billy Goats Gruff, one of Craig's favourite stories. I'd miss the children as much as Maurizio, just in a very different way. All of them had got under my skin and made their way into my heart in the months I'd lived with them and taken care of them.

"There we go." Gabe placed a large cup in front of me. "I got you a double shot of espresso in there."

"Thank you."

"You smell funny." Charlotte didn't try dressing things up and my drunken state was no exception.

Gabe made no effort to correct or chasten her. He placed some brownies on the table. "Tuck in. Brownies are always the answer to problems. Oh, and I got you these." He threw me a packet of hand wipes and some mints."

"Thank you," I repeated.

"No problem, we've all been there." He paused, his cup raised halfway between the saucer and his lips. "Are you okay as in not hurt . . . I mean someone hasn't hurt you, have they? Not everyone is kind or honest . . ."

"I'm fine, thank you." I remembered hearing the brief details of Carrie having had her drink spiked and someone she had once considered a friend attempting to hurt her.

"Okay."

Charlotte's squeal of excitement drew our attention to the presence of Seb, Bea's boyfriend. He scooped up Charlotte and covered her giggling face in kisses before taking the seat opposite Gabe. It was then that he looked at me and seemed to recoil in horror.

"You okay? Do you need a hair of the dog?"

Gabe cussed at him under his breath. "No, she doesn't. We are having coffee and brownies and then Flora is going home, probably for a nap, right?"

I nodded. He didn't need to know that I was going *home* to say my piece and then I was leaving for good.

"What brings you here?" I asked Gabe hoping to move all attention from the state I was in.

He laughed. "What happens in the café stays in the café, right?"

I nodded.

"My wife is in her nesting stage of pregnancy, so I decided it was safer for us both to leave the house and come here."

"Snap!" Seb announced, leaning across and taking a bite of Gabe's brownie before then sipping the coffee from his cup. Neither man acknowledged it while Charlotte giggled at her uncle.

"You sound like wise men," I told them both.

"And your man, Mo, is he not a wise man?" Gabe asked.

I shook my head. "No, he's not."

"Ah. I am not in the habit of offering advice, again, I am not my wife, but whatever has happened between you, he is totally smitten."

I scoffed. Gabe didn't know what he was talking about but he had been nothing but kind to me so I let it slide.

"Look, it's no secret that me and the guy aren't exactly BFFs but Gabe is right. We met him in a bar months ago and he is well into you, so if he has . . ." He covered Charlotte's ears. ". . . been a dick, you might want to hear him out." He uncovered the little girl's ears. "I know you'll find this hard to believe, but even I have made mistakes."

Gabe laughed and I joined in with his laughter. Seb ignored us both.

"But Bea allowed me an opportunity to earn back her trust, so, I dunno, just don't be rash."

"Thank you, both." I smiled at Charlotte who was looking up at me as I got to my feet. "All of you, thank you."

Armed with the wipes and the mints, I headed to the bathroom before going to see Maurizio. I didn't know if I would take their advice, but I absolutely had to talk to him, even if it was to get things off my mind.

When I arrived at the house, I still looked like shit, but I wasn't as drunk, the rain and wind blowing around me had gone some way to tame my hair a little, but it had also left me rather wet and the mints, of which I'd eaten about half, had freshened my breath.

Maurizio's car was absent from its position between Sophie's and mine, which was no longer mine. Seb's and Gabe's words ran around my head and I was glad to have met them because now I was calm and had only one intention. To say my piece.

Knocking on the door, I waited. Sophie pulled it open and smiled at me, concern etched across her face. "Flora, are you okay?" She didn't wait for a response. "You're wet through, let's get you in and dry before this storm hits." She was heading back into the house and I followed. "There's a yellow warning for rain and wind later," she told me, the kettle already being put on.

I watched her and could see her as the woman of the house here, but why wouldn't she be? This had been, was her marital home? How much of the décor here had been her choice?

"Let me grab you a towel and some spare clothes." She scurried off and the sound of a gentle snore alerted me to the sleeping children, cuddled together on the sofa. The image made me smile.

"They went down about ten minutes ago so we won't be disturbed."

"Sophie," I began, but I had no clue where I was taking this.

"There you go, get dry and dressed while I make the tea."

Taking the items she'd gathered for me, I dried my hair and removed my outer clothes, replacing them with a pair of leggings and baggy T-shirt she offered me. Hers. She was taller and far slighter than I was, but the outfit did the job.

"Tea." She offered me a steaming mug and we sat opposite each other at the table that just a few days before had seen her walking in on me being in Maurizio's lap.

"Sophie, why are you being so kind? I left. I was seeing your husband, sleeping with him."

She frowned. "I know. Oh, and he is as good as my ex-husband. The first part of the divorce came today."

My mouth dropped open and I was stunned into silence.

"The benefit of two legal minds is that we get this shit done on a daily basis so legal things aren't problematic."

"Maurizio loves you."

She was the one speechless now, at least for a few seconds. "Not like he loves you."

"I heard him tell Nico."

"You didn't. You heard him venting to Nico, but you need to speak to Mo about all of this."

"I don't understand. You left and didn't see the children, then you saw them infrequently."

She looked guilty.

"I'm not judging you."

"You should be and I am judging me."

"But Maurizio welcomed you back here and then he was speaking of divorce but he refused to explain . . . I don't understand."

"Okay. The stuff you think you heard Mo say, I've already said, you need to speak to him, but me coming back and why he wouldn't explain, well, that I can tell you."

She took a mouthful of her tea and then began to speak.

I sat, mesmerised at her strength and poise as she retold me the events of the months before she returned and the time since then, including her visit to the hospital with Maurizio and her fears for not being around for her children.

"I am so sorry, Sophie."

She nodded and as she rubbed the back of my hand I could have sworn she was comforting me.

"It's shit, but I will know more once I have seen the doctors next week. Mo was going to tell you when he cooked your breakfast. I asked him not to until I had been to the hospital. He told the children this morning about you two."

"He did?" I was stunned and already regretting not being an adult and speaking to him, giving him an opportunity to explain.

Sophie laughed. "Well, he tried to, but the children somehow managed to tie him up in knots about the type of friends who make breakfast for each other, like boyfriend and girlfriend people."

"No!" I threw my hand over my mouth in horror.

"It gets better, Craig told us all that you are his Daddy's girlfriend because he saw you kissing, the day I came back."

I dropped my head to the table and buried my face. A loud crack of thunder made me jump back into a sitting position, causing Sophie to look at me with concern.

"You okay?"

I nodded. "I don't do well with storms." I didn't say any more and she didn't ask, but stroked my hand again. "Are you sure there's nothing between you and Maurizio . . . I know what I heard."

"I know what you think you heard, but there was far more you didn't hear, and me and Mo? Old news, co-parents, friends, no more."

"Did you love him?"

"I'd offer you a glass of wine to do this discussion, but I'm living clean and I think you might not want to partake again so soon."

"That obvious?"

"Oh, yes."

"So, did you love him?"

"Yes. He was my best friend and we had an amazing life together. I am glad the children came along but it was so hard for me, but Mo and I worked well together, although he very much slotted into traditional roles far easier than I did and we hired Bea. When I was seventeen, I lost my virginity on a girl's holiday and it was less than great, however, the next night, my friends hooked up with guys again and I didn't. I chatted with a girl working the bar and I went home with her, and she blew my mind, and everything else. I never saw her again, went home and went off to uni, met Mo and things were good, but there was always something missing for me. I am sure you know I had an affair and ended my marriage because of it?"

I nodded.

"She confirmed that I was gay. I didn't go about ending things in the right way and I hurt Mo, and I will always regret that. I was a mess, confused doesn't even come close, and the children should never have been treated by me the way they were, but I thought they were better off with Mo and Bea, and you. I think I believed that if I was gay and had stuck to my guns they would never have been my children and that I didn't deserve them, but that is not an excuse. You, though, you love him as he should be loved and I have never seen him as happy as he is with you."

"I do love him."

"He loved me and believed he was in love, perhaps he was in some way, however I was what he thought he should want. Marrying me was expected, the house, the children, all expectations, but you, you are what he needs like he needs his next breath. Mo was never short of female attention. I mean, he is the whole package, and I am not saying he didn't enjoy that, but he and I, we both thought we could be a couple for all time. I don't know if you believe in soulmates or not, you are it for Mo. You are the one in almost eight billion for him."

"Eight billion?"

"Yeah, that's the world population give or take a few hundred million, and I think he's yours. Everything between you both is felt from your core, your very being, and now I have said my piece, so, what you do next is up to you, but I would suggest you start by listening to Mo."

"Where is he? I need to speak to him."

"Yes, you do, but before you do, I need to ask you something?"

"Of course." Nothing could have prepared me for what she said next. Another loud clap of thundered seemingly shook the house causing me to jump erratically as hale began to bounce off the windows. I turned back to Sophie, she deserved my full attention.

"I have cancer, I know that. What I don't know is the extent of it, and that is my own fault, but my motivation for fighting this will be my children." Her voice wobbled. "Fighting might not be enough ultimately, and they will of course have their father and family. Nonna will go into loving them overdrive, which I know is hard to imagine being any more than what she already does."

I laughed. "She is very intense. I might need to learn Italian because when she talks about me to Maurizio, she does so in Italian."

Sophie shook her head. "She would love that. So, if the cancer wins our fight, my children will be safe and taken care of physically, financially and emotionally, but the one thing they will never have is a mother's love."

I wanted to halt the flow of her words, from continuing with the heartbreaking scenario of two motherless children, heartbroken from grief, but I couldn't because tears were already silently running down my face and poor Sophie was beginning to gulp as she sobbed, but continued, needing to get these words out.

"I know you and Maurizio will sort this out and probably have children together but I need to know that my children will always have a mother's love and if it can't be me, I want it to be you. Flora, will you please take care of my children and be their mother if there comes a point where I cannot?"

We were both sobbing, trying to stem the noise so as to not wake the children because with all they were going to have to deal with, the last thing they needed was to find their mother and their nanny hysterical at the table. I pulled out a chair to sit next to Sophie as we huddled together. Although the storm was still howling and blowing, the rain interspersed with hale and less frequent bouts of thunder, hopefully the storm was subsiding.

"You're going to be fine. You can fight this." I needed her to be okay, for the children, they needed that.

"I want to believe that, and I will fight it with all I have, but nobody knows the outcome, and knowing that I don't have to worry about my beautiful babies being the children in school with no mummy, the ones who have nobody to make a mother's day card for, nobody to help guide them through life from a mother's perspective will allow me to focus on fighting and beating this cancer."

"Of course," I stammered. "Maurizio and I have never even discussed the possibility of either of us having children, but I swear Craig and Rosie will never not have someone who loves them as a mother would. Together we will help you fight and get through this."

Her words of gratitude were drowned out by the sound of Nico's voice calling Sophie's name. He appeared in the doorway of the room looking ashen and wet through but more than that he looked scared.

The sight of Maddie appearing behind him confused me, although I had been expecting her after the phone call from Ash I had forgotten about.

"What the fuck do you think you are playing at?" Maddie was already striding towards me, leaving me unsure as to whether she was going to hit me or hug me. She did the latter and soaked me through with her wet clothes. "I can't believe you ran away without money, your phone or your coat, and drunk."

Nico stepped closer. "I need everyone to stay calm but Maurizio was looking for you Flora, but with the rain and the wet roads, he's been involved in a car crash."

That numb feeling I'd been searching for before, that feeling hit me right now. I listened as he told me that we needed to get to the hospital, that Carrie had phoned Ash to say Gabe had seen me in the park. He didn't know how Maurizio was, just that he had been taken to hospital in an ambulance.

Arriving at the hospital with Nico and Sophie felt like a dream. Maddie had agreed to stay with the children. Sophie offered words of encouragement and support to me, but I wasn't really listening as I felt oddly detached from it all. Nico seemed angry with me and said very little. I couldn't really blame him. If I hadn't acted so impetuously and perhaps childishly, none of this would have happened. Maurizio wouldn't have been out and looking for me in a storm. That thought did cause a few tears to fall, rather unexpectedly. Was I going to lose someone else I loved in another storm?

Nico pulled into the car park and we ran across to the emergency department. We stood at the desk together as Nico gave his brother's name and we waited for some kind of information.

"He's still with the doctor's, that's all I can tell you at the moment. A doctor will be out to speak to you when they can, but we are busy." She gestured to all of the people behind us, filling every space in the waiting area.

Together we filed away and found a space with one free chair and a vacant wall next to it. Both Nico and I insisted Sophie take the seat and we each slid down the wall and sat on the floor.

"I'm sorry," I told Nico.

He looked confused.

"You're angry with me, you blame me for what's happened."

"I don't blame you, but yeah, your actions have pissed me off, not least because Maurizio and Maddie were out of their minds with worry, and the last thing your sister needs is more worry. It was immature and irresponsible."

"Sorry," I repeated.

"Yeah, well, you already have Maddie's anger so you don't need mine."

"We never did discuss the two of you, did we?"

"Nope, and we're not about to do it now."

"Is she okay?" At least focusing on Maddie prevented me from thinking about the man I loved behind doors with doctors.

"She will be."

"Should we call Carmella?"

Both Nico and Sophie let out a loud *no*, drawing the attention of others nearby.

"Mama does not need to be here and more than that, we do not need her here. I will call her when we know something."

Getting to my feet, I began to pace, my earlier calm dissipating with every passing second. As I completed a length of the waiting room, I turned and looked at the clock. Minutes turned slowly and with every turn my fears rose and my tears began to fall. Sophie and Nico continued to watch me but allowed me to continue for a while longer. As I turned and the clock showed I had been doing this for a solid twenty minutes, I found Nico blocking my way.

"Flora." He placed his hands on my shoulders. "Stop."

It was at that point I realised my face was wet with tears and as Nico pulled me into his embrace the tears came thick and fast, as did my noisy sobs.

"You were right, I am irresponsible, this is all my fault. What if he dies? What will I do?" I turned and saw Sophie's face through the haze of my tears and my hysteria only increased. "What about the children, and you?" Flailing in Nico's hold, I didn't know whether to fight him or flee, but a small voice in my head reminded me that fleeing is what had got us here in the first place. The children didn't deserve this, any of it, and now, because of me, they might lose their father, their mother's life was already at risk due to her cancer. I was incoherent as I imagined the pain Rosie and Craig would be subjected to as orphans, the pain I knew only too well, but at least I had been older, almost a young adult. They were still babies. What would this mean for them and what would it do to the adults they were yet to become? I knew that the adult I was had been adversely affected by the sad events and loss in my childhood. What of my own babies, the ones I hadn't had and never would now. Until Sophie had mentioned children earlier, I hadn't even considered Maurizio and I having children.

My head was banging, possibly the effects of the copious amount of alcohol in my system kicking in, but the stress, worry and crying weren't helping either. I tried to stop crying but I couldn't. The harder I tried, the worse the crying became and I was shaking uncontrollably. My breaths became laboured and I was fighting for every one of them. Shit! I was having a panic attack. I felt myself being lowered to a seat and then the ground as distant voices echoed around me. My vision was hazy and I realised I was probably too far gone to pull this back from going into free fall. Maddie and Maurizio were the only ones who had ever been successful in supporting me in preventing the spiralling, and neither of them were here, well, one was but I had no idea if he was dead or alive.

His voice came to me, words of comfort I couldn't quite make out. This was bad if I was imagining him here, hearing his voice.

"I've got you," he said. "Flora, listen to me, I'm going to stay right here with you, just let me hold you, okay?"

I felt the warmth and aroma that was him as I was rocked from side to side. I was somehow cushioned and wrapped tight.

Time slowed and all thoughts began to leave my mind, my breathing slowed and I entered that place of calm, the one you find just before consciousness finds sleep.

"That's better. Tesoro mio just needed a hug."

Voices began to filter through. Nico, Sophie, some I didn't know, asking if was okay and then one that was unmistakable.

"Maurizio."

"Flora, I am going to let go and then we'll get you up, okay?"

I opened my eyes, the tiniest of cracks and there he was. Was this real? His presence and warmth left me and then hands were helping me to stand, but it wasn't Maurizio in front of me, but Nico. "No," I cried. "Maurizio." Had this been a dream, an illusion? Had I imagined him being there and saying those words to me? My legs threatened to give way again.

"Hey, I'm here."

He was there in front of me, one hand reaching forward to stroke my cheek. Then I took in all of him; his face was bruised, a variety of shades of blue covered his forehead and face, a bandage was secured around his head and his clothes carried blood stains. My gaze dropped to see one arm in a cast and a sling holding it at an angle across his body while his good arm was dropping so he could take my hand in his. Looking down at our hands clasped together, me holding onto him for dear life, I saw his foot in one of those boots.

"You're here."

"Of course I am. Where else would I be if not with you."

I cried again. Happier tears this time.

"Let's get you checked out," he told me. "Then we will go home and you and I need a discussion."

"By discussion you mean to tell me off for running away, don't you?"

"I mean discussion, and then I will tell you off for running away because I have never been so scared in my life as when I couldn't find you and nobody could reach you or tell me you were safe. Then, we, you and I, will do this thing properly."

"Thing?"

"Yes, thing. You and me, us, the future."

A nurse stepped forward. "It looks as though you've had a panic attack, but let's get you checked over and we can get you on your way."

Epilogue

Maurizio

Coming downstairs, I found Nico and Maddie laughing together while Sophie was making drinks in the kitchen. Flora was tidying toys away. The children sat at the table with snacks, chatting to each other and the adults around them.

"You all set for the new woman in your life?" Nico asked.

"I am indeed. She is everything you could ever want on four wheels."

Maddie frowned. "I don't get the obsession you boys have with machines. It's a car that will get you from A to B."

Nico shrugged.

I still hadn't figured the dynamics of their friendship. Maddie was pregnant and had planned on telling the father, but before she got to the bit about the baby, the guy had dumped her, totally cut her loose. He'd told her she had only ever been a bit of fun, and he had the chance of some promotion at work. As far as I knew, he'd moved away with his wife, and as it turned out, the three children he already had with her. Maddie had chosen not to tell him and was planning on bringing the baby up alone. She had relocated here and lived in a small house in the village. Nico, her *friend,* was a regular visitor, as was my mother who loved the idea of another *bambino.* My mother was actually at one with the world. She had been amazing in her support of the children and Sophie. She had voiced concerns about our living arrangements and the pressure that might put on my relationship with Flora, but it was, and always had been short term.

"Flora, are you sure you don't want to come and collect her with me?"

She rolled her eyes as she always did when I called my new car a 'her' or 'she'. "I will if you want me to, but I am going to see Bea and Carrie and the babies in a while."

Her face lit up at the mention of her friends and their babies.

"Ash came back off holiday yesterday so I am picking him up on the way."

"You blowing me off for friends and babies?"

"No, well, maybe just the babies." Her gentle flush was nothing other than endearing as was her honesty. Between Bea, Carrie and now Maddie, my girlfriend was becoming broody. "Take Nico with you and I will get ready to go out while you go and I can see the other woman in your life when you get home."

"Other woman! I'd have thought having your ex-wife and your current squeeze under one roof was quite enough." Nico chuckled and while Sophie and Flora joined in with his laughter, Maddie didn't. Perhaps the other woman reference was still a bit raw for her.

I decided now was the perfect time to leave and as my brother leapt to his feet, he seemed to have done the same.

"Is she as good as you'd hoped? All you wanted and more?" Flora was already rushing across the front of the house towards me while Nico headed for the house. "She is a beauty."

Flora laughed as I surveyed my new car. My last car had been a write off. The tree landing on it as I skidded down the country lane had seen to that. Somebody had been watching over me that day, a guardian angel because I should never have made it out of there alive, but I had. With a slight concussion, a significant cut to my head, a broken arm, muscle damage to my leg and endless bruises and abrasions, I had walked away but the car had paid the price, and I was absolutely okay with that.

"She is. I have an eye for beautiful things."

I pulled her close and trapped her between me and the car that was parked next to hers. I pressed into her, my desire and need for her obvious. My mouth dropped to her ear that I licked and gently nipped before kissing a path down her jaw and along her neck to the place I knew drove her wild. Her breathing became loud and gaspy as I moved lower, my lips moving across her collar bone while my hand that had been cupping her behind began to gather the fabric of her dress until I could manoeuvre my hand into her underwear.

"Shit! You're wet," I groaned as she spread her legs slightly to allow me better access. I didn't need telling twice. Sliding two fingers inside her, I thrusted gently and smiled down at her dazed expression when her body began to contract around my fingers.

"Maurizio."

I slid my fingers along her length and found her clit. Stroking it, I swear she was ready to come already judging by how deeply her nails dug into my shoulders.

The sound of activity from the house behind us, brought her out of her arousal fuelled daze.

"Tell me to stop," I implored her because I didn't want to be discovered in this position but was incapable of stopping where this woman was concerned, that had always been the case.

"Stop," she whispered, but her disappointment was obvious.

"We could take it for a spin, maybe find somewhere secluded and christen it."

She pulled away, her clothing dropping down as she moved, laughing as she did so. "Maybe you ought to park her in the garage . . . no interruptions, and no telling you to stop."

THE END

Have you read Swipe Right For A Knight – A Catfish/Royal Romance?
Turn the page for more...

SWIPE RIGHT FOR A KNIGHT

Have you read Swipe For A Knight?
If you like Royal romance with a catfish storyline, read on...
Live ebook Link: https://books2read.com/b/bao2zv

Gazing down at the beautiful brown eyes staring up at me, I had no option but to smile. That face, that little bundle of squishy goodness never failed to make me smile and even when miserable, I immediately became happy in her presence. Not that I'd known much misery of late.

"You are going to change the world, my darling."

Lorena's eyes sparkled as she gurgled in response. At twelve weeks old, she had me firmly wrapped around her little finger and I had never known instantaneous love until I had set eyes on her.

"You are." I truly believed this child, my niece, had been sent to make her mark on the world. "Someday, you, and you alone will make a change that benefits the world. Maybe it will merely be your presence." She burped, making me laugh. "Okay. I might be romanticising slightly. I'm a born romantic."

She let out a small cry.

"Hey, I've only come to realise that of late myself, so trust me, nobody is more shocked by that than me."

Fidgeting in the crib, she seemed to shake her head.

"Oh, you don't believe me? Well, it had been my plan to come in here and tell you a story and see if that would get you to catch forty winks while the world here goes a little ga-ga but have it your way. Now, you get the story of me. She who swiped right for a knight."

<u>Two Years Before</u>

When we'd first met . . . I laughed at that. Scoffed. We hadn't met, not unless you count online. That first meet was an accidental swipe to the right. Who knew a thumb could land you in so much trouble? Certainly not me.

Anyway, I digress. I swiped right and so did he. I messaged to apologise because he was not the man for me. He was gorgeous, super accomplished, athletic and I was none of those things. I told him it had been a mistake. An accident. I never expected him to respond. He did.

He sent me a crying emoji and a question mark. I looked down at it and felt a warm feeling inside as I watched three dots buzzing away. He was still writing.

I laughed when his next message came.

<Your swipe to the right being accidental wounds me>

I was unsure if he meant any word of that but sensed it was said with good humour. Another message.

<My right swipe was entirely deliberate>

Staring down, I wondered if I should respond. Three dots flashed then disappeared several times making me wonder what he was saying and most likely deleting again.

Nervously, I did the same, typing and deleting before settling on something simple and with hindsight a little dorky.

<*Thank you*>

His response was a series of laughing emojis. The heated red flush crept up my face as embarrassment set in, but I laughed too.

<I just meant that I didn't think you'd be interested in me>

No delay in a response now.

<Why wouldn't I be? You're beautiful>

I laughed again, a little awkwardly. I was average in terms of looks, and in no way beautiful, and was absolutely okay with that.

A message from my sister, Megan, flashed across the top of my screen.

<On my way with a bottle of wine so decide what takeaway we're having>

I sent her a quick thumbs up and returned to my accidental swipe.

<I have to go, dinner with my sister>

I had no idea why I had shared that information, but I had.

<Have fun>

I sent him a quick thumbs up then locked my phone.

"Megan and I . . ." I looked down at my niece, hanging onto my every word. "Megan, or as you call her, Mummy, were halfway through our first bottle of wine and tucking into pizza when she turned the conversation to my love life or lack thereof."

"Any men on your radar?"

"Nope."

She frowned at me. "Why not? You've been single too long and you are so pretty and sweet and funny, it's a waste."

"I am happy as I am." I wasn't, not really. If I was, I wouldn't be on a dating app, would I?

"I could fix you up. Dean . . ."

Again, I gazed down at the baby. "Daddy, that's Daddy."

I picked up my story, Megan discussing her husband and her being able to fix me up.

"Dean has loads of friends and colleagues. I have loads of colleagues, and I could wheedle out the weirdos and dickheads, so you wouldn't have to."

I laughed. "You're too kind." Although I did see that it was a nice thing she was offering to do for me, but I didn't need her to find me a man. I could and I would find my own. Megan and Dean both worked in media. He was a P.R. consultant and no matter how many times they explained what that meant, I still didn't get it. I had less of a clue what my sister's job involved as a runner or production assistant or something at a TV studio for a daytime magazine show.

"Is that a yes?" She eyed me with cautious optimism.

I was ready to agree when my phone sounded with an alert. From where Megan sat she saw the notification.

"Micah says . . ." She picked it up. "He says, hope you've had fun with your sister."

I stared across at her, her eyes full of questions, but I said nothing.

"Maybe I don't need to fix you up, although you said there wasn't anyone and this is a dating site."

There was no judgement in her tone. She was simply stating the facts. I didn't know why I had joined the dating site. Megan had suggested online dating a couple of times and I had always resisted but then one night about a month ago, whilst lonely, I decided to take a look.

She scowled at me now. "I met the guy who owns this site. Nice guy, but the name, pfff."

I laughed at her horrified sounds and expression.

"Single No More, I mean, why?"

I shrugged. "I guess it conveys a sentiment."

"Yes, and makes you sound like a loser or a dickhead, maybe both."

"So, what was the guy like, the owner?"

"I'll tell you about him and allow you to deflect attention from Micah, but know, that I want details."

I nodded. I knew she'd settle for nothing less.

"His name is Jamie Lewis, tall, dark and handsome, and probably never needed to be single in his life. Curly dark hair, a cheeky grin and a glint in his eye."

"You fancied him."

My sister did nothing to deny my accusation.

"Grace, he was bloody gorgeous and funny, you know that combination is my kryptonite!"

She was so dramatic.

"He was appearing on the show to talk about the dying art of meeting someone in a pub or wherever and dating in person from the get-go. He told me, not on camera, that his sister had met her husband because of the online dating app."

"He had his sister on his dating app?" That seemed all kinds of wrong to me.

"He didn't know she was on, didn't know she was his sister, but he didn't give me the details. Anyway, she went to a date night thing they were throwing and met her husband there, although he said her husband wasn't part of the date night. Now, who and what is Micah?"

I told my sister how Micah and I had swiped and matched and the very brief exchange we'd shared. She'd insisted on looking at his profile.

"He's hot."

"He's athletic and his photos all involve physical exertion." I was not a keep fit or active lifestyle kind of girl.

"I'd be up for some physical exertion with him." She sniggered and wiggled her eyebrows making me laugh too.

"You're married."

"I know, and *you* never will be if you don't mingle a little."

Rolling my eyes, I caught my phone that she threw to me just as another message came through.

"What did you do?" I asked her, knowing she'd tampered in some way. Cautiously looking down at his words on the screen I felt mortification.

<For someone who swiped right in error, it seems odd that you would spend your evening telling your sister how attractive you find me>

I threw a cushion at her, but she wasn't fazed by that at all. "You're welcome. I am going for a wee and then we will finish off that bottle and the pizza."

About Elle M Thomas...

Elle M Thomas was born in the north of England and raised near Birmingham, UK where she still lives with her family. She works in local education and writes in her spare time with dreams of becoming a full-time writer.

Whilst still at school, and with a love of writing slightly risqué tales of love and romance, one of her teachers told her that she could be the next Harrold Robins. Elle didn't act on those words for many years. In February 2017, with her first book completed and a dozen others unfinished, she finally took the plunge and self-published the steamy romance, Disaster-in-Waiting.

Elle describes her books as stories filled with chemistry, sensuality, love and sex that she always wanted to read and her characters as three dimensional and flawed.

FOLLOW ELLE ON
SOCIAL MEDIA...

X - (Twitter)

Facebook Author Page

Instagram

Goodreads

TikTok

Printed in Great Britain
by Amazon

41680404R00182